THE CHASE

A BLACK COYOTES MC SERIES

RUBY BLOOM

Copyright © 2022 by Ruby Bloom.
All rights reserved.
No part of this book may be reproduced or transmitted electronically, hard copy photocopying or recording or any other form without permission from the author, except for brief quotations for book reviews. This is a work of fiction, characters, names, places and incidents that resemble anything in real life is purely coincidental.

note

This book contains adult scenes and language that some readers may consider offensive or triggering. This book is for adults only, please store this book accordingly, to prevent it being accessed by under-age readers.

For my daughter, the earth beneath me, you are the grounding force of my life.
For my son, truly the master of your sea.
For my husband, ruler of my heart, you deserve a crown.
For the moments we look at each other when we are out and about and someone behaves recklessly and you raise your eyebrows to comment, knowingly
"that was such a 'Colt' thing to do."

Chapter 1
COLT

Colt Kincade was pretty fucking pleased with himself. Release day. Finally, after five years, five lonely, tedious years. Watching his back, playing the game, biding his time. And now, he was free.

"Kincade, time to go," the guard said to him, collecting him from his cell.

Colt stood and walked out of that little concrete box without a backward glance. In truth, he wanted to bolt out, he wanted to scramble out as fast as he could and puke with relief as soon as he made it out. He didn't do that, though. He kept his cool, just like he'd done over the last five years. He kept his face passive and his body neutral, ever ready, and he strode out as if he couldn't care less. He cared very much. His muscles strained from the effort of it. But he'd made it, finally.

He was walked to the processing area and given back his old clothes. He shrugged into his leather vest, complete with sewn on tags that denoted his position and the name of his motorcycle club. President. Fuck yes. The weight of it on his shoulders felt instantly better. Like he had found his right arm again. His cut was everything to him.

His jeans felt too heavy, too loose. He wanted them to feel just as good, but they didn't. He was built now, but that wasn't solely it. He'd whiled away the long five years by getting trim, getting strong. He'd needed to take care of himself, and ended up in one too many brawls along the way. And that time he got shivved. Yeah, that sucked. But now, he was free. He stood in the room, as the gate buzzed, and a jailer led him out.

As President of the Black Coyotes MC, his release from prison after five years should be a big fucking deal. He expected a party and a half to be waiting for him when he was picked up and taken back to the clubhouse. Sex, drugs and rock and roll. He expected to ball into his clubhouse, be handed a drink, and be welcomed back as a hero. He'd taken one for the club and no mistake. He was the only one who'd ended up doing time after that gun sale gone wrong. That night was a complete shit show. It had been part of the arrangement, Colt did the time, the others got off with no charges. Since he was the President, he'd stepped forward, he'd stepped up, he'd taken it on the chin. Their club wasn't big, they'd had about forty members, he'd done time so they wouldn't have to.

Now he expected topless women everywhere, that he could take his pick from. He anticipated whiskey, top drawer stuff, on the rocks. They'd have Cuban cigars and a fat roll of weed and maybe even a few rows of blow. And part of him did want that, part of him did feel that restlessness, that recklessness, to just let loose, live for the buzz, enjoy the night, as he would have before. Yes, part of him did want to party hard and finally live, after five years of feeling half dead inside. However, the other part of him honestly wanted a hot bath and to lie in his own bed, alone, for the night. Clean, crisp sheets. He shivered involuntarily. That half dead feeling trying to follow him out of the prison. He needed to chase those feelings away quickly, get back to the President the club expected, the President they all deserved.

He stepped out of the gate. The California sunlight touched

his skin, the same sunlight he'd been under inside, but it felt totally different. Outside. Free. The wind felt different, the very air he breathed felt different. It held possibilities, promises, options. He'd had none of them. And yet, he shivered again. The wind was blowing right through him, he felt like a leaf, trembling, tumbling. He felt like an old man. He knew he wasn't strong enough. He couldn't lead them like he had. That self doubt had been planted within him on his first night inside the slammer. And it had grown. And now, standing in the light of day, finally free, he felt it lodged within him. He'd have to keep it choked down, he had to appear brave and strong, hungry for blood. He'd have to appear to be a fucking Rottweiler, while inside he felt like a scrawny Chihuahua. They could still bite, right? Yes, he answered himself, but a Chihuahua didn't stand a chance against a pack of wolves.

He stood and blinked. Looking back at the doorway to the prison, then looking ahead, to the parking lot. He rolled his shoulders, and forced that thought down. Stand tall and stop yapping like a little bitch. He cleared his throat. He could do this, he'd done it every day inside. He expected a motorcade of bikes to come and greet him. Yeah, the whole fucking club should turn up to get him. He wanted to hear the rumble of the straight pipes of their motorcycles. He wanted a real 'fuck you' gesture to the prison, to the authorities, to everything and everyone who'd stood against him. He wanted to ride back in style, larger than life. Hide his insecurities behind all the fanfare.

He basked in these warm thoughts for a moment. Perhaps he could feed off their heat and grow into it all again. The moment swiftly turned into minutes, though. Then he was well aware that it was approaching an hour now. An hour later, he'd been left to stand in the parking lot outside the prison. What the fuck? When he got back, heads would roll for this. Not literally. Unless someone really pissed him off. What were they playing at, leaving their President standing outside?

Finally, he heard something. A car. It approached slowly. In fact, it sounded like the engine was on its last legs. It backfired and spluttered to a halt in front of him. It was a beaten up, rusty old thing. Two guys were in the front. Two teenagers, practically. One was gripping the steering wheel, looking about nervously. The other got out of the car. They had on 'Prospect' cuts. They were the lowest ranking, apprentices, they were nobodies. They barely looked old enough to drive. What the actual fuck? Sending snotty nosed prospects to pick him up? Him, Colt, the President of the Black Coyotes.

"Who the fuck are you?" Colt rudely snarled.

The one who'd stepped out of the car answered, not timidly, almost cockily. "I'm Nails. That's Club. Get in."

Colt ground his jaw. He'd show these two a piece of his mind. When they got back to the clubhouse, he'd fucking pin them up with nails to the wall and have the boys club them. Nails and Club. He almost thought about lashing out at them now. When they offered him the only ride away, he thought better of it.

That was a product of his last five years, he realized, opening the back door and climbing in. He'd learned to pick his fights, to concede, to regroup, and fight his battles when the time was right. His younger self would have picked a fight right there. Now though, he honestly fancied having a doze on the back seat, watching the countryside roll by while the boys drove him home.

They drove north from San Quentin State Prison and pulled up into the clubhouse about three hours later. There was a bar at the front, their biker hangout at the back, with bedrooms on the top floor for members who lived in the clubhouse. Rows of motorcycles lined the front, and cars were outside the bar, also. Members of the public were allowed in the bar, it was open to everyone, it was just a typical dive of a roadside bar. As they rounded the corner, large black gates swung open on a mechanized device. The gate squawked.

It immediately felt off to Colt. There was no welcome party. There was no barbeque in the courtyard, no banners or balloons, no people gathered in a tight group, clapping or shrieking or looking in any way pleased to see him. Fuck. Maybe everyone was gathered inside and it was a surprise. Yes, he thought, that could be it, maybe this was all part of the act, a bluff, make it look like they didn't care, and then spring a good time on him. He swallowed bile in his throat. He hoped that was it. He felt in his bones that wasn't what was going to happen at all.

The prospect driving the car, Club, pulled up outside the entrance and shut off the car engine. Colt stayed where he was.

"Get in there." The prospect nodded. He was young, not yet twenty, Colt guessed, yet with the confidence of a stallion. Where did he get that from, cocky bastard?

So Colt climbed out of the car, slamming the door behind him. He'd be damned if he didn't swagger into that clubhouse like he owned the place. He did own the place. He should. He had, before he'd gone inside. He clenched his jaw together, ensured his cut was on straight, and strode toward the front door.

The prospects immediately flanked him. Like they were prison guards. Fuck. Something was wrong. He knew it. He wouldn't let on, though. He wouldn't give these two the satisfaction.

He balled through the door, plastered a bombastic smile on his face and braced himself. The first thing that he noticed was that it was dark inside. Dark and smoky. And empty. Fuck. There was no one here. He strode around, his boots thudding on the dusty wooden floor, not letting his smile slip.

A part of him was glad to be back. The smell, the leather chairs, the sound of his feet on the floor. It was home, it had been his home. He'd practically grown up here. He'd been a snotty nosed prospect himself, sleeping on that sorry excuse for a couch in the corner. Colt let his gaze linger on it, the old brown leather thing just sitting there. Hell, this club had taken him in when he had nothing and no one. This had been his home, and a part of him was happy to be back. But it was empty. It was missing everything that made it home. His brothers. Laughter, smiles; love. It was devoid of life entirely. He no longer felt at home.

Chapter 2
COLT

"Prospect," Colt snapped. "Whiskey. Ice. Large," he batted out, as if he expected them to immediately do his bidding. They should, if they were really Prospects and he was really the Prez. He was still going to act like he ruled the roost.

They didn't. Fuck. They looked at each other. Then the one called Nails, the scrawnier of the two, relented and moped around to the bar, dragging his heels.

"Jesus, what's up with you two?" He leaned against the bar, appearing casual, while the prospect clattered about getting his drink. They didn't respond.

"The others in church?" Colt asked, nodding to the large, closed wooden door off to the side.

Through that door was the meeting room, the sacred room containing a large hand crafted wooden table, where all the members would sit, and the President would preside over, and they'd decide what reckless carnage they wanted to get up to next. How to make their money, how to build their kingdom, defend it, seek revenge. How to live as they wanted to live. That was the point of the whole motorcycle club in the first place. They could do what they liked, fuck the rest of society. Paying taxes, getting a mortgage, settling down and sleep-walking through life was not the way they lived.

They worked hard, played hard, grafted and outlawed and reaped the rewards of their lucrative, dangerous lifestyles. Fuck yes. A part of him did still feel a thrill in the thought of that. He'd been the one sitting at the head of that table, surrounded by the eager, devoted faces of his brothers. Brothers he would have stood behind, fought for, died for. Brothers he'd done time for. Where were they now?

"Yes. They're in church," the prospect replied sullenly.

"And when the fuck do I get to see them?" Colt snapped back. This impatience, he wasn't faking. Sure, he had a bad feeling about this, but now he was beginning to get annoyed.

Nails slid him a large glass full of dark colored whiskey. He hadn't had a drink the whole time he'd been inside. He brought it up to his lips, breathing in to smell it through his nose. The alcohol burned his nose. The familiar oak smell. This would taste good.

But before he could take a sip, there was a commotion at the door. Someone busting through it. Two other snot nosed, scrawny prospects, shouting, running forward catching up to-

He blinked. A woman. Fuck, he hadn't seen a woman in five years, either. His senses were bombarded. It felt like a punch to his gut, his eyes, his balls all in one go. Black dress. Short, lots of leg on show. Little gold, stupidly high, strappy sandals. Shouting, she was huffing and screaming, she sounded extremely pissed off. He could smell her from the other side of the room. Expensive floral perfume. She had long blonde hair, fancy color job on it. But had a black rag tied around her face, covering her eyes. Or at least it had been, she had obviously fought and struggled and pushed it up so it was halfway up her forehead, her hair all bunched up. She'd been led into the building by the prospects, her hands had been tied together in front of her by a plastic zip tie, but she'd somehow shrugged it off and now was refusing to come quietly. Fucking good for her, he thought.

THE CHASE

He got back into obnoxious Prez mode. "Finally, is this my welcome home present?" Colt drawled cockily, unashamedly eyeing her up and down. He didn't have to fake his interest and attraction to her. Maybe she really was his welcome home present, maybe this was an elaborate role play, maybe these prospects hadn't gotten the memo that he was the fucking President and they'd get their asses ridden when the others got out of church. He had no clue what was going on, but judging from the arrival of her, things were about to get interesting.

He tried to take a sip of the whiskey, wanting to lean cockily at the bar and down it and then take this sweet little morsel to bed with him. But even the fumes coming off his drink caught in his throat, making him cough. Fucking hell. He put the whiskey down.

Her head snapped to him, and she rounded on him, assuming he was in charge. "Hey! Who the fuck do you think you are, kidnapping me like this?"

At least someone could tell who the leader of the pack was, he thought wryly. His former escorts, Nails and Club, gave each other another loaded sideways glance, but then headed over to conflab with the two other prospects who'd hauled the woman in. They looked nervous, like they knew something was going to go down. Like they shouldn't have brought the two of them here, at the same time, together.

"You total dick. If you think you can get away with this, think again," she shouted, strutting toward him on her long, bare legs. Legs he wanted wrapped around his waist. Legs he wanted wrapped around his neck.

He couldn't help but smile. "Feisty, like a little kitten that got wet in a rain storm. Fucking perfect," he drawled. It was true, he didn't mind a little spirit, a little push back. He felt his cock plumping. She was hot. Tiny, a little firecracker, plucked from God knows where, dressed like she was on an evening out. Hell, she sported a vintage leather jacket to boot. A little cropped thing, the finest Italian calf leather. A true classic. Where did she get that? He blinked. Something about it was familiar. Something about her... a memory tugged at him, from the past. He hadn't spent much time dwelling, looking back. It was pulling him further back than the five years he'd done in prison. Further back than he wanted to go.

Colt turned away, both from her and wherever his brain was trying to take him. "Prospect." He snapped his fingers. Yes, it was rude, but that was the life of a prospect. You were treated like dirt, you grafted until you had proved yourself as a true brother. Like an apprentice, but shittier. He'd done it himself, everyone had done their time at the bottom of the ladder. "Whiskey, for the lady," Colt barked.

Nails turned and thought about it for a second. Then shrugged and slouched about behind the bar, fixing her a drink.

Colt ran his tongue around his teeth inside his mouth. He needed a cigarette. He had them in his back pocket. He pulled one out, put it between his lips. The woman stared at him, tutted, huffed, looking at him with burning anger and indignation. As if she was offended by the cigarette. As if that was somehow more serious than this kidnapping. He lit it up with a single, confident flick of the lighter.

Fuck yes. He breathed in deeply, feeling the glow at the end of the cigarette. Feeling the bliss hit his lungs, flit into his veins. Calm him and excite him at the same time.

"Those things will kill you, you do realize," she stated, irritated. She fixed him with the most piercing blue eyes. Fuck, she was beautiful. He wanted to tease her, this little uptight hellcat. He took another deep drag and blew a puff of smoke toward her, letting it out of his nose and his mouth. She was far enough away that it didn't really bother her, but the gesture was plain.

And then he saw something flit across her face that he had not expected. Desire.

Her eyes hooded, for just a second. Her lips parted. Her gaze dropped to his mouth. Lower, raking over his body in one lusty sweep. What the actual fuck?

He did a double take of her. No way would a woman like her look twice at a guy like him. She was beautiful, yes, but intelligent. It oozed out of her, the way she pronounced every letter in the words she spoke, her upper class indignation at something unexpected happening to her. Her diamond earrings. Her hair, it must have cost a bomb. It was no cheap job from a box from the supermarket. She reeked of class and sophistication. She'd probably been on an evening out, at a cocktail bar perhaps, when she was grabbed by those prospects. And why the fuck had she just given him the come-to-bed eyes when she clearly was annoyed with him and everything around her? Yes, he'd been flippant about taking her to bed, he'd thought about it the second she'd marched through the door. She would be sweet, clean, supple. She would be a joy to sink his starved cock into. But no way in hell would she volunteer for that with the likes of him. A dirty old biker, a convicted felon. A no-good bad-boy.

Unless that's what she wanted. That's what she's secretly craved and never had. His cock stiffened in his jeans again. He had to pay attention not to gag on his cigarette now, too.

But he didn't have to respond, as the big wooden door opened up. The prospects immediately jumped to attention. Nails and Club flanked Colt, grabbing his arms. He stuffed his cigarette between his lips before they could restrain his arms and they frog-marched him into the room, into church. He heard the woman kick off again behind him, and didn't need to look to assume the other two prospects had grabbed her, too, and were attempting to march her in. And she was kicking up a fuss. He smiled to himself, liking her attitude.

"Come on, you're our slut now, go in like a good little slut-" one of the Prospects began.

Colt turned around at that.

Her hand whipped out of the prospect's grasp and back handed him across the face. For a second she went white. Like she was shocked and horrified. That was the look of someone who'd never hit anyone before, Colt thought. The prospect, his head slapped round, brought it back with a wince, checking for blood, for damage. Finding none, he still moaned.

"I'm not going fucking anywhere and I'm most definitely not your slut," she said, recovering her cool and tossing her head back with dignity. Then she grabbed their hands and stomped forward like she was the headline model at Paris fashion week, the two prospects at her heel like woebegone, shamed puppies.

Fucking hell, Colt fell a little bit in love with her right then and there. Her spirit, her confidence. He wanted to call her his slut. His head spun and his groin felt like he'd just been punched. It hurt good.

Get it together, Colt, he told himself, this is no time to lose your head because of your dick. He let the prospects lead him in for now. Remembering his lessons from prison. Wait, bide time, figure it out. Wait and see and act later. He pursed his lips to grip the cigarette and blow out smoke at the same time. He let a nonchalant, mildly amused smile play on his lips, let his feet drag in an unhurried way, as if this was all a big joke.

CHAPTER 3
COLT

They were in the inner meeting room, church, as it was known. It was where he had always aspired to be. Growing up, as a scrawny prospect with nothing to his name, he had dreamed of being one of the fully patched members, with a seat at the table. He'd watch the men stride in there, beyond confident, with their big, muscular bodies and heavy boots. These men got what they wanted out of life. He had dreamed of being one of them. He'd been a bony homeless kid when he first showed up here. He'd been dumpster diving behind the pizza place down the road, Rossetti's. He'd been caught, picked up by the scruff of his neck, thrown onto the sidewalk and shouted at by the restaurant owner. The restaurant owner, a man in his thirties, had looked at Colt like he was a cockroach, something disgusting, something to fear and hate. Colt had withered under his glare.

One of the bikers had spotted him. A small group of them had been loitering by the entrance of the biker bar and had watched. This biker had shoulder length, steely gray hair, a pierced ear, and icy blue eyes. His name, it turned out, was Blue. He'd taken a long look at Colt, and then called him over. Colt had nowhere else to go, so he tripped forward, gulping back the tears, the hunger and the loneliness. Blue had said if he swept the floor of the bar, Colt could have a plate of food. Colt had agreed. He was a trembling little squirt of a kid, but he swept the whole floor of the bar, front and back, and the kitchens, too. He'd kept his head down but had been in awe of it all. Turned out Blue was the President of a big, bad ass biker gang, men who did what they wanted, said what they wanted, got what they wanted out of life. Colt had never seen anything like it and instantly fell in love with it. They'd kicked him out after he'd scoffed down a burger and fries. But he came back the next night. And the next. They then threw in the couch for the night, as well as dinner. The couch had been saggy and smelly back then, when he'd been fifteen. But he'd sunk into it like it was goose down and silk. The bikers continued to party around him, but he'd conked out and slept like the dead. They threw him out again in the morning, but, again, his determination was all he had. He'd be back by the early evening. Blue would look out for him, and every day, Colt would come scampering up the road. Every day looking a little better for having had a square meal in him the night before. Blue would put his hand out and pat his shoulder, calling him "son." Blue made him feel human again. And Colt became instantly attached to Blue, seeking his approval, devastated when Blue had to discipline him for an accidental wrongdoing or an adolescent slip up.

The days turned to weeks and they stopped kicking him out. In the morning, he was roused from the couch and given a mop and a bucket, or a sponge, and sent off to do whatever odd jobs he could. The weeks and months and years went by. Colt was taken on as a prospect. Given some mundane jobs, some important jobs. His favorite had been safeguarding Blue's daughter. Fuck, that had been the best time. She didn't know Blue had assigned a member of the MC to watch over her, she didn't even know her daddy was the president of an MC. But in the summers, when she was back from boarding school, and later, college, Colt was her personal shadow. And he'd guarded her like a fucking Fabergé egg. Best times of his life.

THE CHASE

The rest of club life suited him fine. Crazy shit went down, parties, sweet butts, gun fights, territory stealing, police raids... all of it. After Blue's time as President came to an end, it came to Colt. And he thought he'd made it. President, head of the table. Fully patched member of the Black Coyotes. He'd led them for three years. Lived his dreams. He'd insisted on keeping the smelly old couch in the clubhouse, so every day he'd see it and remember where he'd come from. That it was still there, looking saggier and smellier than ever, pulled at something within him.

But it wasn't home anymore. This room, church, it wasn't his table. These weren't his brothers who sat around the table. He didn't recognize any faces. They were younger. Meaner. They looked at him with curled lips and sneers.

The only face he recognized sat in his former seat, at the head of the table. Cleaver was his name. He'd been a tough, cold bastard back in the day. He'd just been an ordinary member of the club when Colt first showed up. Then he'd wormed his way in with the former President, Blue. Colt had never liked Cleaver, he'd often clip him round the ears when Colt had been a scrawny kid. Once Colt had begun to fill out, weight trained with the guys and ate three square meals a day, Cleaver stopped the physical harassing, but kept up the sneers and the jibes. Colt quickly learned to ignore him, especially once Colt overtook Cleaver in height and weight. He didn't give a flying fuck about what the older guy had to say, and mainly stayed out of his way. But Blue had listened to Cleaver. And Cleaver had often taken Blue to one side and whispered in his ear. They'd planned together. In fact, they'd planned that fateful night, the night raid of the white supremacy hate group that had wanted to buy their guns, the Guardians of Purity. The Black Coyotes were going to sell them guns for fuck knows what purposes, but it had all gone wrong. Very wrong. The Feds had been lying in wait. Everyone started shooting. Blue disappeared. Other brothers got shot, arrested... it had been a shit show. Traumatic. Was Blue dead? No one knew. No body was ever found. Colt had been devastated.

After the dust settled, the club had called a vote, to vote in the new President. Colt won. Cleaver seethed about it but had accepted Colt's Presidency. Colt had got on with leading, and Cleaver had done whatever the fuck Colt had told him to do. Until they planned a raid on the Guardians of Purity again. The retribution raid. To take back their guns, take back their dignity and teach those fuckers a lesson. Colt wanted revenge. But it had gone to shit again, and Colt had been incarcerated. Yes, Cleaver had always treated Colt with a cold shoulder and a snarky attitude but he'd never stepped out of line. Now Cleaver had, though. Way out of line.

Colt was dumped onto his knees on the left side of the room. The two prospects holding onto the young woman dragged her forward, dumping her on the right side of the room, opposite him. She was still hissing and spitting like a drowned kitten. What did he have to do with her? Why were they both being dragged into church?

As Colt approached the table, all of this flashed through his mind. How had he gotten to this? Cleaver had stepped so far out of line, he'd stepped right out of his place and into Colt's. And filled the remaining seats with new blood, who clearly supported Cleaver. Well fuck, Colt had been usurped. He'd lost his club. Fuck, he'd lost his home, his family. He had nothing without the Black Coyotes. And he'd be damned if he ever accepted Cleaver as President. It felt like a bitter stab to the chest. A stab and a twist for the sheer hell of it.

"Well, look what the cat dragged in," Cleaver sneered. He had a pointed, rat-like face that Colt had often dreamed of punching. Now, more so than ever.

"Thanks for keeping my seat warm, you can fuck off now," Colt said, keeping his tone firm, casual, confident. He did not in any way expect Cleaver to concede so easily, but he might as well make his position clear.

"Ha, Colt, as cock-sure as ever. There's been a few changes while you were away."

"I see that."

"Spring cleaning, out with the old, in with the new. There's no seat at the table for you any more, old man." Cleaver barked a harsh laugh. A few of the others around the table sneered, too. They looked at him like dirt. They didn't even fucking know him. They weren't true members of the Black Coyotes.

There was a thud and a groan. Colt looked around. One of the men at the table had just slumped forward, his head knocking into the table. Colt blinked, the guy's dark, scruffy brown hair fell forward onto his face.

Colt turned back to Cleaver, a question in his glare.

Cleaver waved his hand as if he was trying to swat a fly. "That's just Skunk. He drinks. Ignore him. We call him that because he's always drunk as a-"

"I get it." Colt frowned. "He drinks? Like to the point of passing out at the table? Looks like a brother needs a brother, if he has a problem, you should help."

Cleaver strode over to the guy, Skunk, and kicked the chair out from under him. The guy crumpled to the floor, completely out of it. A few of the other men around the table snickered.

Colt winced. "What the fuck? That's no way to treat a brother. Take him to rehab, get it sorted out-"

"Fuck you, Colt, you don't call the shots anymore," Cleaver hissed.

It didn't sit well with Colt, how that guy, Skunk, was being treated.

None of it sat well with Colt. He rolled his shoulders back. "Looks like the founding principles of loyalty and respect have been fucking torn up and tossed in the trash in my absence, eh?" Colt parried. He wouldn't just concede without a bit of lip, a bit of a fight. He could see he wouldn't win this battle right here right now, and it stung to admit that to himself, but he knew the truth. And he simply didn't have the manpower to take them all on. He had to back down, he had to give up. There wasn't anything left to fight for. It hurt but he had to keep his wits about him. There was time for licking his wounds later. For now, he had to survive.

Cleaver pursed his lips. "You are the one who got yourself locked up, you are the one who let the others die on your watch, you made that mistake, you nearly ran this club into the ground."

"I took the rap for you! I went down so that no one else had to," Colt hissed back. "And don't even get me started on why I was told everything was fine in prison. People gave me updates saying the Black Coyotes were doing fine…"

"Yes, I fed you false intel so you stayed quiet in there. You thought you would be welcomed back a hero, your President's seat would be dusted off for you and you could just pick up where you left off?" Colt kept his gaze fixed on him, and pulled away from the two prospects who'd been holding his arms. They were easy to shrug off. The stuff Cleaver was telling him, however, was not.

"What the fuck-"

"Well the other brothers all met untimely ends. Unfortunately."

"Fuck, all dead?" The guys he'd been looking forward to seeing, gone. His brothers. His heart howled inside his chest. Blue's blood would be boiling, if he still had blood beating around his body, knowing this is what had happened to the club. He stamped down the swelling grief inside him. He wanted to ask how, when? He wanted

THE CHASE

to ask where they were buried, or where ashes had been scattered. He didn't. He had a feeling he wouldn't like any of the answers, he had a feeling foul play was involved, and Cleaver had orchestrated all of this. He sighed but he kept his chin up.

"Colt, don't worry, I got the club back on track, less members now, about twenty strong, but we now have some fat fingers in some tasty pies."

"Illegal pies? You know Blue wanted to go legit," Colt tutted.

Cleaver stood now, too. "Ah yes, Blue, the resident ghost of the Black Coyotes," he said, commanding the attention of the others at the table. "Disappears without a trace, no body, no word. Yes, let's talk about him." Cleaver began, as if he were telling a bedtime story.

The woman across the room, on her knees, took a breath in. Then stopped herself.

"We'll get to you in a minute, bitch!" Cleaver spat harshly. She immediately pursed her lips and looked down.

Cleaver continued his speech. "The mighty, untouchable Blue led this club, back in the day. Yes, yes, he'd done a good job and the club coffers had filled and everyone had been happy. But some of the outgoings were for Blue's daughter. Her mother was a crack whore who died of an overdose, you know, she was just a flavor of the month to Blue and the kid had gone to live with her mother's parents. But Blue still wanted to keep tabs, so had used club resources to do that. Man hours spent trailing after the spoiled little college brat. Oh yes, and not to mention that Blue's daughter's been receiving Blue's cut of the takings for the last however many years. He's not dead, you see? No body was found. So the money still goes to his account. And to this day, a cut goes out every month, did you know that?"

The men around the table hissed their disapproval.

Colt shrugged. "President's privilege, it's written into the charter.

No dead body? Means Blue's not dead."

"Well, we are tightening the purse strings. Blue is dead to us from this point forward. I don't want to spend any more time or grief thinking or talking about Blue. Anyone fucking breathes the word Blue, and they'll pay. Cutting off Blue's share. Re-writing the charter. No more cut for little miss Blue."

Colt reeled. "That's fucked up-" he began.

"Now, where you come in is that we are on the cusp of a big deal. Huge. Fucking good thing for the club, we'll be fucking rolling in it-"

"What deal?"

"Guardians of Purity, your old friends-"

Colt growled.

"They wanted us to start delivering materials for them to make bombs…"

"Bombs? What the fuck, Cleaver-"

"But they want you out of the picture, they fear retribution, they were the ones who ratted on you in that gun sale five years ago. You sought vengeance on them for what had happened to Blue, they knew you were coming for them. So they played you first, they ratted on you-"

"The fucking dirty little shits!"

"Yeah, so, they won't do the deal until you're dead. I tried to kill you off in prison but that didn't fucking work."

Colt sniffed. No wonder he'd spent a large percentage of the last five years either in solitary confinement, in the 'beast' wing or in the hospital ward.

"As per the charter, you're excommunicated. You run. We chase. We chase you until we catch you and we kill you."

CHAPTER 4
COLT

Colt took a breath and gulped, but kept his gaze steady, unflinching.

"Dirty bombs for a white supremacy hate group? Man, that's not Black Coyotes, you shit face! That's not what we do!"

It all fucking hurt like he'd been stabbed, but he wouldn't show them that.

Cleaver smiled leerily, obviously very pleased with how this was all working out, the drama, the theatricality. "Yes, you know what that means, Colt, you're a wanted man now, your time is up. Anyone who brings you back, dead or alive, gets a reward. You got twenty-four hours head start and then every member of the Black Coyotes can hunt you down, Colt. And believe me, I'm clearing our schedules so that they are all free to go out and fucking chase you to the edge of the earth. I want that deal with the GOP. I'm only not killing you now 'cos we voted on it earlier, the guys want to uphold the charter, excommunicate you and give you a chance to run."

"How fucking kind of you," Colt spat. He stood. He shrugged off his jacket. Grabbed a flip knife from the table. He cut off the President patch on the leather jacket. Hell. Fuck it, he'd go all the way. He cut off all the patches while everyone watched on in stony silence. His leather jacket, his cut, his pride and joy. Now hard, dark, gaping spots where the leather underneath was clean and fresh. Each cut of thread was a cut on his heart strings. But he did it without blinking. Then, he took the cigarette out of his mouth. He pushed up his long-sleeved shirt sleeve. A tattoo at the top of his bicep. The Black Coyotes. He had a bigger one on his back. He'd deal with that one later. He took the cigarette and stubbed it out on the Black Coyotes tattoo on his arm. He did his best not to grimace as the butt burnt his skin. It fucking hurt, though. It burned. He kept the cigarette there until he could smell his burning flesh. A few of the guys around the table looked considerably paler than before. One of them gagged.

"See ya later," Colt said, and went to turn on his heels.

"Whoa fella, not so fast. You have colors on your back, too, am I right?" Cleaver asked with a cruel smile and a glint in his eye.

Fuck.

"We can burn them off for you now, too. Hold him down boys," Cleaver yelled.

Colt struggled but there were arms and hands everywhere, pinning him down, tearing off his long sleeved T-shirt, so he was bare chested. So much for his bravado. So much for his devil-may-care exit.

"Wait, what are you going to do to him?" The woman's voice piped up now. He was surprised. He looked up, and saw her looking on, looking terrified, disheveled but determined. In this light he could see dried tear streaks on her cheeks. He hadn't seen that in the bar.

Cleaver cleared his throat. "Ahh, little miss Blue, I forgot to introduce you. April Rodgers. Yes, that's right, you might as well witness this because this is what will happen to you if you don't cooperate, too."

"What the-" Colt's gaze snapped back to her. This was Blue's daughter. April. Fuck. He thought he'd recognized her. A thousand memories suddenly pounced on him, drowned him. He didn't need any of the MC members to pin him down, he was paralyzed with the sea of the past crashing down on him.

"Oh yes, and April, sweetie, meet Colt, your stalker, your guard dog, poor bastard followed you, panted after you for years..."

She stared back at Colt. The likes of her and him didn't mix, their paths never crossed, and that's something he'd learned to live with. But now their paths had crossed. Here she was, plucked from whatever high end night out in her glamorous life. Kidnapped, roughed up a bit, but unharmed. And not only did she still glow with that warmth Colt had felt years ago, she had some fight in her, too. Some spirit, a sense of indignation. That lusty once over in the bar earlier, he hadn't imagined that. And she was looking at him again now.

His survival instinct kicked up a notch. He had to save himself and he had to save her. As he always had, as he always would. She was getting out alive. He was going to make sure of that.

"Burnt off or cut off? That's your choice, Colt," Cleaver spat.

"You can't be serious," April spat back. "And how is this in any way a lesson for me? I have nothing to do with this stupid biker gang-"

"Shut up, bitch! Your Daddy was the President-"

"No, he wasn't! I... I thought he worked as a diplomat for the government-" April stammered, blanching.

"Pah, is that what he told you? No, Daddy didn't wear suits and brush shoulders with the rich and influential, he was a dirty biker scumbag-"

"He was a biker and a good man," Colt ground out, looking at April, trying to convey in his eyes that he was her ally here.

She looked about, panicked, realization setting in. "The money he sent me... it was dirty money?"

"It was our dirty money," Cleaver corrected her.

She whimpered, but regained her fight after a second, anger flashing in her eyes now. "So what do you want from me? Just cut me off financially and let me go, I have nothing else to give-"

"Yeah, I was going to do that, until I realized you were a hot piece of ass. Now I want you to stay here, with me. With all of us. We'll take good care of you, right boys?" Cleaver licked his lips.

Colt felt sick. The others around the table grinned and leered and snickered. He wouldn't trust them to be good to a woman. They all looked at her like she was a hunk of meat. A cheap hunk of meat. He knew how this worked. The club owned women. When he was President, they were willing, pliant, they loved being part of the biker club, having any of the brothers they wanted, giving them what they needed. And the brothers would happily share. But they treated the women well, the women could basically do what they wanted, they got money, clothes, cars, freedom to come and go, to party and drink and eat and sleep with them all. He hadn't seen any women in the bar earlier. Colt doubted Cleaver treated the club women in that way. He certainly doubted he'd treat April that way.

"If you think I will come willingly into your bed, then you have another thing coming-" April began, sassy, quirking up one neatly manicured eyebrow and looking down her nose at Cleaver like he was a piece of dog shit. Colt bit back a smile. But that was exactly the look he feared she'd give Colt himself, all those years ago. And now she'd really poked the hornet's nest.

"Come willingly? Who said anything about you coming?" Cleaver snickered cruelly. "Who said anything about you being willing?" A vein popped in his temple. "You'll be one of our whores, I think that would be an apt payback for all that money you took, April. Oh, and we'll take that back, too. You can pay back your interest to us in sexual favors." Cleaver licked his lips.

April ground her jaw, Colt could see the little muscles twitch from where he was. She took a breath to respond but Colt interrupted.

"Here's what's going to happen. You aren't going to touch a hair on her head. You aren't going to burn or cut my colors off my back. You're going to let us both walk out of here and then we won't see your fucking ugly mugs ever again. That's what's going to happen," Colt said.

"No-"

"Cleaver, stop. Just stop." Colt played his final cards. "You sit at that table head, then you have the trust of everyone here. You start breaking that trust, and, well, you might not be sitting at that table head for much longer. If he does this to me," Colt said, looking around at the men's faces at the table, "he could do it to you. What does brotherhood mean, anymore, if this is what happens? If this is what you let happen? There's a charter for a reason. So you can all respect your fellow man, and be respected in turn. Otherwise, you'll be next. You voted to let me go, so let me go. No more fucking about, changing the rules, burning my colors off. Let the chase commence," Colt finished quietly.

A heavy silence fell. The men around the table looked down. Cleaver could see that there was that sense of doubt settling in. Cleaver could turn on any one of them just like that, too. They were all thinking of their own necks.

Cleaver licked his lips, realizing he needed to backpedal promptly. "Colt, go now, that's fine, but we'll start chasing you, and when we catch you, we'll take your life. Make no mistake about it," Cleaver said.

Colt shrugged off the two prospect minions who had regained their hold on his arms behind him after the struggle.

"Yeah, fuck you," Colt growled and clambered to his feet. He dared a glance at April. She opened her mouth to say something to him. But he saw the hurt and confusion in her eyes. She was trying to appear fearless but inside she was quaking like a leaf. He knew that feeling.

Colt picked up his cut, with his patches missing, no longer proudly identifying him. Now he was just a nobody with an old leather vest.

Cleaver turned. "April, my darling, now, you will be tied up on the bed in my room and tonight you will be showing your appreciation to each and every brother in turn-"

"I will not-"

"Gag her, too." Cleaver added callously. The brothers of the Black Coyotes MC moved to do Cleaver's bidding. April let out a whimper as they bound her mouth, with what, Colt didn't see.

Colt turned and walked casually toward the door, tossing his now ragged leather cut on, missing his T-shirt but trying to look like a man who didn't give two fucks. He gestured a wave over his shoulder, and didn't look back.

CHAPTER 5
COLT

He didn't look back until he got across the parking lot. He slouched away from the clubhouse, his home, what was his home. The gate was open, no barrier between him and the open road. A guy stood by the gate, clearly meant to be guarding it, but was slumped over, passed out. Colt could see the track marks up his arms from across the forecourt. Standards had slipped. There was no way he'd have let any brother in the MC, not in the least the guy meant to be fucking guarding the clubhouse, use. Cleaver was running a shoddy operation.

Colt saw the line of gleaming Harleys. Where had his ended up? He didn't know. He had nothing. Nothing in his pocket except a packet of cigarettes. A lighter. No money. No phone. Not even a fucking T-shirt. Nowhere to go. He felt like that helpless fifteen year old for a second. But he remembered he wasn't that helpless kid any more. He shivered, though it was a warm afternoon and he had his cut on. He was off the hook, in terms of having to step up and be the brave, arrogant Prez again. He should feel pleased, he could just fuck off into obscurity and have a quiet life, live happily ever after, as long as he kept running. He didn't feel pleased at all.

At the end of the line of Harleys, a prospect was shining up the last one in the row. He looked again. It wasn't a Harley, it was a Triumph. A nice one. It glinted in the late afternoon sun. Colt kept walking casually until he was right next to him. The Prospect was just a skinny kid himself, Colt thought ruefully. He looked back at the clubhouse, and that body movement covered him to make the next one. Swinging his fist into the kid's head. He dropped like a leaf. Colt dragged him into the shade and propped him up against the fence. Colt grabbed the keys from his pocket after a swift pat down. He straddled the motorcycle.

Fuck, that felt good already. It was a sweet ride. He turned the key, the vibrations, the sound, soothing something in him that had been aching for the whole time he'd been in prison. It buzzed through his blood. Freedom. It was within reach. He pulled open the saddle bag that hung on the side. He yanked out a helmet from inside, a proper helmet, with a visor. That would do. He wore a helmet because he'd seen what happened to a human skull when they weren't wearing one. Yeah, fuck that. He shoved on the helmet. He could just roar away and that would be the end.

He looked back over his shoulder. He couldn't hear anything, but he could see the President's bedroom. The room that had been his own bedroom. He thought of Cleaver laying his hands on April. Fucking dick. Was that really how her story was going to end? Becoming a whore of the MC? She was destined for better things. Blue would be turning in his grave, if he was dead after all. Hell, Colt felt himself turning in his own grave and he wasn't even dead and buried.

Colt turned away from the clubhouse and revved, looking up into the sky. Could he leave her? Going back to get her would be trouble. So much trouble. He was nearly at his happy ending. Could he actually do it, leave April? Could he actually live with himself, knowing he had left her?

Suddenly, he was that little scrawny eighteen year old again. The first time he'd seen her, Blue had told him he had a very important job and Colt had been desperate to please him. He would do whatever Blue asked. And Blue had asked him to follow his daughter. She was due home for the summer, staying with her grandparents. Blue wanted him to wait for her at the airport, as she was flying in from some English boarding school. Colt had a beaten up old Wolf Classic motorbike. Barely even a proper motorcycle. It was all he could afford with the measly dollars he had managed to beg, borrow and steal at the time. He had a roof over his head, a space to sleep that was safe enough, and food in his belly. But that had been all he had. It only just ran, and Blue had helped him fix it up.

Colt had been sitting astride his bike in the pick up area of the airport, the hot sun bouncing off the road. He was a lanky thing, long legs and a skinny torso. He had his leather Prospect cut on and he wore it with pride, though it was incredibly hot, and too big for him. He had sneakers on, battered old Converse. His hair was long, floppy, and it always stuck up at the front in a bit of a cowlick. He thought he'd looked incredibly cool, with his cut, on a bike, shades on, waiting for an important person, who he was supposed to watch. He had thought he was the cat's pajamas, for once, a sense of pride in who he was. He was a prospect of the Black Coyotes. People buzzed past him and didn't look twice, but he didn't need their affirmation. He felt good in his own skin. There were fumes in the air, cars were pulling in and out, people coming and going, no one was just there. Except him. He was there, waiting for April. Blue had described her. Blonde hair, about waist length, eyes like his; piercing blue. She'd be sixteen, two years younger than Colt. Colt had his eyes glued to the door and was assessing everyone who matched that description, determined not to miss her.

And then she emerged. His breath hissed out of his lungs. He wouldn't have been surprised if butterflies followed her and rainbows came out over her head. She carried herself differently, her posture was tall, her chin held high. That blonde hair cascaded like golden silk down her back. She had a wheelie suitcase behind her, a leather handbag, wearing a little dress. She was perfection to Colt. At sixteen, she was still lithe, skinny, too, her face was a neatly put together little kitten face of pouty lips, big eyes and a button nose. Her skin, dewy golden perfection. She walked closer, toward Colt. His mouth had dropped open. The blood in his body pumped like a runaway train. He wouldn't be able to say anything, his throat seized up. She flipped some expensive looking sunglasses over her eyes, and looked about, still heading his way. And now she was right in front of him, so close he could touch her. The air around her filled with sunshine and sweetness, her scent was flowers and peaches. Hope, and power, a sense of rightness. Like within her bubble, he could achieve great things. Colt breathed in deep, filling his lungs, taking a hit, wanting to get high off her. And then another. For a split second he thought she was looking at him, right at him, and her mouth opened and he thought she might talk to him. Might smile at him. His heart slammed into his rib cage.

But no. She passed by. To the taxi rank beside him. The taxi driver asked where to, she ducked her head a little to give the driver the address, her voice soft clouds. The taxi driver got out and grabbed her case as she swung herself into the back seat. She hadn't even noticed Colt. But he had noticed her. He had his world flipped over, his heart now beat to a different tattoo. Hers. The poles of his orientation had swapped and there was nothing he could do about it. From that moment he would be hopelessly in love with April.

Colt would be watching, always from afar, watching her as she shone like an angel, and waltzed through a blissful teenage life. The most expensive education to be bought, boarding school in England, then to an exclusive private high school, then Brown University after she'd graduated. She'd come home for the summers and he would count down the days until he could see her again.

April. The skimpy little dresses and skirts she'd wear, very girl-next-door. Innocence that would drive him wild. He'd turn into a rabid dog the nights in the summers he was watching her. It got that bad. Fuck. April. Then she went to get a job in San Francisco after graduating and that was the end. Blue put her on the watch list for an affiliated SF based MC. It sucked. He'd force her out of his mind. Colt had gone back to drinking and whoring and outwardly enjoying the trappings of the MC lifestyle. Inwardly, he often thought about her, where she was, how she was doing. He'd revisit her in his mind only occasionally, normally when he drank too much. He'd wonder where she was, what she was doing. He'd day-dream about her noticing him, on one of the days when he was trailing after her. Wouldn't it have been something if she'd seen him, stopped in her tracks, smiled at him. Hell, sometimes he dared to dream she'd approach him, talk to him. Sometimes he dared to dream she'd kiss him. And more. But she never did.

And now, at the ripe old age of thirty-five, Colt hesitated. Going back to get her would be trouble with a capital T. But maybe he wanted trouble. Maybe he didn't want to end things there. Maybe he had a sense of duty to Blue. Maybe his teenage infatuation needed to be exercised.

He turned off the engine, yanked off the helmet, and headed back. Back to save April. As he always had done, as he always would do.

CHAPTER 6
COLT

He hauled himself up onto a dumpster, on the side of the building. From there, he could climb onto the flat roof of the kitchen. Then, across that, it was another climb to the roof of the main building. Then it was a question of dropping down onto the windowsill of the right bedroom. He'd checked out whether there were any other prospects about the place, or guards, but it seemed all the members were still in church. That suited him just fine. He clung onto the concrete edge of the building, thankful that he'd done so many chin-ups in prison, and lowered himself down. His booted feet touched the windowsill, and he dropped quietly. The window was old, wood, half rotten. He thumped it a few times lightly and lifted the sash. It was as easy as that. He swung himself into the President's bedroom, clambering over the window frame and thudding gently on the floor.

There she was, as he'd predicted. Her wrists were in restraints, tied to the bedpost. Her ankles, too. She was a picture. He couldn't deny it. Her posh clothes all ruffled up, her chic hair all over the place. Tear stained makeup, wild eyes. She was beautiful.

"Christ. Give me strength," he muttered as his body immediately reacted to seeing her there. Adrenaline and desire pumped a heady mixture through his body.

He approached, trying to step quietly, trying to look at her with reassurance. She was gagged, straining against the rag, previous tears streaked her face. He was close now, he bent down to her. Was she scared of him? She seemed wild. Who wouldn't be, given the afternoon she'd had? He hooked a finger under the bandana material of the gag and pulled it off her.

"Colt!" She began desperately, but he interrupted her, shushing her. She immediately was silent, looking up at him with her big, blue eyes.

He forced air into his lungs. "You're leaving with me, now," he hissed. He began untying her wrist ties. She nodded. He had to lean over her to get the other wrist. Then to her ankles. He eyed up her ridiculous heels. "Take these off, we've got to run, to climb."

"No way, these are Manolo's."

He was getting high off being so close to her body, her skin, spread out in front of him. "We have literally seconds, take them off or I'll… fuck them off you." He didn't have time for her sassy arguing back. She wanted sass, he could match her there. His pulse raced. His head spun.

Her eyebrow arched. "If we have literally seconds, how do you think you'll be able to fuck them off me?" She countered.

"I've been in the slammer for years, Kitten, it wouldn't take me long to get myself there." Jesus, he was hard. This was not the time for this. Yet, he felt so fucking alive.

"And what about me?" She batted back.

"What about you, Kitten?"

She pouted. "Selfish."

He played along, smirking. "Selfish the first time. Selfless the next time."

She raised her eyebrows, opened her mouth to say something but was speechless. Yes, he'd won that. Point to him.

"They are fuck shoes anyway," he said, eyeing them and her slender ankles. His erection plumped and pressed uncomfortably into his jeans. So uncomfortable it felt good.

"I beg your pardon?" She said indignantly.

"They are fuck shoes, not for walking in, purely for fucking in. They look good on your feet up in the air-" he continued.

"I don't think-"

"Take them off or I'll fuck them off you," he ground out again, feeling his patience fraying despite how hot it was making him. Yes, he wasn't the scrawny besotted teenager anymore, staring from the shadows. He was the big, bad biker who was going to save her ass. She eyed him up. Clearly despite her wishes, he presented her only option out of this mess, so she obliged, untying the gold strap that looped up her ankle.

"Fine but you can carry them." She shoved them toward him, into the pocket of his cut. Her fingers fumbling on his torso made his breath hitch. The presumptuous minx. He was to carry her shoes now? Fuck it. He would, of course he would. They had to get out of there.

He backed off, away from her, and beckoned her over to the window. "We climb up the drainpipe, over the roof, and basically down the other side, simple enough. Follow me exactly," he said. She nodded and pursed her lips. She grabbed her leather jacket and reached inside, pulling out her phone. She tapped away on it.

He frowned. Firstly, surprised they didn't search her and take her phone off her, and secondly surprised she was calmly on her phone. "Kitten, this isn't the time for updating your social media status or taking a photo for the 'gram'," he drawled.

She stuck her tongue out at him but slipped her phone back into her jacket pocket and zipped it up, as if she were preparing to go out into the cold. It was a hot July day outside.

He almost smiled. He crouched on the window ledge, indicating to her to be quiet with a finger to his lips. Damn, he was still hard. Now she was barefoot and wearing the tiny dress, miles of slender leg on display. He refocused. He lifted himself up, grabbed the drainpipe to the right of the window, and scrambled up onto the roof. It was too high to pull himself up the way he'd dropped down. He turned. Would she have the strength to pull herself up? She was already shimmying up the pipe, her feet able to squeeze in the gap between the brickwork, pulling herself up with her forearms. Great. Once he was standing at the top and looking down, he held out a hand for her which she took, after a fierce look. He pulled her up onto the roof. She followed him silently, he ducked and then hurried. She did the same. It wouldn't be long until they found her gone, the window open. They'd be able to find her pretty soon.

He wordlessly dropped down onto the kitchen roof, turning to help her, offering her his knee as a place to put her foot to help her down. She flashed him another fierce look. Like she didn't want to be helped, she resented him for helping, but she knew she didn't have a choice. He bit his cheek to stop himself from chuckling at her attitude. He'd be enjoying this so much more if they weren't in imminent danger. Hell, who was he kidding, he was enjoying this a lot even though they were in danger. Then onto the dumpster, and down onto the concrete. He turned again to help her, but she'd already landed on the balls of her bare little feet, cat-like. Kitten-like, he corrected himself. His little drowned, spitting kitten.

He licked his lips. They were nearly there. Nearly free. He whispered to her as they cut across the yard, his eyes darting around to see if anyone was watching them. He hopped on the bike.

"Put your shoes back on and we'll ride out," he said, thrusting her shoes back at her.

"I'm not getting on the back of a bike with you," she declared cuttingly.

Colt faltered. "What? So you'd rather stay, get tied up again and-"

"No! Sorry, but... I don't really do this-" She waved her hand at him like she was talking about an object. "This isn't how my life normally goes. I don't know you, you're a convict, you're a biker... why would I go anywhere with you, what have you got to offer a girl like me?" She finished haughtily.

He should have known. He felt the pinch of rejection bite him. Deep. "I can get us outta here."

"That's it? You haven't got a plan, money? Any allies to help? It's just you and that bike?"

"...Yup."

"No, I'm not... this is not..."

He felt the pull of sucking despair, watching everything he wanted slip through his fingers. But his mask didn't slip, he did what any self respecting, cocky MC Prez would do, he rolled the dice, playing his final hand.

"Look, I get it, I'm not the usual white knight prince charming shit, the only relevant skill I can offer right now, the only thing I can put on the table... I can drive fast, that's all I got." He cleared his throat. "And a hot, hard fuck." He felt dizzy saying it, but he held her gaze. "That's what else I can offer. A fast, dangerous ride out of here, wherever you want to go, and a fucking hot as hell ride on my cock. That, I can guarantee."

He watched her face. She considered it for about half a second. Then she laughed out loud. Fuck, that hurt. That would echo around inside his brain for the rest of his miserable fucking life.

She shook her head, almost like he'd told a funny joke. "I ordered an Uber before we climbed out the window. Look, I'm sorry, but I'm not hanging around with a no-hoper ex convict like you, inviting more trouble-"

He continued nonetheless. You could say many things about Colt, but that he gave up easily was not one of them. "Both of us have a price on our heads, if we both go on the run together-"

"I'm not running anywhere, I'm going back to my fiancé, to my life-" She backed away now, heading toward the gate, barely flicking a half-hearted backwards glance at him.

He stood by the bike he'd planned to use as their getaway ride. The poor young kid he'd punched was still out cold. He wordlessly watched her walk away. From him. As he always knew she would. April. Better than him, not looking for him, never going to be his. He watched her slide into the black sedan that had just pulled up by the open gate. She didn't even look back. He stared, wondering if she'd look out the tinted black windows on the passenger side to watch him as she rode off into the sunset, happily ever after. With some fiancé. That wasn't him. That would never be him.

She'd left him. He wanted to howl and rage against the stars that had dictated that this was his fate. His eyes caught something shining on the ground, by the gate. Her shoes. Had she dropped them or dumped them? He stooped, picked them up. The car sailed away, he couldn't even see into the blacked out windows. He realized he probably had an open mouthed stare on his face, watching her go. Fucking great, he was left at the side of the road, staring after her, holding her shoes. What a class A chump he was. He thought about dumping them again right there in the yard. He didn't, of course, they were April's shoes. He slumped over to the bike, and shoved the shoes in the saddle bag. He straddled it, fired it up, shoved the helmet back on his head, and rode out of the yard. He looked left, the way the taxi

THE CHASE

had just driven. He could catch up to them in no time, he knew. He looked right, the road that led out of town. Away from all the drama, toward his sunset and his happily ever after. Except it wasn't happy at all. He looked left, then right again. Which way should he go? He was screwed either way.

CHAPTER 7
APRIL

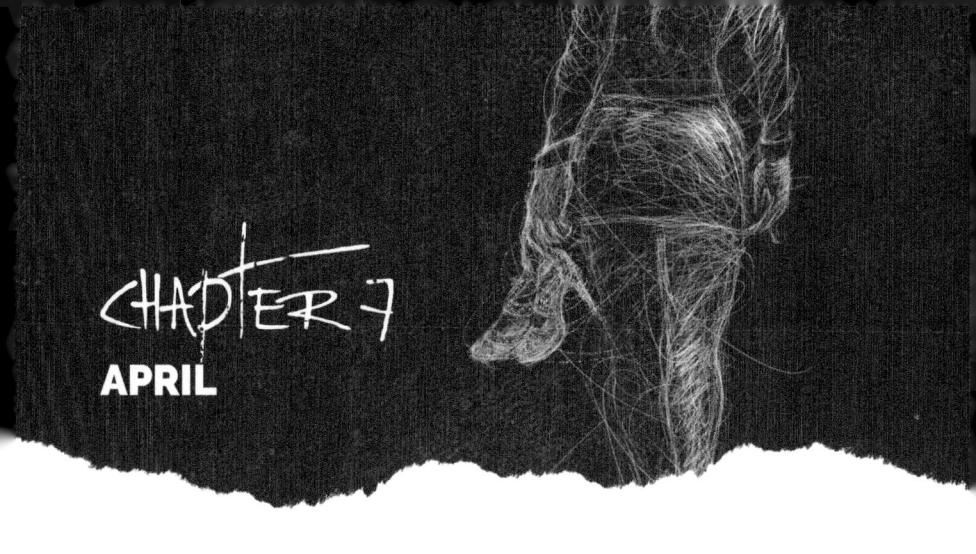

April stared into her vast closet in despair. It was a walk-in, and she had filled it; dresses, trousers, tops, coats, shoes... but she was paralyzed with indecision. What should she wear? It was her fiancé's business launch night. She had to be there, looking good. The culmination of months of hard work and planning for him. He wanted her there to support him. She had to go and stand at his side as he introduced her to all of his investors and potential clients, to look like the smiling, adoring wife-to-be she was. She wanted to go, she shook herself a little, of course she did. She had been looking forward to this night for months. Not only for the night out, in the Creekdale Hotel, no less, the fancy spa and golf resort outside of town.

The night would consist of canapés, champagne, glitz and glamour. But also so she could get her fiancé back, get on with their life together. He'd been working long, late hours for months, for years, really the whole time she'd known him. He'd had this idea in college, he'd told her all about it on their first date in fact. And he'd been so passionate and driven. She'd admired that about him. But it had turned into him putting the business first, always, every time. And she was second. She shouldn't complain, she never complained, it was the right thing to do. But there were nights when she wished he'd just come home, perhaps with a bottle of wine or a bunch of roses, or whisk her out for an unexpected dinner. Or drop everything for a cozy night in. Some impulsive romance. That's what they were missing. That's what they had never really had. Spirit, soul, life. The relationship felt very... on ice. As cool as the champagne she would soon be sipping on. She couldn't bear to think about what had been happening in the bedroom more often than not. She winced. Precisely nothing. Every evening, every minute, every move he made was planned around what would look good for the business.

She had to go tonight, of course she did, but she didn't feel any of her clothes matched her current mood. And all she could think about was a pair of searching brown eyes. And a torso chiseled from rock. And that voice. His husky, gravelly voice, calling her kitten. It was like it had never happened. Like it was a dream. A moment she had snagged, a wrinkle in the space-time continuum and slipped into a parallel universe.

She skimmed the beautiful clothes in her wardrobe absently with her hands. Silk, velvet, cotton, linen, all of it ran through her hands but she didn't really see them. She cocked her head, suddenly remembering something that would fit her mood perfectly. Did she still have them? It had been years since she'd last worn them. She ran her hands through the curtains of various trouser legs, against all the colors, all different cuts, all the materials. Until her hand hit one. Yes. Leather. Here they were. She grabbed onto a pair of leather trousers. Tight leather trousers. They were dark burgundy in color. They had been a very expensive present from her father. She pursed her lips. Who she now realized was a biker. A leader in an outlaw motorcycle club. She'd honestly believed he worked for the government. That's why he was never around, that's why she lived with her grandparents during the summer and went to boarding school. She couldn't quite wrap her head around it. But now the leather jacket made sense. The gift he'd given her for her fifteenth birthday. And these burgundy leather trousers. High waisted, they fit like a glove. She'd only worn them a few times. She had loads of other gifts from him, too. Her father, an omnipotent stranger.

Her last twenty-four hours flashed in front of her eyes. She'd need time to process it all. She'd think of it later, she told herself. She'd lied to Hugo, her fiancé, she said she'd been out late and decided to stay over at a friend's house. She had hoped to assign it all to a crazy, silly dream and forget it had happened and move on with her life. She didn't need to think about the biker who'd rescued her. The guy who had apparently been some sort of bodyguard to her all throughout her teenage years. Jeez. She didn't recognize him. But he seemed to recognize her.

It had started out as a nightmare, taken, roughly manhandled, blindfolded. She felt blinding panic and she couldn't breathe. And then he had been there, and he had rescued her, and she was saved. The look in the eyes of the man at the bar. His smoldering brown eyes, clocking her. Gosh, she had been scared until that point. But she saw him and... her fight returned. Her resolve. Her strength. He looked at her and she had almost melted at his feet. Melted and reformed again. Hell, to be with a man like that. What a woman she would be if she was with a man like that. He'd puffed on a cigarette, something she hated, but he'd made it look delicious. He'd smiled, said something to the others in the room. If she'd been kidnapped to spend a night with a man like him, then maybe she wouldn't have fought so hard in the van. He was solid muscle. Tall, he had shoulders that could hold a woman up and worship her without getting sore arms, and thighs that could drill into her all night without getting a cramp. Two of the things her fiancé had complained about the last time they had been intimate a few months ago. When Colt had thudded down into the room wearing that leather cut on his torso... it was too much. The biker had a chest to die for, abs, that 'V' of muscle that sat above the hips, leading the eye down, down to his lower region. And he'd probably be massive down there, too. God, her thoughts spiraled.

She swallowed. Her mouth was dry. She was very aware she stood wrapped in a towel after her shower and nothing else. She was meant to forget all about it and pretend it had never happened. She was meant to be picking something to wear, getting dressed for the business launch... the importance of that drifted away like sand in the wind. She was thinking of him instead. That biker, Colt. The look he'd given her when they were both frog-marched in. It was a heavy look, a meaningful look. It said to her 'don't worry, I'll come back for you.' And he did. Just as she was beginning to panic, when she realized she'd been strapped to that bed and literally couldn't move her arms and legs. She'd felt bile rising in her throat and a panicked sob had bubbled up but had been silenced by that awful gag, and she'd almost lost it. And then he had thudded into the room. Thudded into her heart. He had come back for her. And she had laughed at him and left him. She regretted that. Out of all the things about the last twenty-four hours, she regretted that. She shook her head, he probably wasn't sparing a second thought on her, he had thick skin. He'd been usurped from the top spot of the club, that was probably his bigger worry.

She held the leather trousers in her hand. What would Colt like her to wear? Would he like the silk dress, or the leather trousers? Any man would like either, she wasn't ignorant, she knew she had a good figure, and her long blonde hair and clear skin did catch the eyes of the men she met. She knew that, she'd flaunt it sometimes when she needed to. She was modest about it as a default, though. Colt had certainly seemed to appreciate her. She remembered when she'd put her foot down onto his thigh when lowering herself off the roof. She'd almost stood on his very large and very obvious erection. Somehow she felt closer to him again, with those leather trousers, and for some reason, she wanted that. Needed that. What if she had gotten on his bike and ridden off with him? She bit her tongue. Part of her regretted not going with him. At the time, she'd thought he was a bad man, just like all the other bikers. But as soon as she'd gotten in that taxi and looked back at him, there by the bike, holding her shoes, she'd felt instant regret. What adventures would have been waiting for her? For them?

It was silly, a silly fantasy. She knew that. There wouldn't have been a 'them'. He probably had ridden straight to some other clubhouse or bar and got drunk and then got whatever woman he'd wanted. He probably would have dropped her off up the road and ridden off. She'd panicked and she'd wanted to return to safety, to her fiancé, to her job and her life and forget the whole silly kidnapping ordeal. She'd panicked and dropped her shoes in the process of clambering into the car. Her precious Manolo's, well, they had been precious, they weren't so much any more. She found that they meant less to her, after meeting Colt.

She unhooked the leather trousers from the hanger, and in one move, let the fluffy white towel fall off her. She was naked in front of the wardrobe mirror. She'd already done her hair and makeup. Glamorous. She reached for her underwear drawer, since she'd need a little thong for these trousers. She slipped one on, wriggling it up her hips, snapping it into place. The material lightly grazed her clitoris. She was sensitive, she realized. She felt wetness spread into the crotch of the thong already. Her fingers drifted down and skimmed over herself. She moaned involuntarily. Primed, turned on, ready. More so than she had been aware of. She pushed further and slipped a finger inside herself. Warm, pliant, wet, she moaned. She hadn't touched herself for a while, either. But now she found she wanted to. She closed her eyes and imagined Colt. Imagined him watching her, with those melting brown eyes of his. She sped up with her finger, slipped another inside herself to join her first, and rubbed her clit in the process. She groaned and felt tension leaving her. Tension she didn't know she had. In her jaw, in her shoulders, uncoiling within herself, replaced with physical need. The need built up within her. She bit her lip, whimpered, sped up.

"April! Are you nearly ready?" Hugo shouted up the stairs. Crap. She jumped, yanking her fingers off herself. She should have been dressed by now.

"Uh... almost... I..." She stammered. She let the waistband on the thong snap back, and she wiped her wet fingers on the towel on the floor. She was burning but would not get satisfaction tonight, she thought sadly. Maybe afterwards, when they were home. She grabbed the leather trousers and her body hummed with the friction as she slipped them on. She promised herself she was going to come, tonight. She needed it. She burned inside. She was either going to persuade Hugo to give her what she wanted, or she was going to give it to herself.

She heard his footsteps coming up the stairs, and scanned the closet quickly. What the hell went with burgundy leather trousers? She found a leopard print silk halter-neck top. Sassy, sexy. She pulled it on. It didn't need a bra, she was fairly petite up top, perky rather than buxom. Then reached for some heels. She was missing her favorite pair. Oh crap, the ones she'd dropped escaping from the clubhouse. She blinked, what had Colt said about them? Fuck shoes? She imagined herself wearing them, and only them, and him above her, drilling into her, pounding her breathless-

THE CHASE

Hugo burst through the door. "April, what on earth are you wearing?"

She whimpered again, and realized a flush was creeping into her cheeks. God, caught in the act of fantasizing about another man. She'd known Hugo had been stomping up the stairs, approaching and yet her thoughts had tumbled wildly down that rabbit hole. She was bursting for sexual release. Instead, she was facing a man all buttoned up in his neat, expensive suit. Not a hair out of place. A waft of heavy, expensive aftershave hit her. It smelled too sweet. She had liked it, but now, she felt repelled by it.

"What am I wearing? You want me to change? You want to undress me?" Gosh she needed to get her thoughts under control.

"No, have you been drinking?" He frowned at her, looking displeased. His eyes raked her up and down. "Why aren't you wearing one of your pretty dresses? We're going to be late, we'll go as soon as you change."

"I'm not changing. Undress me if you don't like it." She challenged him, lifted her chin, suddenly defiant, speaking to him as she hadn't before, the desire coursing through her making her bold, reckless. She knew he wouldn't, she didn't even want him to… she didn't want him. The thought smacked her in the head.

"What? No, I don't know what's gotten into you-"

She reached for her second favorite pair of shoes. Black Jimmy Choo stiletto peep toes. She strapped herself into them. Hugo watched, flustered, his mind not on her. She stood up, grabbed her little designer handbag from the dressing table. Throbbing inside. Reeling. "Let's go then." She pouted.

CHAPTER 8
APRIL

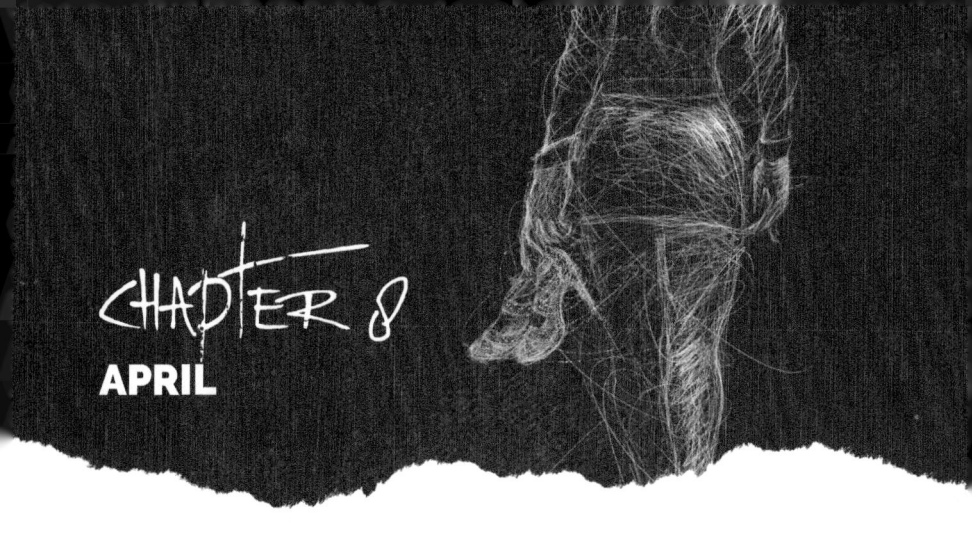

April stood and sipped her Cosmopolitan cocktail delicately. Then took a much larger gulp. God, she felt like getting drunk tonight. She didn't often drink to excess, just occasionally she'd let her hair down. Hugo didn't like it when she drank. Once or twice she had done it to wind him up, rebel against his expectations. Why, she didn't know. She stared into the tiny little martini glass at the depleted drink. She felt off tonight, not quite right. Moody, like she wanted to sulk, to stomp her foot and piss off Hugo. Tonight was not the night for it, she knew that. She wanted to go home, have a nice hot bath and bring herself to climax, day dreaming of Colt. Good girls like her weren't supposed to want bad things, like him, but here she was, wanting him so much it ached.

Hugo laughed loudly a few feet away from her. He was surrounded by a group of other men in suits who looked exactly like he did. Shiny watches, expensive aftershave, neatly buttoned up. Starched and stiff and like they'd give the fuck of a creaky ironing board. They guffawed together, congratulating themselves on their investment, their ideas, their success. She had found it attractive. She realized she was thinking in the past tense. Once upon a time, she had found Hugo, and everything he stood for, to be attractive. Not anymore. She had admired his drive, and appreciated his neatness. He was always clean, polite. He did the right things, wined her and dined her at the beginning. Her grandparents approved. She'd moved into her condo, a beautiful two story place in a sought after neighborhood. He'd shown appreciation and respect for her career, too. Her aspirations to make partner one day at the law firm she worked for. She looked at him now. His confidence was now arrogance. His body, once she had thought it well proportioned, now seemed weak. Everything he was now seemed so unimportant and unattractive. Gosh, she really needed to come. Then she'd be a lot less moody and resentful. She needed to snap out of this. Step up, be the supportive fiancée.

She downed the rest of the Cosmopolitan, and scanned the room. She'd head over to the bar, get another drink. Hugo was over there now, an abundance of martini glasses and high balls were being added to a tray in front of him. That would do the trick. But her eyes stuttered on something in the crowd. Someone, who stood out like a sore thumb.

Oh my God, she thought.

Colt.

Striding through the gaggle of neatly dressed, well groomed professionals. She let out a stuttered gasp. Her heart jumped in her chest. Air whooshed from her lungs.

Colt was coming toward her. His eyes were fixed on her. Melting her.

He was wearing the same jeans and leather vest from yesterday. The threads were still there from the patches he'd cut off. He'd found a T-shirt from somewhere, a white thing. His face was bruised, a dark, purple mark around his cheekbone, a cut on his eyebrow. He looked like he hadn't shaved, hadn't slept, hadn't eaten. He was the definition of disheveled. He wore it well. He looked hot. Rolled in like a thundercloud. She realized she needed to breathe, she had no air left in her.

"Kitten," he purred, as he approached her, his gaze was molten chocolate. A few people turned to look at who on earth he was addressing. With such a nickname, as well. They looked on, perplexed, frowning, disapproving.

"Colt, I-" She began, unsure what she was going to say.

"Who are you?" Hugo's indignant tone cut through her own utterance. She turned, he was now at her side, looking at Colt with disgust. "I'm sorry, you must have the wrong place, I'm sure you aren't on the guest list," Hugo said haughtily. It was enough to put off any other normal person. Impolite, condescending. A lesser person would have cringed back into their shell. Apologized and shuffled off. Colt didn't even blink. He didn't even deign to look at Hugo, in fact, his eyes were fixed on April.

"April, we gotta go. They're coming here," he said.

She swallowed. She knew instantly who he meant, the MC.

She'd wanted to step back into her old life and pretend the silly kidnapping had never happened. Pretend she hadn't been about to be gang raped and imprisoned for the foreseeable future at a biker clubhouse as their resident whore. How she had let herself get to that position, she didn't want to think about. But in one sentence, he had suddenly brought it all back to her. The kidnapping flashed in front of her eyes. The panic. Being manhandled. Being tied up. She felt sick. She was in so much danger. How could she not have acted? What the hell was she doing here sipping cocktails, playing let's pretend?

"They are here? Are you sure?" She stuttered back to Colt, also ignoring Hugo.

"Please leave before I call security," Hugo insisted coldly. "I'm sure my fiancé has never met you before." His gaze swept pointedly over Colt.

Colt's jaw flexed, she almost missed it in the low light.

"No, Hugo, it's alright, I know him, this is Colt-"

"How?" Hugo interrupted, looking at April incredulously.

"Ah... he was a friend of my father's-" April tried to be diplomatic, defuse the situation. Her eyes flitted between the two men. Hugo was shorter, softer, cleanly shaven, cold, stiff. Unwelcoming, unaccepting. Colt was pulsing with heat, bringing thunderous darkness, his appearance was undeniably a mess. A hot mess. Tall and strong, and angry, and full of life.

"I'm going and I'm taking April with me," Colt stated simply.

"What is the meaning of this?" Hugo was going red with rage now. He was realizing people were looking and he was embarrassed.

Whereas Colt was just focused solely on her. "Hugo, we need to listen to him, we need to-" She began but Hugo cut her off again.

"Look, I don't know who you think you are but-" Hugo tried to sound authoritative.

"No, Hugo, it turns out I'm in trouble with some of my father's... er... associates, and they think they need to collect a debt, that I do not owe, by the way... Colt helped me out yesterday but we need to take him seriously and leave before something bad happens," she hissed, feeling slightly panicky.

Hugo looked at her like she had uttered something unspeakable. "We are not leaving my business launch. I am not leaving," he rasped out.

She bit her lip. Colt glanced between the two of them.

Hugo turned to the tray on the bar and swiped up a drink. He paused for dramatic affect and then downed it, smacking his lips.

"I'm not leaving here," he repeated, dramatically. Too bad the drink he downed was a bright pink Cosmopolitan. It had about as much bad-assery as a puff of candy floss in a summer breeze.

April almost laughed out loud at Hugo's attempt of bravado. If it wasn't for the gravity of the situation, she would have guffawed.

Colt looked on without blinking. He gave off an aura of calm, she felt it, soothing her.

Hugo grabbed another drink, another bright pink martini glass. "I said, get out."

That was his big power play, the final gauntlet that he had laid down. Someone gasped nearby. April was aware people were looking on.

Colt smiled, a curling half-smile. April braced herself. He reached behind the bar and grabbed the first thing he could get his hands on, a very expensive bottle of vodka. He ripped the pourer out with his teeth and took a huge swig. He then backhanded the tray of cocktails off the bar, like swatting a fly, sending ice and glass shattering all over the floor. All over Hugo.

Colt turned to April, like nothing had happened. "Be seeing you soon, Kitten," he said casually.

He turned and strode out of the hall, bottle of vodka in hand. A security guard tried to catch up with him and stop him by the door. April watched on as Colt spat out a plume of fine mist of vodka at him, through his teeth, covering the security guard in a spray of burning alcohol. The guard cried out and his hands came to his eyes. That had to sting, April thought with a cringe. Colt was free to ball out of the room with no one stopping him.

Now that was a display of bad-assery.

April turned around and saw Hugo, pink liquid staining his once crisp, white shirt. Sticky wetness covering his crotch, dripping down his temple. His eyes were fixed on her, and he was cold with rage.

"You!" he spat.

"Hugo, listen, Colt was being serious, I'm in trouble-"

"I don't care, April! You've ruined the night! My launch-" He took a step forward but slipped in his dress shoes on the wet floor. He went sliding to the side and landed awkwardly on his knee caps. Someone tutted nearby. People looked on in silence.

"Hugo, I'm asking for your help here, I'm asking you to trust me and believe me-"

"April, I'm sorry, but this is nonsense, I don't want any part in this. Of course I'm not going to just up and leave with you! I think we've reached the end of the line here, don't you?"

She took a breath and then realized what he was saying. "You're dumping me?" Her voice was high-pitched with disbelief.

"There's no need to be dramatic, we are obviously at different stages-"

April felt a surge of pure wrath. "I don't fucking believe this!" she snarled.

Hugo's eyebrows shot up. "Language April! Look, let's call it off, I'll arrange a courier to come and pick up the ring and drop your things back at your apartment-"

April opened her mouth but no sound came out. She couldn't believe it. Four years and now it was over just like that? She didn't feel hurt, she felt mad. The one time she needed him in her corner, to believe her and take a chance on her and help her. And he'd hung her out to dry. She blinked furiously, trying to make sense of it all.

"I think it's for the best really, April, don't you?" She heard him say.

She looked down at her hand, at the large diamond engagement ring he'd given her that she wore on her left hand ring finger. She wrenched it off with her other hand.

"Here, have it back," she spat, tossing it on the floor amongst the smashed glass and ice. She took a deep breath in and yelled, "I

THE CHASE

was going to dump you anyway, you lazy, selfish asshole!" Her voice cracked, betraying her emotion. She wasn't sad, she was angry. Her hand felt lighter without the ring on it. Her heart felt lighter without Hugo's grease on it. She took a breath. Her chest felt lighter.

She had a moment of clarity, a moment of realization then. She didn't want to spend a second longer with these people. Judging, tutting, gasping. She didn't want to spend a moment longer with Hugo, cold, unwelcoming; judging Colt for what he was wearing, what he was saying. Hugo, now focusing all his social embarrassment on her. Blaming her. When she had done nothing wrong.

She took a breath in. She wasn't sure what she was going to say, but she was fully prepared to lash out with her tongue. She didn't get the opportunity.

The fire alarm went off.

Loud. Continuous beeping.

People gasped and screamed.

Security lights came on.

"Quick!"

"Fire!"

"To the exits!" people yelled and hurried toward the doors. The launch, forgotten. Social nicety forgotten. People pushed and shrieked. Her foot got stamped on by a stiletto heel. The glamour and slickness of the evening, long forgotten, too. Was it even a real fire or just a drill? She couldn't help but feel it was related to the trouble she was in. Was this the MC already, literally smoking her out of the building? She stopped and diverted to the coatroom, nabbing her leather jacket on the way out. She didn't go anywhere without it.

CHAPTER 1
APRIL

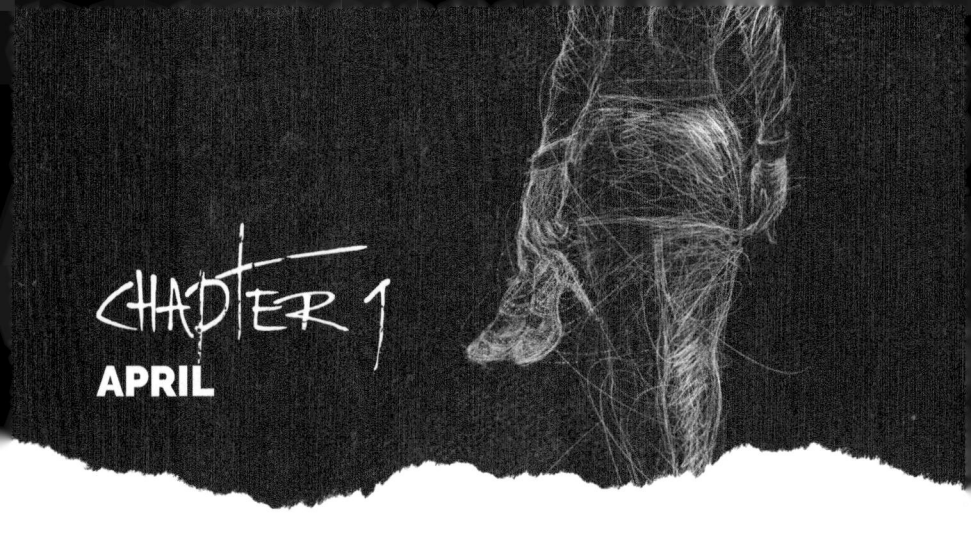

She could hear Hugo across the parking lot, mouthing off about how the criminal who just came and gate-crashed his launch probably had set the fire alarm off. Everyone had gathered in the parking garage of the hotel. Guests from Hugo's business launch, but also other hotel guests, other evening guests. There were other conference rooms and they were obviously being used for other evening functions. Lots of people, well dressed, glamorous, now reduced to milling around outside. Cooks and cleaners and waiters were filing out of the building, too. Someone had a clipboard, and started counting the staff, and trying to get guests to stand still in one place. April didn't know what to do. She felt creeping dread growing in the pit of her stomach. She looked around. Were the MC there, hiding in the shadows? Blocking the exits to the hotel?

She was standing alone. She looked on at the glittering crowd and sighed. She can't run from this, from what happened the other night. From the truth about her father. She can't run from where she came from, though her whole life had been an attempt to do just that. She had always sensed it with her grandparents. With the expensive schools and the trips away. They were always trying to keep her distracted, on the move, moving forwards, moving upwards. Away from her roots. Because as it turned out, they were dirty roots.

She turned from the crowd and there in the darkness, at the other side of the parking lot, in between two cars, a figure crouched. Fear gripped her for a second. Was it Cleaver? Or another MC member? His face then lit up briefly as he inhaled on a cigarette.

Colt.

She instantly puffed out a breath in relief. She pursed her lips, feeling sheepish, and grudgingly walked over to him. Away from who she was, away from the people she had stood shoulder to shoulder with. It was time to embrace her roots. It was time to put her head on straight and think her way out of this mess.

"Hey, Kitten," he murmured, but he didn't stand up. He looked up at her. His eyes lingered more than was necessary. He tilted his chin in a nod, beckoning her to crouch down with him. She could barely see him in the darkness. She was realizing this is her life now, crouching in shadows, looking over her shoulder, being chased. The threat was real. She dipped down low.

He blew out a plume of cigarette smoke by tilting his head back and forcefully blowing it up, above her head. He looked so hot doing that, the way his neck moved, his lips pouting together. Almost like a kiss. She shook herself. What an inappropriate thought. But God, would she love to be kissed by him. Jesus, she needed to stop. Now was not the time.

"Where's your rock?" he asked huskily, breathing in, wincing a little, the tip of the cigarette glowing orange.

April blinked, unsure what he was referring to at first. He nodded down to her hand. Her ringless finger. "He… we broke it off," she said, her voice quiet. Not because she was sad but because she was appalled at how little she actually cared that her future wouldn't have Hugo in it. She realized she didn't actually mind at all. No, she was quiet because she felt embarrassed in front of Colt. Her pride was hurt. She was almost sulking about it. She'd left Colt standing at the side of the road because she deemed herself better than him. Turned from him and his offer of safety because she thought she could do better. She realized her mistake now, she was wrong to turn down the freedom he had offered her. It was more than what she had waiting for her with Hugo.

Colt held the smoke in his lungs thoughtfully for a moment. She almost began to worry. Then he ejected it again, above her head, in a plume. She thought she saw a flicker of amusement in his face. Maybe not amusement, triumph. He scanned her face and she felt very exposed. She broke his gaze and looked down.

"Best to leave them to it, they are not from our world," he said finally.

"I'm not sure you and I are from the same world, Colt. But I believe right now we are in the same boat. They are coming to get us, aren't they?" she asked.

He breathed in and blew out again on his cigarette, making her wait for his response. She almost lost her patience, this guy had a serious attitude. Everything on his terms, and everyone else around him fit in with that. She would find it impressive, sexy even, if she wasn't feeling so panicked by the urgency of the predicament.

He stubbed the cigarette out on the ground and flicked the butt away. She pursed her lips, saving her lecture on littering for another time.

He nodded to a brown paper bag at his feet. "Put those on." He instructed.

She opened her mouth to argue back. What on earth could possibly be in the bag that would warrant taking time away from escaping? She blinked into the bag. A pair of black biker boots stared back at her. She reached in and pulled them out. They weren't new, but they looked hardly worn. They were her size.

"I guessed you'd be wearing another pair of obscene shoes."

"You got me some boots?"

"I figured if you're going on the run... you need a decent pair of boots." He almost looked bashful.

She was touched. Genuinely impressed by the thoughtfulness and care that went into him finding her a pair of cute little boots in her size. It looked like he hadn't slept or eaten since she'd last seen him, but somehow he'd managed to get her some boots. She was speechless.

She looked up at him. His gaze was fixed on her feet, currently in her little black peep toe Jimmy Choo's. He growled.

"Fuck shoes," he muttered hungrily.

She raised her eyebrows. "Do you have some sort of foot fetish or something? Because it's weird..."

"Not until I saw yours," he growled back. He cleared his throat, shifted, turned away. Almost like he'd said too much. "I was left standing at the side of the road holding your last pair of heels. I learn from my mistakes, I'm not asking you to run anywhere in fuck shoes again."

She didn't know what to say to that. She sat down. She didn't have any socks but she wouldn't mention it. He kept his head down, almost as if she were changing clothes or something. Like he knew he shouldn't look, no matter how much he wanted to, or he was preserving her dignity. If he liked her feet, he was showing great restraint in not looking.

She cleared her throat as she laced up the boots. "Aren't you raging drunk by now anyway?" she asked haughtily.

He looked straight at her then, frowning, puzzled.

"The Grey Goose? Haven't you guzzled it all by now?"

"You mean this bottle?" He twitched his hand. April peered

THE CHASE

through the darkness. There was the bottle, in his hand. He held it loosely. It had a rag stuffed in the top. She frowned.

He got out his lighter with the other hand. Flicked it once. His face lit up in the orange glow. His gaze was fixed on her. The rag caught, burning with a flighty yellow flame. He stood, took a few running steps and threw it. Overarm. She watched it hurl through the air, a look of dumb horror frozen on her face. It smashed through a hotel window. The fire catching, spreading instantly, illuminating the room with an orange gleam. She gaped back at him.

He smiled. He was crouched down next to her, he looked straight back at her and smiled.

"You just... but the fire alarm... there wasn't a real fire..."

He simply shrugged. "There is now. Relax, everyone's out, I heard them say everyone is accounted for."

"Then why..."

"Wouldn't want to waste good alcohol."

"I thought you'd have drunk it."

He shook his head once. "No, turns out I can't hold a drink since getting out of prison." He licked his lips, as his eyes darted around. "The MC is coming. They know you're here. If you want to do this... I can get us both far away from here. We run," he said quietly, looking at her intently.

"You came to warn me? To help me?" She stammered. "You could have just disappeared and you'd probably be far away and safe by now. I was so rude to you, I laughed in your face-"

He shrugged again. "Yes."

"But you came back for me anyway?"

"Yes."

April almost laughed out loud. "And to think, I judged you for being a dirty, rowdy, bad boy ex con biker-"

"Kitten, I'll say again what I said before, I can give you a fast ride and a hot, hard fuck. That's all there is to it. Now, do you want it or not?"

She gaped. She wanted to get out of here and trusted him to do that at least. Once they were out of harm's way, she could collect herself, assess her options, make a plan. She could walk away from him, and get back to her life, her job. As for the other part, she couldn't. A hot, hard fuck? She couldn't want that, could she? Her mouth felt suddenly dry. She knew she did but she couldn't.

"I'll take the ride out of here-"

"Kitten, I will be fucking you, you know that, don't you?"

She was speechless. She thought she'd feel indignation. She didn't, she felt a thrill creep up her spine. She wanted him. She was surprised by him. Here he was, all rugged, just out of prison, cast out by his outlaw motorcycle club. Fresh from nonchalantly torching a hotel. She had a million assumptions about him. Here she was assuming she'd ditch him as soon as they had got a safe distance away. And yet, he'd bought her sensible shoes and he hadn't drunk a drop of alcohol. He'd come back to rescue her, but in the same breath, had cockily told her, not asked her, but outright told her, that he would be fucking her. It sent pangs all over her body and her mind. He was a Rubik's cube and she thought she'd had it all lined up, only to find she was far from the final solution.

"I'm…"

"Save it for later, Kitten, right now, we've gotta move. Toss your phone," he said.

"What?" she said. Her phone was like her right arm.

"Get rid of it, toss it over there, they'll track it. If you want to disappear, you gotta let it go," he said. She understood, she did, her brain got that. But her heart… something pulled. To throw away her phone was to throw away who she was. All her emails, access to the internet, social media... in that moment, it hit her. His words echoed in her head, gotta let it go.

"Okay, fine," she said, and it took great strength, but she did exactly that. A simple gesture, in the end. She threw it like a ball, it soared into the darkness and clattered to the ground somewhere. And she was free. Cut loose.

"Good, now we run."

"Colt, I have one request."

"What, Kitten?"

"There is something I need to do... we need to go to the bus station."

Chapter 10
APRIL

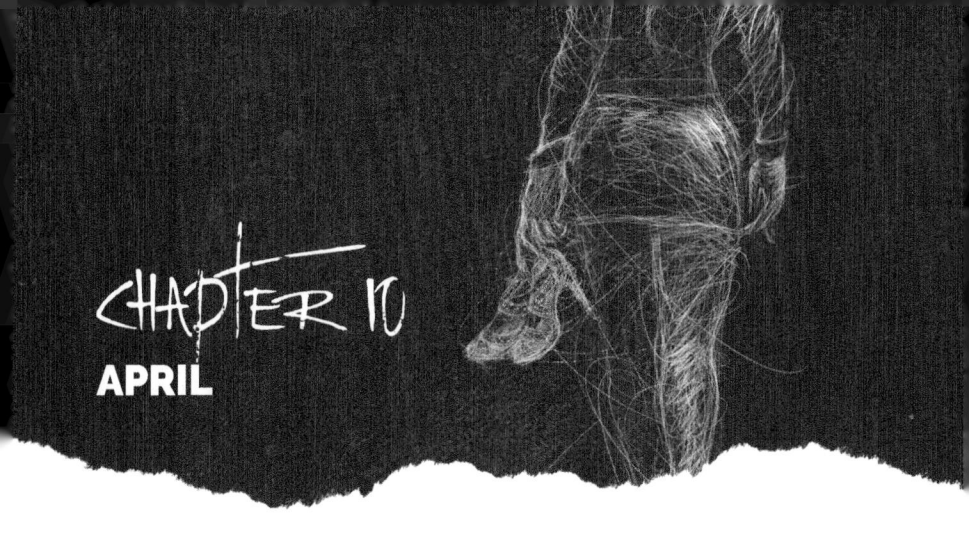

He raised both his eyebrows and jerked his head back. "Why the fuck... no."

"It's important."

"What? No, we can't loop back around-"

"Colt, I need to get something from there. My father..." She paused and took a shaky breath. She felt tears welling in her eyes and swiped them away quickly.

"Shit, Kitten, I'm sorry-"

"Christ, this has been such an ordeal," she muttered, more to herself.

"Blue's death was a fucking shitshow, I'm sorry-"

"It's not that! He's not... It's-" She paused and wondered how much she should continue. How much to say. She didn't know this man, she didn't trust him yet, not fully. Enough to get a ride on his bike, sure, but with everything else she was thinking right now... no, not yet.

She cleared her throat. "My father said if I ever needed it, there was help, waiting. An emergency package of sorts. He said if I ever needed to get away... I'd always laughed it off to be honest but he insisted I knew that he'd left me something. At the bus station. I have the key to one of the luggage lockers. It's stitched into the lining on my jacket here." She tapped her torso.

Colt nodded slowly. She knew it would mean navigating around downtown, a risky place. He had managed to avoid the MC while he'd tracked her to the hotel, but going back downtown with the MC on their bikes and in active pursuit… she knew it wasn't smart. But she wanted to go back and get this thing. Whatever it was. It might be helpful, or it might be something really useless. It held sentimental value to her, she had to convince him-

"Sure, Kitten, we'll swing by the bus station," he said quietly.

She gave him a penetrating look that he shifted under uncomfortably. She was surprised he'd relented. He wasn't an ogre, he was human, he did have a heart. "Then where?" she asked, with big wide eyes.

"Where? Over the state line," he ground out. His eyes were hidden in the darkness. His whole face was.

She raised her eyebrows. "Then where?" she practically whispered.

"Don't know," he said simply. "One step at a time. Let's grab this package or whatever it is Blue left for you, then let's get the fuck out of here."

"Okay. Thanks," she said, almost hesitantly. She had expected more push back from him.

"Maybe I can pee at the bus station?" she asked hopefully.

"Oh no, you go into that bus station, you grab the package from the locker and you run out, do you hear me? Straight back on the bike and then we don't stop until we are over the state line."

"But that will take hours! We'll be riding all night!" she exclaimed. "I assumed you had a car or something-"

"Nope. Bike. MC Prez, remember…" he said sarcastically, pounding his fist into his chest.

She huffed.

THE CHASE

"Now, we move." He nodded his head, indicating for her to follow. He began to slink off around the car, crouching still.

She took a breath in and pushed it out. She had to follow, she had no choice. She wouldn't turn into a hysterical needy princess that required rescuing, even though that is exactly what she felt like. She had to keep her cool. She followed him, crouching like he did, keeping low. They slunk around the back of the hotel by the dumpsters. Doing anything with Colt seemed to involve sneaking by dumpsters. It must be the staff entrance or delivery entrance or something. Her mind whirled hysterically. She tried to follow. Her heart was beating in her chest. Louder and louder. Quicker. He seemed calm, outwardly as nonchalant as ever. But she could sense his urgency, his alertness now, which was different from when they were crouched, chatting. She was struggling to breathe, moving quietly and carefully in a hunched position.

Now he sprinted across the concrete. She followed blindly, thankful for the boots. They ran across the concourse, lit by streetlights. Colt headed to the steep grassy bank. He kept running, up the verge, throwing himself into the bushes at the top of the peak. She followed, panic surging now.

Branches scratched her. Her lungs felt like they were going to burst.

But then strong, warm hands brushed her face. Brushed the branches out of her hair, pulled her forwards. Colt. She calmed. Closer to the center of the bush, there were less leaves and little snaggly twigs. She could breathe. She couldn't see him, but she sensed him. His warm presence.

"My bike is about a hundred feet down the road, on the left. I cut a hole in the fence here. We run, we do not stop running. You will get on the bike behind me, you will put the helmet on your head, and you will hold on. Okay? You hold on tight, both hands, do you hear me? Keep your head down and you don't look up." His voice was low but insistent. She heard urgency. She also heard bike engines. That ripping sound of multiple engines.

She opened her mouth to take a breath but couldn't. She gulped. She felt the bikes getting closer, the noise getting louder.

"Hey," he said, and now his hands were on her face, holding her cheek, holding her chin. He forced her to look right at him. In the darkness of the bush she couldn't see much at all, except two shiny orbs of warmth in front of her. His eyes bored into her. "I will not let anything happen to you, April," he insisted. "Okay?" he asked her, releasing her chin.

She nodded. She remembered it was dark and he probably couldn't see. "Okay," she croaked. She breathed finally. She trusted him.

"Now." He disappeared. She felt the branches move, the bushes shake. She followed.

Squeezing through a small opening in the metal fence, her top caught and she pulled herself loose. Out in the open, she turned left, like he'd said. He was up ahead of her, running flat out. She did the same. Not her usual jog. Not keeping with her breathing, calm and controlled, in through the nose, out through the mouth. Like how she ran in her designer lycra with her ear buds in on a Saturday morning. No, this was rasping, furious, pumping her legs like she hadn't done since she was a kid on the playground. The motorcycles sounded so close, like a swarm of bees coming up behind her. Ahead of her, he was at the bike. He batted on a helmet, and swung his leg over the seat. Held out a helmet for her, like a relay baton.

Finally, she was there, too. She slammed the helmet onto her head, and she hopped onto the back of the bike. She tentatively put her hands on his hips.

THE CHASE

He started the engine. The sound, the vibrations beneath her. She whimpered, not even hearing it herself, and then wrapped her arms around his waist, squeezing like a bear hug, burying her face as much as she could in the back of his leather jacket. He revved the engine and they shot away. Away from the danger and the panic and her life.

He was going fast. Faster than she'd ever gone before on the road, Colt was clearly breaking the speed limit. She felt tears streaming from her eyes and closed them. She clenched her thighs together, gripping his rear with her body, clinging onto him.

Thank fuck she'd worn the leather trousers, she thought to herself.

CHAPTER 11
COLT

Hours later, he felt a tapping on his shoulder. He thought he might have heard her saying his name, too. It was too hard to hear over the noise of the bike. They had streaked away into the night. He'd weaved down residential streets and broader, main roads. He had to admit, he fucking loved it. These streets were his streets. He may not be Prez any more but he was still the fucking king of the road. He'd grown up on these streets, literally living and sleeping on them, riding pedal bikes then mopeds then his Harley. He had owned these streets. He rode like they were still his. He knew them like the back of his hand. Some things had changed, most hadn't. It brought back memories of when they'd all ridden together, his MC. Two rows side by side. He remembered yanking the bike up onto the back wheel and roaring like a rampant lion through the town. Or sliding, smoke coming off his back wheels, looking behind and seeing his brothers grinning back at him. Fuck, his brothers. He didn't want to think of them, didn't want to remember them. He had thought they'd all be there for him when he got out. They weren't. One day, he'd be brave enough to ask what had happened to them. How they died. Today was not that day. And he didn't think that day would be coming anytime soon. He felt a lump in his throat and focused on the road, the thrum of the bike under him. They were his streets, he hadn't been here for five years, but they were still his streets, he reminded himself. Roaring on that beautiful bike made him feel whole again, though a lot had been broken. To ride a bike like that took strength, bravery, and attitude. You had to commit, it was ride or die. He chose to ride.

She followed his instructions perfectly, she'd clung onto him and not looked back. He was glad, because he'd seen the MC riders in his mirrors a few times. He'd been lucky with being able to dart down streets and traffic lights impeding their progress. He wouldn't tell her how close the MC had been. He wouldn't think of what might have happened if they'd been caught.

They hadn't left the city limits yet. He doubled back at times. He had wanted to shake them off his tail before committing to any highway out of the state. He needed to know they weren't going to follow them. Colt had been zigzagging around the city, his route erratic, not following any obvious plan, not sticking to any road or route. They'd been at it for hours but hadn't traveled far. He wanted the MC confused, unable to guess where he was heading. How he hadn't been stopped by police for speeding, he didn't know. Maybe the cops knew what was going on. Mainly they had left the MC to their own devices back in his day. The local Chief had been accepting bribes from them to look the other way, he didn't know who the Chief of Police was these days.

Why had she tapped him on the shoulder? She wanted to stop, probably. He eyed the road ahead, and checked behind in the mirrors. Nothing, it looked safe. He pulled into a quieter road, and then to the side of the road, there was just forest on the other side. The sky was lit up with the glow of the city from the yellow of the streetlights. He cut the engine.

With the bike engine turned off, the quiet of the night was suddenly deafening. His wrists felt tight, his butt was numb. He hadn't ridden in five years, but he'd been intensely focused on getting away.

"Fuck," he breathed out involuntarily.

"If I had a dollar for every time you swore…" Her playful voice came from behind him. He couldn't help it, a huge grin spread across his face.

"You could buy me a sweet new bike- " He began. He felt her hands digging into his stomach, her nails biting into his abs. More than was needed for her to shimmy off the bike safely. He shivered. Yes, it was a definite raking down of her nails on his torso. He fucking loved it. She swung her leg over and came to stand beside him. Oh he wanted to scoop her up, wrap her up in his arms. To treasure. To ravage. The pull between such extremes, treating her softly, gently, with care, and then wanting to fuck her brains out and ruin her so that no one else could have her… they tugged at his heart, his soul. His very skin. He felt torn.

She stood with her hands on her hips, all wild, raw sass. He guessed she'd enjoyed the ride. Probably hadn't felt anything like it in her life. "Have you ever ridden before?" he asked.

"A motorcycle?" she asked, and there was the most subtle cock of her eyebrow. Fuck. She was playing with him. His balls tightened. He smirked back at her.

"No, not a motorbike before, it was… exhilarating," she said. She got it. He could see it. Bikes divided people, some loved them. The freedom, the roar, the power underneath, becoming a part of you. Others hated them, too noisy, too dangerous, a nuisance. He would bet any money in the world April had belonged to that camp, hating them before. But he could see the change on her face, the surprise, the effects of the adrenaline, the wind, the freedom, the power. She had caught the bug. She was experiencing the same high that he was. And it seemed to be bolstering her libido, just like it was with him.

She licked her lips. "I feel like I've been blown away…"

He had to look away, watching her lips say the word 'blown' had caused his dick to stir. He was already sporting a semi from the vibrations of the ride.

"I really need to pee, I know you said after we got out of the state but…." she said, tossing her hair out of the helmet, hanging it on the handlebars.

He had to pee as well before he got too hard. He swung his leg over the bike, and took a few steps away. He tried very hard not to think about her, about her cocked eyebrow when she'd made that innuendo about riding. Or about her lips when she'd said 'blown'. He tried not to think about what could happen if he turned around, with his jeans still open… too late. He had an image of her straddling him, both of them straddling the bike. Oh sweet fucking Christ. Being back on a bike had made him ballsy. He finished peeing, shook himself, tucked himself back in and zipped up while he still could. He turned to face her and saw her practically tapping her foot, arms crossed, looking angry. Looking fucking cute with how ruffled she was.

"I can't believe you just did that. I'm right here!" she huffed.

He smiled. "Yeah, now your turn. Let's get going," he said, mirroring her body language, crossing his arms, tapping his foot, but he was smirking broadly. She just got huffier. Now he really wanted to just bend her over and slam into her, deep and repeatedly. Fuck.

He let it go to his head, he felt momentarily high off of it, and gave her a wink, then turned away.

She huffed loudly and turned her back to the fence. He couldn't quite believe April was panty-less so close to him. April. That beautiful, untouchable girl he'd trailed after, watching. Always watching. Now they were riding off into the night, it was both thrilling and terrifying.

He did a quick sweep of the bike and put on his helmet. It was in good working condition, they had enough gas. That prospect buffing it up the other day had taken good care of it before Colt had punched his lights out. Poor kid. Colt hoped he was okay. They had a long ride ahead of them. A sleepless night, it would take them until dawn to get out of California. He'd relish every second with her pressed up against his back.

"Colt, was that the fast, dangerous ride you promised me?"

He turned to see April. She was looking at him now with a glint in her eyes. A glint he'd seen in the bar when she'd first laid eyes on him. Desire. She didn't take her gaze off him. She wanted more from him. He watched as she waited. He felt a surge of recklessness. Sure, she'd burned him before, but he was a dumb motherfucker and wanted to get burned again. What the hell? He felt a haze of delirium settle about him, felt a coil of excitement unraveling in the pit of his stomach. Why should he not throw the dice again after all?

He smirked. "Kitten, that was just the warm up lap."

And he knew she saw it on his face, too. A satisfied smile quickly spread but then she regained composure, and raised an eyebrow, putting her hands on her hips. Oh he could eat her up right now.

"What about the hot, hard fuck?" She tossed her hair over her shoulder. Her eyes now finally left his face and raked over him. He cleared his throat. It felt sticky with desire. She knew what she wanted, she knew her worth, she knew she was a beautiful woman, standing in front of a man who wanted her, she trusted herself and she wasn't afraid to go after what she wanted. It was the hottest thing he'd ever seen.

His heart was pounding in his chest. His vision pulsed with how much blood was pumping through his veins. And it was surging to his cock. He ripped off his helmet again.

"Are you asking me for a hot, hard fuck, April Rodgers?" He asked, folding his arms over his chest. She unzipped her leather jacket. His lips curled in a smile. "Fuck, you in that jacket…" He lost the rest of his thoughts. But then she reached behind her neck and grabbed the ribbon securing her halter-neck top. The bow undid after she gave it a tug. Colt could only watch on as her top fell down, bunching round her waist, her breasts now out for him to see. Her leather jacket was still on. He stared, unashamedly. As if the meaning of life was down there. The meaning of his life *was* down there.

He didn't think. His body reacted as if it was a reflex. He swung his leg off the bike and stood. He pulled down his jeans and his hard, dark red cock bobbed free. His jeans got caught up mid thigh but that was all he needed. He drank in the sight before him, April, her tits out and her nipples all swollen and perky for him.

"Yes, Prez, I'm asking you for a hot, hard fuck," she said, looking up at him, biting her lip and smiling.

No need to ask him twice.

CHAPTER 12
APRIL

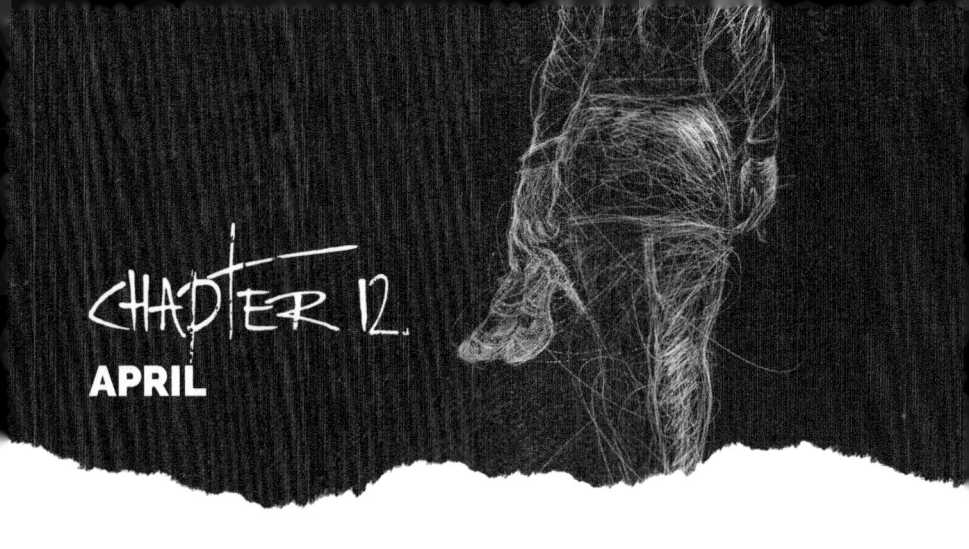

She hadn't ever felt like this. Ever. Free. On the edge. Running from an MC. Those bikes, roaring behind them. Terrifying yes, but now that they'd stopped, she could recognize that tingling in her gut for what it was, as well - excitement. Her skin had felt the cool air whipping across her face. Her hair was all mussed up from the helmet and being in the wind. And she was there with him. He was fast becoming undone. In control, and yet undone at the same time. Like a bonfire, about to smolder and burn. The women of his life before must have been strong, beautiful women. To be able to feed him like this, to slake his desire. If this was how he loved, they would have been infinitely energetic, giving. She was in awe, envious, and suddenly intrigued.

When he had winked at her, she had realized it could be her. She could be one of those women. Even for a short moment in time. She looked at him, the adrenaline in her blood making her reckless, making her needy. She was worried she had blown it by being stuck up and snobby. But she saw he would forgive her. He would give her a second chance. Probably it was his dick doing the talking in his head right now, but either way, she wanted to capitalize on it. That bike ride had blown away everything about herself that she had once held to be important. And she was free to seek what she actually wanted.

He released his jeans and approached her. She quivered with excitement, suddenly all action. And fear. This had escalated quickly. She had made this happen and now that she was strapped in for the ride, she realized how extreme the roller coaster actually could be. She wanted her mind blown. She wanted this.

She was dizzy with the speed this was going at. She wanted to see him, taste him. Savor him. But no. She was just going to feel him. In one place, and one place only. She wanted to run her hands over his abs, grab his ass. She hadn't been able to admire his body, and she wanted to see his shoulders, his pecs, his stomach, the rolling muscles. She wanted all of him.

"Yeah, you better get those fucking leather pants off your ass right now," Colt ground out, his hands yanking down his own jeans further.

No one had spoken to her like this before. It sent sparks up her spine. She floundered, bending quickly, peeling down her pants, realizing she wouldn't be able to get them over her boots. Then he was in front of her, pushing her lightly so she bumped against the seat of the bike, from the side. Should she worry the bike would topple over? She sat a little on the side of the seat, half leaning on it, suddenly breathless, looking up at him. Looking to him for direction. His hands were there, holding her foot, ripping at the laces of her boots, pulling them off like she was a doll and they were toy shoes. Tossing them over his head. He wasn't worried about the bike, so she wouldn't either. Then off came her pants, he pulled at them like she wouldn't need to wear them again.

Then his hand went to her boobs, and he cupped and lifted them. She arched her back. She'd never been handled like this, and never in this position, perched on the side of a bike in the cool night air. His other hand hitched up one of her legs, gluing it to his waist, hooking it around his hips. He took his other hand off her boobs and sent it between her legs, and she knew what he'd find there. He moved aside her thong, it rucked against the side of her leg.

And then his rough fingers touched her. She shivered and gasped. His fingers felt hard against her soft, wet skin. He swiped them along her crease, then delved into her folds, seeking firmly. She trembled. Never, never had she felt this.

"Kitten, so wet for me," he purred and then his other hand went to his cock, partly obscured still by his jeans. April wanted to see it, to hold it and stroke it, but she couldn't. "Hold on to the seat of the bike. Hold on hard, April," he said.

She watched as his face clouded over. No, not clouded, it darkened like octopus ink squirting into the ocean. In a matter of seconds. The air crackled between them. Their gazes locked together. Almost daring each other to move. He was waiting for her. Though something was consuming him, the man almost gone, replaced by a creature of darkness that wanted her blood. The last rational thread held him back, forced him to breathe, and to wait.

She could tell him no. She knew that, this was the moment when she could, but she didn't want to. She wanted more, she wanted all of it. She hadn't thought he'd honestly just go ahead, right here, right now. But that was the kind of man he was. Now here they were and she was burning and melting for him and the only way out was to fall with him. So she did.

She moved first. She leaned forward, toward him, as he stood beside the bike.

He lunged forward to meet her, snagged her lips and kissed her. Hard. She tried to keep up, to respond, but he wasn't kissing, he was devouring her. She could only hold still and let him. She closed her eyes and threw herself into the moment. He kept going. And going. Like teenagers, discovering their first throes of desire.

He was insatiable, his stamina, his need for her thrilled her. This was all beyond what she had thought this could be. This was going to be beyond how she thought two people could make love to each other. Or fuck, it wouldn't be making love, it would be raw, animalistic fucking. She knew that, since she hadn't done either in the last few years. She had neither been made love to or fucked, she realized now. She hadn't been doing it right. She hadn't been doing any of it right. Her old life was a meaningless, almost funny memory that no longer fit. And this felt shockingly, ridiculously more right than anything she had felt for a long, long time. She had never felt this before. But she did now. And it thrilled her.

Chapter 13
COLT

Fuck, he'd forgotten how to do this. He was being too rough with this kiss, he just wanted to taste her, to eat her. He forced his tongue inside her mouth and growled. Then he pulled back and looked at her. Her legs bare, one cocked up under his hand, around his waist. Her pussy, wet, dark pink, beckoned to him. She trembled beneath him.

He took her all in. Her nipples peaked like bullets, poking out from under her leather jacket. He felt his control scatter. He gave it up, surrendered it, and let his animal brain take over. Fuck. He wanted to fuck. He wanted her.

So he held the base of his throbbing cock. And put his head to her wet cunt entrance. It called him home. He didn't wait, he didn't think any longer. He plunged in.

Wet heat gripped him like a vice. He didn't pause to think. His body began to move on instinct. Nothing about this was conscious thought, nothing about this involved his rational, human brain. It was raw, old, ingrained in his bones and DNA. Ingrained in what made him an animal. He had to fuck her.

He barely heard but she was screaming with each impact. He held her hips and slammed. Her boobs jumped. Her body jarred. Again. Again.

And again. His hips pistoning with a spirit of their own.

Fuck her.

Own her.

Selfish.

Selfish fucking monster.

Beast.

Fucking animal.

But it was good.

It felt so fucking good. So right. So perfect.

Something was stirring in him.

Between them.

The fabric of the universe was shifting. Something profound, the darkness within him. The doubt, the fragility, moving away. Like fog from the sun's warm rays, something holy and true and real was changing. It was so potent he felt he could shatter the sky with it.

His eyes were closed now. His world was black, warm, wet. Fully engulfed in her. He felt something scratching his skin. Not a scratch, light flutters. His neck. Her fingernails. He kept going.

And it built.

Harder.

Faster.

He couldn't stop. He wouldn't stop. This was his. He wanted it so he'd take it. He chased it, he'd catch it. This was his moment. All that was right in the world was telling him this was his. He needed it. He'd earned it.

And there. There it was.

"Fuck!" he roared, as it splintered through him. The hardest orgasm he'd had in years. And he squirted into her. He pinioned his hips deep and poured himself into her. His cum shooting deep within her warm, wet core.

The Chase

His hearing caught up with him first. He heard her gasping pants. She sounded hurt. Fuck. He was panting, too, rasping oxygen in. His heartbeat banging in his ears. He opened his eyes. Everything was spinning. Hell, he had water in his eyes. That was how hard he'd come. He blinked and wiped them with the heel of this hand.

Fuck. She was trembling, shaking. Wait, had she come? Fuck no. She hadn't. He'd been so selfish in getting what he wanted. Her face was wild, her eyes half closed with lust. She looked half undone. He'd done that. Fuck. He had to finish her. He pulled out. The cool night air surrounded his wet cock. Wetness seeped out of her.

Wetness. Fuck. His cum. He'd come inside her. Sweet fucking Christ. He'd never done that in his life. Shit. Awareness rolled in. He was shocked. He'd let himself go so damn quick and so damn hard.

He put his hand down between her legs. She gasped. She was sensitive. Yeah, because she hadn't come yet, dumbass. He forced himself to take a breath and start righting the wrongs. First priority, her. He traced his two fingers along her crease, her swollen, wet folds. Then he dipped into her. She felt perfect. Full of his cum. He felt like a barbarian.

She groaned and rocked slightly on his fingers, her eyelids closing. He groaned, too. He pulled his fingers out and looked at the gooey, wet stickiness that hung off them. His cum. Inside her.

He couldn't help himself. He smiled. He was a fucking selfish, dimwitted bastard but he loved that he'd come inside her. Inside April. Fuck.

"Please, Colt," she hissed. His awareness snapped to her.

"Sorry, Kitten, I'll give you what you need," he said simply, and plunged his wet fingers back inside her. He shamelessly finger fucked her, like how he had with his cock, like how he should have if he had been able to keep going. He positioned his thumb to skim her swollen clit on every stroke.

"Oh God," she snarled, and tilted her head back, her golden hair cascaded down her back. "Colt, oh, God." She wheezed in between gasps.

"Come," he commanded. She was writhing like she was trying to escape. Colt knew why. She'd never been touched like this before. College douche had probably pawed at her like a lame fox. It seemed she hadn't been serviced properly, and he would do the honors. Fuck, it was a dream. A privilege. To be knuckle deep in a wet, begging, pliant April. Now that he was thinking with his brain again and not his dick, he was beginning to wonder if he shouldn't have planned this a bit more... waited. Until they had more time. A bed. Seduce her. Treat her well. Roses, silk sheets and champagne. Well, not that, he was a biker after all but just... something better than a quickie on the bike on the roadside.

"Colt, don't stop, this is the most-" she whined again, pulling him back from inside his head. God. His senses flared, she was everywhere around him. He could smell, touch, taste, and hear April. Under his fingers, April. Getting under his skin, April. Had he slowed down? He shook his head and continued his onslaught, focusing on her changing face. As her mouth opened up, her face muscles tensed. Yes, this was it. Her eyes slammed shut and she stuttered. Electrocuted. By an orgasm he had caused.

"Yeah," he ground out as she clenched and released. Again. Clenched and released. Her fingernails clawed lightly at him. He held her down. Clenched and released a final time.

He looked at her, resting his forehead on hers. Sharing each other's breaths. She gazed back at him, her blue eyes brighter than ice.

The Chase

His heartbeat pounded in his ears still. He smelled her shampoo, her skin, sweet and soft.

Colt cleared his throat. "I'm... that was... I'd not normally..." He felt shame crashing down in him. It was heavy, it threatened to suffocate him. He knew he needed to apologize, but he somehow couldn't form the words.

She watched him with big, wide eyes, and said nothing.

"I've never come inside someone bare before, I always use protection. You clean and covered? I mean we're okay?" he asked urgently.

"I..." she blinked and looked up, as if she was doing math in her head. "Yes. I... yes, clean, covered," she said.

He breathed with relief, but felt a little sting. That caught him by surprise, for what? It was fine, she was on birth control, so why did that pinch?

"I'll get some for..." He felt a sense of duty to do the right thing, even though the horse had already bolted. But he trailed off, would there be a next time? Fuck, he both wanted it and dreaded it.

Then another sound cut through their night. A far off rumble. Colt immediately stiffened.

"What's that noise?" she asked, but the tone in her voice said she already knew, already dreaded the answer.

"Straight pipes. The MC," he said, his eyes hardening, clearing, coming back into focus, freezing the waves of shame in place for now.

She gulped. " We better-"

"Yup, get on." He turned and searched the ground, finding her boots, her pants, tossing them to her. She paused, took a deep breath.

"What's up?" he asked, frowning.

She threw him a look. "Just taking a moment to realize what we did..."

He set his jaw with a grunt. Fuck, was she having second thoughts already?

"I just had unprotected sex with an ex-con biker I hardly know on his bike on the roadside while being chased by a motorcycle club-"

"Not my bike," Colt cut in.

"What?"

"Stole it." He shrugged, nonchalant. She gawked for a second. He wanted to push her to her knees and shove his semi in that gape. He could go again. He didn't, he resisted, his head was too fucked up from all of this.

"Great, fucked by a biker on a stolen bike on the side of the road-"

"Alright, alright, we gotta fucking go. You can list your regrets in your Dear Diary later on." He got on the bike, anguish and disappointment taking hold within him. But he pushed it down. Just another feeling to lock out. Just another thing he could dwell on in the dead of the night. But right now he needed to act. And act fast. To save his hide. And April's. Of course. Once again, here he was with April front and center in his life. Maybe only for the next twenty-four hours. Maybe for longer. He hoped longer. No point denying it, he was still as into her as he was as an eighteen year old kid. He'd had a taste of the forbidden fruit. And God help him, he wanted more.

She approached behind him, strapping on her helmet. It was good that the saddle bag had a spare helmet in it. The owner must have an ol' lady or a regular that rode frequently on the back. A backpack was the term for it, though he wasn't going to call April that right now. She sure as hell wouldn't appreciate it. He didn't turn to look at April, just stayed where he was and licked his lips, knowing what was to come. Her hands on his body. She first held his shoulders to get her leg over the saddle, then, once settled, she scooted closer to his body and her arms spidered in towards him. Under his cut. Her palms on

THE CHASE

his hips. Her fingernails, again, massaging his sharp V of muscles for a second. He groaned out loud. He could go again.

"Are you okay? Did I hurt you?" she asked.

Fuck, he hadn't meant to make a sound. He started up the bike, and it roared to life beneath them. That was better.

Riding off into the moonlight with April, freshly fucked, on the back of his bike. The stuff of his teenage dreams. Being forced out of the Black Coyotes with a reward on his back. The stuff of his teenage nightmares. Out of prison and already deep in trouble. The ride ahead of them would provide space and time for him to process it all. It would take the rest of the night to get out of California. He planned to head up the eighty, from San Francisco to Nevada, make them think they were heading to Vegas maybe. But he was going to loop back around, head north, connect to highway five, up to Oregon. He swallowed and set his jaw. He revved the bike and they shot off into the darkness.

Chapter 14
APRIL

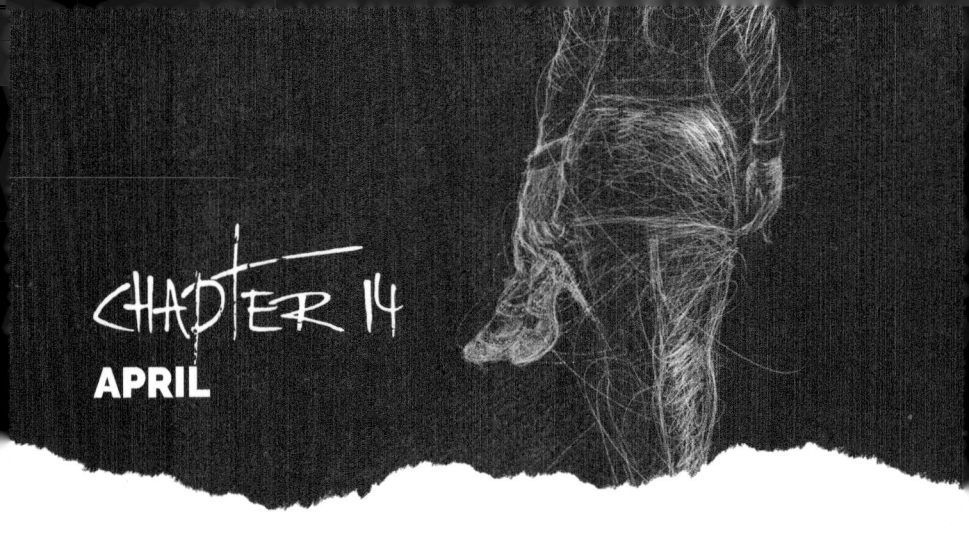

She woke up with a start. Had she actually been asleep? She had thought not, but now she realized it was that milky light of dawn. It had been dark before. She was numb. Her hands, her arms practically locked in a curled position from hanging onto him. She realized she'd been clenching her jaw, because it hurt. They had pulled into a rest stop. There were pine trees. It felt cool, fresher. Oregon. The bike had stopped, the noises changed. There wasn't the lashing of the wind, and the intensity of the loud noise anymore, the engine was deafeningly silent. Luckily the bike had a back rest. She didn't think she could have lasted all those hours without it. She stretched a little in the seat, turning her head, trying to move.

Holy hell. Her inner thighs ached. Her hips… oh God. It all came flashing back to her. Taking his cock on the roadside like her life depended on it. She'd never felt that desperation, that thrill. He had completely lost control, and she'd gone along for the ride. Her lips curved into a smile remembering. It had been the wildest thing she had ever done.

After that pit stop last night, they rode to the bus station. The stop at the bus station had been dicey. The bike was noisy, and people had looked as they passed. It wasn't busy, being late at night, but there were still people in the parking lot.

She'd hopped off and scurried into the building to get to the lockers in the waiting area. Colt had circled round until she came back out. He was constantly looking over his shoulder. Head on swivel. He had taken an indirect route there. Her heart pounded in her chest, her mouth dry. What if the MC had people waiting at the bus station? What if he wasn't there when she came out?

She opened the locker and her hands closed blindly on what was inside. A heavy, black sports bag. She didn't look inside it, she slung it over her shoulder and hurried out.

And there he was. He pulled up. They strapped the bag to the back with bungee cords from the saddlebag. He hopped off to help her. "Get on, I'll strap this up and then, we go," he said. "What's in it?" he asked, looping the cord around the backrest and over the bag, securing it.

She swung herself onto the bike. "I didn't look, I just wanted to hurry."

He nodded. "Now we go, and we don't stop. Got it?"

She nodded as she put on her helmet. He moved in front of her, swung himself onto the bike and scooted back into her crotch. The heat from his body enveloped her like a blanket. Then, he revved the engine and they sped away.

And by the looks of things, they had successfully made it through the night, through California and into Oregon. They'd stopped in what looked like a cemetery. It was peaceful, there were graves and some mausoleums in front of them.

She looked up, looked for him. Colt was walking over to a metal, half height tap that poked out of the ground. It was meant to be used for maintenance, watering the flowers. He laid his cut on the bike, and pulled off his T-shirt, too. She watched his back as he stalked toward the water tap. He looked like a wild beast. Wide shoulders

THE CHASE

tapered into a lean waist, muscles rolled like ropes under his skin. His back had a Black Coyotes image tattooed on it. It looked fearsome, an animal skull, she guessed a coyote, stared blankly back at her. He hunkered down on his haunches by the water tap and turned it on. She heard his groan from back where she was. His hands reached out and cupped some water, he drank, it dribbled down the outside of his throat. Trickling down onto his chest. Hell, his chest. Solid pectorals, small, neat, erect nipples. One with a little silver barbell through it horizontally. Rolls of abs. That V down to his groin. Dark wispy hair that trailed down the center of his stomach, spread then below his belly button and disappeared under the waistline of some black underpants, which in turn disappeared beneath the waistline of his jeans.

She was salivating. Despite how sore she was, how tired, how emotionally and physically spent, she was still salivating for him. Whatever happened from here, she'd have this to remember and fantasize about. To tap into when she wanted to feel alive, wild and free. Because that was how she felt right now, and she had no idea how much she'd needed to feel this.

She had been determined to get rid of this guy as soon as he got her out of harm's way. He was a no good convict, a member of the MC gang, a bad man that she had wanted nothing to do with. And yet… the events of last night had made her doubt herself. Now, watching him wash himself at the tap, watching his hands touch his body, wipe down his arms, his chest, splash into his hair, she had changed her mind. She had to admit it to herself, she didn't want to just walk away.

Why not? Why should she not want more? She felt greedy. She bit the inside of her cheek. She'd been thinking about this through the night. Maybe she didn't go her own way after all. Maybe she wanted to go on an adventure… with him. She was an ambitious, tenacious person. Once she saw something she wanted, she pursued it without mercy. She was selfish and proud and sought out what she wanted with single minded determination. She was flawed, yes. But it's how she got what she wanted out of life. That's how she'd got her job, how she'd got to be top of her class in college, how she made it through law school. She'd chased the entrepreneurial boyfriend until she had a ring on her finger. All of that looked silly now, superfluous, but she still felt that drive within her. Only now, she was going to be chasing after Colt.

He looked over and caught her gazing at him. She closed her mouth, and got off the bike, stiffly, shakily, and dragged the helmet off her head. The cool morning air felt nice on her sticky forehead. He stalked back to the bike and her.

He cleared his throat. "I'm going to drop you off in the nearest town, we crossed the state line, we're out of their territory, so hopefully that will cool things off -"

She smoothed down her crumpled top and leather trousers and raised her chin. She wished she looked and felt a little fresher, a little bit more appealing. But she wasn't going to let that hold her back. "I have a better idea. Instead of you dropping me off, why don't we go on the run... together?"

His mouth fell open. He quickly tried to regain his neutral, devil-may-care face but April saw something flicker across it before he could guard against it.

"I was planning on driving around for the next few weeks, maybe months, no plans, no fancy places to stay, just trying to keep off the MC's radar-" he said.

"Yes, I think we'd have more luck doing this together."

"I don't know-"

"That was your original intention, wasn't it? We'd run together.

THE CHASE

If I hadn't ordered that Uber back at the clubhouse, we would have headed off together."

"Yes, but you put me firmly in my place by hightailing it outta there-"

"Well, I've changed my mind, I want to stay with you, run with you."

He swiped at his forehead, wiping water off him. "Like some sorta Bonnie and Clyde thing? I'm sure an educated woman like yourself doesn't want to get mixed up with a loser like me," he said wryly, quoting her comment from the other day right back at her.

She pursed her lips but didn't even blink. "I said that about you. I regret that, and I apologize," she added, with a twinkle in her eye. "And things didn't end well for Bonnie and Clyde, right? I wouldn't want that."

He smiled, stepping up to her, close. Very close. She felt his breath on her face. "Last night change things for you?" he asked.

She licked her lips and looked away.

"You want more?"

She paused for a moment. She knew what she wanted, she knew her worth, she knew she was a beautiful woman, standing in front of a man, she trusted herself and her judgment and wasn't afraid to go after what she wanted.

She looked back at him and straight in his eyes. "Yes," she replied to him simply, unashamed.

Colt reeled his head back. "Look, Kitten, you were right, I'm empty handed right now, I have nothing to offer you, nothing for you..." He faded off. His throat constricted.

"I want to stick with you," she repeated quietly, biting her lower lip.

He watched her do that. Watched with his big brown eyes, and adjusted his jeans. She was sure, if she looked down, she'd see a bulge there.

"I'm not what you are looking for," he replied quietly, looking away, his modesty, his insecurity taking her by surprise.

She took a breath. Now was not the moment to back down, she knew it. She had to be brave here. She had to be bold.

He risked a glance up. She stared him down, defiantly.

"Don't make me beg, Colt, that's not my style. I want to stick with you."

"You want more of this?" He indicated to his torso.

He was shirtless. And now that he was giving her permission to look, her eyes roved shamelessly over him. Despite himself, he smiled at her reaction. That little puff of pride almost undid her. She was sure that women had always loved his body. She was sure he had been arrogant about it in the past. But right now, the little gesture of modesty was endearing. In prison he must have worked hard to keep it toned. He had a tattoo over his shoulder and pec spreading down his arm. His nipple bar. She shamelessly stared. He seemed fascinated by her fascination.

"Do I want more? Yes. I want more from you, Colt. I want more of you," she said, looking him straight in the eye. Straight into his soul.

"Fuck," he said simply. The heat simmered there, between them, her eyes had glazed over, imagining what they could be like together. Imagining last night again, but less hurried, on a bed. With more touching. His breath on her damp skin, the heat of his thighs. He reached out a hand, cupping her chin, swiping a thumb over her lip in what she was realizing was a unicorn-rare display of tender affection from him.

A car turned into the cemetery, a noisy car, exhaust popping away. It was far up ahead, but it broke their connection, and they both turned, surprised, remembering their situation.

THE CHASE

"We should go," he said. The moment was broken. But the stage had already been set.

He grabbed at his T-shirt and cut, shrugging them on quickly. She repositioned herself on the back of the bike and he hopped on. Again, pressing herself forwards into his warm back. A place that felt much more like home than she'd ever thought it would be.

CHAPTER 15
APRIL

She had been incredibly uncomfortable on the bike for the second leg of their journey. First, she had just begun to loosen up after the night of clinging onto Colt's back like a baby monkey. Second, she was turned on. She couldn't believe it, in a situation like this. Now, in the middle of a crisis, in the middle of her life unraveling and a sleepless night spent on the back of a bike with a felon, she was feeling lusty, needy. She had arched her hips a little and felt the vibrations of the bike humming through her. She had pressed her thighs around his hips, around his neat, tight buttocks. She had looked him right in the eye and said she wanted him. She couldn't believe her brazenness.

But she couldn't deny she was desperate to get off the bike. Everything hurt. Every part of her body either hummed with pain or hummed with desire. All in all, she felt incredibly uncomfortable.

But then thankfully, after only fifteen minutes back on the road, they entered a small town and slowed down. They pulled into a car repair shop, the bike purring to a stop. The garage had its doors open, there were four bays, one had a car in it, jacked up already. There were no workers, except one, a man with gray hair and a giant gray mustache and beard. He sported a pot belly and a leather jacket. Without any patches, she noticed. Like Colt's.

Colt pulled up next to the office building, a single story unit to the side of the garage. He shut off the engine and yanked off his helmet. April took that as her cue to do the same, reluctantly shifting away from Colt's body. She was about to rise off the bike but his hand caught her wrist, urging her to stay seated. Her body screamed to stand but she followed his lead.

"Colt... as I live and breathe..." The old man slurred in a thick southern accent.

"Millhaus." Colt nodded a greeting, but it was curt.

The old man, Millhaus, sauntered over to them. She felt Colt bristle. She'd assumed this guy was a friend, why would Colt take them to somewhere where they weren't welcome?

"You told me, the last time you saw me, that you'd kill me. You said if I ever showed my face around California again, you'd put a bullet-"

"Yeah, I know what I said. Years have passed, old man, times have changed," Colt cut him off.

"What? Your time behind bars made you reflective? Repentant? I never thought I'd see the day when the great Colt Kincade would be penitent about his previous hot-headedness," Millhaus drawled.

"Something like that. You keep up to date then, knowing I did time," Colt replied.

"Always got one ear to the ground." Millhaus nodded.

Colt almost kissed his teeth. "Then you'll have heard about the Black Coyotes. The ah... change in leadership?" Colt winced, sounding as though he hated saying the words. April sat quietly on the back of the bike, trying to read his body language through his thighs and his back, peering over his shoulder curiously.

"Sure did. Cleaver's a dick. A rat's dick. A mangy rat's dick. There's one way that MC is heading. Down," Millhaus said.

Colt nodded. "Then we have something in common. I happen to

agree."

Millhaus chuckled then and Colt visibly relaxed.

"Look, I didn't vote you in as the next Prez because I thought you were too young-" Millhaus gushed, as if he'd been holding it in.

"I know-"

"My loyalty was with Blue-"

"I know, it's all ancient history, old man." Colt waved Millhaus' nervous babble away. Millhaus stilled, sighed, nodded once. Colt sat back on the bike, more casually this time.

"Sweet ride," Millhaus said, opening his arms, nodding to the bike they were on. Colt released her wrist and began to shift to get up himself. She took that as her cue to do the same.

"Sure is. It's one of theirs. I stole it. Got a price on my head, got excommunicated," he said, bringing Millhaus up to speed.

Millhaus nodded slowly, looking curiously at Colt. "And you came here, why?"

Colt sighed and stretched. "I can't ride that thing round the states on the run, brother. My back ain't what it used to be, besides, I got a backpack." He nodded now to April. She wasn't sure what he meant, a backpack? Did he mean her? Should she be offended by this? She returned both of their stares with proud defiance.

"Your ol' lady? Nice." Millhaus hissed through a slightly leery smile at her. Her eyes darted back to Colt, who widened his, nodding discreetly at her. He was telling her to play along. She breathed out. Fine, she'd play the obedient biker bitch.

She smiled bashfully, fluttered her eyelashes, looked down, then back up at Millhaus as if he were Brad Pitt. He was most certainly not Brad Pitt.

But Millhaus appreciated the gesture and smiled back at her.

"Need a cage. Any old rust bucket will do. As long as it goes fast.

Trade you this bike for it. Though, you'll have to hide it well, I'm sure the MC is on our tail. They'll come here. A cage and your discretion, that we were never here," Colt said.

They both squared up to each other. Men doing a deal. April rolled her eyes. How long was it going to take to establish whose dick was bigger? She bet Colt's was anyway, she thought with a slight flush.

They bartered back and forth for a moment, April switched off. She needed to pee. She needed food, a change of clothes, hell, a shower. She started trying to think ahead. She had no idea what a cage was. By the names they were tossing about, it sounded like a car. That would be a start, they could at least carry supplies in a car, maybe even sleep in it… they didn't have any luggage. She turned to the sports bag still strapped to the back of the bike. They had that, and the saddle bags that were full of whatever the other biker had put in it. That was it. They didn't have anything else.

"As I said, sure the bike's sweet but I'll have to strip it down, the parts are what I can use. That takes time, labor… I don't have cars just sitting around fully tuned up and ready to go…" Millhaus was saying, shaking his head. Colt coaxed, she gave him that, he knew how to negotiate. He had the gift of the gab, charming, suddenly he was Millhaus's best friend. The old man was warming to him, relenting.

"Well… now here is a bit of a wild card, might suit you Colt… I got an old Ford here…"

They were walking inside the garage, Millhaus trying to persuade them to go with the oldest, worst cars that he could spare. Colt turning his nose up at them all. Not good enough. Not fast enough. Too unreliable.

Despite Colt's pickiness, April thought Colt had made the right call coming here. Even though it seemed that Millhaus and Colt had previously been at odds, they were now united. Now both cast out of favor of the Black Coyotes. They walked past a sectioned off area in the garage. April peered in, there was something large, van like, under a dust sheet.

"What's in here?" she piped up.

They both turned to her, surprised. Maybe she wasn't meant to speak, but to hell with that.

Millhaus shrugged. "My son, he had this grand plan to drive coast to coast or something like that, and he fixed up an old VW campervan, did a sweet job of it…" Millhaus beckoned Colt in, and April followed. "But then he fucked off to Asia, to find himself or some such shit that the kids are always going on about these days." Millhaus tutted and shook his head.

"Let's see it." Colt asked.

Millhaus was obviously proud of what his son had done, and without much persuasion he yanked the dust sheet off.

A beautiful, vintage, cherry red VW glinted back at them. April gasped. Colt kept his cool but she could tell his interest was piqued.

"Yeah, he kitted it out with a bed, a little camper stove and the engine is top notch, too…" Millhaus began reeling off the stats and Colt looked suitably impressed. Millhaus went to reposition the dust sheet. Colt took a breath.

"Oh no, this is strictly off limits, Colt." Millhaus preempted Colt's question. "I promised I'd keep it for him here, he spent hours on it, and all his money on the parts-"

"But he fucked off to Asia," Colt reminded Millhaus. "It would serve us well, we could camp in it so no need for motels, it would purr like a panther with the engine it's got-"

Millhaus frowned. "My son will be back for it. Don't push me on this Colt, it's off the table."

Colt paused and flicked a gaze at April. She knew Colt had his mind set on the VW.

"Fine, of course," Colt said, easily relenting. Too easily. "Let's take another look at the Ford…" April was instantly suspicious. He was planning something, she could tell.

Chapter 16
APRIL

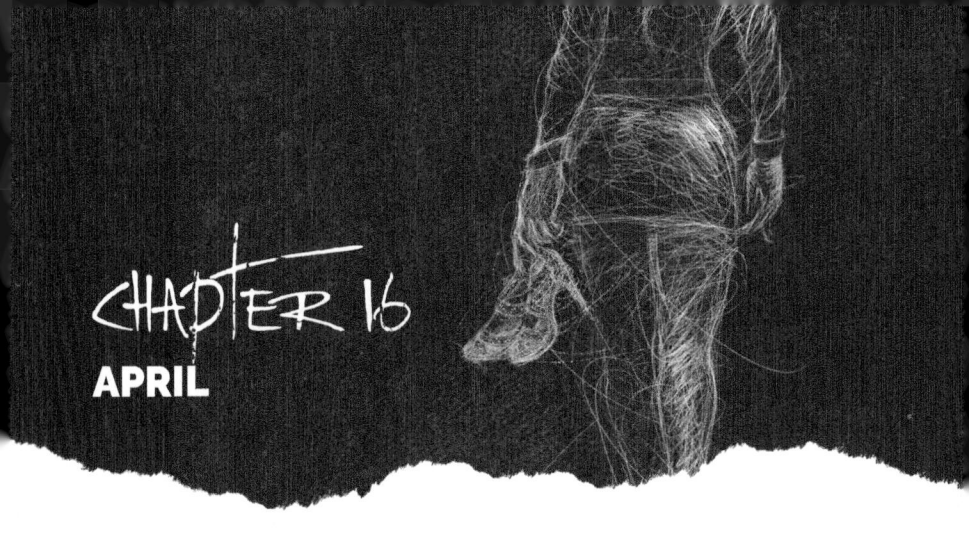

April frowned. They doubled back in the garage, left the VW, wrapped up again in its dust sheet, to stare again at some completely average looking car instead. What was Colt up to? He flashed her a heated gaze.

They all eyed up the non-descript Ford again.

"What do you think, Kitten?" he asked her.

She stared at him, nonplussed for a second. Then she saw him raise an eyebrow, widen his eyes. She guessed he wanted her to play along again.

"Yes, I like it, Colt, I think we should take it. We should get on the road again..."

Millhaus looked hopefully at Colt. He schooled his face to look as though he was reluctantly considering it, then acquiesced with a chin lift. "You want this one? Then it's a sure thing, Kitten."

"Ahh, the lady has chosen! Well now, little missy, I'll just get the keys and you can drive the Ford right outta here..." Millhaus looked elated, he clearly thought he'd done a good deal.

April gave him her prettiest smile in return. "That would be lovely, thank you very much."

He bustled away with a spring in his step.

April turned on Colt and stammered, "Colt, what are we-"

"We're going to take the VW," he said to her in a low voice, eyes fixed on Millhaus' retreating back.

She gaped. "How?"

Colt flicked his gaze back to her and blinked. "We get in, we drive off."

April shook her head. "Colt, I don't think-"

"Come on, we're just borrowing it. We'll aim to give it back one day."

April rolled her eyes and huffed. She wasn't sure she was comfortable with this idea. "Colt, I really don't think-"

But he was already dragging the dust sheet back off the VW. She knew no matter how much she tried to reason with him, stomp her foot or huff, he wouldn't change his mind. He had a gleeful, smug smile on his face as he flashed her a glance and watched her come to terms with not getting her way. Something she wasn't used to.

She eyed the VW warily. It was a cute camper van, and could be cozy inside, but there was no space for hair dryers, the kind of clothes she'd be used to packing, no ensuite, none of the comforts she was used to. No dressing table to do her makeup. Hell, she didn't even have any of these things with her, but the reality of being on the run was laid bare for her in that instant. It would mean long hours of driving, cramped conditions, one bed… she swallowed. She wished she could change her clothes, brush her hair, her teeth. Maybe they could stop and grab a few essentials? Her mind whirred away as she watched Colt bunching up the dust sheet.

She stifled a panicked sob and turned her attention to the sports bag that she'd slung over her shoulder as they'd begun their tour of the garage. Maybe her father had put a change of clothes in there. Something to cheer her up. A bottle of water even. She held the bag with one hand and pulled at the zipper with the other.

The Chase

She peered inside. Stacks of $100 bills peered back. "Err…" she said out loud. She blinked and looked again.

Yes, the bag was full of stacks of clean, unwrinkled $100 bills. The stacks were bundles of… she did some quick estimations… $10,000 probably. There were multiple bundles in here. More than ten. That was $100,000. More than twenty, easily. She calmly zipped up the bag again and cleared her throat.

"Colt…" She said, her voice shaking a little. He turned, clearly curious about the tone of her voice. She scurried over to him, tugging at the zipper on the sports bag she had slung over her shoulder. He hunkered forward, his expression exasperated, probably he was thinking, what now? She opened the bag a little, enough for him to peer in. He looked. Blinked. Looked some more. Then he looked up at her.

"Holy fuck," he said simply.

"Yes," she replied. "I thought maybe there'd be some water in the bag, a change of clothes, so I took a look…"

"We could buy a whole new wardrobe of clothes," Colt said. "We could buy this fucking VW campervan."

She nodded. He looked up at her again, regarding her carefully.

"You didn't hesitate to show me," he said, almost surprised.

"What do you mean?"

He nodded to the bag. "The money. I could have taken it, left you… it would have been the smart thing to not have shown me."

She tilted her head. "I trust you," she said simply, and in her heart she knew it was true. He was an ex-con, former Prez of an outlaw biker club. She should have been careful, should have kept her cards close to her chest. But she didn't. She knew there was more to him. She knew she could trust him. He was all of those things but he was also a man with chocolate brown eyes and thick brown hair and warm, golden skin. A man who had protected her and saved her, who smiled at her and had fucked her. Yes, roughly, furiously, selfishly at first. But it had been what she had wanted, what she had craved. He provided her with everything she needed. Everything she wanted. The thought struck her like a baseball bat to the head. In 24 hours he had done more for her than her former fiancé ever had. She was just beginning to peel off his tough biker layer to find a genuine, caring, rough around the edges, but intriguing man underneath. She trusted him, with her body, with more than her body, she realized. The money, yes, but more, much more. She stared at the stacks of money in the bag, not seeing them, staring through them.

"Throw it in the back, we'll be out of here in a second," Colt said, after fixing her with a penetrating stare.

"Okay." She nodded, letting go of the mild panic that had built up inside of her. She blew out another breath, blowing away the fear.

Colt already had some sort of tool that looked like a thin chisel in his hand, that he had shoved down the gap where the window was, and was wriggling it around. The lock clicked, and Colt pulled the driver's door open.

"Fuck yeah," he said, eyes roving over the dashboard.

He pulled himself up into the driver's seat and turned to her. "Get in, Kitten."

She bit her lips. "Can you leave him a note, saying sorry, we'll take good care of it and aim to return it-"

Colt looked at her with a deadpan expression. She thought he was going to say no. Then he mellowed. "Sure, Kitten."

She had an idea. "Can we give him some cash, as compensation, or like a deposit maybe…"

He puffed out a breath. "You are fucking cute, you know that, don't you?" He smiled at her.

THE CHASE

She blushed a little.

They revved out of the garage in the VW leaving Millhaus behind with a resigned, unsurprised, "ahh fuck", a scrunched up dust sheet and a neat little stack of crisp notes.

Hours later, they stopped at a store. He loped off to buy cigarettes from the gas station nearby, then crossed the parking lot, head on swivel the whole time, but there was no MC. She bought useful things, towels, bedding, and clothes. Burner phones for them both. She bought frivolous stuff, too. She wanted to put a smile on Colt's face. Fairy lights, scatter cushions, scented candles. A new life. A whole new, cheaper, more minimal life for herself. And for that moody, difficult ex-con that she'd thrown herself in with. A few days ago, she'd been a corporate lawyer, Brown University alumni, she had a fiancé, she was a trendy, young professional, decked out in designer clothes with hundreds of followers on social media. But now she felt lighter, freer, more invigorated than she had ever felt. She bought underwear, which brought color to her face. Yes, she was going on the run from an MC in a van with a felon, and she was doing so with sexy underwear. She didn't do things by halves, she was an all or nothing girl after all.

CHAPTER 17
COLT

They were on the road again. It was dusk, Colt was behind the wheel, and April sat next to him in the passenger's seat. He missed the bike and the instant hit of bravado it gave him, but this was the better option for them both. More practical, more comfortable. He tutted to himself, he sounded like an old man. What happened to the dirty biker that he was? April had made him shower at a truck stop, for a start. They both smelled of the shower gel she'd bought. It was some sort of floral scent. Colt had lathered it all over his body, making a welcome change from prison soap. He'd taken a second to imagine her hands lathering it over her own body. He'd gotten hard, despite the shower being a mere dribble of cold water, his hand had slid over his cock, gripped it hard, using extra shower gel to slide up and down his shaft.

He was thinking about April, and what she'd said to him when they had stopped. When she had stood up in front of him, asked to go on the run with him, then asked him for sex. Yes, her outfit was creased, her hair was a mess, her makeup smudged, but she still looked smoking hot. Like he'd bedded her long and hard the night before. If only, he thought with a wryness. And when he'd challenged her, called her out on turning up her nose at him, she'd apologized. He was impressed she hadn't backed down there, she'd been honest, taken it on the chin. She'd just stood there anyway and asked for what she had wanted. It was the hottest thing he'd ever seen.

But he'd tried to talk himself down, talk her out of this harebrained idea of hers; running together, spending more time together, repeating what they had done... together. As he uttered the words about how he was a bad guy, trouble, he wished it wasn't true. He had felt a deep regret that turned his voice gruff. He hoped it sounded like tough nonchalance. The opposite was the case, he had never felt so invested in what she had been about to say next.

And the way she had looked at him, biting her lips, desire pooling in her eyes. He had a sudden urge to feel those teeth biting the base of his hard cock. He looked down, the surge of desire engulfing him. He almost groaned out loud. What was fucking wrong with him? He was like a horny teenager again. He knew his body looked good, he'd always taken care of it as soon as he'd been able to gain a bit of muscle after he had started working out at the clubhouse, but in prison he'd lost himself in mindless repetitions of deadlifts with dumbbells, squats... he was in the best shape of his life. It fucking figured though, if college boy had been her fiancé, she probably hadn't had much to look at in the body department underneath his shirt and suit. He liked that she liked him physically. She'd probably never been with a man like him. She probably hadn't ever even dreamed she'd do what they did last night. She'd probably never done some of the things he wanted to do to her. That sent his mind whirling away, and he let himself, for a split second, imagine her, naked, on top of him, grinding against him, moaning for more. He imagined his hard cock plunging deep into her, her pussy swallowing him wetly as they both watched. Right there in that sorry excuse for a shower, he gripped his rock hard cock. He pumped once, clenching his teeth. He wanted to wait, but he knew he needed to build up his stamina for her, being in prison for five years, he knew he would not be able to last long enough to satisfy her. He'd blown his load too early already, he didn't want to repeat that.

If they had had more time, he would have finished himself off thinking of her in the shower. But they didn't. He changed into the clothes she'd got for him. A cheap white T-shirt and some blue jeans. They felt very much not like his own. And some sort of douchey leather shoes. She'd called them boat shoes. They were college boy shoes. He hated them on principle but found they were actually pretty comfortable. She'd got the right size for him. He'd slipped on the black boxer briefs and wondered if she'd imagined him in them when she was buying them. What size he would take. What he would look like in them. What he would look like taking them off. He hoped she had had some thoughts like that.

He was conflicted. Torn inside. It was April, the angel he watched from the shadows. The pure young thing he was sent to protect. He was dirt to her, not worthy of her time. Let alone… a lover. As he thought about that, goosebumps rose on his arms. Being with her, being balls deep inside of her, feeling her warmth clenching around him as he drove himself home inside her… it was too much. Had it really happened just yesterday? He was getting lost in his own head, something that had crept up on him in prison. The intrusive thoughts he couldn't seem to block out, that he couldn't turn down. Whirring away in his mind on repeat.

He had dreamed of being with April, of course, as a teenager. A complete self indulgent fantasy to occupy his mind and his hand during lonely nights. He had never thought it could actually become a reality.

But she had come back to him, not as a pure thing existing in a higher universe. But as a woman, flesh and blood, soft, strokable hair and wanton sighs. Her own power coursing through her veins. That had swept over him with a long lashed gaze of female desire. And possibility had been born. In his mind, in his heart. In his body. She was no longer an angel. And he was no longer dirt. She was a woman, and he was a man.

He'd taken a risk, played his cards, played his soul on the line by offering her himself. He'd done it under a veneer of bravado, cocky confidence and cavalier brashness.

But she'd said yes. She had wanted him. He knew it was only skin deep. She wanted what he was, a hunk of muscle, who would take her roughly and touch her like no one else before. She didn't want him for who he was, but he'd take it. He wanted to see her on her back, to hear her scream and gasp as he plunged into her, taking her. The wild, wild thoughts filled his head as he drove on.

She had nodded off almost as soon as they'd started moving. He had planned to drive for hours into the night, but he was bone tired. He blinked furiously and put the window down to let the dusk air in. It was no good, they had to stop. He'd wanted to talk to her about where they should lay low for the night. But he didn't have the heart to wake her. They were over the state line, they were in a new set of wheels, they had loads of stuff to help them run, to help them survive. He'd been moody about it earlier, her wanting to shop for stuff, but he saw the wiseness in April's plan here. Yes, they could now drive for days. They could blend into the crowd, disappear. It was better than just trail blazing away into the sunset only to run out of gas a few hours later.

Colt's eyelids were drooping. He was struggling to keep his head upright. His hands on the wheel even. Everything wanted to sag to

The Chase

the floor. He needed to sleep. He pulled off the highway, checking his mirrors obsessively. No MC came roaring into view, the roads were quiet. The night was peaceful.

They were at the coast, the Pacific ocean highway hugging the dramatic cliff line. After five years in prison, he couldn't wait to see it in the daylight. In the growing dusk it was already beautiful. He pulled off the highway, onto a smaller road, closer to the ocean. Stopping the van, he lay his head back against the headrest. Finally, a moment of peace.

He climbed out the van, his legs jelly, his back beyond stiff. Time to see what April had made of the back of the van, he thought wryly. He heard the ocean waves, the faint whisper of the wind, and that was blissfully all he could hear. He walked back to the van, stretching his back and neck, feeling a thousand years old. He opened the doors, and blew out a low whistle.

Fairy lights. That was the first thing he noticed. A string of them around the sides and top. Pretty little lights with a warm glow, like fireflies. Then the bed, she'd got a duvet and pillows. Ah, multiple pillows. He'd had one thin pillow back in prison. She'd made the whole thing look fucking cute. He blinked, was he really going to be sharing a bed with her? Fuck. He went back to the cab and opened her door slowly. She was fast asleep. He leaned over, undid her seatbelt, and scooped her up in his arms. Carefully carrying her back, he realized how small she was. Her head lolled a bit, but her hands clenched on his shirt, like a baby sloth. He liked that he could protect her, care for her, keep her safe. He liked that feeling.

He had to climb up and into the van, crouching, with her in his arms, to get her to the bed. Not an easy maneuver and his back did not thank him for it. But he got them both there. He collapsed down with her on the mattress, turning his body as he sank down with her.

Not on top of her, though he sorely wanted to.

The mattress was the softest thing Colt had ever felt. His aching limbs were sucked into it and he felt his body sighing with relief. He forced himself upright before he fell asleep and pulled off her shoes, her little brand new sneakers. He should have put her under the covers, but he hadn't thought that far ahead. He closed the doors, locking them. They were safe, for now. He laid back down on the mattress and stared up at the ceiling of the van. It smelled good in there. She'd bought something and now it smelled of something calming, lavender? No, something more like tea leaves, not sweet, more musky. He liked it. The fairy lights twinkled above him. He should turn them off but he had no idea how. He looked to the side, and April was there, breathing heavily, eyelashes fanned over her cheeks. He couldn't quite believe it. He was on the same mattress as April. Oh, if the circumstances were different, the things he would do to her to make up for the other night. To make his dreams come true. He rested his head back on the multiple pillows, and was painfully aware of the mere inches between them. Glad he was used to sleeping on a narrow bunk, he crossed his hands in front of him, as he had every night for the last five years. And he closed his eyes. And sleep immediately took him.

CHAPTER 18
COLT

COLT WOKE WITH a gasp. It felt like he had fallen back into his body with a thud. A painful thud. He felt stiff all over, stiff but well-rested. He hadn't woken up feeling rested in the last five years. His sleep had been a state of frozen paralysis in prison; still as a statue on his narrow bunk, not fully awake yet ever ready to pounce if there was a threat. Not fully asleep but his brain numb and his body still. But now he had slept well. He knew what time it would be, he didn't need to check any clock. 7:00 a.m. had been ingrained into him in prison. He felt hot and sweaty, and very aware he was in the same set of clothes as yesterday. He dared a glance to his side. April was sprawled out on her side, one arm up over her head, her mouth slightly open, breathing deeply.

Colt sat up. He hadn't moved from his rigid position all night. He never did, too many years of sleeping in a confined space, he wasn't one to spread out and sprawl carefree like April was. He opened the door quietly. The morning was beautiful, the sky was blue, and far down below, waves were crashing. The sunlight was strong. Colt's spirit soared. Freedom. It was fresh and new. He emerged from the back of the van and stretched, beguiled by the beautiful morning. He immediately yanked his shirt off. He had to move, he had the urge to use his body. He was barefoot, too, he must have kicked off his shoes in the night. In just his jeans, he dropped to the ground and did push ups. He found solace in the familiar moves, but excitement in the new location. Push ups, sit ups, squats. He went through his usual routine, the morning sun heating his skin, the breeze cooling him.

He turned suddenly, feeling a set of eyes on him. April. She was wide awake, sitting up in the bed inside the van, watching him. He smiled to himself and rose to stand at his full height, flexing his pecs a little as he did so. He sauntered over to her until his legs bumped into the doorframe of the van. Her eyes roving over him, she did a double take at his nipple piercing, a tiny silver bar through his left nipple. He felt his cock begin to harden and his confidence surge.

"When you're done eye-fucking me, we could get some coffee," he said.

She gulped and tore her eyes from his torso to his face. "Eye... pardon? I wasn't... I was just-"

"Ha, don't lie to me, I can see it all over your face, Kitten."

She looked away, her pride dented from being caught.

"I'm going to be honest, I didn't think you'd be the type of woman to be interested in the likes of this." He looked down at his own body.

She tilted her head back. "You're right, a week ago if I'd seen you walking toward me on a dark night, I'd have crossed the road to avoid you," she said.

He turned to move away from her, feeling a stab of disappointment. Maybe she had changed her mind about what she'd said yesterday.

"And yet... I would have thought about you once I'd made it home, safe and sound." He turned back to look at her. "Once I was in my bed, all alone, wide awake..." She returned his gaze now.

He almost choked. Was she implying she'd have touched herself, thinking about him? Was she teasing him? "Well, you weren't alone, were you? College Boy was there to do your bidding-"

"Or not able to, as was the case. Hence why I'd be dreaming of a man like you..."

He came closer, crawling into the van on his knees, like a predator. He didn't stop until he was inches from her. His hand found her cheek, and he looked down at her. He could rip her clothes off right now and get down to it. That possibility hovered there, in the air between them, sizzling. He breathed in and out. Once. Twice. He'd fucked it up the first time, going in too hot, and he wanted it differently. He wanted to cherish her with sweet gentle kisses, but tarnish her with his cum all over her face.

He should take her then and there. He should just rip her clothes off and sink himself into her. He would have done that years before, without any hesitation. Hell, he'd have done that only yesterday. But now, he felt differently. He wasn't ready to try again. How had he completely lost control of himself? He could have hurt her. It had been stupid and reckless. He felt so unworthy. He needed her to snatch herself away from his needy, grasping hands. She wasn't, she was opening herself up and giving him easier access. To the point where his brain and his self-shame had caught up with him and was pulling back from the brink.

She deserved better than him. She wasn't like the girls he had with before, mostly club girls, with alcohol and drugs involved. Girls who wore very little and were keen to please, keen to belong, keen to count their self worth by how long they could keep a man like him interested. April was different. She respected herself, she was intelligent, she had grown up with a sense of self-worth. So when she said she wanted him, it meant so much more. She didn't say anything. She had that look on her face again. Her eyes turned darker, her jaw dropped a little, her lips parted.

He undid the top button on his jeans. What was he doing? He

didn't know. He couldn't risk it again. He didn't want to lose himself again like that. With her.

He should stop himself, back away now. He couldn't.

"We should talk about what happened yesterday…" she began to say. She shifted in the bed, all soft sheets and cotton freshness against her golden, warm skin.

He really didn't fucking want to talk about what happened yesterday. He wanted to repeat what happened yesterday. And yet, he knew he'd regret it later. He wasn't worthy, he wasn't strong enough. He was tearing himself apart inside.

He put his lips to hers and kissed her. Really kissed her, opening his mouth and lapping his tongue inside. She moaned, her skin was so soft against his, her breath was warm against his lips, sweet on his tongue. It turned him the fuck on. He pulled back and she held on. His resolve melted like wax under a flame.

"Am I making you wet?" he asked her. His self control scattering, particle by particle on the gentle, warm breeze.

"What a question to ask! I-" she began, but suddenly he was kissing her again.

He put his hand roughly between her thighs. She squealed, shocked, but opened her legs for him. He undid her jeans and pulled them down a little, over her butt. Then he slipped his finger over the cotton of her briefs, right to where her folds were. He couldn't stay away, he'd swear he touched heaven there the night before, he was drawn to it like a bee to honey. The cotton was damp.

"Jesus, you are melting for me. You want me bad," he ground out between clenched teeth, butting his head lightly against her forehead. Despite his brain screaming no, his body couldn't stop. He had to tarnish her. Ravage her. Ruin her. He had to feel her. He slipped a finger beneath the cotton, tracing the line of her slit, he dipped his finger into her damp core. Her eyelids fluttered. He clenched his teeth and traced circles over her clit.

He put his ear to her mouth then. "You want me, don't you, Kitten?"

She practically shuddered.

He then pinched her clit, his fingers becoming rougher. Not teasing, but pushing, driving. He couldn't find the strength to hold back.

"What do you want, April?" he asked, roughly rubbing her.

She let out a strangled cry. "I want-"

"Tell me you don't want this." He almost wanted her to say it. To pull him back. "Tell me to stop."

"Don't stop, I want you, I want this-" she whispered breathily, her eyelids fluttering. Fuck, he thought. He had to stop, he had to stop. Cherish her. Treasure her.

"Once I take you over the edge Kitten, there's no coming back. No one else will be able to give it to you like I will."

"Please, I want it."

"Yes you do, but I won't give it to you yet." He pulled his fingers away. Everything was screaming now, his ears deafened by the noise in his head. Her cotton briefs snapped back wetly.

She yelped with anguish. "I was almost-"

"I know," he said with ragged desperation. He didn't want to give it to her like this. She deserved better. He couldn't give it to her like this. His body was hot, his balls felt like they would explode, his hard dick rubbed on the inside of his jeans painfully. Her whispering those words while his fingers felt her hot, wet slit… that was something he would treasure to the end of his days.

"Colt, wait, please…"

"Begging me now, Kitten? I thought that wasn't your style." He had to hide behind his bravado, hide behind the pretence of teasing her like a cocky biker Prez would.

She cried out in frustration, reaching down to touch herself.

He caught her wrist. "Good things come to those who wait. Believe me, I'll be good. I'll be the best you've ever had. Just wait."

He couldn't resist a final touch. He licked her fingers and guided her wrist down, his hand covering hers, his hand guiding hers under her briefs. He caught one of her fingers with his and pushed it into herself. She felt how wet she was, she closed her eyes and purred.

"I'll be so good you'll never be satisfied with anyone else," he whispered, already out of his mind with how much he wanted her. He had to stop talking before he said anything else he'd regret.

"We need to talk… about what happened yesterday…" she slurred.

It broke the spell. Enough now, he told himself. Colt removed both of their fingers from her warm, wet slit. He sighed and removed her hand completely from inside her jeans. He didn't want to talk, he just wanted to feel. To fuck. To ravish and devour her until he was spent. But he knew he couldn't.

He backed away. "I gotta shower."

CHAPTER 11
APRIL

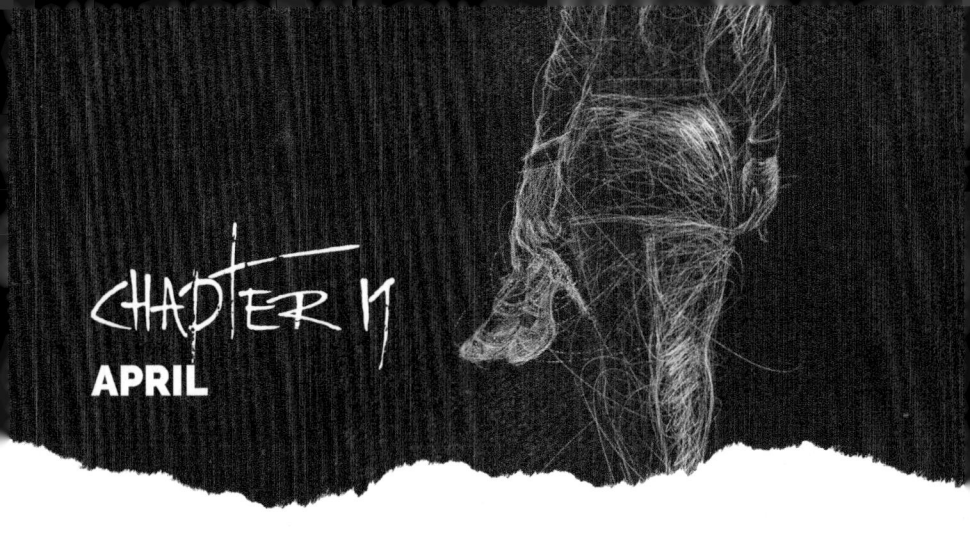

After showering, they both wordlessly climbed into the van and drove off in stony silence.

She was sulking. She couldn't believe he'd pulled back. April always got what she wanted. In her life, if she saw something she wanted, she'd get it. She worked hard to get where she was in life. The good corporate job with the big salary that meant she could have the great condo with the shiny car. The friends and the things she'd do with those friends. Cocktail evenings, brunches, fancy restaurants, nice clothes and shoes. She saw it, she wanted it, she got it. Simple as that. Until now.

She wanted Colt. Their first time was too rushed and crazy, she wanted more. Was he teasing her? She hadn't thought he'd have the willpower to resist. To deny her. When she'd looked at him, her mouth had watered, she hadn't considered that he'd turn her down.

This morning she had gained some clarity. If this man was somehow a trusted associate of her father, then he couldn't be bad. He could be trusted. He wasn't the bad guy she had painted him as when she'd first met him. And, despite everything, she couldn't not feel that heat. There was something about him that brought her to life. Something almost primeval. Wrapped up in a rough exterior, with a dash of hot-headed impulsiveness, and a hint at some inner uncertainty in himself, he'd shown her nothing but kindness. She could trust him enough to get her the hell away from this MC debacle. She could trust him enough to be her lover, if it could be described as that. But she wanted to trust him with more. He was undeniably very attractive but it wasn't just that. It was something more, something else that animated him. Determination. Survival instinct. A thirst for more. A desire to chase after what he wanted, to catch it, to own it. She recognized it there in him.

She wanted to trust him to give her something she hadn't had before. To let herself go completely, to breathe life back into her, to relinquish control, and just free-wheel for a bit. Coast. She wanted to trust him to take the reins.

She took in a deep breath and expelled it, gazing without actually seeing the scenery passing by. Her eyes weren't focused on anything in particular. It wasn't exactly comfortable silence. She could sense his unease. His eyes flicked to the rear-view mirror often. He didn't seem to relax into the car seat, he was uptight. Hand resting on the gearstick even though he wouldn't be needing it for a while. Not resting, hovering. Tapping occasionally. They had been driving most of the morning like this. Neither of them talking. Neither of them mentioning what happened earlier. Or what didn't happen.

April felt she had to break the ice. "Sorry I can't drive stick shift."

He turned with a flick of his head to her, but didn't take his eyes off the road. "It's okay," he muttered.

She held her breath but he didn't say anything else. She bit the inside of her cheek. "So, are we going to stop for lunch soon?"

"Uh huh," he murmured back.

This was not going how she'd intended. "Colt, are you okay?" she asked.

He huffed. "I'm gagging for a smoke, my back is sore after sleeping on that mattress-"

"That mattress is pretty expensive memory foam. You're probably stiff still after the all night bike ride and now driving again… and the fucking, which we still haven't talked about, by the way-" April paused and shot him a glance, leaving space for him to interject.

Colt only pursed his lips in response.

"And it doesn't help that you have nicotine withdrawal… maybe you could use this time to cut down on your smoking?" she suggested, trying to sound optimistic.

"Nope, ain't going to happen," came his surly response.

She rolled her eyes. "It's incredibly unappealing, you know, in a sexual partner." She peeked at him from the side of her eye. "… Like kissing an ashtray."

"You regretting it already?" he asked, jutting his jaw out. She breathed out, finally, they were actually talking about it. For a man that exuded confidence, he seemed to doubt himself. Think the worst.

She frowned. "I only regret that you didn't follow through this morning. I wanted round two," she said, almost challenging him to come up with another excuse.

He blew out a breath. "April I… fuck, I fucked up, okay? I completely lost control last night and that wasn't fucking cool-"

"Colt-"

"I damn near forced myself on you, I was too rough, probably hurt you…"

She held up her hand to stop him. "No, you didn't hurt me, I wanted it Colt, I wanted you. I loved it that you lost control like that with me. Colt."

His eyes flicked to her quickly, then back to the road. "A bit of a change of pace from College Douche?" He visibly relaxed. He let a slight smile spread onto his face.

April threw her head back against the headrest. "Ha, a whole different ball game." She laughed.

Colt smirked now. "More where that came from."

She glanced sideways at him and their gazes met briefly. The seed had been planted now, for connection. Companionship. For more. She felt like before it had been a dry desert between them. Hot but barren. And now the rains had begun, a gentle patter for now. Making a difference already though. Softening the dry earth, moistening the air. Providing conditions for things to grow, to flourish. She felt a change. A softening. The life she had led was a buzzing, angry, hot mess, and now things were calmer. Now that they were talking, she wanted to continue. "Colt, did you really follow me, all those years ago?"

CHAPTER 20
COLT

He smiled hesitantly. "I was tasked with guarding you... Blue said it was about ensuring you weren't kidnapped... the MC had a few enemies... enemies in powerful places, they could have hurt you... to get back at Blue and the MC. You could have been a negotiating tool... it was important for the club that I kept you safe... I mean, that you were kept safe, and I was tasked with doing that..." He was murmuring now, reluctant to expose himself, but wanting to hear more of her thoughts, wanting to hear her laugh again.

He saw she was smiling. He shifted in his seat, he felt lighter. She was happy, she was okay with what had gone down between them. Even if he still had mixed feelings about it, he was happy she was happy.

She pursed her lips, amused. "Did you come to spring break?"

"Which time, Mexico or Florida?"

"You came to both?"

"Mexico, you and your girlfriends decided to go to some dive of a bar where a total douchebag decided to spike your drinks and your friend, the curvy one-"

"Elaine-"

"She puked and passed out and none of you could pick her up and you were all wasted. You'd lost your phone -"

"Oh my God, you were there! This local teenager helped carry Elaine back… oh… that was you?"

He raised his eyebrows in response.

"You came out to Mexico… to protect me?"

"Got my passport 'specially for that," he mumbled. "Came in handy for when you did that summer in Costa Rica-"

"The turtle sanctuary? You came there, too?" she squawked with disbelief.

"Yeah, I didn't hang around the sanctuary, that was boring as fuck, I stayed in the town-"

"The whole summer, you stayed there?"

"Where you went, I went, April."

"But I never noticed you…"

He shrugged. "I don't know why you would. I was a scrawny nobody tasked with watching you from afar. I kept myself busy though, got the MC hooked up with some sweet supply chains that summer. Your daddy was so pleased with me, called me enterprising-"

He still remembered the swell of pride when Blue had heard his news. The warmth that went straight to his gut that he'd impressed them by negotiating and organizing the drug pipeline for the MC through Costa Rica. He came back feeling like a Mafia Don.

She watched him carefully, trying to interpret the well-veiled emotions that were flitting through his mind. "You were there for me the whole time?" she asked quietly.

"Got you out of trouble a few times," he said with a wry smile.

She raised an eyebrow. "Like?"

He rolled his eyes. "How about the time you snuck out to that senior's house party and your girlfriends took something they shouldn't have and that red headed friend of yours passed out in the pool-"

"Jessica-"

"I had to drag her ass out of there and give her CPR-"

"Oh God, I forgot about that!"

"Yeah, not your proudest moment."

"Okay, I'm sure you've got yourself into some sticky situations-"

"Plenty," he said with a devil-may-care wink and a grin. He was enjoying reminiscing with her.

She raised one perfectly manicured eyebrow. "Did you come to prom?" she asked.

He grunted with a smile. "I rode behind your limo and made sure you got there, then I hung around outside until you got to Becky's after party-"

"I remember feeling so grown up, wearing heels and that dress-"

"Fuck, Kitten, your prom dress." He whistled.

She smiled. "You remember my dress?"

"It gave me wet dreams for months, thinking of you in that dress." He smiled as if he were joking. He wasn't, he had literally jerked himself off in the parking lot after watching her walk around in that slinky dress.

"God, I should have left that building, stepped outside, opened my eyes and found you that night," she said, licking her lips. It was his turn to raise his eyebrows.

April continued, "Instead, I was blinded by a teenage crush for Harrison-"

"He was a fucking moron." Colt's face darkened instantly.

"I know, star quarterback, senior... when he asked me to be his date, I just got starstruck-"

"He didn't deserve you."

"And when I found out he'd been screwing that cheerleader…" she said, shaking her head, flattening her lips. "I should've known better. Oh well, he got mugged by a gang a few days later-"

"He didn't get mugged by a gang," Colt muttered quietly.

April opened her mouth but then did a double take at him. His knuckles clenched on the steering wheel and a tendon flexed in his jaw. She could figure it out. He wasn't ashamed. When he found out that douchebag was two-timing April, especially after she'd slept with him for the first time, her first time... given him her innocence, fuck, he was getting mad just remembering it now.

"Did you... have anything to do with his injuries, Colt?" she asked directly.

He pursed his lips together. "I had everything to do with his injuries."

"Colt."

"Yeah, Blue was pissed, too, said I should have left it alone, that you needed to learn the hard way... I couldn't just sit back and watch that guy fuck around... he hurt you. I hurt him. Karma," Colt replied. He hoped she didn't think he was a monster, violent, untameable.

"I wish I'd have opened my eyes and seen you, Colt. Back then... I would have thanked you..."

"I wouldn't have listened," he replied. "I would have bent you over my bike and fucked your prom dress off you," he spat, the van speeding up slightly under his foot.

"Like the other night then, some little boys never grow up," she said playfully, giving him a sideways glance.

"Oh, I grew up alright, and I'm not that little boy anymore," he growled.

She took a breath. "I bet you were a real looker back then."

"No, I was scrawny-"

"All big brown eyes-"

"All big dick, no technique, but stamina and perseverance-"

He took a breath. All this walking down memory lane was

confusing him inside. His teenage feelings of awe and wonder for her, his self loathing, were mixing with his adult feelings of lust, jaded desperation and betrayal. He felt too much, that was his problem. He shook his head to clear the thoughts that had entangled him. He shouldn't give a fuck. Yeah, he was done with memory lane. It was the path ahead that he feared more. It both terrified and excited him.

CHAPTER 21
APRIL

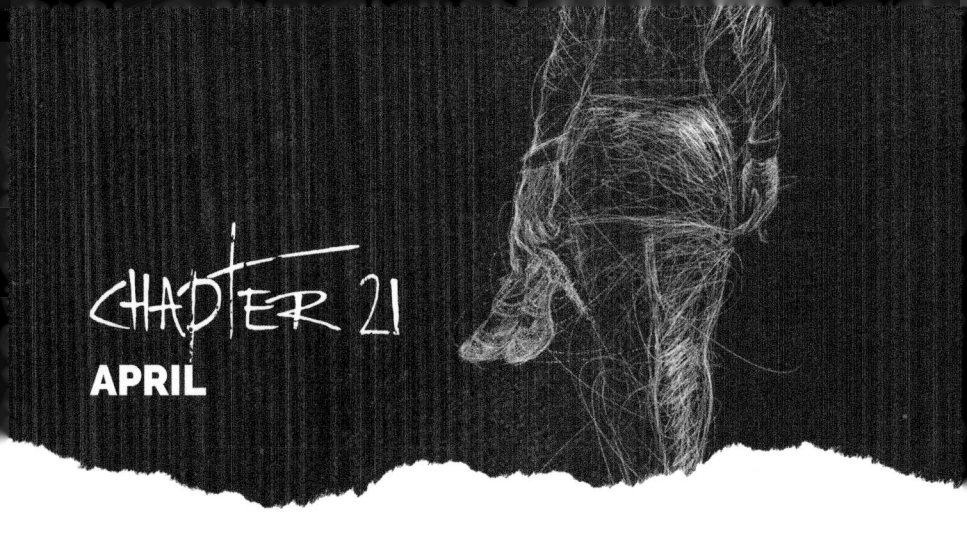

Pain shafted through his face. She saw it. She could recognize it. Thinking of the past wasn't his most favorite thing to do then. She wanted to keep him talking, she didn't want him to withdraw into himself again, as he seemed to do sometimes, she wanted more of him. She cleared her throat and changed the subject.

"So, why join a MC in the first place? I don't get it." She shrugged.

His eyes opened wide with disbelief. "Don't get it? Kitten, I don't get why not?" He smirked.

"It sounds like a philosophical experiment, except with illegal stuff happening…"

Colt blew out an exaggerated breath. He tilted his head for a second, appearing deep in thought. "Well, yeah, I guess that's not an unfair assessment. It's a bunch of men that have gotten together and said fuck you to the system."

"I see."

"… And from big risks, comes big rewards. Yeah, running guns for the cartel isn't legal, and it may not be moral, or safe, but it'll make you more than you could earn in a year in one trip. Then, you come back to the clubhouse and party hard. Free booze, a room upstairs, food, free women…"

"Free women… what exactly do you mean?" She curled an eyebrow up, narrowing her eyes.

Colt shifted in his seat. "Well, the sweet butts are there to serve you, in any way you'd want. They do the cooking and the cleaning. They live in, and they pay us back in sex."

"So literally… prostitutes."

"Well, they kind of become family, like the cousin you love to hate, they belong to the club, you could claim them if you want them to be your ol' lady…"

"A wife?"

"Kinda, more flexible than legal marriage, but your ol' lady is your other half. There are no rings involved, you go to the members, you say I wanna claim, whatever her name is, anyone object? No, okay, she's yours now. Your property."

"Property?" April said in a low voice.

"Yeah."

"Like a slave?" she continued, throwing him a glare.

Colt felt it and scratched his neck. "Well, she could leave if she wanted to."

"But she doesn't earn any money, she gets paid by being allowed somewhere to sleep and eat, and she has to cook, clean and fuck to earn that."

He pursed his lips. "Yeah."

"You hear yourself, right?" she said, smiling incredulously.

He dipped his head and blew out again. "I get it, it belongs in a different century… but where there are bikers, there will be women who want that and will do anything to have a piece of the pie. You get that, April, right?" He flung it back to her with a teasing smile.

She gnashed her teeth. "Touché," she said. Yes, she was one of those women right now, and yes, she saw the irony. "So the ladies have to do all the cleaning and cooking and-"

"The sweet butts, yes, the ol' ladies, no."

"So the men make the sweet butts their ol' ladies-"

"Not really, no one wants to have one of the ladies who have been passed around. Tends to cause drama."

She tossed her hair out of her face, trying a different angle. "And so what's with the leather thing?"

"It's a cut, it has the club colors on it, the emblem, position, and name. You gotta represent, gotta wear your club colors."

"… That's what you cut off, right, all the name badges and stuff?"

He looked at her for a moment. Maybe they weren't called badges, it made it sound like a Boy Scout or something, collecting badges. And a Boy Scout, Colt was not. She tried not to blush.

"So, do you earn money, as well?" she asked.

"Well, sometimes, you can earn a bonus, but usually it all goes into one big pot, which is divided up between the members, or invested to better the club, or make new connections…"

"Really, it's a group of disillusioned men and women with self esteem issues who got together to try out some slightly communist principles and who take part in illegal-"

Colt interrupted now, his voice louder, his face taking on some color. "It's more than that, yeah there's shady stuff, and yeah I see that women's rights still has a way to go in the MC, but it's a family. I'd die for my brothers, and in turn they'd die for me. They have my back, when no one else would. When society labels you a fuck up and casts you out with no safety net, no family or attentive teacher or thorough social worker or lenient insurance payout…" He cleared his throat of the emotion but she heard it creeping in there. "Yeah, the sweet butts can cause drama, but it's free pussy, on tap, all of them willing, there to make your wildest dreams come true. And some of the guys love 'em. You know? They fall in love, they get knocked up, they get betrayed, they support each other, just like any other relationship."

"And can anyone join?"

He scratched his stubble with his thumb. "Only men. And only if you have a bike. And actually… some MCs have outdated rules like no blacks, no gays…"

"Are you joking?"

"It's written in the charter, which was created in a different time-"

"Times change and rules need to change, too."

"I hear you, I agree, it was on the list of things to do, to change, we just never got around to it."

"Too busy whoring and drinking and partying-"

"Well, yes."

"And drugs, too?"

"Yes."

"You did drugs?"

"I wasn't a junkie, but you could get yourself some premium weed, or blow. I never went stronger and I never encouraged that as Prez, because it made the guys sloppy, but if you wanted it harder…"

"Sounds idyllic, Colt," she said sarcastically.

"I hear you, I do, if I were Prez again, I'd do things differently. We all gotta start somewhere." He shook his head and smiled again. "But I was never alone, and for an orphan, that was a powerful thing. Somebody cared for me, I got food, and a place to sleep, my own room. That was great. I had women dropping to their knees at my feet, when the only other interactions I had was laughing in my face. I didn't have parents, I was in foster homes, some okay, some not okay. I ran away from the last one. But at the MC, I could stand tall, I had money in my pocket and wheels and I was a man, you know? I could achieve things, I could get shit done. People looked up to me, respected me, and I took it seriously. I wanted to be the best Prez for them, to better them, as I had been bettered myself…"

She looked sideways at Colt as he drove. His stance was relaxed, his energy was flowing, he was animated and alive. Happy. Talking about MC life, Colt was a different man. "I had a home," he said, finally.

She could relate to some of that, she realized. She knew what he meant, about being someone to be proud of, someone who belonged. It hit closer to the mark than she felt comfortable disclosing. Her mother had died when she was a baby, her grandparents had done everything for her, but they were very much not her parents. It was in her ambition and drive to succeed and be an overachiever, that she found her place, that she found she could stand tall and be somebody. A woman of means, intelligence, and wit, who got what she wanted. An independent woman, a proud woman. A woman who saw where she wanted to be, and how to get herself there. Who could get shit done, as Colt had eloquently put it. She sighed. She had looked down on Colt at the beginning, but she was now aware of how they were on equal footing. They had always been, she was just blind and ignorant. Some aspects of this MC life he described sounded positively barbaric, but some of it… she saw the spark in his eye and she felt it in her own heart, too. He cleared his throat and she was aware he had stopped talking. She had been too busy thinking and eating humble pie.

"You ready to go off grid?" he asked, his gaze flicking sideways to her in the passenger seat.

She'd been watching the trees pass by as they zoomed along, eating up the miles as they meandered deeper into the state, further from the highway. "Am I ready?" she repeated, turning to him. She nodded and cleared her throat. "It feels good to be heading away from... things." She shrugged her shoulders.

He watched her for a moment, understanding flickering in his eyes. "It feels good to be out."

She took a deep breath, relishing in the freedom in front of her. She wanted to feel it, smell it. "Can we... can we put the windows down for a second?" she asked.

He blinked at her.

"I just want to... feel..." She tried to articulate, looking down, scared of what she would see in his eyes.

But then she heard the noise of him rolling down his window, so she immediately did the same and the car was filled with the roar of the wind buffeting in from outside. Instantly, the smell of pine trees, of forest and earth rushed in. The warmer air. It was sweet.

"Yeah!" She raised her voice, grinning from ear to ear despite herself. She stuck her head out of the window and howled, "Yahoo!"

"Yeehaaaah!" He did the same. She heard him yapping a series of wolf-like howls himself, grinning. "See April, you were born for MC life!" he shouted over the noise of the wind. "Blue's daughter is a real wild child at heart after all!"

She tossed her hair, letting the wind pull at it. No one had ever compared her to her father before. No one had ever mentioned her father before. She felt a shot of pride, affection and realization as she blushed and looked away from Colt, feeling too exposed. She really had been a total imbecile to dismiss him at the beginning. She felt her world tip off its axis and Colt was the one holding the globe. And the most shocking thing was she didn't mind. She liked it. She let the wind slap her face, she closed her eyes and embraced it all. Yes, they were on the run from the MC with a price on their heads, barely any possessions between them and if they were caught, then they'd be killed. But they had a fast car. They had their wits. They had each other.

With miles of open road and nights of secluded intimacy ahead, April felt excited, truly excited for the first time in her life. She had no idea what was going to happen between the two of them, but she hoped it was something. She didn't just want a hot, hard fuck anymore. She was intrigued by the man beside her, she wanted to get to know him more. He was a dangerous man who torched a hotel and stole a van. He could be violent, he had been the president of an outlaw motorcycle club. He had done time in prison, and yet she felt safe with him. She knew he'd never hurt her and would do anything to protect her. She felt like his partner in crime. For the first time in a long time, she felt like she was right where she needed to be.

CHAPTER 22
COLT

THE SKY HAD clouded over by the time they pulled off the highway. They'd been driving most of the afternoon. It was cooler, the sky was heavy, threatening rain. They stopped for a break. The thrill of earlier had clouded over like the sky. As the miles and the hours passed, he'd felt his growing irritation. His back was hurting him more than he was letting on. It was tiredness. It was the emotional toll of finding out his former brothers were all gone. Fuck, it was nicotine withdrawal.

She settled herself, seated cross legged in the back of the van, letting him be for now. She had flung the doors open and let the fresh air in. She nursed a can of orange soda like it was an expensive whiskey. And she watched him prowl.

He stalked over to a fence about ten angry paces away, patting down the pockets in his jeans. He pulled out his lighter and a pack of cigarettes. He put one between his lips, holding it loosely, with his mouth open. He flicked the lighter, his face glowed orange and he shielded his flame from the breeze with one hand as he took a deep drag. He closed his eyes with pleasure and relief for a moment. April looked on. Colt opened his eyes and saw her watching.

"I should quit, I know. It's bad for me, I know," he snapped impatiently.

"I wasn't going to mention it."

He took another drag. He was moody, irritated. But he wanted to be irritated, and hated himself for it. That carefree man who'd chatted easily with her and that howled with delight out of the open windows was gone. He wanted her to hate him, to leave him, to make it easier for him. He wanted to rip out the wiring in his brain that couldn't just let it be.

Her nostrils flared as she smelled the smoke from where she was. She licked her lips. He watched her. She watched him. He clicked his neck and looked at her like a lion eyeing up his prey. Almost as if she'd dared him to, he grasped the bottom hem of his shirt and yanked it over his head.

"That better, Kitten? I'm only worth looking at when I'm shirtless?" Then he sauntered closer.

He wanted her to scold him, shame him, make him feel like the monster he thought he was. But the expression on her face told him she wouldn't do that. He both hated and loved her for it. Why couldn't she just tell him he was a fuck up and saunter off into the distance to a taxi, leave him to fester? He wanted her to and yet he didn't want her to. He already knew that she wouldn't do that, her guard was dropping, and she was willing to let him in. He was terrified.

She cleared her throat. "I want to know the story behind the nipple piercing." She nodded to the little silver bar that caught the light.

His eyebrows shot up and he looked down disarmingly, surprised. "Same as the story behind that little ear piercing of yours." He shrugged. He felt he'd disclosed too much to her earlier. He'd basically stalked her relentlessly, he was there for all of the big moments in her teenage life. He regretted he had been so open earlier. He didn't want to talk about the past. He felt moodier than the gray, threatening sky up above them.

She frowned and gazed up at him with those blue, blue eyes. "I got this done when my friends and I took a trip to Atlantic City... wait, you came?"

He nodded once. She absent-mindedly twisted the dainty little diamond in her tragus. "We all got piercings..." She drifted off.

Colt couldn't keep his foul mood up when she was around him. He couldn't keep hating himself when she was there. He resigned himself to telling her more. Hell, she already owned his heart and soul. What was one more slither of his flesh?

"Yeah, the other girls got their belly buttons done, thank fuck you wanted your ear otherwise your dad would have actually killed me... I had to check it out, ensure the place was decent... plus one of the guys at that gym by the beach had really helped me improve my squat form and he had a nipple piercing and I thought it looked bad ass at the time..."

"It looks great, Colt. How does it feel?" she asked, reaching out with her fingers as if she wanted to pluck it. His balls tightened at the thought of her pulling it. With her fingers. With her teeth. The jolt that would cause... "I don't just like you shirtless, Colt, for the record. I mean, I like you shirtless. Despite me desperately not wanting to, I still find you attractive smoking..." She tossed her hair back and took a breath. "I want to see that combination of pleasure and relief on your face when you come deep inside me." She finished, speaking fast. She looked up at him, shocked at herself. She'd clearly never talked dirty before. That she'd tried for him melted his self-loathing.

He took a deep drag and smirked. He no longer felt full of rage, she had successfully massaged his ego enough to believe maybe he didn't have to hate himself and hate the world in that moment. He swaggered toward her, until he stood right in front of her.

April swallowed and gazed up at his torso. She locked her eyes on him, and opened her legs from her cross legged stance. She scooted to the end of the van, hanging her legs over the edge of the drop down. She reached out and put a hand on his hip bone, underneath a thick rope of his muscle. His body was warm, her hand felt cold. She pulled him in between her legs. He resisted at first. She planted her other hand firmly on his other hip and pulled. He let himself move forward so that he was standing inside her legs. She moved her palms to the front of his stomach. His muscles rippled briefly. She dared a look up to his face. He had the cigarette in between his teeth, his lips bared, his head nodded forward, hanging off her every move. He was staring at her hands on his stomach. She licked her lips, leaned forward and pressed them against the muscles. Beside his belly button. Over wispy dark hair that grew downwards leading her lower. Urging her lower.

"Fuck, April," he whispered.

She bit him lightly, bit the small amount of soft flesh on top of his muscle, gathered it between her front teeth and tugged slightly. It would be oh so easy to let her continue. Why was he pulling back?

"No, April." He grunted. His head tipped back and she reached for the low slung waistband of his jeans. He clamped his hand on hers, stopping her. "I hate that you make me want you like this..." he whispered.

"Like what?" Her hands pressed the bulge at her eye level.

"Like this... roughly, furiously, desperately... I don't want to lose control again..." He breathed.

"But I want you like this," April countered quickly. She looked up at him, pleading with her eyes. She told him she didn't beg, but here she was, begging him.

"You deserve silk sheets and champagne..."

"I don't want that... I want you... take me, Colt, roughly, furiously, desperately..." she whispered into his skin. "I felt it, too, you know, when we were together. I feel that power, that rawness... the darkness.

The Chase

Like something biblical, something God forgot to do anything with in the book of Genesis, when you moved in me…" She breathed and he could have sworn his soul sighed along with her.

Well fuck. He clasped the cigarette in between his teeth and blew a plume of smoke away from her. Looking down at her, he put one hand on her face, his fingers holding her chin. Then he moved his hand so his fingers tangled in her hair. He fisted his hand, pulling her hair. It was no longer in a neat ponytail. One of her hands trailed up his torso, to his nipple with the bar through it. She pulled it lightly, watching his reaction. He rolled his eyes with pleasure.

"Yes, April," he found himself gasping. Her name over his lips felt like a prayer to all that was good in the world. A little smile of her own played on her face. Lips that were caressing his skin. He tossed the half smoked cigarette away without a second thought. He thrust his other hand into her hair, bumping her face against him. Her nimble fingers were undoing the button of his jeans; ripping the zipper open and tugging them down. He felt her breath, hot little pants on his lower stomach. Her hunger was powerful, shocking to him. He fucking loved that she wanted him that much… it undid him. Completely undid him.

He shivered in anticipation, barely controlling the desire coursing through him. She clamped her mouth down on his steel hard cock through his briefs. He cried out loud. Her hot, wet mouth was almost too much. Almost. He started moving his hips, thrusting his cock into her face, hard. He felt like a dog in heat. An animal. A savage bastard. The devil himself, climbing out of hell to chase after what he wanted. Again.

"April, no," he said again, shaking his head, yet unable to stop. "You don't deserve this…"

Her hands were pulling at the elastic of his briefs, trying to pull them down.

He was close to losing his load. Coming too soon. Again. Taking what he didn't deserve.

"Trust me, Colt," she whispered. His eyes slammed into the back of his skull.

"It's not a question of trust, Kitten, I-"

"It is."

"Fuck, April." He squeezed his eyes shut. For a split second he imagined what it would feel like to have her lips close around his throbbing hard cock. Bare skin, not just on top of his briefs. Wet heat. Slipping inch by inch. Watching her lips stretch around his cock. Her cheeks hollow, pulling him in further. Then to hit the back of her tight throat. To look down and see her eyes water slightly from the effort. Her mouth engulfing him.

He pulled his hands off her head, grabbing hers at his waist. He restrained her.

"Colt, no, let me," she pleaded, her voice pinched with frustration.

"April, April..." He was practically chanting her name. His eyes were shut, he was straining to keep her fingers off him, straining to keep himself from falling off the edge.

"Colt..." She was saying his name now, too. His ears rang from his pounding heart. Wait, was she saying something else?

"Bikes, Colt, is that the sound of...?"

His eyes snapped open. "... Straight pipes," he finished her sentence. His body slammed into sobriety like a concrete wall. He took a breath. Back in control. Back inside himself, off that edge.

"Get in, let's go," he husked out. He pulled himself away from her, from what they'd done, and what they had almost done. That moment was gone. He reacted on auto pilot. Fight or flight. Flight mode. Get the hell away. He yanked up his jeans, as April scrambled up.

The Chase

The rumble of motorcycles could be heard far off. Time to run. He jumped into the cab of the van, pleased to find April in the passenger seat, slamming her door.

"Drive fast and hard, Colt," she said.

So he did.

CHAPTER 23
COLT

COLT DROVE HARD and fast for days. They went north into Washington, then looped back down again, through Idaho. Then Utah, Nevada. Colt didn't want to get stuck up against the coast or the Canadian border. He said he didn't want them to think they were just headed due north. Or straight east. So they snaked about through the states. April said she saw more of the US than she'd ever seen before.

They'd stopped to eat at a truck stop but at that moment, he heard the far off sound of a bike. Multiple bikes. The loud kind with straight pipes.

The MC.

They were coming.

They were near.

Pulling off the highway, into the truck stop they were just about to leave.

So close. Their driving around in circles hadn't thrown the MC off their tail.

Colt edged the van toward the on ramp, checking everywhere before pulling out. The sound had stopped. The bikes were still and out of view. Colt hit the gas and they were on the highway again. April glued her eyes to the road, but no bikes followed them.

As the evening drew to a close and the gray of dusk began to bite, April's eyes drooped. It was becoming routine. She finally succumbed to sleep, her head lolling to rest lightly on the window. When he was certain she was out, he allowed himself to think about it. What kept happening whenever they got close. The brush of her hand against his, the breath on her lips that coasted over him when they stood too close. Why he choked. Again. Why he couldn't just drop his pants and get on with it like he should have been able to. Like he wanted to. Hell, like he'd bragged to her, "a good fuck with a bad ass biker". He'd delivered a frantic, teenage quickie and then nothing more. She had asked him for it. Begged him for it. Her sassy words of "don't make me beg, begging isn't my style..." rang in his ears. He knew he was getting lost in his own head, he felt it, spiraling downwards, round and round, but he couldn't stop it.

The first time, he'd let loose and he'd been terrified he'd broken the universe. The power balance, the difference between light and dark and right and wrong. He'd come too quickly and ruined himself. The second time, he'd backed down, because... He took a deep breath in through his nose, instantly taken back to that moment he had his index and middle fingers thrust roughly inside her. Oh fuck. It had felt good. So warm, so wet, so silky soft inside that tight little cunt of hers. It promised to be everything he had dreamed of. Everything he thought it was but hadn't taken the time to properly appreciate when he'd quickly binged on her. He had stopped then because he knew he was rushing it. He didn't want to rush it again. To force things. And he felt he was forcing. Her little breathy screams would play on his mind. Haunt him. He was glad he checked in with her afterwards that she was okay. She said she liked it. He didn't want it to be like that again, rushed, needy. Dirty. But at the same time, he wanted it exactly like that. Hard, fast, pounding into her like she was his and only his. Skin slapping skin. Wet skin. Fuck. He was getting hard thinking about it. So why hadn't he just followed through and made it happen?

Because it was her, the voice in his head answered. His ultimate teenage fantasy, fucking her. But not just that, her coming to him willingly, wanting him hot and hard, rough and dirty. In the back of a van, on the side of the road. Ripping his jeans off to get to him. In his wildest dreams only had he imagined undressing her, peeling pretty little garments off her. He hadn't foreseen her pawing to get inside his pants. Her telling him not to stop. Begging him. Her little mewls, her utterances of 'Colt, please'. Her confession that she'd imagine a man like him when touching herself. Telling him she wanted to see the pleasure on his face as he came. He wasn't sure he was good enough for her. He wasn't sure he deserved her. No, he was sure, he was one hundred percent certain that he did not deserve her.

But when she was looking hungrily at him from beneath those dark lashes of hers, he felt like the king of the world. Like a god. She made him feel fucking invincible. Like he could actually deserve her. He could glimpse it. It was within the realm of imagination. But then his self-doubt caught up with him. She only wants you to scratch a one-time itch. She only wants to try you out, take you for a spin, have a wild ride, then walk away. She won't want to have anything more to do with you. That's what the voice in the back of his head said to him. And that was the truth of it. That was what it all came down to, he realized with a sinking feeling in his soul. He wanted more. He wanted more than just a hot, hard fuck with the untouchable April. It wasn't just a one and done thing for him. He had thought he'd be able to handle that one night in heaven, one blaze of glory. One slice of the pie. One puff of the cigarette, but as he knew only too well, once you had one puff, you wanted more. You craved it, your body burned for it. And that was how he felt now about April. He wanted more. He wanted her more than once. More than just a few times. He wanted her forever. He wanted her roughly, and gently and everything in between. He already knew he was insatiable when it came to her. Addicted. Obsessed even. He'd watched from the shadows as a teenager, whispered her name like a forbidden prayer in the darkness. Knowing she would always haunt him. Yet he embraced it. He thought he didn't matter enough for his deadly addiction to be a problem.

But it was a problem now because he knew he wouldn't be able to give her up. Once he'd had her fully, that would be it. She would always be his. And, even if she wasn't his, she would be his. He wanted to cut loose the thrashing, starving, raging animal within him and let it loose on her. But he knew once he had let it loose, that was it. It would never come back in the cage. He would never be able to call it back, lock it up. It would be forever hers. And she would leave him empty. It wasn't a dilemma, though. He wasn't thinking about what he should do. He knew what he would do. He'd give in. Let her have his passion, his hunger, his soul. He'd fling open both doors of the cage and let her take it all.

He let his gaze drift to her, still fast asleep. Maybe it would be enough for her, too. He barely dared to hope for it. If all of this had happened five years ago, before prison, before he heard of the demise of the MC, he would have aimed mercilessly for her. Cockily. Like the arrogant asshole MC Prez he had been. With his brothers at his back and his position at the head of the table. He would have pursued her with single-mindedness, with certainty that they would end up in bed together and that she'd love it. He wasn't that man anymore, he was an imposter, an empty shell of a man. Could he conjure up any of that bravado now? He would try at least. Like he did in the meeting room of the MC. He'd fake it until he made it.

He glanced at the clock on the dashboard. It was late. He turned off the highway. Off the next road, and the next, until they were in the middle of nowhere. Then he parked up at some half empty campsite. The silence filled his ears. He let out a sigh. He was tired. His body ached again. He got out of the van, closing the door quietly, pressing it shut rather than slamming it. He stood and it felt like each of his vertebrae cracked back into place. Fuck. He'd have to do something about his back. Especially if he wanted to give her the ride of her life. To give himself the ride of his life, too. The night air was cool, damp almost. He smelled the mist and the road and the trees.

He opened up the back of the van to the little love nest she'd created. Fairy lights softly bathed the interior with warmth. The quiet of the softness inside. Had she meant for it to be so intimate? It was pure coziness. It was heaven after his prison bunk. The last few nights of sleep, he had been numb by the time he'd collapsed inside it. As was their routine now, he took a step back and turned to go to the passenger side. He opened the door slowly. He was engulfed by her scent as he leaned over her to undo her seatbelt. He knew it would be wrong to breathe in deeply, but fuck it, he did it anyway. He took a deep drag of her as he carefully unclipped her seatbelt and fed it back into its reel so that it didn't snap back loudly or drag over her. Then he firmly scooped her up and into the van. She sighed but didn't wake. In fact, she nestled into his chest. Her little murmur against his chest sent a tightness straight to his cock. Fuck. He wanted more, but it was looking like it would be the same as usual; passing out fully clothed on top of the duvet.

Again, he took off his boots and her shoes. He wanted to get out of his jeans. He laid back, fuck it felt good, and lifted his butt to shimmy out of the pants. Yep, his dick was semi hard. He gave it a quick, hard squeeze over his briefs, and stifled a groan of desire. He whipped off his socks, and lay back down in his T-shirt and briefs. She was on top of the duvet in her clothes, but he wasn't about to undress her, he wanted that experience to be enjoyable for both of them, when and if it ever happened. He wanted to rip her clothes off right before sinking himself in her wet heat. He wanted her to watch him do it. He wanted to feel her hands ripping the clothes off him, too. Ah hell, he was fully hard now. It felt wrong to touch himself right next to her sleeping body. He'd close his eyes to go to sleep. He'd let that oblivion claim him, that empty wasteland of purgatory, neither calming nor frightful, that empty place he went to every night. Except the last few nights, where he had dreamed of her. He turned his head, cracked open an eye and took one last look at her, fast asleep next to him. He had a feeling he would see her again in his dreams as soon as he closed his eyes. The idea of that both soothed and excited him. He turned his head back to center, took a breath, closed his eyes and plunged in.

He woke slowly, but was immediately aware it was too early. It was still dark, still night time. The fairy lights twinkled above him, bathing everything in a golden glow.

What had woken him? Then he felt it. A stabbing, tight pain in his shoulder blade right next to his spine. He sighed and shifted slightly. It was warm in the van. The air was quiet but close. His T-shirt stuck to him, it felt claustrophobic on his skin. He dragged the cotton over his stomach, upwards, raised his arms and yanked it off over his head. He shifted his head to see if April was still sleeping soundly.

He had to muffle his groan with his hand.

THE CHASE

Fuck Christ. She was undressed. She must have woken up and been too hot, too. He saw skin. Miles of her luscious, soft skin. She'd kicked off the covers and was lying on her side, facing him. He let out a noise like he had taken too big a bite on a cake and his mouth was full of something large and delicious. Black cotton panties hugged her hips. A black bra clung to her breasts. He continued his trail up her body to her face. Then her eyes snapped open.

CHAPTER 24
APRIL

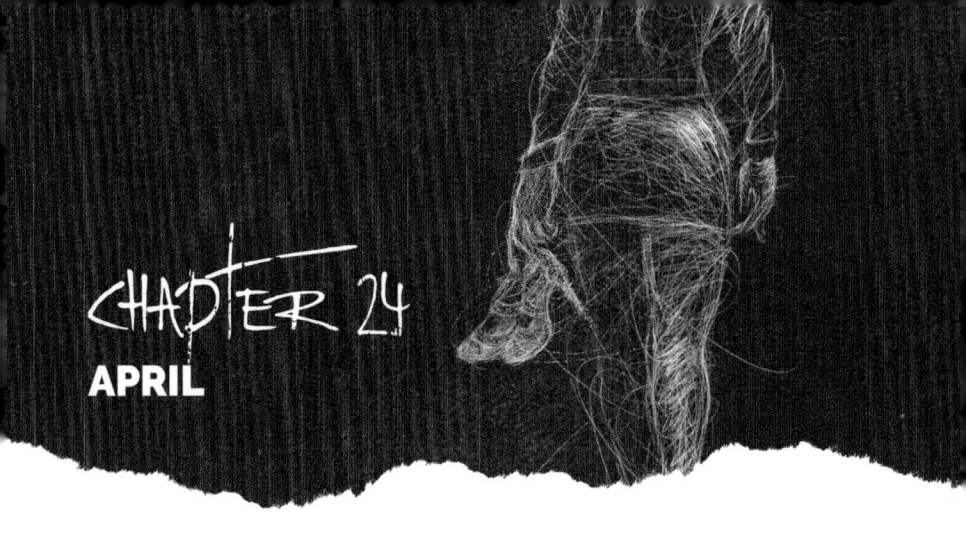

She woke up suddenly. Something had startled her awake. She blinked. She had pulled off her clothes earlier. Colt had obviously carried her from the seat to the bed again. He'd laid her down fully clothed. She was grateful for that. She had tried to stay awake, she desperately wanted them to go to bed together. To undress, to get close. But that never happened.

When she had woken earlier, she'd restlessly yanked her clothes off. She wasn't too hot again, so what had woken her? She was met by two dark, wide open eyes gazing back at her. Intensely. Looking hungry. Ravenous. She swallowed loudly.

"You okay?" she whispered.

He grunted in a casual tone that did not match the intensity of his gaze. "Shoulder hurts." He shrugged his right one once.

He obviously didn't realize how much his eyes were saying to her. Screaming to her. He didn't take his eyes off her. She felt his warm breath on her skin. They must have rolled close to each other at some point in the night. She had to capitalize on this moment, no way could she let this pass. Before he got lost in his own head again. Before he started hesitating and pulling away. They were both in their underwear, mere inches from each other. She knew he wasn't going to initiate it, something was holding him back. Thinking she was too good for him, or not wanting to hurt her. Whatever it was, it was resulting in frustration for both of them and she'd be damned if she let it go on any longer.

"Your right shoulder? Probably all the driving. Roll over and I'll give you a massage," she instructed.

He breathed, in and out, once. His chest rising and falling. Was he hesitating? He just kept gazing at her, devouring her. After a long moment, he shifted. He did roll onto his front. His bare back was now exposed. Muscles, broad shoulders, tapering in a beautiful arch to a narrower waist. Sinew bunched on either side of his spine. And those black briefs, clinging to his perfectly round orbs, topped by two little dimples where his hip bones were. Her gaze swept him up and down. And up again. Now it was her turn to devour him with her eyes. He turned his head to her. She pushed herself up to sit and straddled his back.

He let out a muffled grunt as she lowered her weight to sit on his butt. She adjusted herself a little lower, on his upper thighs. She breathed out and looked at his back. The Black Coyotes MC tattoo covering it spanned from his shoulder blades to his middle lower back. The skull of a coyote, eye sockets, empty and staring. In the middle of a circle, a motorcycle tire with the lettering 'Black Coyotes' around the top and 'California' across the bottom. Exactly the same shape and design as what had been on the back of his cut. It was bold, haunting, and the shapes were black against his skin. His skin was smooth. She used the fingers on one hand to trace the outline.

He flinched under her touch. "Tickles," he mumbled. He was trying to sound grumpy. But he wasn't, she could tell. She went back over the outline again with a firmer touch.

"We need to get this tattoo covered up. If they do catch up with us... it would be better if they don't take it off you by some gory method..."

"They'd have to catch us first," he said.

She murmured, "I'll hit up Instagram, see if I can find someone good..."

"We'd need them to keep quiet-"

Her hands danced over his back and went to his right shoulder. She didn't know massage, had no training or particular skill. She'd just wanted an excuse to get her hands on him. She pushed her thumbs into the hard flesh over his right shoulder blade. He sucked in a sharp breath.

"Sorry, did that hurt?"

"Yes, but that's the right spot."

She used less pressure, rubbing her thumbs upwards and he groaned into the pillow. He mumbled something.

"You okay?" she whispered.

He arched his back, she shamelessly watched his lower back dimple up as he shifted momentarily. His hand disappeared under him.

She frowned, what was he doing? Then it clicked. He had to adjust himself. She smiled. He must have been lying with his dick at an awkward angle. And it must be getting hard. And he had felt the need to touch it. She felt a proud sense of ownership. She had done that.

He groaned again now but it was unmistakably a groan of pleasure. His butt cheeks squeezed as he shifted his hips. Thrusting the mattress, oh so subtly. Did he think she didn't know what he was doing? He was dry humping the mattress under him. The friction of the bed and his weight must be getting him off. She was shocked. And yet, not shocked at all. She lowered her face down, closer to his back, her hands still massaging his shoulder, though less deliberately.

She couldn't resist, she opened her mouth and sunk her teeth into the flesh on his back.

He bridled. "April! Fuck, I-"

"Keep going, Colt," she interrupted him with a hiss, and immediately licked the skin that had been between her teeth moments before. She was shocked at her aggression. She felt dizzy with it.

His thrusts became more overt, more wild. She needed more contact to hold on. She sunk her body down onto his. Her front plastered to his back.

He tried to turn his head to see. Maybe he caught a glimpse of her boobs pressed up against him.

"Kiss me," he demanded. She leaned forward and sideways and their lips locked. He almost bit her with urgency.

She felt it now, too. A runaway train, carriage-less and free and careening downhill. Getting faster and faster. She pressed her pussy into his hip bone, rubbing herself against him. He must have felt what she was doing, as he let out a guttural sound from deep within him. Yes, they were both running wild and free now, together.

He put his arm back over his head now, as if he were reaching behind himself to scratch an itch. Except he grabbed onto her forearm, pinning her in place above him, tugging her slightly to force her to ride his backside.

"Use me, Kitten," he growled from within the pillows. "I'm yours, use me."

His utterance had her mind spiraling out, the sense of urgency, of desperation was pulling at her veins, clawing in her core. She wanted him deep inside her, chasing away that feeling, hounding it until it ceased. But she would take this opportunity to get whatever satisfaction she could. She had seen he was bothered by his own feelings of inadequacy, of insecurity, how it was crippling him, how it was whirling around in his mind, over and over again, on repeat. She thrust against him, and in the same rhythm he was thrusting himself against the mattress. She wouldn't let him get stuck in his head tonight.

"We're backwards," she managed to huff.

She was his, dammit. She surprised herself with how true it was. And he was hers. Her heart was getting caught up in this. She felt it with each of their joint thrusts. She was drilling herself and him together. Hammering their souls together. Tight.

She wanted it, she loved it, feeling her heart and soul again in the first place. Wanting. Yearning. Feeling. Loving. In whatever capacity this was. Yes, loving. Loving him. Wanting him. He'd spent years watching her and wanting her, and she'd been oblivious. And now she wanted him.

"Kitten, this is how fucking much I fucking want you. You make me do fucked up things..." He made a violent noise in his throat. "Show me how much you want me," he demanded, pounding his hips.

She ran her hand down her body, she had to let go and let them both tumble. She pressed her whole self into him. Her breasts against his writhing back, her pussy into his butt. Within her, she felt shuddering darkness and a howl she barely heard.

CHAPTER 25
COLT

Animal.

Savage.

Fucking brute.

But he carried on anyway. He didn't fucking care. He ground his hips into the mattress again.

Again.

Again.

It felt so good. It felt so wrong. How had she ended up on top of him, behind him? Rubbing her hips against him. He laid underneath her, a mindless wreck of a man. No longer a man. An animal. She built him up and cut him down all in one move.

"Fuck fuck fuck…" he heard himself chant. What were they doing? Rutting like their lives depended on it. How unhinged had they become together, they weren't even the right way around. And he heard her yowl, felt her shudder, and knew that she had driven herself over the edge.

He was a burning fuse. He knew it, he felt it. He needed this. He was about to blow. He allowed himself to. He felt he could now. He reared up, unable to take it anymore.

"I need to come," he rasped. April moved to the side as he grabbed himself. Dick, balls and all. And he yanked once. Hard. And came.

Hard.

He felt his juice shooting out of his engorged cock. He came everywhere. He almost choked on the bliss of it. He heard himself groan. He felt his eyes sting with stars.

He forced them open to watch the streaks of cum spit on himself. On the sheets. On her. She looked at him with wide, wild eyes as his cum spurted onto her. Her thigh and stomach. Marking her. Fucking animal. But she was his now. He hated himself and loved himself at the same time. Hated what he'd done. Loved what he'd done. He'd come in a burning trail of desire so palpable he practically choked on it.

"Fuck me." He looked on at what he'd done, his work of art. Panting, chest heaving. He heard her heavy breathing, too. He ran a hand through his hair, pulling it back from his face. He was a sweaty mess. He felt the liquid heroin of quenched desire in his blood.

But now his rationality was catching up. Again. Thoughts and logic thundering along like a heavy truck, bringing up the rear defiantly. He'd just dry humped a mattress, then come all over April. What was he, thirteen? An inexperienced loser? He had said he would wait for a bed, he would wait to do it properly.

Fuck, they hadn't even had sex. He was feeling like a god when he hadn't even found the ultimate satisfaction. And damn, now she was just covered in sticky cum. She'd had to ride his ass, literally, to get herself off. What the fuck had he done? Yet again, he'd fucked it up. He met her eyes and couldn't face what he thought he saw. Surprise, shock. Complete disbelief.

"Colt, that was-"

"Kitten I- "

"...one of the hottest moments of my life," she spoke over him to finish.

"I... what?"

"I'm... that was... you let me... and then we... and you..." she gestured to the glistening liquid on her body.

He raised an eyebrow. Damn, that was the last thing he expected her to say. "What was the other hottest moment of your life?" he asked, buying time to assemble the shreds of his tough guy persona. She smiled coyly. It went straight to his cock. Filthy thoughts thundered through his brain. He wanted to fuck her so badly it hurt.

"When you plunged your fingers inside me and begged me to stop you... when you yanked off my boots and lifted my leg and plunged into me on the back of a stolen bike..." she said, raising her chin with defiance, letting a finger of hers lightly trail through a droplet of his cum on her stomach. Daring him. Goading him. She wanted more. She was loving this and she wanted more.

He was a dead man.

"Fuck." He breathed out of his lungs. He felt a warm buzz pulsing out of his chest. He knew that feeling. He'd felt it before. He'd follow her into the fiery pits of hell if she asked him to. He had to get out of there before it was too late and he did or said something stupid.

"Gotta have a smoke," he managed to wheeze out. His body jolted into action. He grabbed his jeans and scrambled down the bed, toward the backdoor. His pulse hammered in his ears. His legs felt boneless. Stumbling out of the van, he slammed the door behind him. Goddamn, his briefs were damp. The cool night air nipped at his body. He peeled off his underwear, wiped himself down with them, then chucked them on the ground. Naked, he had a quick glance around.

Things were quiet, thankfully, no one was about. He should have checked before he'd stripped. But he never learned, always acted first, then thought later. Fucking animal.

He put on his jeans, commando. Not that they did much to stop the night chill from enveloping him. He patted his pockets until he found the cigarettes and lighter. He plucked one out with his thumb and forefinger, jabbed it in his mouth and lit it. He inhaled deeply. With the nicotine entering his blood and the hot smoke at the back of his throat, he started to pace.

Fuck, he should just own what happened. It was hot. April seemed to enjoy herself, he had enjoyed himself. Face down in soft sheets that smelled of her, thrusting wildly, not holding back. Indulging himself in his desire for her. And her, rubbing herself all over him, pushing herself into him, needing him for her own pleasure. Both of them united in their chase. He raised his head. The moon was out, maybe a full moon. Or almost full. It was half hidden behind some fluffy clouds, lit up from behind. It looked moody. Haunting but beautiful.

He should go back in the van and have hot, sweet sex with her, tenderly and deeply, for what was left of the night. He needed to just stop, now. The endless cycle of hating himself, ruminating on the things he'd done, or not done, on how he wanted it to be. He was beginning to annoy himself. What was he doing out here, smoking? He flicked ash off the tip of his cigarette and stared at it. She said she didn't like it. He'd cut back, avoiding doing it around her. Pussy whipped already. But no one had ever cared enough about him to tell him to quit. Until now. He'd finish this one then go back in. If she was still up for it, he'd take what he wanted, what he'd always wanted. Her.

He blew out a plume of smoke and tossed the cigarette away. Did she have condoms? He didn't, would she have bought any? If so, where did she put them? He'd buy some, at the next stop, keep a few in

THE CHASE

his wallet, he thought with a smile. He felt himself beginning to get hard at the thought. He took a moment, looked up at the moon and thanked his lucky stars that he was even able to think about condoms and April in the same sentence.

CHAPTER 26
APRIL

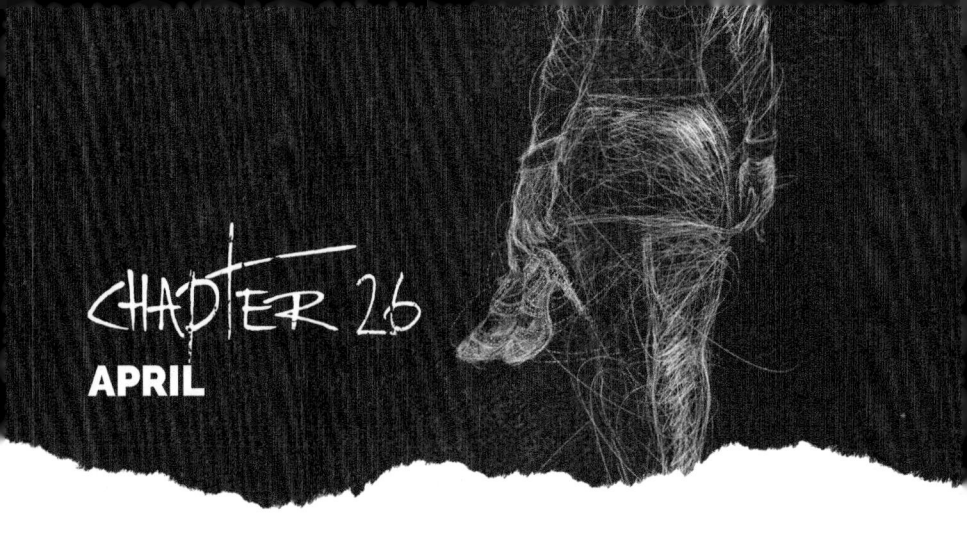

He slammed the back door of the van on his way out. Not because he was angry, just because he was a heavy handed biker. Who had just come all over her. Jesus, she was glad he got out for a moment. She needed to collect her thoughts, which spurted around her head messily just like his cum had. And was now all over the place with the potential to cause trouble.

She was having a hard time remembering this was just a fast ride with a bad boy. A taste of the other side of the tracks, crazy sex, then return to normality. But now she knew she was in trouble because she preferred this side of the tracks. Turned out she was falling for this biker bad boy, because he was a good man, after all.

She looked down at her stomach and dipped her index finger in the glistening cluster of droplets there, again. Colt's cum. She knew she was in trouble because she had the overwhelming desire to take that wetness and slide it into herself. She wanted him there. His life essence, deep within her. She wanted his seed. And damn her, she wanted it to grow. What the hell was she thinking? A future with Colt? She couldn't deny herself, because the thought alone was turning her on. Her body, yes, and her heart, her soul. She wanted him, she could see herself loving him. She was halfway there.

If they weren't on the run, in this van, what would it be like to be with a man like Colt? To do normal things, like grocery shopping. To go on a date with him, sit across from each other, a candle between them on the table. To clean the house together, divide the work. Maybe he'd do the vacuuming and she'd dust. Maybe they'd argue about which way dishes would go in the dishwasher. She smiled, trying to imagine that. He'd say he didn't give a fuck and stick them in all over the place. Trying for a baby with him. Showing him that positive stick. Where was this coming from? She would have said she hypothetically wanted kids, if anyone had asked. She was still young, there was time for that. She wasn't working on any timeline. She wanted babies in the generic sense, an idea but no actual plan. Had she wanted Hugo's babies? No, she had not. What a sign that was. But she wanted Colt's babies. A lewd act some would consider disrespectful, him coming all over her. But it had stirred something in her that she hadn't felt before. It should have happened after they had made love or something, not rutted like deer together and then him blowing his load all over her. None of this made any sense, but she felt it, clear as day.

Colt suddenly burst back through the van door. "April."

"Colt, I–"

"Pipes. I hear straight pipes," he hissed urgently.

Her cozy musings shattered instantly. She felt sweat run down her spine. Her mouth went dry, her heart galloped. "No! How are they finding us?" she wailed.

"Help me, we'll push the van into the bushes, then hide."

She scrambled into action, grabbing Colt's discarded white shirt as she passed. Tumbling out of the van, she threw on the T-shirt over her underwear. She heard the pipes now, too. Coming closer. They were on the main road.

He'd released the parking brake. "It's going to be heavy, but I

THE CHASE

think if we just tuck it into the bush there..." He started pushing the van, throwing his weight into it. Her heart hammered in her chest. He already had the van rolling slowly forward into the bushes, but she joined in too.

"Just past the first branches here so they can't see..." he whispered. She threw her weight into it and, with some clips of the branches against the wing mirrors, it rolled behind the first few fronds of the pine tree. "Good, now, follow me." He suddenly stooped and grabbed his discarded briefs from the ground, then scrambled over to the van. She followed, clumsily, feeling like her legs didn't belong to her. He grabbed her hand. His was warm and strong, and he placed his other hand on the top of her head. "Under. Now," he instructed firmly.

She frowned. "Under... what... down there? But I-"

Too late, he'd scooted down himself and pulled her with him, protecting her head with that hand.

She tasted dirt. She smelled oil or gas or something. She could barely move. Somehow he half dragged her under the tiny gap between the ground and the van. She faced him, panicking. He gazed at her reassuringly. He didn't look away.

Bike engines cut out at the turn off of the road. The night sounded deafeningly quiet. Her heart slammed against her rib cage. She was worried there wasn't room for her lungs to expand in the cramped space they were in. She could hardly see anything. She focused on his eyes. He still had his hand on the top of her head. She focused on the warmth of it. The slight pulse she felt from his heart through his hand. Slower than hers. Steadier. Calmer. She let it calm her.

" ... I'm just saying, we don't even know what vehicle we're looking for-"

"I know, but Cleaver said his intel was that it could be a camper van or something--"

"Yeah, yeah, I'm just saying to you-"

"Well don't be saying it to anyone else, unless you want to be skinned alive."

The two voices came closer. "This isn't the shit I signed up for, man."

"What do you mean?"

"I mean fucking dirty bombs, kidnapping women, fucking chasing the former Prez just cos Cleaver wants to line his pockets-"

"Buddy, you can't let anyone else hear what you're saying..."

"I know, I just... I thought it would be fun, easy... booze and women and good times."

"Yeah, well, the women left when the money dried up-"

"And when Cleaver started getting rough with them-"

"Yeah, fuck... that, too."

"You know, I heard good things about this guy, Colt, when he was Prez- "

"Sounds like it was the golden age, don't it?"

"Yeah, so if he did come back, if he did challenge Cleaver-"

"Buddy, don't say it..."

"But I'm just saying man, I'd back him."

"Well, unfortunately we're meant to find him and kill him."

"As I said, we don't even know what we're looking for."

"Just look for signs-"

"What signs?"

"I don't fucking know!"

The pair continued to bicker as they kept walking, continuing out of earshot. Colt stayed stock still. She wanted to breathe a sigh of relief but Colt didn't move. She focused on her breathing. On his breathing. Then she heard their voices again. Of course they looped back. She hadn't thought. That's why it was good to be on the run with

THE CHASE

him and not by herself.

"You wanna wait until morning? Wait by the entrance to see if they come in or out, or keep going up the highway?"

"Screw this, man, let's go, nothing outta the ordinary here."

"Yeah."

"Let's go. Wish we'd gone to that bar back on the highway."

"Yeah, there'll be another - hey, tomorrow night we'll check out campsites, then hit up a bar..."

Their footsteps faded as they walked off to where they had left their bikes. April continued to breathe shallowly. In and out again. In and out. She heard Colt's breath, too. Longer, slower. Then bike engines started up. And began to fade. They were gone.

CHAPTER 23
APRIL

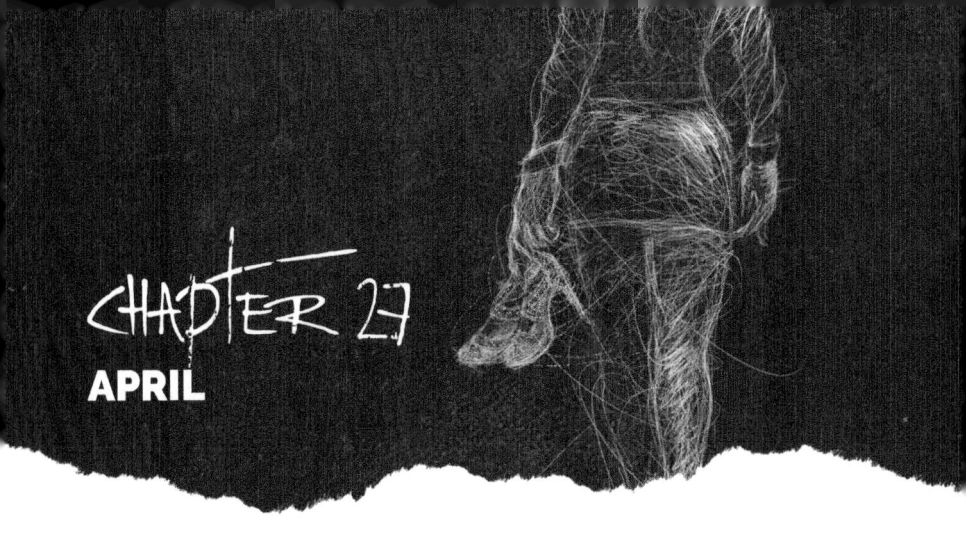

"Tonight, we're wild camping," Colt said firmly, as he steered the van out toward the exit early the next morning. It was just after dawn, they were back in Oregon again. They had both waited under the van for what had felt like hours to April. Her legs had gone numb with the cool predawn air. She thought she could feel damp from the ground seeping into her skin. Her muscles and limbs stiffened and she felt like she was made of clay.

Finally, Colt moved. He'd been stock still the whole time. She had become intimately familiar with his beautiful burning bright eyes, every hair of his beard, every pore of his skin. But then he'd moved, urging her to be silent with a finger to his lips and an imploring gaze. She followed his lead, feeling like a little girl, clinging to him, relying on him to make meaning from what happened. She was reminded of the seriousness of the game they were playing. This chase wasn't just a question of hide and seek, of a fun, carefree road trip and camping. They wouldn't all laugh and pat each other on the backs if they were caught. She and Colt might end up dead. She could be dragged back to the clubhouse to be raped.

They had crept into their van, in the bushes. After a shower and a silent breakfast of an apple and a banana each, they'd set off. The sun was just rising, the sky was a milky blue. April felt like she'd been up all night and it should be lunchtime already. She had her chin propped on her elbow as she watched the trees roll past them in the window.

"We're wild camping, and we're heading back down the highway," Colt repeated when he got no response from her.

She blinked, raised her head and turned back into the cab, toward Colt. She took a breath, forced her teeth to unclench and tried to relax. She risked a glance at him and could see stress in the lines around his eyes, in the white knuckles on the steering wheel.

"What's wild camping?" she asked.

"No campsite, no facilities."

"Huh... isn't that illegal?"

Colt blinked. "Do you think I give a fuck?"

"No facilities... no toilets, no showers?" she suddenly realized.

"Yeah, I didn't think you'd be happy," he said with a wry grin. She took a breath, about to protest out of habit, about to insist on a basic level of comfort, she could hear her shrill voice now in her head. It felt like her old self. She wasn't that person anymore. She expelled the breath forcefully.

"Good idea," she heard herself quietly agreeing.

"That's it? No pushback from my little pampered Kitten?" He smirked now.

She raised her eyebrows. "Oh, you want an argument?"

"I like your spirit, I told you."

"Well fine, you want me spitting like a kitten, here we go, brace yourself..." She took a big breath.

"I'm braced." He smiled.

"I'm not having us driving all day and most of the night again. How's that? Your shoulder is hurt and we both get grouchy and I fall asleep and we never get an evening together... so whatever we do, wherever we are, I want us to stop and actually enjoy the evening." She took a breath and peered sideways at him. He was amused.

'You want to enjoy your evening, huh?"

She set her jaw, knowing he wouldn't want to discuss what happened last night. "We're on the run from an MC that's dead set on killing us, but so far all that we do is you drive and I sleep."

"Come on Kitten, that's not all we do, is it?" he asked, his voice suddenly liquid caramel.

A hot blush bloomed on her cheeks. "I... I mean..." Why was she the one getting embarrassed here? Last night he was the one who'd come by basically dry humping the mattress. Her mind flooded with the image of his naked back, arching under her. His hot skin, his groans. And her own need, to get a release by rutting herself against him.

He had no shame. Something had changed from last time. He didn't seem to care that their latest foray into physicality happened how it did. She closed her eyes and imagined him rearing up above her. The glimpse of his large, engorged cock. Then the jets of hot liquid. She closed her eyes and gulped loudly. No, he didn't need to show shame. She shouldn't, either. It had been the hottest thing... then the disarming thoughts that had followed. Wanting him, a future, a home with him. A family with him. She pinched her lips shut before she said anything out loud that she shouldn't say.

Colt's voice cut through her thoughts, providing an ice bucket of reality. "I'm hoping those guys headed up the highway like they said... they didn't seem too smart..." Colt muttered, his eyes scouring the road, left and right. She couldn't see any men on bikes.

"I think we're clear," she said tentatively. He made a noise of agreement in his throat.

"For now. They'll be back. They've got intel from somewhere, they know we're in a van..."

"I wonder if…" she began to say, then trailed off, throwing him a guilty glance.

He flexed his jaw. "What, Kitten? If there is something you need to tell me, about how they might be getting intel…"

She shook her head, that furtive look gone from her face. "No, nothing, I just thought, maybe we should hide somewhere for a bit, get off the road…"

"Yeah, but they'll be looking for us when we need to stop, buy food or something… get gas… they'll be waiting for us…" He took a deep breath in and sighed while turning onto the highway. She watched him drive for a bit, falling into companionable silence. He held the steering wheel lightly in one hand, his elbow resting on the window ledge. The other hand was on the gear stick. His strong fingers lightly grasping the knob. His legs stretched out in front of him. His thighs spread a little. He drove with confident ease. She felt comfortable being driven by him.

It was at odds with his hesitancy to get physical with her again. Why was he holding back? Was that why he'd pulled back when her lips had been inches from his hard cock and she'd been thirsty to taste him? Why he'd snapped her panties back into place? Why he'd been ashamed, embarrassed that very first night, when he had let it all go? The way he drove the van told her a lot about him. She was getting a thin slice of him and all of his layers. He had this bad boy exterior, leather clad swagger that had immediately captured her attention. And that bad boy who didn't give a fuck was still there, still doing his thing, still breaking the law, acting uncivilized, taking what he wanted. But then that deeper, wiser layer was there, too. He wore his helmet on the bike, made sure she wore hers, checked the buckle twice. He looked over his shoulder, he read the map. Didn't drink any alcohol. A layer that had known fear, pain, betrayal, only made him more in her eyes. More of a man, more of a human, more to admire. More to love. April wanted to take a giant bite from the whole cake, all the layers. All the frosting. All of him. She wanted all of him.

They'd looped back around over the state line into California again. They stopped for gas in a small town near a national park. They stopped early that evening, in a clearing, with a shallow stream. The water pattered over gray, smooth stones, plunging into a deeper pool. It was so quiet. She could hear the stream, babbling softly. Forget staying here for the night, she could stay forever.

"Make yourself useful, Kitten, and find some firewood," he said in his bossy tone once they'd parked up, nodding in the direction of the trees.

Her mouth dropped open for a second, but then she snapped it shut. She rolled her eyes, then mocked dramatically, "Fine, Scout leader, I'll get firewood."

He smiled, enjoying her playfulness. "Good, dry stuff, of different sizes-"

"Yes, yes, I know the basics of making a fire-"

It was his turn to raise his eyebrows. "Do you now?"

She shrugged. "Well, I've seen enough movies about people making fires..." she quipped playfully.

"Right, it's just like in the movies." He chuckled.

"I was also a Girl Scout," she said mockingly.

He scoffed. "Course you were."

She grinned and walked away with a little skip in her step. He chuckled, she wouldn't have thought she could make him chuckle. And she wouldn't have thought that it would have meant so much to her. But it did. It really did.

Chapter 28

COLT

The fire snapped, breaking the quiet of the night. The smell of the burning wood filled his nostrils. It reminded him of the bonfires they would have in the courtyard back at the club house. His brothers, standing around, watching the roaring flames. Great BBQ food, a few beers, a few puffs on a good quality joint or two. Warming himself against the quieter, glowing embers as the night came to a close. Some nameless sweet butt tucked under his arm, a full stomach, all the drink he wanted. They were all gone. His brothers. His family. Not by blood. By choice. It was all gone, it hit him like a punch in the gut. Everything he'd worked for and defended, taken from him. All his brothers, killed or missing. He rubbed at the tightness in his chest.

"You okay?" A calm, soft voice said nearby.

Colt turned and looked at April, cross-legged in front of the fire. On the picnic blanket, wearing a large fleece. No shoes, just thick socks. He looked at her hard. Yes, he missed most of his old life painfully, except for one thing. Her. He was glad she was here. He'd swap any of those nameless, faceless lays for her.

"Yeah, I'm okay. Just thinking about my brothers… the MC." He cleared his throat, trying to refocus. He rubbed the back of his neck. Did he want to get into it with her, here and now? No, he wanted to enjoy this moment. Who knew how long he'd get to have her like this? He could talk about his brothers another time.

"You want to talk about it?" she asked quietly.

"No," he replied without hesitation. "Just like you don't want to talk about the kidnapping, and how you were almost raped, and how you feel about your daddy being dead-"

She shook her head. "It's not that... it's complicated... I can't..." she stuttered.

"I get it. It's fine. We don't need to talk about any of that," he said as he leaned into her. Feeling bold, he put an arm around her shoulders and scooped her into him, closer. He had not realized how much he just needed that. How much that made him feel. Home. Whole. Her body, her heat, her sweet scent in his nostrils.

She shivered and snuggled into his chest. "There is something I want to talk about. Colt, why are you making me wait?"

He bit his lip. Why was he making them both wait? He stroked his thumb up her arm, under her neckline on her fleece. He was reluctant to put it into words. But it was no use. He had to be honest with himself. With her.

He cleared his throat. "You deserve better than me."

She pursed her lips. "But I want you. I know you want me."

"It's not that simple, Kitten... you want me now, yes, but after this whole ordeal, then what?" Colt let his temper lash out slightly.

She went to take a breath to argue back but Colt cut her off.

"April, girls like you don't end up with guys like me. I might feature on your fuck list, a fun life experience you can chalk up and move on from, but frankly, I'm too old and too tired for games anymore."

She leveled him a penetrating stare. "You lied to me," she said eventually.

Now that was something he wouldn't stand for. "What?"

"You said you had nothing to offer me, except a dangerous ride and a hot fuck, remember?"

He growled. "Well, I'm a no-good felon, remember?"

"I mean the bit where you said you had nothing to offer me. You have so much more to offer me, Colt. I want more from you, I want it all from you. You are a good man-"

"Are you joking?" he asked, incredulously. "I'm a washed up loser ex-con without a penny to my name, no home, no bike. I'm fucking living in a stolen van right now-"

"Colt, stop whining, I don't need a man with money. I'm looking for a man who excites me, who respects me above all else. A guy who can let me into his heart and trusts me... that's why we haven't had sex again, isn't it? Because I've already slipped in between the cracks in your heart and you didn't want me to?"

He reeled.

"You want me more than just physically, I know it. I feel the same about you, and that's why you can't go back to just a quick fuck with me anymore, because it would be more than that... you've let me in already, you didn't mean to but now-"

"Fuck April, I-" He didn't know what to say. "I don't want to be one and done with you," he finished quietly.

She licked her lips. "You wouldn't be one and done for me... maybe at the start, yes, I'm adult enough to admit I thought this would be a fling... Honestly, I'm surprised by how much I want you. Physically, yes, but Colt... I have a feeling we could go... we could go all the way..."

He gulped.

"You can fuck me hard and make me come all over you," she paused and licked her lips and it undid him, "and you can also hold me close and gently make love to me, you can do both, I know it."

It was like she was looking into his soul. There were women in his past who he had been attracted to, and he'd take what he wanted. But he didn't care about or respect them. He wanted April more than his next breath but he couldn't help feeling she deserved better. If they were talking about going the distance, he couldn't keep a girl like April happy in the long term. Could he?

"You could do so much better than me, College Boy for example-"

"He wanted success. Money and influence were his true loves. He cared, but he didn't want me, really. He wanted the status of having a good looking attorney on his arm. I want you, Colt," she reaffirmed.

"I'm a washed up broken wreck, April."

"You're not broken. Prison didn't break you. Your tough childhood didn't break you. The MC betraying you - that was a betrayal you weren't expecting. You'll get back up," she said quietly.

"I suppose you're the woman who can fix me up?" he said sarcastically, not looking at her.

She shook her head. "No, you'll fix yourself. I haven't lost like you have, I don't know what that feels like. I was brought up by my grandparents, but that wasn't much of a hardship, they were loving and good to me. The hardest thing I've ever had to overcome is… the kidnapping, being tied up, now being on the run… I went back home and pretended like it had never happened. A terrible coping mechanism, I know, but I didn't even want to think about it. I'm sure this will take you years to overcome, but you'll get there, it just takes time. Do what you need to do, find a therapist, road trip across the States, go sky diving or do whatever you need to do. I'll wait, and you'll sort your shit out, I'm sure of it."

He saw it then, she had let him into her heart, too. She respected him, trusted him. She'd walked away from everything in her life, putting her faith in him. A well educated woman with a job, a house, a car, a sense of such self worth - that didn't happen for a guy like him. But she had.

He blew out. Nodded once. He needed to change the story, he needed to step up and be the man she wanted him to be. The man he wanted to be. He had been holding back, but now, he needed to let go. Pull out the battery on that whining thing in his head telling him he wasn't enough. He needed to take action and seize what it was he had wanted all along. He could trust her with his heart and soul, and he could respect her heart by holding it tenderly and loving it fiercely. She was there in front of him, all he needed to do was take her.

Chapter 21
COLT

"I need a smoke," he muttered finally, after a deep, pensive silence staring into the flames, mulling it over in his mind.

"I took your lighter," she replied, her tone was even, keeping her eyes fixed on the bright red embers.

He frowned at her. "Well, can I have it?"

She turned then to look at him. "Come and get it. I hid it."

His eyebrows shot upwards. "Where?"

"On me."

He contemplated her with his dark eyes.

"Come and get it," she repeated quietly, taunting him. She looked at him apprehensively, unsure how he would react.

He reached out for her and she pulled away, just out of his reach.

"Don't play with me," he growled.

"You can't use your hands. If you want it that much, you have to use your mouth," she said. "Your lips... your teeth... your tongue."

He almost swayed with dizziness. "You are playing with fire, Kitten."

"I know. Come and get me."

He turned to face her and leaned forward, his heart hammering in his ribcage. Closer than he ever dared to go. He'd been here before but only in the hot throes of desire. This was calm. He was in control.

His lips hovered a whisper above her lips. While she looked calm from where he had sat, he now knew she wasn't. Her face had a slight flush, her eyes a glossy sheen, and her breath fluttered on her lips, in and out, rapidly. She opened her lips and her gaze dropped to his mouth.

He brought his lips down to meet hers. Lightly. Softly. And kissed her. A short kiss, just a taste. He pulled away and flicked his eyes up to her, checking her reaction. This was not a lust fueled, desperate devouring like in the past. This was deliberate, purposeful. He half expected her to laugh and pull away and say she didn't want him after all. Half expected it, half wanted it, feared it. She had closed her eyes. Not squeezed shut, but closed in a blissed out, gentle way. She liked it. She wanted it.

Colt smiled to himself and brought his lips down onto hers again. This time harder. This time he used his tongue, flicking it inside her mouth. She groaned and responded, mirroring his actions. Bolstered by her response, he opened his mouth wider, and savored the taste of her. The pace picked up, but he still felt in control. He wanted this, it wasn't carnal lust or his animal brain seeking this, it was him. His soul, his heart. Her hot, wet mouth consuming him, her tongue following his, the occasional clash of their teeth, it got his blood thumping down to his cock. He felt himself with his hand.

She made a noise and pulled away. "Remember, no hands," she breathed, batting his hand away from his groin.

That turned his thoughts primal. But he felt at one with it, he felt whole, wanting more. All of him was pulling in the same direction now. Not torn inside, but working in harmony. Toward this. Toward her. Toward having her. He growled and launched himself at her. He fastened his mouth on her neck. That tendon that ran from her ear down to her collarbone. He nibbled, like she was a juicy piece of fruit

THE CHASE

and he was hungry. Starving. His lips sucked, too. He stuck to one spot, certain he'd leave a mark, then moved down, rooting down her neck. She smelled good. She felt warm, soft. He heard her gasp and moan. He felt her hands on his arms, pulling him in. He smiled and batted her hands away.

"'No hands,' he growled back at her. She let out a muffled chuckle.

He moved lower, following the tendon down her collarbone, and heard her breath catch in her throat.

"Am I getting warmer?" he breathed into her skin. The heat coming off her was roasting.

"Yes, Colt, yes," she rushed to reply.

He pulled off her long enough to glance at her face. Her eyes were closed, she was biting her bottom lip, her face flushed in the firelight. He nuzzled down again and went straight for her breasts. Fuck this, he was going in. No more games. With himself or with her. He couldn't take it anymore. She wanted him and he wanted her and that was enough for him. With his teeth he bit the top of her T-shirt, pulling it away from her and down. It was baggy, it had some give in it. And it gave.

He dove into her now accessible cleavage. He stopped short when his mouth felt something cold and plastic. His lighter. He'd forgotten all about that. He gripped it with his teeth, extracted it from its perch nestled between her breasts and spat it onto the ground beside them. He didn't even look at it or where it had landed, he dove straight back into her cleavage.

Two warm, soft globes met his mouth. She was the perfect size, not so massive that they required strength to lift, but enough to fill his mouth. He'd grabbed them that first time, but hadn't appreciated them as they deserved. He battled with her bra, pushing it aside with his nose, rooting like a hungry newborn.

He couldn't get her bra out of the way and growled with frustration. He bit down on her nipple through the bra she was wearing. She squealed, actually fucking squealed. And that's when he lost it. His savage animal was taking over. His mind and his heart were happy to sit back now and just enjoy the ride. His inner savage was hungry.

He reached his hands out and gripped her upper thighs as she gasped out, "Colt, no hands."

"Fuck no hands, Kitten," he ground out through his teeth. "Get this shit off. I'm going to taste you, Kitten." He yanked at her leggings, grabbing a handful of material and pulling. They peeled down, exposing the miles of her naked legs. He spotted those little cotton panties tangled up in the leggings, too. They drove him wild. His hand snatched them and he got them to her ankles, his blood pulsing in his body. Like a gladiator in the ring, about to meet his match, his heart pounded. Her legs were caught together by the leggings. She was at his mercy, which turned him on further but he wanted her legs spread and wrapped around his head. Kneeling, he yanked them off her completely. He looked back up at her. She'd snapped her arms out of her fleece, yanked off her shirt and was currently reaching around her back to remove her bra.

Colt reached a hand forward and grabbed the black material. As soon as it was undone, he pulled it off and tossed it aside. Her pert tits tumbled free, revealing little, dark pink nipples. They were in his mouth quicker than lightning. He held them both, one hand on each. He licked and suckled on both together like a starving man. Their softness, their warmth, their pert fullness in his palms, making him want to cry. What right did a dirty bastard like him have to touch something so pure? To hell with that. He was done with that. He had no right but he was going to fucking do it anyway. She was his. She simply shuddered under him. Gasping, her eyes hooded.

THE CHASE

He tore his mouth off her breasts, and sat back on his heels.

"Here Kitten," he rasped, grabbing her ankles, pulling her so she slid down, reclining. He surveyed her body beneath him. So much soft, supple skin. She was beautiful. Little petite waist, her rib cage just visible, giving way to her toned stomach. He remembered when he'd come all over her the other night, painting that little stomach with him. Fuck yes. He reared up above her and shouted out, no words, just a yelp to the night sky above them, he felt so fucking alive. He grinned down at her wolfishly, and then howled, literally like a werewolf, at the moon.

She giggled beneath him, bringing him back down to earth. His cock strained in his jeans. He had to open them up to relieve the pressure. He snapped the button at his waist and yanked the zipper, bunching them down his thighs. She looked on with wide eyes, panting. He saw her chest rising and falling rapidly, a wild animal caught in a trap. And he was about to tame her. Break her. Claim her.

He shrugged out of his leather cut and pulled off his T-shirt. "Put this over your shoulders, Kitten." He held it out for her and she took it in her hands. Impatient, slightly trembling hands, he noticed triumphantly.

"I'm not cold," she said with effort. He allowed a smile on his face and then his gaze honed in on her pussy. His cock surged. He wanted to look and stare and memorize each inch of it. It was his. A neat, clipped triangle of hair pointing him down to two perfect lips and her little clit just peeking out from between them. Maybe it wouldn't ordinarily peek out, but she was aroused. It was a perfect, delicious, little pussy. This all felt so right, so much better than just mindless groping in the dark.

"How are you so neat?" He muttered, more to himself.

"Laser hair removal." She shrugged, nonchalant.

He didn't know what that meant and in that moment, he didn't care.

"Kitten," he bit out, "I want you to come in my filthy, ex-con, biker mouth." He held her hips, and brought his lips down to meet them. He tasted her and groaned in ecstasy. He was hooked.

CHAPTER 30
APRIL

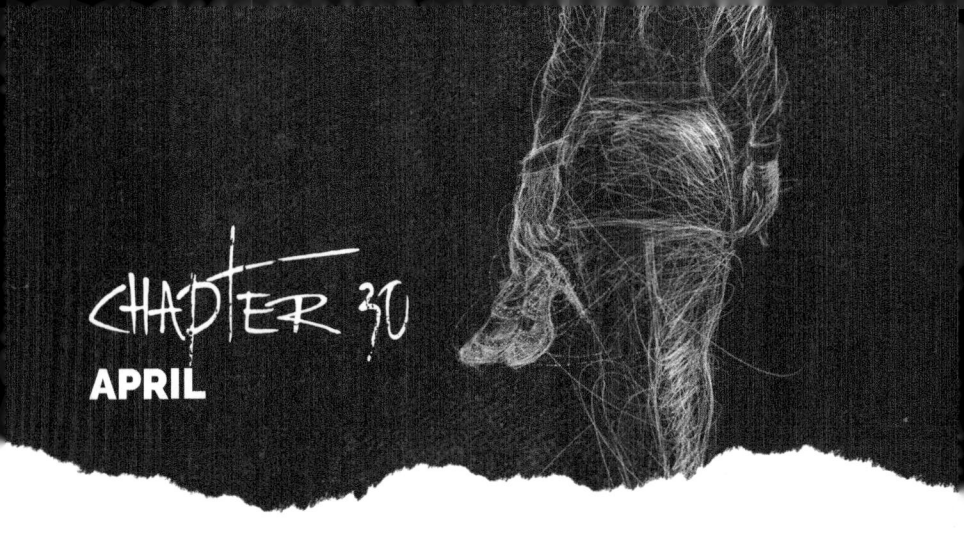

APRIL FOUGHT BACK another gasp as his mouth finally, finally made contact with her pussy. She had been burning, pulsing with need for him. She'd felt it zapping along her tendons, into her fingers, up her thighs, into her core. He'd sucked her breasts like no man ever had before, and now he was literally feasting on her pussy. She'd never felt anything like it. He lifted her hips to his mouth as if he were drinking from the holy grail. His hot tongue licked her, hard and plentifully, from front to back. He kissed her left lip, and then her right lip, nibbled and sucked them into his mouth. He dipped his tongue inside her, then moved on to her clit. She hadn't ever been licked like this. She felt special, he was worshiping her body with such utter devotion. She had never felt that. She'd always been very aware of the 'favor' her partner was doing her. A favor that would require her to repay. A transaction. Almost a chore. Hugo had never had time for it. And previously, it would have been skittish college boys experimenting.

It was very obvious Colt didn't need to experiment. He knew what he was doing. He knew every contour and how to traverse it with ease. With skill. With flair. She was left to lie back and enjoy it. To let go of everything and just shudder in his cut. She tipped her head back and closed her eyes. The smell of him surrounded her. It was like being inside his chest, under his skin. Safe, warm. She was being consumed by him, devoured. His prey, his food, his nourishment. She loved how he cherished her, as if she was all he needed. This was the only place she wanted to be. The heat from the fire, his ministrations and from the leather surrounding her brought her skin to a light perspiration. Dew formed on her skin and then drew in the cooler night air. She opened her eyes and saw the canopy of stars against the indigo blackness of the sky. The outline of the pine trees. It was surreal. Her soul soared free and became a part of the night as she felt the pull within her tighten and tighten under his lapping tongue. She heard the groan escape her lips. She shuttered her eyes and saw a darker kind of black to the night sky above her. She bit the leather of his cut, feeling like she was biting down on his flesh. He was dominant. Her bite was her submission.

And then she came. In a shuddering, screeching impact. Her teeth rattled. Her body tensed and released, pulsing. Pleasure and relief. Biting her. She then heard him. Had he been talking the whole time?

"Yeah, Kitten, all over my face, your cum tastes so good, Kitten, so sweet, good little Kitten... " he chanted quietly, licking slowly now, final strokes. He pulled away and looked down at her. His face was wet. His nose, chin and lips glistened in the firelight. April had not known anything more erotic. Until he crashed up her body and pushed his face into hers.

"Taste it, Kitten, taste how much you wanted me, how much you liked what I did to you..." He pressed his face into hers and kissed her, open mouthed, wet from her juices. She tasted herself, relished in it, savored it. But she wanted more. She reached out her hand, gripping onto the belt loops of his half hanging off jeans. He hesitated, his eyes boring into her. April took a deep, purposeful breath and tugged again.

He nodded once. "Yeah. Fuck yes," he said in reply to her silent

THE CHASE

demand. He kneeled between her legs and pushed his jeans down off his ankles. He'd relinquished his boots at some point. His hard cock slapped against his stomach. She gaped hungrily, laying eyes on it. It was just what she'd hoped for, large, heavy, with a vein pulsing down its length. His balls hung heavily. His pubic hair was dark, thick and unruly. She practically gurgled. He was watching her face, watching her reaction carefully. He clearly liked how he was affecting her. He smirked and straddled her. She opened her lips, letting them part of their own accord, leaning closer to him. Then, before she was ready, he took her head in both his hands and thrust his cock in between her lips.

The groan he emitted pulled deep within her. The part of her that he'd just awoken, the part that was warm and wet and alive, had its own voice, and spoke to her. He thrust in again, deep. All the way to the back of her throat. His balls hit her chin as she gagged. He threw his head back and roared.

"Yes, Kitten, take it, swallow my hard cock, " he rasped, freeing a hand from her hair to grip her chin. He angled her head up. She closed her eyes automatically. "No, open your eyes, I want to watch you," he huffed.

She couldn't breathe, couldn't think. She almost panicked initially, she brought a hand to his stomach, about to push him away. But she took a moment. His cock plunged into her mercilessly. He was shamelessly using her mouth. Fucking her face. She struggled to breathe around it, felt her eyes welling up with the repeated impact at the back of her throat, but he held on. So she held on, too.

"Yes, cry for me, Kitten. Oh fuck, you look so fucking good. So fucking right for me..." he fixed his gaze on her.

She'd only known looking away, closing her eyes. Ignoring sounds of skin slapping, wetness dripping. Keep it hidden, turn away, like it's something dirty. But Colt wanted to see it all, hear it all, feel it all. It was so bold, so shameless. He had a taste now and wanted more and she loved it.

He plunged in but she wanted to suck. She felt emboldened. She pushed lightly on his hard lower stomach. He paused enough for her to fasten her mouth around his head and suck with all her might.

"Oh yes," Colt stuttered. She sucked like his cock head was a popsicle, using her tongue to stroke, occasionally flicking the tip on the ring around his head. She didn't need to do it very long. "I'm going to come," he hissed, closing his eyes and –

She felt hot liquid filling her mouth. She smiled and lapped it up, sucking it out as he ejaculated, as he gasped and shuddered above her. Enjoying the power over him in that moment.

She pulled away once he'd stopped, his dick softer now, warm and wet. He fixed her with his gaze, stroked her cheek. He looked at her like she was beautiful, through glassy eyes. She could see it plain as day on his face, he was in love. Did he know he was so open?

His gaze snagged on her lips. "You got a drop of my cum on your chin," he said thickly.

April snapped her eyes wide and started. "Oh, sorry, I…"

"What are you apologizing for? It's hot. April, that was so fucking hot."

She smiled.

"Let's go again," he said.

Her eyebrows shot up. "Again?"

"Yeah, let me guess, college dick was a once a night kinda guy?"

"Well, yes. Once a week, once a month, more like-"

"Douchebag. Well I'm not a once a night kinda guy. I'm more like… as many fucking times as my body can manage it until the sun comes up kinda guy."

"I see that," she said with a little smile, her eyes watching as he got hard again. She was fascinated. His heavy cock slowly but steadily pumping up again to a large, angry-looking rod of hard flesh covered in a soft velvet sheath.

"This time, instead of no hands, we do only hands," he said. She shivered. He noticed. "In the van," he added.

"No sex?" She couldn't help herself from asking.

He came close to her, his head now right in front of her. His forehead touched hers, she felt his warmth on her face. "April, I want to know every inch of you, I want to taste and touch every inch. I want to fuck every inch of you. I don't want to rush this. I want to enjoy memorizing every inch of you. This isn't just me wetting my dick inside you. And when I do take you with my cock, I will stroke your hot, wet cunt until you clench up and come again and again and milk me until I'm shooting out stardust, I'll be that empty. Do you understand?"

She bit her lip and closed her eyes and nodded, as she let him haul her to her feet, and tripped over to the van door. She had to remind herself to breathe again, as they climbed into the back of the van, and he swung the door shut behind them. Her world went black. A warm, safe, happy, black, where she just existed, and he worshiped her.

CHAPTER 31
COLT

THE NEXT DAY, Colt sauntered out of the convenience store like he ruled the town. Standing tall, swinging a white plastic bag, humming to himself like the happy fucker he was. They'd been driving a few hours, the day was young. He'd told her to wait in the van as he'd made a quick dash. He opened his driver side door and hopped in.

"Did you get the trail mix? I need a snack," April eagerly chattered. He passed her the bag without thinking.

She pounced gratefully, peering inside, reaching her hand in... She paused, blinked. He remembered.

In the store, he'd meandered over to the condom section. Trying to look casual, eyeing the offerings. He hadn't bought these in years. He grabbed a big box of thin feel.

April had taken the box out of the bag and was reading it.

"Ahh... I just..." he trailed off. Why was he embarrassed suddenly? Why was he searching for an excuse?

She turned the box over and read the back. Why did he buy a giant box? That maybe seemed too presumptuous, like they'd definitely be using a lot. Should he have gotten ribbed, for her pleasure? He wanted the ground to swallow him up.

She looked up at him, bit her bottom lip for a fraction of a second, then she took a deep breath. He braced himself. "I didn't want you to use any," she said finally.

"I... what?"

"I was thinking about it, and I don't want you to use any condoms," she repeated.

He frowned and blinked, computing what she was saying. "You want me to pull out? I can try but, Kitten, I don't think-"

"No, I don't want you to pull out," she replied.

His eyebrows shot up. "You want anal? Fu-uck... I didn't think... but I mean sure I can, Jesus, the thought of your tight, little-"

"No, not that!" she replied, rolling her eyes. "I've never done that and that's not what I meant."

"Woah, never? Well, that's something we definitely should-" He began, he was smiling now, heat flooding his face, making his eyes dance. He adjusted his crotch. She didn't doubt this conversation would make him hard.

"No, what I mean is, when we have sex, I want you to come inside me. Again," she said.

Those simple words left him speechless. They echoed inside his head. Inside her, she said. He remembered himself releasing into her, his juices squirting deep inside her that first rushed time.

"Kitten, I know that first time we did... but that was an accident, I wasn't thinking, we should be safe-"

She took a breath. "I'm clean, I had a test just a few weeks ago, actually, and Hugo and I haven't... slept together since then."

"I was tested yearly as part of a routine check up in jail, so I'm clean, too, but..." He trailed off, looking at her. He was quiet, thinking. She couldn't fathom the look on his face. "But why did you get tested a few weeks ago?"

She pursed her lips together. "I didn't trust him fully, there were a few incidents... he always came up with a perfectly reasonable excuse afterwards but at the time it felt... off... he insisted on using condoms even though I was taking birth control-"

"Why?" He exclaimed loudly, frowning.

"He said he preferred not to have the mess-"

"Ha!" He burst out a laugh, this guy was a grade A jackass, Colt thought. "Are you kidding me? The mess is one of the best parts of it, fuck yeah..." he said, biting his own lips now. He was imagining them together, remembering what had happened in the back of the van, he was hard and his cock was getting wet with pre-cum now. She smiled, a little bashful, then looked up at him through her eyelashes.

"I want you to come inside me," she repeated.

He cleared his throat. "Kitten, I can certainly do that, gladly..." He trailed off. "Before that first time with you... I've never... without a wrap..." He trailed off.

She looked up at him. "Never? You'd been that self controlled, that careful?"

He shrugged in response.

"I want you to fill me up with your cum, Colt," she said with a croak. "I think about it every night, I want to feel you inside me, just you, nothing between us-"

"April, Jesus I-" He palmed his groin, letting out a strangled sound.

"I'm not on birth control. I can track my cycle and let you know when I'm safe-"

"Fuck. Christ, April," he replied. Now there was the element of risk, a risk of pregnancy with her... he was harder than he'd ever been in his life. He realized a secret part of him would thank the gods and all the heavens if that should happen. His cock flexed, screaming to be let out. "What if-" he slurred, drunk off desire.

"We'd figure that out when or if we got there," she replied, matter of factly. She'd obviously been thinking about this. That was hot in itself.

"You're not on birth control? The other night… you said we were safe…" he said slowly, part of his brain wanting to understand, the other part wanting to rip off her clothes and breed her right here.

"I know, I… I count the days, I know when I'm going to be fertile, when the egg is released, so we'd avoid those days, and when my period is due…"

"Right, right… all eggs and full moons and hippy dippy mother nature shit like that." He'd heard about this, this was ringing a bell from conversations the sweet butts had back in the MC when he'd been fucking anyone who'd have him.

She laughed, tipping her head back. "Not really full moons but, that kind of thing… anyway, as long as we avoid certain days we'd be safe enough I think…"

"It's not a sure thing, though, is it? It's not 100% effective."

She shook her head. "No. But I mean, if that should happen, it wouldn't necessarily be a bad thing…"

Colt frowned at her. "Do you mean, you'd want to…"

"I'd keep your baby, Colt," she said quietly.

He was speechless. Utterly tetherless in a beautiful blue sea. Floating, under a spell. In a whole new plane of existence that he hadn't known about until that very moment.

"I have nothing to give a kid right now, April, I can't… that can't happen," he whispered, disappointment creeping in. They shouldn't risk it.

"There you go thinking so little of yourself. You are a good man Colt, you'd make a great father-"

"Hell, April-"

"Look, I guess I just wanted to say, you wouldn't have to worry about me refusing to let you see it or anything. If it didn't work out between us, you'd always be the father, and I'd hope we'd both always be there for them-"

His head was whirling. Desire was still pumping through his veins and now he was imagining her pregnant, imagining them together, with a little baby. He felt a tugging inside him, a pull so strong, so completely innate within him.

"April, we are on the run from a dangerous MC who wants us dead, we have nothing except a hunk of cash from your daddy and a stolen van... we live day to day right now, we couldn't have a kid..."

"I've been thinking about this, right now we're just driving aimlessly. Somehow, they know we're in a van. They must, they keep following us, they are always a few steps behind but we haven't been able to shake them off. We need to stop. We need to turn around and face them, head on. We need to win back our freedom. We need to deal with this."

He shook his head, his dick forgotten. They were worrying about a future that would never happen, a kid that would never exist, most likely. It left a bitter taste in his mouth.

"What is the answer, then? Wear condoms? Well, I got a box full-"

"No, silly," she said, cuffing his shoulder lightly. "We stop running. We turn around and start chasing them back. We get even. We get the MC to stop following us. We get off their wanted list." She said it calmly, as if it were about deciding to go shopping that day. No big deal. She looked up at him.

"April, sweetheart, these men aren't messing around, they will find us, they will kill me and they'll drag you back to-"

"No, there's got to be a way. We just can't see it yet. We must think. That is what we will do. We need to find somewhere quiet, get off the road, get your ink sorted out, stop running, and think," she said.

He blinked at her. His Kitten wasn't a kitten at all, he realized. She was a lioness. She was sophisticated, calm, strong. She was cunning, fearless, lethal. She assumed they could get themselves out of this mess. She didn't just have an idea, she didn't just have a hope and a prayer. She knew it, deep inside, she was certain. He hadn't considered it before, he'd just been thinking about pumping the gas and surviving the day and her sexy little body beside him for the ride. He hadn't even dreamed that they could somehow solve the problem. He admired her confidence, her cool, calm approach. Just find a way out. We can't see it yet, but if we think about it, we'll figure it out. That self assured confidence was the most beautiful part of her.

"Then, once we have dealt with them, we have a future together, if that is what you want, if that is what we both want…"

"A future… together?" He hadn't even dared to hope.

"Yes, we could go anywhere, do anything. I've got my law degree, no one can take that away from me. I could just sell my condo and we get something else…"

"Well fuck, Kitten…" In front of his eyes his lioness stretched and roared. Not a kitten, the goddamn queen of the pack. The quickest, the deadliest. She wasn't going after a quick kill, taking down the runt of the herd, and surviving for another day. No, she wanted the whole fucking herd, dead at her feet.

"We can do this Colt, we've just got to think, get one move ahead, hell, more than one. We've got to catch them out and then we'll be free. We can strategize this."

He saw the value now in an education, her upbringing, what it was that kept people like her on the straight and narrow. How it gave her this sense of being able to solve anything. He basked in it, having never felt it within himself. She was right, she could do her job anywhere. He felt the doubt lifting for good this time. He could be anything she wanted him to be, anywhere she wanted to go. Would she honestly give up her old life for him?

"But your friends, your life? Partying in fancy bars, your career, the city?"

She shrugged. "To hell with that, I already let that all go the moment I got on the back of the bike with you, Colt. I'd rather be with someone and be happy than in the city surrounded by all that and be miserable."

He smirked. "Hey, are you saying I make you happy?"

She smirked, too, and tried to hide it. "Well, I haven't given you a full road test yet, so the jury is still out on that. What if, with a bed and champagne and all the bells and whistles, you are a terrible lay after all?" she joked.

"Oh I'm good," he purred, unable to wipe the grin off his face.

She beamed at his cocky confidence. "Yes, this is what I've been trying to say. I like you, I want you, I-"

He leaned forward, and kissed her on the lips, mouth open, tongue chasing hers. He didn't hold back, his hand came up to her face. "Yes," he finally replied.

"Yes... to what?"

He smiled. "All of it, yes, no wraps, yes, I'll keep you full of cum and so constantly fuck-drunk you won't be able to walk-"

"Colt!" she squealed.

"Yes, let's get off the road and think. Yes, let's get even with the MC, show them they messed with the wrong people. Yes, get on with our lives… together. Yes..." He trailed off to kiss her again.

"I've never heard that expression before, fuck-drunk," she mused.

"No? You know when you melt in a puddle of cum after orgasming so many times in a row and your legs don't work and your brain doesn't work 'cause you've fucked so hard and fast for so long?"

"Such a dirty mouth!" She pretended to scold him.

"You like it."

"I like it from you… in moderation, I think."

"Kitten, I'll burn your ears off with dirty talk while I fucking pound you as you come until you gush."

Chapter 32
COLT

"This place." She thrust her phone in front of his nose suddenly. They were laying on the mattress in the back of the van. The morning was fresh. The air, cool and clean, birds tweeting. The sound of cars swooshing along a nearby road drifted in through the open back door.

He started at her sudden burst. If he was being honest with himself, he'd been asleep. Or dozing at least. He snapped his eyes open but couldn't focus on the website on the phone a few inches from his face.

"I can't see-" he began.

"It's perfect!" She beamed. A smile on her face, she was excited, a slight flush showing him she was pleased with herself.

She was cute. He smiled. "Let me see," he said, grabbing the phone and holding it at a distance so he could actually see what was on the screen.

"The Pines," he read out loud. "A mindfulness and yoga luxury retreat... rehabilitate your soul..." He scanned the website.

"It would be good, it's off the beaten path in the middle of nowhere. It's exclusive... I think some celebrities have been there, there's security so we'd be safe..."

"I mean… it looks like it would be full of stuck up dicks," he said, looking at the website, the tastefully shot photographs of a pristine lake and little log cabins hidden in the trees. It looked very yuppie bougie, like a place he wouldn't be welcomed.

She remained undeterred. "It would be fine, we pretend we're married and we're honeymooning-"

"What?" He gulped, his eyes widening.

"-And we've been on the road too long after quitting our jobs in the city-"

"Slow down, slow down", he interjected, "these elaborate stories will probably unravel at some stage... What kinda job in the city would I have? Janitor?" he said sarcastically.

She shook her head. "Okay, we'll figure it out and practice our story, but I think this would be a great place to get off the road for a while." She looked at him with anticipation shining in her eyes. "I think we need to stop being chased and… just stand still," she finished quietly. But he absolutely understood. He felt they needed to pause. To stop running.

He ran his hand over his jaw stubble thoughtfully. "It does seem like a good place…" He drifted off, thinking.

"I can call and check availability?" She practically bounced with excitement.

He sighed. "Go on," he said, before he regretted it, continuing to scroll through the photos.

She grabbed back the phone. "Okay, I'll send you the link so you can keep looking at the website." She pulled herself up and hopped out of the van.

He rolled over, hearing his phone beep somewhere in his pocket. He didn't reach for it though. The place looked high end, douchey but decent enough. And like she said, it was safe, a good place to hide. It looked like a place that would have a decent bed. That was a key criteria for him. A fucking big bed where he could throw her down and ravage her to his heart's content. Fucking rail her hard, stroke into her, long and deep...

"Fuck," he groaned into his pillow, he got hard thinking about it. No more pussy footing around this time. He had decided, he knew where he wanted to be. Balls deep in her tight, hot, wet-

"I did it! We got one of the executive cabins, minimum booking was a week, so I went with that -"

"A week?" he exclaimed, sitting up now.

"Yes, I said we were newly married and road tripping but you had a nervous breakdown, so we wanted to take some time to ground ourselves and be in one place."

"Sounds douchey enough."

She started tidying her clothes, animatedly talking about it. She was looking forward to it. He was glad they were doing something she wanted to do. She hadn't complained the whole time, but he could see it in her eyes. There had been times when she was tired and scared. She wasn't used to wearing cheap clothes and going to laundromats. Making do with regular coffee and baked beans for dinner. She'd done a good job of not once complaining. But she deserved luxury. Hell, he did, too, damn it. And he'd ensure they both got what they desired.

"Wear your khakis and your boat shoes, so we fit in," she said with a smile.

He rolled his eyes but reached for the pants she'd bought for him but hadn't worn. He thought he'd take it one step further and, instead of a T-shirt, he grabbed one of the polo shirts she'd got him. He shucked it on and then walked around to the passenger side, where she stood. She'd opened the door but stood stretching from side to side, her head stooped as she scrolled on her phone. As he approached, she looked up. And her eyes swept up and down over him.

Her eyes lit up. He liked that he'd pleased her. He made her proud, he saw it on her face. He felt a warmth in the pit of his stomach. He felt proud of himself.

She smiled and he returned it. "You like me dressed up as a douchebag, huh?" He smiled. "You like me as a boring, average Joe?" He strutted forward.

"I mean, I like you no matter what you're wearing…" She trailed off breathlessly.

"But you think I clean up well enough, huh?"

She lightly swatted his chest playfully, looked down bashfully and then straight back up again. "Don't worry, I know that underneath is still my bad, dangerous biker." She smiled up at him through long lashes.

"Fuck, yeah." He grunted, grabbing his now quickly hardening cock through those preppy clothes. "You'll have to fuck the bad boy back into me to remind me of my true colors."

She smiled at him playfully, bit her bottom lip and nodded. "That, I can do."

CHAPTER 22
COLT

HOURS LATER, THEY pulled up to the entrance of The Pines. It was off a long, straight road, a tiny wooden sign the only clue of its existence. Colt slowed gently, glancing at his rear view mirror to ensure no one was on the road and watching them turn off. No, it was empty, dusk had fallen, it was almost dark.

They were later than intended, they had taken a longer route, avoiding the highway. Colt didn't want to moan but his shoulder was hurting, his legs were stiff, he wanted to get the fuck out of these pants. They had no give in them, he felt restricted. The neck of his polo felt tight. He wanted to get naked, get April on her back in bed and fuck her into oblivion. Then maybe have a bath and fuck her again. That's what he wanted.

The sound of the van changed as he turned onto the gravel drive, tires crunching. He took it slow.

She was twirling something shiny on her finger. A ring. He'd just bought it for her in the town they'd driven through on their way to the Pines. Colt had seen the little jewelers on the main street and slammed on his brakes. April complained, of course, until she realized what he was doing. He parked the van haphazardly outside the store and strolled in like he owned it. The shop assistant flicked his gaze over Colt and frowned, unsure of what to make of him. Colt had taken it all in stride though, by walking up to him, pulling out a wad of cash, slapping it down on the counter and telling him he wanted to see engagement rings. The man lifted an eyebrow but hurried into sales mode, unlocking cabinets to get out rings. Colt had turned to her with a wink and a melting smile, and said, "Pick one, Kitten, and it's yours."

And she had, gleefully, picked a cute halo diamond, gold band. He nodded his approval, the clerk whisked it away, checked sizes, and popped it in a little black box. Colt had pushed the pile of cash over, picked it up, taken it out of the box again and given it to her. He told the clerk to keep the box. April slipped it over her finger and smiled up at him. He'd smiled back, knowing that she wanted it to be real. He smiled back because he wanted it to be real, too. They left the jewelry store, jumped back in the van and got on the road again. They sat in comfortable silence until he pulled onto the road to the resort. April twirled the ring around her finger, thinking he couldn't see her doing it. Trying to act nonchalant. But he knew.

Now they drove up the dark driveway at a crawl. She peered ahead, leaning forward, to get a glimpse of the place. "Nice and discreet," April said beside him. "I guess that's why it's popular with celebrities."

Colt peered out, too. Pine trees hemmed in the drive that was getting narrower and bumpier as they progressed. After a while they came to a barrier with a little booth beside it. A man in uniform scurried out. Security. Potentially a good thing, though it immediately made the hairs on Colt's neck rise. It felt a little like prison. It wasn't to keep them locked in. This was different, he told himself. He felt the need to run, to jack-knife the van around, put his foot down and get the hell out of there. But April would be so pissed off if he blew this. He pulled to a stop next to the gate and took a deliberate breath in and out again.

The security guard, a plump man of about fifty, with a dour face, signaled to roll down the window. Colt wanted to give him attitude, he could already tell the security guard thought the uniform gave him power. The power to be a dick, just like some of the guards in prison. Colt wanted to bring him down a peg, but again held back. He clenched his fist on the steering wheel.

Wisely, April spoke up across him at the security guard, who ducked to peer at her after flashing Colt a nice, judge-laden sneer. Fucker, Colt thought. "Oh, hi there," April said, all sunshine and roses. The security guard mellowed immediately.

"Good evening, ma'am," he replied with what he obviously thought was a kind smile.

April tucked a strand of hair behind her ear. "We're a little later than we intended, we're staying in one of the cabins for a week..."

"You have a reservation, ma'am?" the security guard replied, then eyed Colt again, mistrust in his eyes. The polo and chinos clearly couldn't mask the blatant disrespect and the desire Colt had to punch him in the throat. Colt grinned and cracked his knuckles. April ignored him, turned on her brightest smile, and leaned over a little further. Colt realized the fucker could see down her now gaping shirt. He set his jaw as the guard's eyes lingered longer than was polite.

"Yes sir, of course we have a reservation," April chirped.

"Check in time was an hour ago."

Colt clocked his name badge. Dwight. Prick name. Any name he had would have been a prick name in Colt's book.

"I know, I'm sorry-"

"I'll have to check in with the manager..."

Colt ground his teeth as the man made a big deal out of getting his walkie talkie off his utility belt. He turned from them as if he were dealing with some sort of spy shit.

"For fuck's sake," Colt muttered under his breath.

"Play nice, Colt," she whispered back in a low warning, still wearing her spotlight smile.

"I could just deck him and ram through the barrier -"

"Oh yes, we'd definitely be allowed to check in late then, wouldn't we? God, we'd probably be upgraded to the luxury suite," she whispered back scathingly.

Colt growled. She was right, of course. Play nice, he repeated in his head, play nice.

Dwight turned back, obviously having had the all clear, and instructed them to proceed through the barrier. Colt wound up the window with a smug smile, just about held in the desire to wind his middle finger up with it, and drove through the now open barrier.

A sprawling wooden cabin, low lit from hidden lights under the pine tree fronds came into view as he swung the van around to the front. It wasn't a rough, rustic little cabin, it was weathered but expertly cut planks and expensive looking. Huge floor to ceiling windows with black frames. Very new-age chic.

Colt got out and slammed the door. His own feet, in those leather boat shoes, caught his eye. He couldn't wait to get naked.

April joined him and together they strolled into the lobby.

"Good evening, good evening, Mr. and Mrs. Black." A gray haired, older man came forward to shake their hands. Colt gripped the man's limp, cold hand with his own large, calloused, warm one. His tattoos laced his arm to his wrists, and he caught the man eyeing them. Colt watched closely as he shook April's hand, too, gently, almost with a caress. Was everyone who worked here a dick?

"So happy you made it, you must have had a long drive," he said, sounding smarmy.

"Yes, we are so glad to be here." April still had the energy for her sunshine smile, Colt was impressed. He was swiftly losing the will to care about being polite, he was tired and uncomfortable and this place was everything that had shunned him. Everything that had pushed him to the MC in the first place. Everything the MC had stood against. It made his skin crawl.

"Yes, we've got you in one of our executive cabins, you can drive your vehicle around the site to get there, you're in one of the furthest ones, by the back of the lake. Speed limit is twenty MPH," he added, throwing a loaded glance at Colt. He sucked his teeth like he had a bitter pill in his mouth. This douchebag was assuming he'd break the speed limit. Yeah, well he would now, Colt thought, just to piss him off.

"We have our spa facilities available, here is a map of the site... the pool is here, sauna, steam room, jacuzzi... our treatment rooms are here-"

"Ah, can we book a massage for tomorrow? My husband has such a sore shoulder..."

Colt threw April a glance.

"Yes, yes, we do couple's massages... I'll introduce you to our concierge who will be able to book that for you... we also have yoga studios here, again, our concierge can book that for you, and our restaurant is here-" he indicated with a shiny silver metal pen, on the map he'd laid out on the reception desk with a flourish. Colt wanted to grab that pen and stab it through the guy's hand. Self absorbed prick. "I'm afraid it's closed this evening, we advocate an early evening meal, as it's best for digestion..."

April's face fell. "Oh, could we get room service food at all? We haven't had any dinner-"

"I'm not sure we can-"

"Yes, we can." A different voice came from behind them. A

younger man in a navy suit stepped forward, speaking over the older man.

Colt immediately sensed the manager was riled up. Ah, the younger man was a threat. There was obviously a history of simmering irritation in this relationship. Colt immediately liked the younger guy just for having irritated the older guy.

"Ah, this is our concierge-"

"Ash." The younger man introduced himself with a chin nod and strode around the desk. He was younger and a little shorter than Colt, leaner. He had longish brown hair, a sort of wild young punk look going on. He wouldn't look out of place in a skate park. He looked out of place in the suit, but not awkward about it. He owned it. Colt respected that. Ash pushed past the older man slightly and picked up the phone, cutting the older man off. Colt felt April's eyes on Ash. Yeah, he was a pretty boy, no mistaking it, dark hair, bone structure of a Ken doll or a dancer or a model or something. High cheekbones, straight nose. His dark blue eyes flicked over April, and Colt almost got jealous. But then Ash's eyes flicked over Colt with the same attention. Sexual attention. Colt hadn't expected that. They all stared at each other while the phone rang. The older man giving Ash a disapproving frown. Ash giving April and Colt the eye as if he was asking them to come to bed. April blinked, doing a double take, she'd seen it, too. Colt watching them all in a mixture of fascination, jealousy and amusement.

"Yeah, kitchen?" Ash, the enigmatic concierge asked. Colt could just about hear someone else talking on the other end of the phone. "Yeah, appreciate you've already cleaned up, you got leftovers? For some guests?" The faint murmur of the person at the other end of the line rattled on. "It's fine, I'll plate it up, have you got any food or not?" he demanded. Ash paused and listened. Colt saw a tattoo on his wrist

THE CHASE

as he held the phone up. Something delicate and simple. A fern leaf? He couldn't quite see.

"Fine. Thanks." Ash clicked the phone down and stared the older man down with a heated glare for a second. Colt liked his attitude. It said, 'see, you said no and I did it anyway, fuck you, old man'. Then Ash turned to Colt and April with his professional face. "Yes, we'll bring a cold platter to your cabin."

April smiled warmly. "Thank you so much."

Ash shrugged. "It's fine. I'll start at nine a.m. tomorrow, we can book massages, yoga, and excursions or experiences then."

"Okay, thanks."

The older duty manager jumped back in, to regain some semblance of control. "We'll continue now with the orientation. There are no board shorts allowed in the pool or spa, fitted trunks only-"

Colt flicked April a look now, too. A thunderous look that said what the fuck.

"Hey, how about we do orientation tomorrow morning, too?" Ash interrupted the older man again. "They've been on the road for hours, they are hungry and tired, they probably want to get to their room and get to bed..." Ash's eyes hooded for a split second and flicked between April and Colt. Perceptive guy. Horny, too, clearly with the attitude of a champion. Colt liked him more and more.

"Yes we are... to um..." she let out a breathy little hiccup that went straight to Colt's cock. Ash saw. "... get to our room..."

"Fine, I'll see you at nine tomorrow, here, in the lobby. Welcome to The Pines and enjoy your evening, Mr. and Mrs. Black." Ash nodded at them both, stared down at the older duty manager, and stalked out. He might as well have done a mic drop.

"Great," Colt ground out, pleased things were moving along. Had they finally checked into this damn place yet?

"You have to excuse him... he's my nephew, my brother's son... he's working here for the summer... I've taken him on as a favor really... he's a bit... at risk of going off the tracks... "

"Seems like he gets shit done to me," Colt countered. April gave him a look.

"Well, we are just so looking forward to our week here, we'll drive our van to our cabin-" April plucked the silver key, on a large disk of wood, out of the manager's hand before he could throw some other rule or information at them. "So, thanks, we'll be back in the morning." April trilled, backing out of the reception area. She grabbed Colt's arm and attempted to pull his stiff, immovable self out with her before any other drama unfolded.

CHAPTER 34
COLT

"What the fuck is this place? Fucking rules-" Colt yanked his driver door open, plunked himself down in the seat and slammed the door shut behind him.

"Colt, shut up and drive," April breathed.

One glance at her and he did just that. The fluster in the lobby was long forgotten. She had one thing on her mind and one thing only. Her lips parted and he caught a glimpse of her little tongue darting out. Her cheeks looked warm, her eyes glassy. Oh hell yes. This was it.

He gripped the steering wheel with white knuckles, and he drove the van along the lake side road. It was dark, he caught glimpses of other cabins, lights on, casting an orange glow from their windows. It reeked of tamed wilderness. The inky black of the lake pulled his gaze in, but only for a moment. Colt single-mindedly drove up to their cabin. Number fourteen, a signpost of the cabin number, lit from below.

He pulled up and turned off the van engine. Silence swooped in. Colt looked over to April as it enveloped them like a blanket. It was just the two of them at a cabin by the lake. It was just them in the whole fucking world.

"Out. Now," Colt rasped, needing to move before he was tempted to act on his impulse to pounce on her immediately and drag her into his lap. He wanted to plunge into her and ruin them both.

April licked then bit her lip and breathed out. She nodded once and then started fumbling with the door handle, snatching it open. He practically fell out of the van himself. His feet didn't feel like his. His knees were like water. He rounded the van and bumped straight into April.

He grabbed her shoulders. "Where do you think you are going?" he hissed.

Her eyes were wide in the dark. "I… our bags… our stuff, should we unpack?"

"No. Inside. Now," he demanded roughly. For a moment he thought of the box of condoms in the glove compartment but then he remembered her bold, determined voice. "I don't want you to use one. I want you to come in me, Colt." His eyes rolled back in his head and he groaned, his balls pulling upwards. Focus Colt, he told himself. Fucking keep it together.

She seemed to be shivering. His animal instincts kicked in. Sweet fuck, he had to get inside her, possess her. He spun her around so her back was to his chest, and he slapped one of her ass cheeks firmly, propelling her forward.

The silent night carried her whimper across the lake. Across the world, it felt like. They staggered up onto the wooden porch, their footfalls echoing on the boards.

"Where's the key?" he spat out, crashing into the back of her as she stopped suddenly. His legs weren't working properly and couldn't stop himself from plowing into her. Feeling her smaller, warm body against him, he let his weight propel her into the door.

"Oof." She had the air knocked out of her by his larger body.

"Key, April," he prompted, his hands roving over her body. He grabbed her ass first, right in front of his groin. He wasn't stopping

THE CHASE

himself now. Using his thumbs over the top of her leggings, he spread her cheeks. His cock had been hard since they'd got back in the van, pressing into the zipper of the damn khakis. He smashed his hips into her spread cheeks. She railed and let out a desperate mewl and he nearly lost it.

"Key, fuck April-"

"Colt, oh my... please-"

She turned her face and looked up at his. He leaned forward and took her mouth roughly. Colt shoved his tongue in between her lips. Her hot, soft lips met his. Pure fucking ecstasy. One hand of his left her ass and held her face up to his by her chin.

He had to get her inside, otherwise he'd take her right here on the porch.

"Colt, I want you-" she began to pull away from his kiss, rubbing her nose against his stubble covered chin. He was in despair with his impatience.

"You're going to fucking get me right fucking now-" His other hand groped her hip, skimming it up to her breast, which he roughly and shamelessly grabbed. "Key?"

"In my... oh Colt..." she huffed, a little frown line appearing on her forehead.

"Where, April?"

She let out a needy yelp and pushed her butt back into his hard cock.

"Fuck," he ground out, dropping his head forward to her shoulders.

"My pocket, Colt..." He barely heard her.

"Get the door open." He nipped her neck, rough, then soft. Then rough again.

She fumbled with the door handle, plucking the key from her front right pocket. The large keychain got caught in the small pocket of her leggings, then released with a light snap.

Colt wanted to snap the elastic of her waistband against her butt. He reached his hands down and tugged, doing just that. She gasped as she aimed the silver key at the lock. Colt did it again, pulling the waistband down. It snapped back against her bare ass. Her panties were caught up in the leggings.

His hand came to his waist now and he ripped his pants open, the button popping out of the buttonhole, the zipper practically unzipping on its own with the bulge of his aching, leaking cock. He yanked the polo shirt off, tugged the khakis and his briefs down to just below his butt, too.

He pressed his freed cock into her butt cheeks. They both nearly lost it then and there, shivering from need and anticipation. "April-"

"It's unlocked, it's unlocked," she slurred. Colt pushed into her from behind, she opened the handle and they both swung into the cabin in a free fall. For a moment, he wanted to fall to the floor and into her in one fluid motion. And hit home. Root deep. Fall out of his skin and into her.

But he caught them both. His khakis were still high enough for him to use his feet. She was falling forward though, and he caught her, scrambling to close the door behind him. She locked the door and had him up against it, kissing him hard.

This is it. This is when it happens, he thought. He wanted it, now is the time. He regained his sense of direction, and switched places with her, pushing her back against the door, one arm coming up to brace himself. He spun her to face him, roughly holding her. Their breaths mingled as their foreheads touched and their eyes connected.

He was aware of the quiet around them. The low lighting, from some table lamps around the room. It smelled of wood and leather, expensive. Yes, this was more like what April deserved. He didn't waste time looking around, the cabin could wait.

Then their mouths connected and there was no more calmness. He devoured her. Smiling into her mouth, she also smiled back at him. They kissed.

He pulled down the rest of her leggings, stepping on the gusset with his foot. Refusing to pull his lips off hers, he pulled his pants down, too. He yanked off the stupid boat shoes then his khakis and briefs with them. She was pulling up her T-shirt and her bra came off, too.

He felt like he'd lost the ability to move in any way that wasn't like a bull in a china shop. He gripped the backs of her thighs, hiking her up, wrapping her legs around his waist. She crossed them behind him, locking her to him.

"Oh yes, Kitten," he managed to purr in her ear. He smirked when he saw her face and how she was already too far gone to reply. With her braced against the back of the door, it gave him a free hand to grip the base of his cock, and without any further fanfare, he plunged inside her.

Chapter 35
APRIL

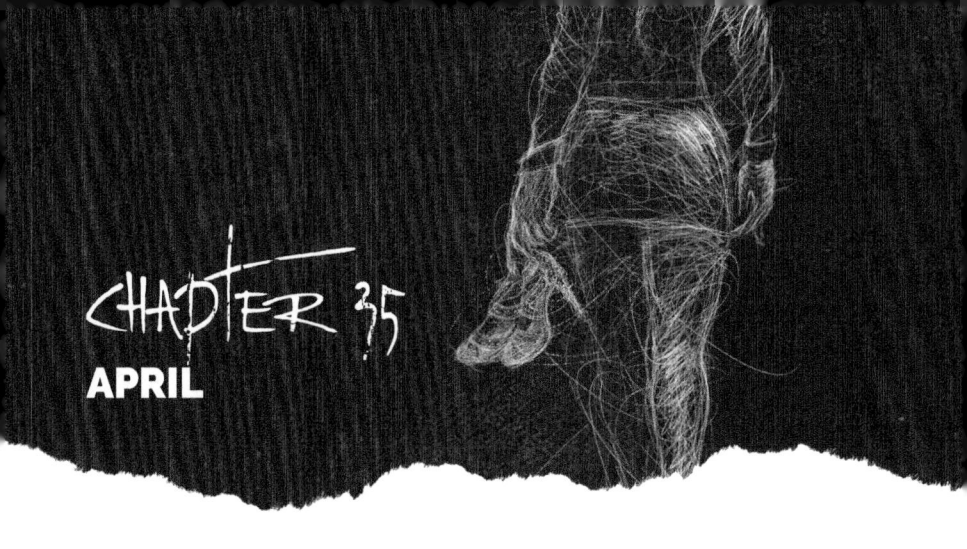

She felt complete. The piece she'd been chasing was finally there. She felt full with him in her, he was a big boy. But not just physically, she felt full inside her heart and soul.

She breathed heavily. He was still, after pushing into her, he waited, panting. She felt his heart thumping in his chest. Hers was in her throat. Her body took over and her pussy clamped down on him. She wanted him there forever.

"Oh fuck, so hot, so wet ..." he whispered on an outward breath.

She had been anticipating this all day, all week. Since she'd first laid eyes on him. There was no need for foreplay, there was no need for him to get her warmed up. They were both already there, the days of loaded stares, electric touches. The dry humping incident, the night by the fire… it all came together at this moment.

He held her up, strong and sure. Her back slammed into the wooden door firmly. She'd have a bruise in the morning but she didn't care. The door rattled in the frame with each thrust. He flicked his hips and the last inch went deep, straight to her core, hitting her G-spot. She shuddered, and her muscles clenched up. She came, like an elastic band snapping as he delivered her to the other side.

"Colt," she said and her eyes fluttered open. She saw him, right in front of her, with his face clenched up.

"Yes, Kitten, fuck, you squeezed me so good, fucking massaged my cock to pulp..."

He pulled out and lowered her down so her feet touched the floor.

"No... no, stay inside..." she pleaded.

"I'm coming back, Kitten, I'm going to fucking rail you-"

But her knees weren't working. She slithered down his body, past his groin, and he came down with her. She held onto him, pulling him down.

"I wanted to make it to the bed but," he groaned, "fuck it." He settled between her legs right there on the floor.

She lay back and bent her legs as he planted himself on the floor, on his knees. He didn't even blink about any discomfort, the hardness of the wood. He lightly spanked her needy pussy with his cock head, holding his cock in one fist. He gripped it hard and pumped once, twice. She had to watch. She couldn't tear her eyes away. He was perfect. "Yes, Colt. Yes," was all she could utter.

"Yes?" he asked. How could he ask, of course she wanted him. She sought his gaze and found it. She saw his mirth, he was amused. Holding her in a state of desperation. Her neediness for him feeling like a palpable thing. He held her there and reveled in it. And she loved him even more, needed him even more. His confidence, his self assuredness to hold her there, was intoxicating. She loved it and she loved him.

She reached and closed a hand around his. She pulled and he released his, so she could grab his cock and pull him into her. She took his throbbing, weeping head, and put it to her welcoming pussy. She gripped his butt cheeks and pulled him into her. She felt every smooth, fat inch of him. She wanted him to the hilt, to feel the base of him against her. But something stopped him from going further. She cried in frustration until she realized it was his hand. His thumb, flicking her clit. He thrust at the same time as he flicked. She reared up with her hips pushing back against him, timing her thrust to his. They met in the middle. Each of their torsos clenching, their stomach muscles working, each gaining a light sheen of sweat. It didn't take long. She began to quiver, her pace stuttered. He pushed in extra hard, saving no energy. There was no returning from this, no going back, it was a one way deal, and they both knew it. Her mouth opened and her body shook. Her mind and soul smashed into the physical realm as she cried out loud and came.

Hard.

Long.

Violently.

It hurt from how hard it was.

He roared above her and came, too.

Inside her.

Like an animal, he planted himself as deep as possible, shook and emptied himself into her. She felt every pulse. She knew his cock was shooting deep. Her body welcomed it, sucking him up, thirsty for it.

She lay her head back, now aware of the hardwood floor. Aware of the silence of the room. No sound but her thumping heart and his labored breathing. She felt the cool air against her sweaty skin, the hot slickness between her thighs. Her legs trembled for a moment as an aftershock swept through her.

She released her hands from his firm butt. They were tight from clenching, gripping and pulling him. Had she left marks on his butt cheeks? She wanted to leave marks. She wanted to be as imprinted into him as he was in her. She was aware of her back bone against the wood floor. Would she bruise there, too? She wanted to bruise. She wanted to have marks on her skin to match the ones that he'd made in her heart. The imprint of him that she wanted to tattoo on her skin.

She suddenly got it now. The tattoos. A need to declare, to stand and be counted. She formed the idea of getting him tattooed onto her skin somehow...

"Kitten that was... un-fucking-believable," he rasped out, his voice like sandpaper.

"Yes," she found her throat sticking, too.

He pulled out as his cock softened. She instantly missed him as his cum seeped out of her. She let out a sound, mourning his departure. But then a knock sounded on the door.

He pushed himself into a kneeling position. Then, up onto his feet, letting out a groan as he unsteadily rose.

"Room service," a voice behind the door said.

"Too old for fucking on a hardwood floor," he said as he staggered slightly, but grinned from ear to ear. His eyes were alive and dancing, a slight flush to his face. She couldn't help but grin back, pushing herself up to a sitting position.

Colt padded to the door, which wasn't far, they'd only made it a few feet into the room. He bent down and retrieved his pants, which he shucked on without his briefs. There was a knock at the door again, three short wraps.

"Yes, yes, I'm coming," Colt said, wearing his chinos undone and hugging his hips, his paler skin and hair of his pubic region on display. April watched, half horrified, half hypnotized as he answered the door in his state of blatant post-sex undress.

It was the concierge, Ash. Looking as buttoned up and put together as a man could possibly be, contrasting Colt almost comically, carrying a tray covered in a series of silver cloches.

April grabbed the throw blanket off the bed and scrambled to her feet.

Ash's face remained deadpan as he handed the tray to Colt, who took it wordlessly. Ash's gaze drifted up and down Colt, lingering knowingly. Ash looked hungrily at Colt.

"Yeah, you don't need to say anything, Ash," Colt said, cutting off any witty quip Ash might have come up with. Ash grinned and his eyebrows flew up. Colt turned and kicked the door closed with the heel of his foot.

Later, April sat back and watched as Colt lounged in the white, fluffy robe and took a sip of his tea. Yes, tea, she shook her head slightly. She had found a kettle and brewed them both a cup of orange blossom green tea. Colt was dutifully drinking it out of a china tea cup she had passed to him. She insisted it would be good for their digestion. Colt had wordlessly accepted her offering and they smiled at each other with amusement.

She absently twirled her ring around on her ring finger. She knew it wasn't real, but... After battening her pinging heartstrings back into place inside her chest, she had glided around that store earlier, looking at rings on their dainty little velvet ring pads. She picked one easily, it had called to her. A gold band, with a halo diamond, surrounded by other smaller diamonds. She knew this wasn't real, she had almost not picked that one because she loved it too much. It was exactly what she'd want if they were getting married for real. Which they weren't, it was just for show. Just for a disguise at the retreat. But then she had thought, taking a page from Colt's book, fuck it. That's the one she wanted, so that's what she'd get.

The food was good. "Cajun okra fries... tomato basil sourdough bruschetta... cumin beetroot dip..." April read from the little menu card she'd snatched up as she helped herself. Colt attacked the food under the cloches, too. She'd then found the terry cloth robes on the bathroom door, happily snuggled into one, and surprisingly Colt had followed her lead. Now he was reclined on the bed, holding the little saucer that matched the cup as he downed the final gulps of his tea.

April raised her eyebrows, she was nowhere near finished with hers. She smiled at him. "Like it? You want more?" she asked him.

He frowned. "No, I want dinner finished so we can fuck in the shower," he answered with a side smirk, all confidence now. It suited him.

April choked on a mouthful of her tea.

"Then, finally, in bed. This is the kind of bed you deserve, the kind of bed I always imagined you in..." he trailed off, shyly.

She didn't want him to get trapped inside his head again and lose his nerve. "Have you seen the shower?" she asked, putting down her cup of tea on the bedside table nearest where she was sitting. As she stood the robe started to open, automatically she went to adjust it, and tighten it around her. Then, thinking better of it, she let it drop to the floor.

Colt held her gaze as she stood there, naked. His smirk slid off his face and he looked at her like she was dessert. Something chocolatey and sinful to be savored. She smiled, loving her power over him. Loving how he reacted to her, wanted her. She hadn't had sex twice in the same night for a long time. Hadn't felt the need to, or been with anyone who had felt the need for her. To be so unsatisfied the first time, to ignore any physical discomfort, tiredness, to want to climb that mountain again. Only it didn't feel like a chore, like a hill to climb. With Colt, it felt like a breeze. It felt easy, like being in the van with him, or on the back of that bike. More than easy, thrilling. No doubt about if they'd make it to the top of the hill or not. No question they would get there. Of course they would, together. With Colt, it was a chase, April mused as he stood and shucked off his robe, too. But they were now together side by side and running downhill. Holding hands, tumbling, tripping, laughing. Caught up in each other.

April tried to hold his gaze, but his body pulled her eyeballs as if they were magnetized. His body was a piece of art to be admired. And by the sound of it, no one had properly. It sounded like these 'sweet butts' had willingly picked the flesh from his bones with their grasping claws, all take, take, take. Not giving or appreciating. Well, that changed now.

"Colt, let's take a shower," she breathed, and nodded toward the bathroom. He stayed standing stock still. April moved forward. She tugged on his hand, leading him, naked ass and all, into the bathroom.

She clicked on the light and Colt whistled, looking around. Yes, the bathroom was lovely. Pale marble from floor to ceiling. A huge jacuzzi tub, dual vanity, his and hers, a huge walk in shower with a large shower head. It smelled of jasmine and vanilla. The lights were dim, not bright and clinical, more soft and sensual.

April turned on the shower. Hot water sluicing out of the giant chrome shower head, steaming. Colt's eyes never left her, watching her the whole time. This big, dark, tattooed man, muscles rippling, stood still watching her like his life depended on it. She pushed him then, and was delighted when he followed the momentum, straight under the hot water. He gasped and sighed, lifting his head and let the hot water cascade around him. His hair went almost black, and so much longer weighed down with the water. His nipple bar glinted. The light dusting of wispy, dark hair on his chest and stomach clung darkly to him. She stood outside the shower area and just watched. In this bathroom that reeked of comfort and civility, it was like bringing a wild animal indoors. Strikingly incongruous, visually beautiful. April was captivated by him.

CHAPTER 36
COLT

THE MORNING CAME gently, percolating through the cocoon of white sheets and softness that enveloped him. Colt kept his eyes closed and woke up slowly, reveling in the memories of last night that drifted back to him as he came to. She had given him the space to enjoy the shower by himself for a bit last night. She seemed to have been very happy to continue watching from outside the enclosure. The glass had steamed up, the air had gotten hot and heavy with water droplets. Colt had wiped water from his eyes, blew out and sent droplets of water everywhere. "Coming in, Kitten?" he had asked in a deep voice. "Or are you enjoying the view too much?" He smiled playfully at her.

He felt like a new man, reborn, re-formed from the clay that had forged him. In different hands, her hands, he'd been taken back to the beginning and re-made stronger, better. He felt confidence flowing through him again. And was braver than before. Before prison and all the shit that had gone down. When he was in his heyday, VP in the MC, under Blue. When girls were dropping at his feet, and the guys were doing whatever the fuck he told them to do. When the town let him go where he wanted, cops let him race down the highway. Back then he had been cock-sure, ballsy. But that was because of his youth. Now, he was older and wiser. He felt powerful, it came from having been through shit and coming out the other side. Nothing could hurt him now, not like before. That trembling Chihuahua that had stepped out of prison, blinking in the bright sunlight, waiting like a lost puppy for someone to come and get him... That man was gone. The guy who had felt too worthless to kiss April, or make love to her properly. Declared he wanted to fuck her but too scared to follow through on his promise without screwing it up, that man was gone. He wasn't the Chihuahua, he wasn't even a fucking Rottweiler. He was a lion, king of the jungle, with a big fuck-off attitude. And his fierce, beautiful, lethal lioness by his side.

It felt like he'd shucked off the grumpy, unsure outer layer and blossomed. They had showered together, washing every inch of each other. Luxuriating in each other's bodies and the privacy and comfort of their surroundings. In the shower, steam had swirled around them. They had shampooed each other's hair and scrubbed each other's bodies with the fancy bath products provided. When they had felt too hot, they had finally exited the shower, wrapping each other in soft, fluffy towels. Then they climbed onto the bed, he pushed her underneath him, and began the slow process of worshiping every inch of her skin. No part of her went unappreciated. Her breasts, her stomach, her forearms, her calves. And she returned the favor by rolling on top, straddling and touching him, tenderly, lovingly. He had watched her hand come out to stroke his ribs, his pecs, his collarbone. The scar on his abdomen from when some bastard had tried to shiv him when he was in prison. His nipples, flicking his barbell gently. His balls, cupping, rolling them in her palm, enjoying their weight. Parts of him had never been touched that way. Tenderly, with care, like she loved him. He looked up at her, curiously, questioning in his eyes. Trusting her, but not understanding. She said his unassuming modesty was beguiling. He didn't know what that meant, but she seemed happy, so he was happy. It was a crime that no one had taken the time to love

THE CHASE

him like this, she claimed. But she wasn't complaining, she would do it, gladly, without restraint, she joked. After licking and nibbling each other's bodies, learning them like their own, they had had sex again. Deep, roaring sex that knocks planets out of their orbits. He thought maybe it would be that slow, tender sex they hadn't yet had, but it wasn't. It had been less desperate, less urgent, but still pounding heat, slamming hearts, gasping, screaming, shivering.

"Come back to bed Colt, we've got time before meeting with the concierge at nine," she said quietly, pulling him out of his thoughts. She wasn't begging, not trying to persuade him, more like an instruction. He was already under the covers by the time she finished speaking.

"Good morning madam, sir." Ash nodded to them the next morning from behind the reception desk. When they finally emerged Ash looked fresh faced, clean shaven. He still had his long, skater boy hair but was otherwise crisp in his freshly pressed suit.

Colt glanced sideways at April. She looked freshly fucked. He was very proud of himself, and stuck his chest out like a prize peacock. Ash flicked his blue eyes between them both knowingly.

"Morning." Colt nodded, trying not to smile smugly.

"Ah, Mr. and Mrs. Black." Colt turned to see the douchebag manager from last night scurrying over. Colt simmered at the sight of him.

"Can we see some of the classes and experiences you offer, please?" April took over. Colt ground his jaw, maybe April could hear his teeth gnashing together already. It was probably for the best that she was organizing things, if he wanted to avoid punching the manager in the face anytime soon.

"Yes, of course." The manager bustled forward. Ash raised his eyebrows.

"With your concierge," April added firmly.

The manager looked crestfallen. "Ah, of course."

"Privately," April added. "We have a delicate request." She smiled sweetly, and it was the manager's turn for his eyebrows to hit the ceiling. Ash smiled like the cat who had got the canary and professionally swept them into a meeting room behind the reception area.

Colt cleared his throat. "How did you end up working here with your uncle?"

Ash flashed them both a devilishly handsome smile. "My parents banished me basically, it was work here or go to conversion therapy at the local church…"

"That sounds positively draconian." April looked concerned. Colt loved it when she used fancy words.

"What did you do?" Colt asked quietly. He settled into a chair to hear the story, stretching his legs out in front of him and crossing them at his ankles. He crossed his arms over his chest and regarded the younger man in front of him.

Ash shrugged, kept his expression neutral and cocked his head to the left. "I fucked the girl next door."

Colt didn't blink.

Ash tilted his head to the right. "And the boy next door on the other side."

Colts eyebrows flickered.

"At the same time," Ash continued. "And took photographs of it, then submitted it for my college photography competition. Then got kicked out of college…"

Colt was going red in the face from holding in his laugh. He pressed his lips together and his cheeks puffed out until he could take it no more. A guffaw burst out of him. He turned to look at April, who was looking at Ash with a surprised but amused grin, too. She flashed Colt a smile. All three of them laughed together.

"Well, fuck," Colt said immediately, humor in his voice.

"So, do you want to hear the yoga schedule?" Ash said, not missing a beat.

Colt smiled. Ash had an attitude, too, unashamed. Shit, he'd make a great Prospect, if Colt was still running the MC, he'd welcome Ash into the fold. But he wasn't. That sobered him. He listened while April and Ash talked animatedly about the facilities and the yoga schedules. Silently mulling things over in his head. Thinking of how Ash could benefit from a sponsor, how the MC life could have helped to focus himself, what an asset this open minded, personable guy could be... It stabbed him in the gut, how much Colt missed the MC.

"Okay, so I'll book you in for the intermediate level morning sun salute... and Colt you'll be in the beginner warrior warm up..."

"Wait, hang on... me... doing yoga?" he stuttered. How much had he tuned out for?

"Yes, don't worry, there's a gift shop here that we can buy you some yoga leggings in," April said with a coy, playful smile.

"I-" he began to argue, but April cut him off.

"We can also get you a speedo for the spa, no board shorts, remember?"

Colt opened then closed his mouth. "Spa... Speedo..." He repeated as if they were foreign words.

"Yep." Ash popped the P and ran a glance down Colt. "Couples massages, too, for today, you've got extra deep tissue for tomorrow, as well, Mr. Black-"

Colt gritted his teeth. So many rules, and a schedule to follow.

How did some people come here voluntarily on vacation?

"Now, you're all booked for breakfast, lunch and dinner. Tonight it's the raw food special tasting menu-"

Colt interrupted Ash now. "Raw?"

"Tomorrow, your morning yoga will finish at nine a.m. for you both."

"Finish... sorry, did I fucking hear correctly, finish at nine?"

"Yes, it starts at seven-thirty," Ash continued.

"What the -"

"My husband is just so excited to learn-" April jumped in.

"You can go to breakfast after yoga, then you have some downtime..." Ash practically undressed them both with his eyes.

Colt rolled his.

"Most guests choose leisure activities in the afternoon, like kayaking, or a hot air balloon ride-"

Colt nodded to Ash's wrist. "Your tattoo," he said simply.

Ash glanced at the fern leaf on his wrist that poked out of his shirt sleeve. "Yeah?" Ash replied, attitude dripping off him, daring them to comment, to judge.

Fine, Colt would spell it out for Ash, since he was clearly being defiant. "Where did you get it?" Colt asked.

Ash glanced down at his wrist. "Locally."

April stepped in. "My husband needs to get some work done on a tattoo, we were hoping you could recommend a local tattoo artist?"

Ash's gaze flicked over them again. "There's no tattoo studio in town, I'm afraid."

"Then where did you get yours done?" Colt asked again.

"A friend... he's recently certified but hasn't got a space or anything, he's got the equipment though-"

"He any good?" Colt asked.

Ash unbuttoned his sleeve and shoved the white shirt material up his arm, revealing a very neat, stylized fern leaf.

"He take cash? He have time for me?"

Ash's eyebrows shifted up a notch. "I could ask him."

"Do." Colt nodded.

Ash got out his phone and tapped away. Then put it down, nodding. "Done."

Colt watched Ash a moment longer. "How well do you know him?" Colt asked.

Ash smiled devilishly. "I'm fucking him," he said, half proud, half daring Colt or April to recoil.

Colt kept his face neutral without any effort. He couldn't care less if two guys were fucking, it wasn't anything that bothered him. "That'll be my afternoon leisure activity. Getting a tattoo fixed."

Ash nodded. "So evening meal is early as you know, then afterwards there's a fireside chat…"

"What now?"

"Where all the guests come together for a mindfulness session-"

"I don't-"

"We do a mindfulness body scan, and a gratitude thanking-"

Colt gritted his teeth. "Course you do."

"So if there is anything else you need," Ash paused and gave them both a heated look, "here's my personal phone number." He slid two business cards over the table, one to Colt, one to April. Bold move, Colt thought.

Colt cleared his throat. "Do you offer all the guests your personal number, or are we special?"

Ash smiled sinfully. "Most of them don't pick up what I'm laying down. Are you catching my drift?" Ash asked suddenly.

Colt didn't glance at April, he went ahead and answered for the both of them. "Not this time, no." Colt shook his head.

Ash shrugged, unperturbed. He didn't blush, he didn't look embarrassed, he didn't look ashamed. Good for him.

"Well, enjoy your stay, I'll get back to you about an appointment with Dane, for your tattoo."

"Thanks, Ash." April nodded, and they all stood while Ash waved them out of the room. Colt let April out first, like the gentleman he most definitely fucking wasn't. He followed. Colt's eyes caught on April's butt as she walked ahead in her jeans. Yes. He wanted in. He reached forward and pinched, then massaged, then lightly slapped.

"Colt!" she exclaimed, whirling around, grabbing his hand, eyes wide but a smile on her lips.

"Come on, Kitten, let's go, I wanna fuck you." He was a drug addict needing his next hit already, he was getting withdrawal symptoms.

CHAPTER 27
APRIL

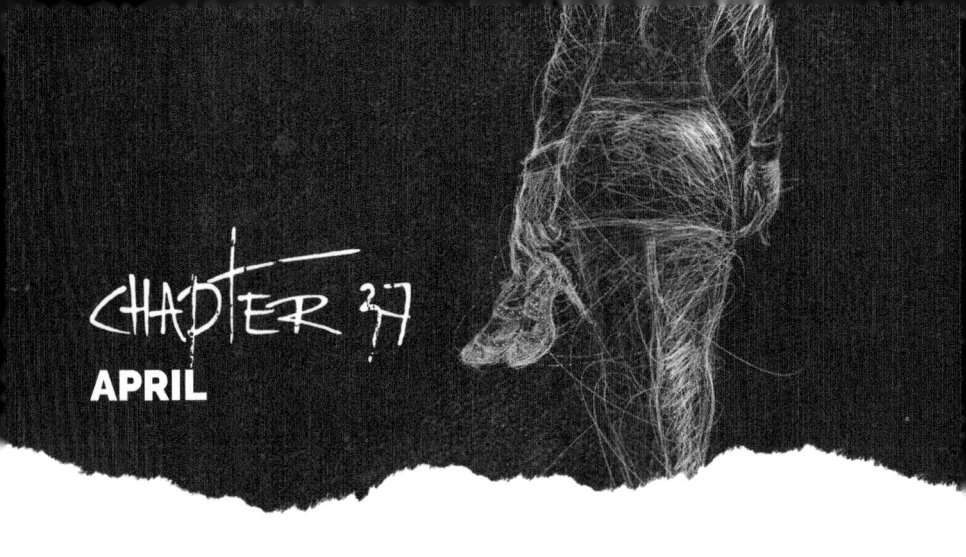

APRIL WATCHED COLT tapping away impatiently on his phone. He'd been quiet since dinner. To be fair, though, she'd been quiet after dinner, too. The raw food, four course taster dinner had been that night. She hadn't had a whole meal of raw food before. It had been shiny, cold, crunchy and all in all, unsatisfying. Colt had barely hid his displeasure. And they'd got a glimpse of the other guests, too. Colt had been right. They were all city yuppies. Some couples were about their age and some older. All of them douches, as Colt liked to label them. The dining room had been low lit, that was part of the dining experience. She smiled when she replayed Colt rolling his eyes again as the waiter had explained each dish. A low chatter, like they were in a museum or an art gallery was the backing track.

"We promote a whole foods diet built on raw, unrefined plants, vegetables, nuts and seeds. Here we have a wheat berry cultured kombucha, artisanal red pepper flake, olive and cashew cheese, courgette noodles, parmesan crisps, basil pesto, organic Thai coconut lemongrass soup, Ceylon cinnamon custard…"

April ran her tongue around her mouth. Some of it was tasty. Some gimmicky. All of it had been small, little dainty bites. One particular dish had come out and Colt had immediately put the whole thing in his mouth, before the waiter had set the plate on the table, it was so small. He'd take thirty seconds to finish one of the plates of food and then he'd crossed his arms over his chest. He was trying hard not to get grumpy. April saw it and appreciated that he was trying at least. He was trying not to have a smoke, and he'd gone to yoga earlier that afternoon, too. In his new yoga pants.

When he had seen them, that had been funny. And his speedo, too. True to his word, Ash had the gift shop deliver them and a bikini for her. They were the right size, Ash didn't even have to ask. Unsurprising considering how much he'd ogled them both with his eyes. Colt had held up the skimpy black swim briefs with incredulity stamped on his face. He'd held up her two-piece black bikini, too, and was miffed about how he wanted her to wear it for his eyes only.

But he'd put the leggings on and loped off to his first yoga class with only minimal grumbling. Like a moody eight year old on his way to school.

She hadn't heard how it had gone. She'd asked, but only received grunts in return.

When the waiter had brought them their final course, Colt had snorted. "Final plate? I'm still hungry." He could be grumpy when he wanted to be. She smiled, imagining him as an old man, imagining herself with him as they grew old and gray. She shook her head, trying to shake the image out of her mind. She shouldn't be so silly, she could only dream of being with him that long. For them to grow old together? Who was she kidding, of course she wanted that. She'd said as much to Colt, she'd said she wanted it all. And hadn't he said he wanted it, too? Not just with the few words he'd spoken on the subject, but with his kisses, the way he held her, the way he touched her. If she wasn't mistaken, that was a forever kind of loving her. Now they were back in their room, she was on the sofa, and he had spread himself out on the bed, tapping away on his phone.

THE CHASE

"Colt," she spoke up before she lost herself in planning out her wedding vows and the names of their children.

He grunted, not looking up from his phone. She licked her lips and tried again. "Hey mister grumpy, what are you up to?" she asked. She was minorly irked, moody, for some reason, not quite herself. Maybe it was her period, she suddenly thought. Yes! She didn't have her cycle tracker app because she tossed her old phone away, which meant she had no idea what day of the month it was, but she was pretty sure she was due any day now. She sighed with relief, that was it, that was why she was feeling so off. She'd have to warn him, they'd need to not have sex for a few days, which she imagined he wouldn't be too pleased about...

He flicked his eyes up to her, then suddenly pulled himself up, out of the bed.

"Gotta go," he muttered, stomping past her.

"What?" she blubbered, incredulous. He shrugged on his jacket, his face closed off.

She felt mounting anger at his attitude. "Colt, wait." That inexplicable irritation, the dissatisfaction, the wildness in her spoiling for a fight. It was new to her. It was his influence, maybe, she thought, his impulsivity and wildness, rubbing off on her.

"I'll be back later," he said and headed toward the door.

She flared with the physical rush of anger. And then in its wake, a stabbing in her chest. The anger turned to hurt. April couldn't believe it, he slammed the door behind him. Those happy images of them growing old together shattering in front of her eyes. She knew she was being emotional, and felt very hormonal, now that she thought of it. But still, she was hurt. The hot prick of tears began to threaten behind her eyes. She could either give in to them, or chase him down. Chase after him, and her new dreams of being by his side. The old her would have probably gotten huffy and collapsed on the bed. She would have settled on her role as the victim, the one who had been wronged. The girl who got what she wanted and had a privileged life would have seen this as a betrayal and given in to the tears. That girl would have seen such rude abruptness as a personal insult, a snub against who she was, and would have felt affronted by his attitude. But April felt new power in her soul. A strength and willingness to face a fight. She wanted to confront Colt, face him, and bring him back into line. No way was she walking away and giving up on her dreams so quickly and easily. No way was she letting his grumpy attitude fester into something they couldn't overcome. She slammed her feet into her sneakers by the door and trotted out after him, determination coursing through her.

"Colt," she yelled out, facing the darkness of the night. She looked up and down the path, squinting back in the direction of the restaurant and reception area. "Colt!" She couldn't see him.

"Kitten, go back inside," came a low rumble from behind. She whirled around and found Colt peering quizzically from the side of the cabin. He had an unlit cigarette balanced between his lips.

She was relieved to find him. She didn't like being alone out here, the woods yawned hungrily, threatening to suck her in. Colt seemed perfectly at home, skulking in the shadows. She did not. She felt a renewed wave of irritation. "Don't you tell me to go back inside," she began, taking a deep breath in. Here goes, she stalked up to him and faced him. "Colt, your attitude has sucked all evening. Here we are having our first day in this swanky resort. I thought we'd have a nice time here, safe, cozy, a chance to get to know each other a little better... this isn't a cheap place and I feel like you're not really embracing this." April took a breath.

Colt smirked. She couldn't believe it. He had the audacity to flash those even, shiny teeth at her.

THE CHASE

"Colt! Don't laugh, this isn't funny!" she scolded.

He reached out and cuffed her chin with his fist affectionately. "Fuck, do you have any idea how cute you are when you're all riled up like this? How fucking cute?" He trailed off, his eyes snagging on her lips. He dragged his gaze off her, turned and loped into the woods.

"Colt! There isn't a path back there! Where are you going?" she yelled, trying to hide the panic in those last few words as she realized she'd be left standing alone in the dark. To hell with that. She bolted after him, somehow stumbling over brambles and branches that Colt seemed to effortlessly bypass.

"Kitten, what are you doing out here? Go back, you haven't even got a jacket on," he said gently. He wasn't rising to her emotional, frantic tirade and that was winding her up even more. She was spoiling for a fight.

"No." She scowled back at him. "I'm not just going to skip back inside, Colt, we need to talk."

He calmly carried on walking. The brambles thinned out and she was able to catch up to walk alongside him.

"I'm lighting up," he threatened, bringing the lighter up to the end of the cigarette, shielding it from the cool night air. He paused and glanced sideways at her.

She huffed. "Go ahead, you think that's going to put me off from this? Well it isn't. I feel like you are being really grumpy and ungrateful-"

"Ungrateful?" he repeated. He flicked the lighter, took a drag on the cigarette. The tip glowed orange, bright in the increasing gloom around them. April shivered. Damn, she should have put on her hoodie. He took a deep breath in. She watched, determined not to find it fascinating. She failed, it was hypnotizing, watching him smoke. He angled his head up, and blew a plume of smoke into the air. He was like a dragon. Ferocious. Dangerous. She felt a pull and a tingle in her core.

"Fuck me, I needed that," he said, taking another drag. April watched the glow reflect in his eyes. "Now, ungrateful I won't accept," he replied calmly.

April felt momentarily confused. What? Oh, returning to the conversation from before. Before she got distracted with how hot he looked smoking. Christ she suddenly wanted him to smoke a cigarette like that while they were having sex, him wearing his biker boots and his leather cut and nothing else…God what was wrong with her, that was a sick, twisted thought. Deplorable. Wasn't it? She shook her head.

"Did you see the size of the dinner? A fucking raw food taster menu? They could have served that at feeding time in a petting zoo, April-"

"Now that's taking it too far-" she began but her stomach rumbled loudly, giving her away.

Colt tilted his head. "See? You're still hungry," he stated with a smug grin on his face, visible through the darkness.

"No, well, I…" she began, but her protest died on her lips. "Okay, I thought dinner tonight was … lacking, but that doesn't mean you have to be moody with me."

He took another drag, and then threw his arm over her shoulder, pulling her into a side embrace. "Oh Kitten, did I upset you? I apologize for that." He planted a kiss on her forehead. The fight was leaving her, goddammit.

"It took a lot of effort to find this place, somewhere where we could hide, regroup, give your shoulder a rest, take a bit of time to get to know each other..."

"To properly fuck each other?" he corrected her. She heard the grin in his voice.

She huffed. "Well, yes, in not so crude language, yes-"

"I am grateful Kitten, I'm sorry, the massage earlier was incredible, the yoga I had no fucking idea what I was meant to do but I'll go again tomorrow and I do see how it can do a person a lot of good," he continued.

She nuzzled into his underarm, glad of the sense of safety his body gave her. Relief that he wasn't wanting to run from her, palpable in her body. She shouldn't have doubted him. She needed to be strong, to not be governed by her emotions, or her sense of superiority. That wasn't her anymore, she needed to remember that. Colt was not a man of constant compliments. He wasn't all roses and rainbows. He was her dirty bad boy biker who got grumpy and swore. And she wouldn't change him for the world.

He huffed now. "I don't like the amount of rules here, the security guard and the pain in the ass manager and all the set times for shit. It reminds me of being in prison."

"It's not meant to be a prison," she countered but she was beginning to understand now.

"I know, but I'd rather it was just me and you and a cabin in the woods, than all this other shit and people interfering..." he sighed.

"I wish that, too, but we need all those people right now-"

"Yeah." He blew out a plume.

"One day," she continued before she chickened out, "one day maybe it will just be us, in a cabin in the woods."

He moved his arm off her shoulder and groped her butt. "Fuck yeah, I hope so," he murmured and she grinned into the darkness, glad he couldn't see how happy that made her.

"Why in the world are we sneaking through the woods in the dark at night?" she questioned. He pulled out his phone but held it with the screen angled away from her. She realized they had managed to walk to a road.

"It was only meant to be me sneaking through the woods in the dark. You are the one who came stomping out here after me-"

"Because you wouldn't talk to me, you just told me to stay inside like a good little woman should."

"Well, sorry for assuming you'd get cold out here. I was right though, huh? You're cold and pissed about tramping through the woods in the dark-"

"Which brings me back to my original question, what are you doing?"

He paused, then replied flatly, "Meeting someone."

April rolled her eyes and scoffed. "Well that's cleared things up... not!"

"What, are we in the third grade or something?"

"What are you... are you doing something illegal?"

He stopped in his tracks now. "April please... like getting drugs? Is that what you are thinking?" He sounded angry.

April swallowed. "I have no idea! That's why I keep asking but you are just being grumpy... I just don't know!"

"Fuck's sake," he yelled out. At that moment, his phone lit up and vibrated in his hand. In the blue light of the phone she could see how pissed off he was. She shouldn't have let him think that she doubted him, she didn't.

THE CHASE

"Yes?" He hissed down the phone. She heard a voice at the other end of the line but couldn't hear any words.

"Yep. Yeah," he said. The voice murmured again. "Got it." He ended the call and flicked his cigarette away. They now stood in silence, in the dark, glowering at each other.

Until she heard the rumble of a motorcycle. She flinched then froze.

CHAPTER 38
APRIL

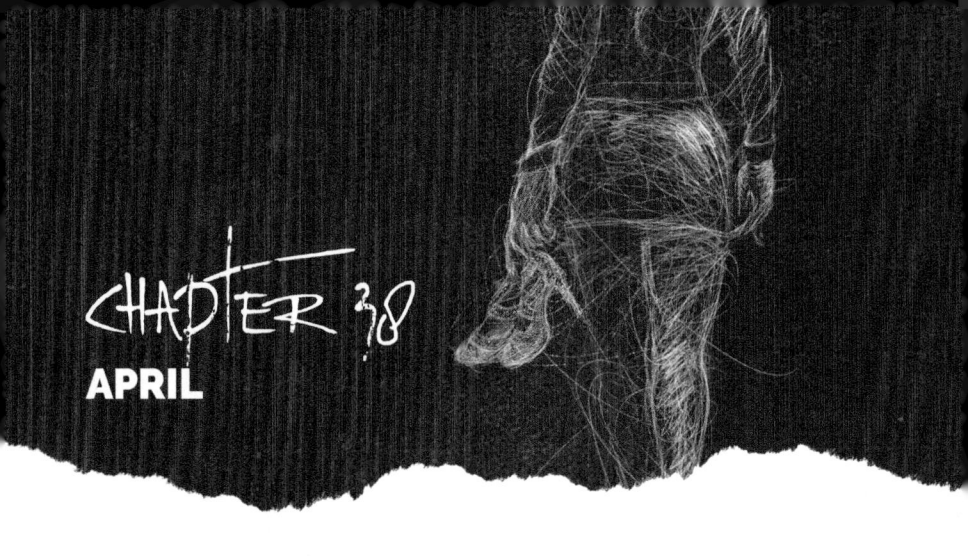

"Colt." Her heart pounded in her ribcage.

"What?" he said roughly, folding his arms over his chest.

She felt a rising panic. Had he sold her out? She whimpered. No, no, no. He couldn't have. She felt her breath catch in her throat. Her emotions running wild inside her. She stumbled back. Half thinking about running, but she knew she'd never make it. It was all over. She braced herself for the hell that was to come, throwing her hands up to her face.

The bike got closer. Colt didn't move. She let out a little sob.

The bike came to a stop in front of Colt. She peered out from between her hands, and saw Colt hand money to the rider, who was dressed all in black. The rider handed him a brown paper bag. She was confused. The rider then drove off.

"Kitten, take your hands away from your face," he said, gently now.

"No," she whimpered.

"Come on, it's okay," he said soothingly. She felt his warm, strong hand on her arm, gently but firmly prying it off her face.

"Double cheeseburger with bacon?" he asked quietly.

"No… what?" She wailed initially, then processed what he'd said. She peeped out from her hands. The smell hit her first, warm beef, cheese. Bacon.

"Oh god," she moaned with longing. He was using his phone as a flashlight now, and she could see him smiling at her.

"Come on, Kitten," he cajoled. He offered her a little foiled wrapped package of warm burger goodness.

"I..." she began, but didn't know what to say next. She suddenly felt like she wanted to cry. God, it was her period. She was all over the place, mentally and emotionally, tonight.

"Here's what's going to happen," he began, talking with quiet, calm authority. "You and I are going to eat. Then I am going to fuck you, hard, right here, in the dark, so you never, ever forget how I feel about you. Despite how grumpy I may seem, do you understand me?"

"Colt, I..."

"And you are going to fuck me back so that I never ever forget to treat you with the utmost respect and gentility, is that alright with you, Kitten?"

She watched with an open mouth as he ripped the foil wrapper off his burger with one swipe, opened his mouth wide and took a huge bite. April was reminded of a T Rex in one of those dinosaur movies, ripping it's teeth into a hunk of meat, tossing it back to swallow it.

She gaped like a fish for a second. Then sniffed up her threatening tears and nodded frantically. Then remembered they were in the dark and found her voice. "Yes, Colt."

She followed his lead, clawing at the foil around her warm burger, and finally sunk her teeth into the fluffy bun. Juicy meat, cheese and a pickle relish filled her mouth and she groaned out loud at the explosion of flavors.

Colt had his half devoured burger in one hand, and reached out his other hand toward her. He snagged her jeans and popped them open.

"Some days I may be quiet, I may be a fucking moody bastard. I'm sorry, that's who I am. It's not going to be all sunshine and rainbows, Kitten, but don't you forget how I feel about you. Ignore me when I'm in a mood. I'm sorry, but that's not something that's going to change anytime soon. And at the same time, I'll put up with your shit, too, okay, when you want to yell at me or huff at me or tell me off for being a moody bastard who has told you to go back in the house."

She nodded, the emotional turmoil within her calming. Changing realms from intangible thoughts to tangible heat.

"Here's your dick, little Kitten. Here it will always be." He opened his jeans. "Off, now," he commanded through a mouthful of burger, pulling her jeans. "Eat and off," he added. "Kitten, I'll never stop, I'll always be here for you, even if I'm a grumpy bastard, I'll still be right here for you, never forget that."

She smiled, gulped, and looked down at her jeans. She felt a thousand things click into place within her. He was there, he always would be, forever. She shook her head and tried to focus on the moment.

She couldn't eat and wiggle out of her jeans. Colt saw her struggle. "Just eat, Kitten." He changed his instructions, putting his burger fully in his mouth now, holding it there as he yanked her jeans down her butt. They ended up at her knees before getting stuck but Colt bunched them there. He pulled what was left of the burger from his mouth, and chewed the giant mouthful. April tried to breathe and eat her burger while her heart blossomed in her chest and her pulse pounded around her body. She felt flushed, now unaware of the cold night air that had been pinching before. The delicious food was heaven, the anticipation of what was about to happen was just as juicy. Her senses were about to be bombarded. He shoved the last of his burger into his mouth and his hands went to his own jeans. She heard the jingle of the buttons and zipper.

He grabbed her by the shoulders and spun her around, like a rag doll in his hands. She whirled around and staggered into the darkness as he pushed her off the road. With her pants around her knees and her burger in her hand, she couldn't move fast or far.

"Finish your dinner April, like a good little kitten. Then, I'll finish us both," he growled in her ear, his breath hot against her cheek.

"Ump." She shoved in another mouthful and chewed frantically. She wasn't able to breathe properly between mouthfuls and even that was turning her on.

Colt was behind her, pressing against her back with his chest. She felt a tree in front of her. With one hand she braced herself against the tree, as Colt bent her forwards slightly. She arched her back, sticking her rear out further for him. She heard a murmur of appreciation from him. He leaned over her and kissed her roughly, biting her ear, the back of her neck in the same ravenous way he'd eaten the burger moments before. She didn't recognize herself and loved it.

His hands came out, and one spanked her ass with a firm zap. She squealed as she felt the sting.

"That's for nearly ruining your surprise, Kitten. Keep chewing." She did. He swatted her again. "That's for doubting me, thinking I was up to some sort of illegal, shady shit. I wasn't."

He swatted again. The sting was tingly hot now. She moaned around a mouthful of burger.

"That's for not finishing the burger quick enough, for making those noises, Kitten, my cock's getting jealous, swallow that burger and take my cock like the good little kitten I know you can be."

She was loving this confident Colt, who was master of his body and soul. Who demanded what he wanted and expected it to be delivered.

She took another bite.

She felt one of his hands skimming up her top, pushing up her bra. It was rucked up awkwardly now but it meant he had a handful of one of her tits and he squeezed, jiggled. Then his fingers found her nipple. He pinched, rolled, pulled it. She almost thought about tossing the burger away to enjoy what he was doing with his hand. Almost, but it was an epic burger.

His breathing was turning erratic. She turned her head and caught a glimpse of him. He had his other hand around his cock and he was pumping. Hard. She pushed back off the tree, pressing her ass into his cock. He gasped and shoved it in between her cheeks, not entering her, just skimming over her entrance, the length of her crease. He was wet, she was wet.

She popped the rest of the burger in her mouth, and put her hand on the tree trunk.

"Swallow it, April, then swallow me. With your cunt," Colt purred. She'd never thought she'd be so turned on and be eating a burger, of all things. But it was absolutely delicious. She almost gagged on the massive mouthful and Colt pushed his cock right up to her entrance, straining there, quivering in the starting gates.

"April, don't tease me," he warned. She chewed and swallowed finally. Then she put her hand between her legs and pushed his hard cock into her.

They both purred now. Then he was off. Colt didn't hold back. It was merciless. She couldn't open her legs very far because of her jeans, so he wasn't as deep as he could be, but it was so good to feel him entering and pulling out fully each time. One hand yanked one of her tits, pinching her nipple and refusing to let go. She'd never felt the blissful agony of such rough handling of her boobs, she was close to coming from that alone. God, it was like he was just tightening a coil within her. His other hand on her hip, pulling her back, slamming her ass against his hips.

"Yes, yes, take it April. Never fucking doubt me again. I will never let you down, fucking know it, tell me you know it." He was babbling endlessly, chanting the same thing over and over.

"I don't doubt... Colt, I won't ever..." She found herself murmuring back. She meant every word, every feeling. With every slam of his body into hers, she felt their souls forming together, becoming one, as was always the case when they came together.

"Ah fuck Kitten... coming, I'm-" he spluttered. And he suddenly convulsed, bent over her back. He mercilessly spanked her clit with his fingers now, tapping with each of his spasms and it sent her over the edge. She convulsed under him, mirroring his noise.

The roaring in her ears mixed with his frantic gasps as he sucked air in. The night air rushed in. He smiled and pulled her up so that they were both standing. She leaned her head back against his shoulder. His hand tilted her chin back and he kissed her. Devoured her mouth through a smile that she returned. He was happy, joyful. Far from that closed off, self-deprecating man she had met, or even the grumpy grouch from earlier.

"You needed that, huh?" she asked.

CHAPTER 31
APRIL

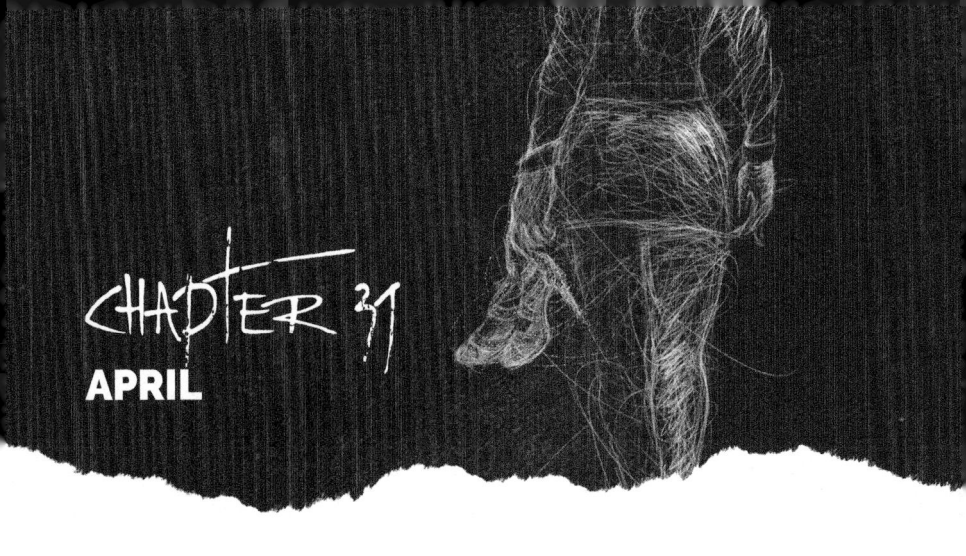

"The sex, the food or the cigarette?" Colt nuzzled into her hair. "Maybe I was in a bad mood 'cause I'd been without you all afternoon," he said between dipping his tongue into her mouth.

She smiled at his playfulness. They got dressed and rejoined the road. But as soon as they stepped onto the pavement, bam, an explosion of light forced her eyes shut and she spun away.

"Freeze! Don't move!" Was shouted from behind the lights. She had the confused thought that she was going to be arrested for eating the burger.

"For fuck's sake!" Colt bellowed. She squinted her eyes open and saw the security guard, Dwight, tumbling over from the vehicle he'd pulled up in. A golf cart. With particularly bright lights.

"It's just a fucking burger because raw night sucked ass!" Colt roared, anger coursing off him.

"No one breaches the perimeter! It's my job to guard the perimeter!" Dwight yelled back.

Jesus. April swallowed loudly and stepped in to defuse the situation before these two killed each other. "Dwight, so sorry, there's been a big misunderstanding, we didn't realize that the delivery driver did not come up the main road."

"Ma'am, it's my job," he said, calming down a notch to speak to her. Colt squared up to him aggressively. April grabbed his arm.

"I've called for backup now-" Dwight said, almost sulkily, clearly annoyed that the situation was a minor infringement and not the invasion he had initially thought. Another motorcycle sound ripped closer.

April tried not to shudder. She'd have to be careful, that noise could trigger a panic attack. The motorcycle approached, slowed, and came to a stop in front of them. April blinked, it was Ash, on a beat up old Harley. She knew nothing about bikes and it was dark but she could still tell it was on its last legs.

Colt laughed out loud. "The concierge? You've got to be fucking kidding me."

April piped up with her middle class indignation. "Maybe this place isn't as secure as we were led to believe, if the only security back up is the concierge?" She glared at Dwight.

Ash didn't seem fazed. "You'd be surprised. I'm a black belt in karate," Ash said drolly.

"Is there anything this kid doesn't get involved in?" Colt rocked back on his heels.

Ash looked around, assessed the situation and didn't bat an eyelid. "You called for backup because they ordered takeout?" His voice was even but you could hear his annoyance. Dwight shrugged.

Ash turned back to Colt. "You can't have deliveries coming, we take the privacy of this place seriously. You need anything, it comes through me," Ash said.

Colt replied with a single chin lift. "Sure. Got it for next time."

Dwight cleared his throat self importantly. "I'll leave you to discuss penalties with these two." He simpered, raising his eyebrows disapprovingly when he said "these two".

Colt snorted. "Penalties? What are you going to do, spank me?"

Colt mocked.

"Don't tempt me," Ash muttered under his breath.

Colt guffawed. April smiled, pleased that these two had struck up a friendship of sorts. Colt was happy to tease Ash, Ash was happy to be teased, he was unashamedly himself. Open, unafraid.

"Well, I hope you are being paid well for all of these double shifts you're working," April joked.

Ash snorted. "I'm not being paid. I'm here as punishment, remember?"

Colt squared his jaw and frowned. "You're not getting paid?"

April heard the anger in his voice. She loved that about him. He got involved. He wouldn't be able to let that lie. It's what had made him a good President before, a good MC brother. Colt liked Ash, she could see that, she knew he found Ash to be just as rebellious, just as disrespectful, just as much of a survivor as Colt was himself.

"Why else do you think you can hear the crankshaft and the exhaust leaking on my ride?" Ash sounded sullen. April suspected his attitude hid the hurt.

"Jesus Christ, why are you putting up with this shit?" Colt asked.

Ash looked down at his feet, the first sign of humility she'd seen from him.

Colt spoke quieter now to Ash. "Just say fuck 'em, I'll help you fix the crankshaft, ride her hard into the sunset and never look back." Colt put a hand on Ash's shoulder. For a moment Ash looked like a lost little boy. He was young but his confidence and his attitude glossed that over previously. Colt offered him the safety and comfort to drop his guard for a moment, and it melted April's heart.

Ash looked up at Colt. "Turning my back on my family... it's final, isn't it? My sister... I wouldn't want to leave her, my parents... I think they might change, come around with some time..." He took a shaky breath.

"Time changes some things. But sometimes it changes nothing at all," Colt replied, sounding older than his thirty-five years.

She moved forward and squeezed her hand on Ash's arm, wanting to show him she was supporting him, too. Wanting Colt to know she saw what he was doing, and wanted to stand alongside him and help.

"Colt will take a look at your bike tomorrow, Ash." She cleared her throat, emotion had stuck it together.

"You've got your tattoo appointment tomorrow." Ash raised his chin, clearing his throat, getting back to business. Colt removed his hand from Ash's shoulder. Ash continued, "Dane said he was up for it. He'll have his equipment ready-"

"Great, what time?"

"Two o'clock."

Colt shrugged. "Fine, thanks. But I'll be free before that-"

"You've got your deep tissue shoulder massage then lunch-"

"Fuck, you know my schedule better than I do." Colt gave Ash a half smile. He returned it. "After my tattoo then-"

"You'll be hurting-"

"Fuck that, your crank shaft is hurting me more than a bit of extra ink on my skin will." Colt shrugged.

Ash hesitated, running his eyes once over Colt, and herself, one last time. "Okay then," Ash said finally.

"Some vacation this will be for you, Mr. Black." April smiled at them both, joking to try to relieve the heaviness that Ash seemed to be struggling with. "You'll be either underneath a bike covered in oil, or underneath a tattoo needle covered in blood."

Ash cleared his throat. "Or underneath April covered in-"

Colt stopped him saying any more with a light punch to the arm and a roll of his eyes.

Chapter 40
COLT

Dane was fucking good, actually. He was a young, slight guy with hair that was shaved on the sides but long on top, so that it fell forward or could form a mohawk if he gelled it. He'd taken a look with quiet thoughtfulness at the existing tattoos all over Colt's body. Dane had inspected the cigarette burns over the smaller tattoo on his bicep with a hiss. They'd have to wait until the burns had fully healed before considering that one, he'd said. Colt had shrugged, that was fine, he didn't care, as long as the yawning skull was covered up, and the lettering, which his clumsy cigarette burns had achieved anyway. Dane had continued the rest of his inspection. Dane's pale, long fingers roving and fluttering over Colt's naked torso. Colt trusted Dane enough to show him his back. The black coyote tattoo, his former MC's insignia, the coyote skull. Gazing blankly out of empty eye sockets. Hide it, Colt had said. Dane had paused thoughtfully and then replied, what if instead of hiding it under another tattoo, they hid it in plain sight. Dane had hesitated, but then shared his idea further; flesh out the skull. Have a snarling, living coyote face on top of the skull. Colt liked it. There was still an emotional connection for Colt to the Black Coyotes MC. He'd worn that insignia on his back so proudly. It had meant home, family. But now he found it to be as cold and empty as the fucking coyote skull. Flesh it out, what a fucking good idea. Create more, from less.

If he was still in charge of the MC, he'd update the insignia. Everyone would have to get updates to their tattoos. It would be a good opportunity for them to prove their loyalty. Start fresh. Cleaver would be history, kicked out. Stop all the shit the MC was currently caught up in. Bring Ash in to Prospect.

Hell, as he thought of all these changes, lying half naked under the needle of this skinny young tattoo artist, Colt felt a stabbing pain. Cold and brutal. But it wasn't from the tattoo gun. It was from thinking about home. About what had been done to his family. About how he burned to fix it. He shook his head to shake that out of him. It was hopeless. He'd turned his back and ran away. Fucking run away, chased out by them. Turn around and never look back, they said to him. He'd already won, he was already living the dream. Ridden off with April, into the sunset. Beautiful, untouchable April in his bed every night. Sucking his cock, riding him until she couldn't speak and he couldn't, either.

Sweet fuck, he got hard right there. He was lying on his stomach on Dane's kitchen table, as the kid didn't have his own studio yet. He had the gun, the ink, all the equipment, gloves. Colt had been satisfied that it was all clean, but it just meant he was face down on a towel, with a raging hard on.

Colt was winning at life, for now. Could he stay ahead, though, that was the question. He was satisfying her for now, yes, he knew he made her happy. Fuck only knew why, but when she smiled at him, it lit his world. And he knew it was a genuine one, she was truly content. But they couldn't stay at The Pines forever. They couldn't run forever. She said that they'd figure it out. She said she was going to think. And he didn't doubt, when April set her mind to something, it happened. She was that kind of woman. Colt imagined her in a suit and heels.

Hell, she'd get shit done. She could fucking run for President of the United States, and the country would be a better place for it. He had faith that she'd be able to come up with a plan. But he was sure it meant running and hiding. Getting fake IDs and going to the other side of the country. Hell, maybe even the other side of the world. It would be the end of his involvement with the Black Coyotes MC.

"It's going to be fearsome. Snarling," Dane said from above, cutting into Colt's thoughts. "It's going to be a warning. But it's also a mark of what you've been through, what you've survived. You are who you are because life has thrown shit at you that has turned you into this aggressive, fearless, rare coyote. And you're going to need to channel that again, sometime, no doubt. But it's here, waiting for you when you need it."

Colt didn't say anything, Dane didn't seem to need any answer. He was saying it more to himself. Colt eventually spoke up. "I want another one," he muttered into the towel.

"Huh?" Dane said, almost surprised to hear Colt, like he'd forgotten he was there. Dane was a bit of a daydreamer. Colt thought he and Ash made a strange couple. He couldn't see it lasting long.

"Want another tattoo. Down here." Colt indicated to his front groin.

Dane's eyebrows rose a fraction of an inch. "What would you have? It'd be sensitive, the lower stomach area, or even your hip bone-"

"I don't care. I want a kitten, a little black kitten, just the silhouette, no cartoony shit."

Dane nodded. "Okay, I'll draw up some sketches, we can talk them through tomorrow."

Colt felt a little lightheaded, imagining having that little reminder of April in such a soft, vulnerable area. "Fuck it, and another tattoo. A lioness, with big, wise eyes that say don't fuck with me."

"Okay..." Dane's imagination was instantly whistling away, Colt could see it in his eyes. "Where?"

"I dunno... on my lower back?" Colt suggested, twisting to look and see.

Dane pursed his lips. "How about high up, on your butt cheek here, so it pokes out the top when you're wearing pants, but is only really visible and appreciated in all its glory when you've got your pants off..."

Colt thought about it. "Yeah, I like that idea. A lioness on my ass cheek, my upper thigh, my lower hip-" Colt starts indicating with his hand on his body.

"Yes, exactly." Dane follows his hand with his. "Head here, I imagine her looking back at us perhaps, as she slinks away, body all sinew. Her eyes saying 'fuck with my pride and I'll rip you to pieces and slurp the flesh off your bones and leave your carcass to rot in the desert'," Dane finished intensely, caught up in the drama of his imagination.

"Er... yes, that," Colt said, slightly worried about Dane's love for the macabre. He'd be a cool Prospect, too, actually. A resident tattoo artist, someone clever, steady handed, introverted and pensive. They always had a lot to bring to the table, the quiet ones. Dane might want to beef up a bit, but that's why they had a weights room... Damn it. Colt couldn't stop thinking like the Prez of the MC. It's who he was. He needed to snap out of it, but he just couldn't.

So Colt would lay there, musing away. Dane cleaned and wrapped the area he'd worked on that day, and Colt would head back to the Pines. He'd wanted to drive the van, but April had said no, keep the van off the road. It made sense, but it meant Ash called a taxi for Colt. He hated getting driven into town, he felt like a pussy. Colt hated anything that made him feel powerless and trapped. And riding in a taxi the short few miles into town did just that. But he'd put up with it for now, he had to.

The mornings started early, six a.m. wake up. They had fallen into a comfortable routine, and Colt loved it. Days ran into a second week, after they agreed to extend their stay. A routine, who would have thought it? He woke up in the mornings and could not wait for the day to begin. The alarm would sound, he'd reach over for April, and either pull her over him, like a second blanket, or he'd snuggle into her, bury his face in her hair and press against her warm, soft little body. But then she'd start stirring and they'd wake up together. The first few days Colt would wake up with a raging hard on and a sexual appetite to match and he'd mercilessly get down to the serious task of fucking her.

But they both learned that hard, messy sex before an hour and a half of yoga wasn't the best idea. April complained that his cum kept leaking out of her. While the thought of that drove him half wild, they decided to hold off until after yoga and breakfast. Colt was getting into the whole yoga thing. The stretches were really helping his body, he felt more connected, stronger. Like his body was beginning to work right for the first time in forever. He focused on the present, letting any thoughts of his brothers and the MC come and go.

He let go of what wouldn't serve him that day, and focused on how he was going to move forward. He stood still, breathed deep, and stretched hard. He heard his heart beating and felt the breath in his lungs. He listened to the positive affirmations that the instructor said. He noticed how beautiful the morning was when he walked out of the studio. He left the yoga classes feeling more put together and capable and ready for the day than he'd ever felt in his life. At first he'd hated admitting it to April. But then he'd embraced it, rolled with it and now was thoroughly enjoying it. Even the yoga pants were becoming quite comfortable.

Colt would then go down to the restaurant and meet April for breakfast, feeling light and limber and in control of his mindset. She'd smile and greet him with a civilized kiss on the cheek. They would eat breakfast, he had no clue what half of it was and he no longer cared. At first they'd start off calmly, chatting about their classes, how they were, nibbling delicately on dark rye bread and fruit pieces. Then Colt would start getting ravenous, but not for food. April, too, he'd notice her lips hang off her spoon, a fraction of a second longer than she should or needed to. Her eyes lingering on his lips. His hands. She'd cross her legs, fidget in her seat, change legs. He'd start shoveling food into his mouth for what he knew was about to come.

Then they'd be too distracted for any more food, and they'd stumble out of the restaurant like love sick teenagers, eyes only for each other. Colt's cock would be plumping in those fucking pants, and she'd get breathy and giggly. And they'd finally trip back into their cabin, slamming the door behind them.

Then came manic undressing like their clothes were burning their skin. Sometimes they took a shower, sometimes not. Colt insisted on making it to the bed though. That was his one rule. Once there, any bets were off as far as gentlemanly behavior from Colt was concerned. They'd go hard, April screaming by the end with every ferocious pound. He couldn't get enough. He couldn't get deep enough, he couldn't give her enough of him. And the release, when he caught up to it, was teeth shattering.

Colt also just loved the aftermath, too, though. Lying there, most often sweaty and pulsing and panting. Alive and living the dream, with a satiated April stretched out beside him. Full of his cum, smiling languidly back at him. He got high off it. They'd finally get up again around mid morning. April did some of the other classes. Her favorite was sound therapy. She described it like she went into a room and lied down and listened to someone playing a giant gong. Colt couldn't face something like that. He'd work on Ash's bike, or get a massage on his shoulder, which already felt better. Or he'd go into town to see Dane, get some work done on his tattoos.

Once he got back to the Pines, he'd meet April in the spa. He had to be careful of his tattoo work and couldn't get that wet, but he'd go and sit at the side of the jacuzzi, dangling his feet into the hot, fizzing water, his calves and feet welcoming the feel. He liked it when she was there alone, and he could talk to her openly. Murmur about how he'd missed her and what he wanted to do to her. She'd be relaxed and lethargic after her yoga or Pilates, mindfulness and sound therapy shit or whatever else it was she'd done that afternoon. She'd smile and bat her eyelashes, that would be dark and clumped together from the water, her skin glowing and pink from the heat. Sometimes, though, April wasn't alone, there were others with her. Colt could sometimes hear giggling and squeals before he'd even left the changing room. He'd walk out into the spa and groan a little.

The spa was all white marble with gold accents. It smelled of rosemary and eucalyptus. There was a big pool for swimming, and three hot tubs to the side. There were saunas on the other side, and treatment rooms where he'd go for his massages. But April was always in the jacuzzi. If she was there with a gaggle of other ladies, he'd go over, smile and wave and give her a kiss. He'd wink to the others, and stroke April's check tenderly.

He made a show of it, he liked to make the other ladies raise their eyebrows and giggle. He liked to make April flustered and blushing. Then he'd go and lay on one of the loungers. He'd just close his eyes and tune out the gossipy women, listen to the water ebbing, music, just soak up the calm and thank his lucky stars he wasn't in prison or dead.

There was a couple their age that Colt had taken an immediate dislike to. When he saw April in the jacuzzi with them he'd grind his teeth, ignore them completely as he bent down to April and grabbed her chin or her neck. He'd kiss her possessively, roughly, and fix them with a cold glare. Then stalk over to a lounger immediately. He didn't care how uncomfortable it made them. Or how unpopular it made him. Something about them made him feel slimy. The woman had lip fillers that made her look like a guppy, bleached blonde hair, and wore all of her makeup in the pool. Her mascara always seemed gloopy and smudged. And she wore her jewelry, too. Big, gold hoops in her ears, necklaces around her neck, and bangles on her wrists that jingled every time she gestured with her hands, which was often as she talked a lot.

The guy with her was a sleazy ass, too. He had a mustache, which he clearly thought made him look more edgy or something. It didn't, it made him look like a goat. He also wore his big silver Rolex in the water. They clearly felt they had to prove something and couldn't be without their status symbols. Their teeth were both bleached an unnatural paper white and Colt had the urge to punch him hard.

One particular day, after Colt had got the last bit of the black coyote fleshed out on his back, he'd gone to join April in the spa and the couple had been there. "Oh, your husband is just so good looking." The woman squeaked in her New York drawl as Colt loped over to them.

"Now, now honey bun, you making me jealous?" The mustache

THE CHASE

guy laughed out loud. Too loud, too desperate. Colt didn't even think, he just dropped to his knees and kissed April from the poolside.

"Stay, Mr. Black, we want to get to know you!" The woman trilled and jabbed a claw-like manicured fingernail his way.

"Yeah, come on buddy, let's talk business, man to man."

Colt snorted like a raging bull. Preparing to charge. He looked to April to say, get me out of here. April had a mischievous little smirk on her face. "Yes, come in here, Mr. Black, let me introduce you to Clarissa and Miles."

Colt gave her a loaded look. Fine, you want to play, he thought. I'll fucking play.

CHAPTER 41
APRIL

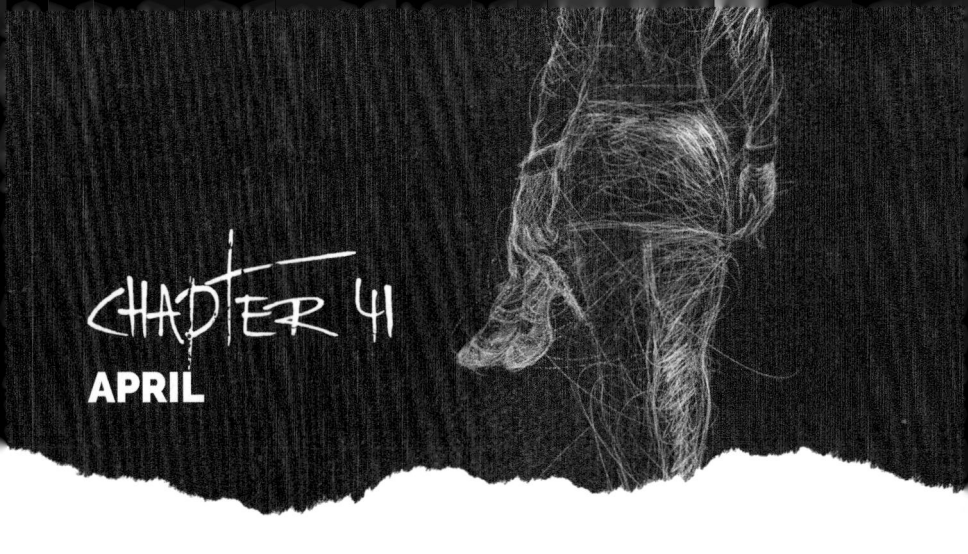

April bit the inside of her cheek to stop herself from laughing. She wanted to watch Colt squirm a little, try to play nice.

"Hi guys." Colt plastered an obviously fake smile on his face and sat down on the edge of the jacuzzi next to April, planting his feet on the seat in the water where the others sat. April hoped this wasn't a terrible mistake.

"Get in here, you!" Clarissa cackled, and Colt got an eye full of huge fake tits as she jiggled in an attempt to entice him as if he were a dog responding to a bone. April noticed smugly that he didn't glance down at Clarissa's tits. He was the definition of nonchalant. He was only a foaming beast about her own tits.

"Ahh, sorry, sugar, I can't." Colt bent sideways to show the large white dressing Dane had conscientiously taped onto his back, covering the whole of the coyote tattoo.

"Ahh, tattoos!" Clarissa squealed with delight.

"So man, what do you do for a living?" Miles butted in, clearly put out that Clarissa was blatantly ogling Colt. He couldn't help it, being sat on the side of the pool in those ridiculously skimpy speedos, he looked like he was modeling the latest swimwear for the front cover of a men's fashion magazine.

"You aren't an underwear model are you?" Clarissa gasped, "You could be. April, you lucky girl, you!"

April smiled like the cat who ate the canary. He smiled at April, it appeared he liked that he could give her that.

Colt laughed. "No, I'm a porn star." Clarissa stopped mid-gape. Miles choked on jacuzzi water. April clamped her lips together to stop herself from laughing. Colt held them all there, enjoying the shock, awe and horror. "Nah, not really, I'm a carpenter. Upcycled furniture…" he said. April was pleased he'd remembered the lines they'd practiced in case this question should come up. He followed her script.

"Ooh," cooed Clarissa, who had been flapping her hand as if she couldn't breathe since he'd said the word upcycled. "I love all that kind of stuff, all the vintage shabby chic stuff, we commissioned our coffee table. Miles, do you remember-"

"Yeah, honey, so you own a business? I'm a stockbroker myself, Wall Street, of course-"

"Course." Colt bared his teeth.

"You employ a team of carpenters? The corporate tax is a pain in the ass, isn't it? Where are you based?"

"I get my hands dirty enough," Colt replied ambiguously to all of Miles' questions at once. April swirled the bubbling water in front of her, she was enjoying this, but she could see Colt's patience wearing thin with each second.

"Well, we'll see you later on, we better get ready for dinner, darling," April said, standing up in the jacuzzi. Colt's eyes darted to her, and he suddenly looked hungry. She recognized that half-hooded expression, she saw his pupils dilating. She ran a hand down over her arms, on the pretense of wiping the water off her. In reality, she wanted him to appreciate her slick with water in her little black bikini top, to want her. April dared a glance at Miles, he saw, too, he was practically licking his lips. Colt caught it, as well, and looked like he was about to tear the limbs off him.

Miles stood, too. He had a hairless, tattoo-less body with limited muscle definition. Colt could have knocked him out in one swing, April thought smugly.

"Yes, us, too, we'll walk with you. April, speaking of getting ready, I'm getting my nails done in town tomorrow..." Clarissa clambered out of the jacuzzi, too, grabbing her arm and drawing her into a discussion about nail salons. April didn't listen, she kept an ear on Miles and Colt, hovering to step in if she needed to.

Miles regarded him thoughtfully. "Hey, buddy, I've been meaning to ask you, your vest, the leather one that you're always wearing, I've been looking for one myself like that… What's the brand?"

Colt stared at him for an inordinate amount of time. "No brand," Colt said finally.

Miles snorted. "Well then, where did you buy it?"

"Yard sale. It's second hand," Colt mumbled.

"Dude, you may think I'm crazy for saying this but… I think it might have belonged to a motorcycle gang member!"

Colt fixed him with a stare. April pursed her lips, trying to listen over Clarissa's inane babble.

"What?" Colt said, buying time.

"Well, I heard these guys, you know, they join a motorcycle gang, get up to all sorts of illegal shit, well, each member has a name, like a road name, like Axel or Midnight or something, and they have their names and emblems sewn on..."

"Oh, right?" Colt feigned interest.

Miles spoke like he was talking about a government conspiracy, loving his role of storyteller. "I know your jacket has… provenance."

"Provenance?"

"Yeah, you know, like was owned by someone before you, it has history of ownership, like an antique, or a work of art... it could have been worn by a murderer, or a drug dealer-"

"Right."

"Speaking of..." Miles laughed and lowered his voice, attempting to draw Colt in close, but April was amused to see Colt walking along too fast to join Miles in a conspiratorial huddle. "I hit the blow too hard, it's why we're here, Clarissa thought I needed help, stupid bitch, she says I'm not me when I've taken it, but fuck, I'm needing a hit now my friend, I can tell you..." Miles pursed, eyeing Colt, who said nothing, gave nothing away. "You wouldn't happen to know anyone I could call, or have any yourself, just a little hit, just to get me through, this place is a fucking nightmare and she's making me crazy-"

"No drugs," Colt simply stated and kept walking.

Miles almost cried out loud, but turned it into a loud, fake laugh, and caught up with Colt's pace. "Fuck man. Fuck. I wish it was the old man of that jacket I was speaking to-"

"Can't help you with that."

"Jeez, we've all seen your tattoos, could be a biker or a drug dealing criminal yourself, you sure look the part." Miles tried to joke.

April held her breath. Colt didn't laugh. Her and Clarissa were closer now, Miles cleared his throat, changing the subject. "I've thought about getting a tattoo myself before. I think they look great, they're expensive, too, huh? Well, I wasn't sure what I'd actually get-"

"Then you don't need a tattoo." Colt stopped in his tracks and turned to face Miles.

"I... what?"

"If you don't know what you want to get tattooed, then there is nothing to tattoo." April and Clarissa had caught up with them now. Colt radiated wild energy, something dangerous and unpredictable, like electricity crackling. "I tattoo my skin because I have to get that darkness out of me. I need it on my skin, otherwise it is under my skin, festering in my heart, poisoning my blood, burnt onto my eyelids so there is no relenting, even in sleep. That's what my tattoos are for. If there was something you have, something not even safe to keep in a safe, something you couldn't lose, something you would run back into a burning building for… That is what you get tattooed on your skin."

Colt said nothing more. They all blinked at him.

Miles leaned closer and whispered conspiratorially. "Hey listen, I know this is meant to be a tee-total retreat but, er… we managed to smuggle in a bottle of Don Julio 1942 tequila, expensive stuff, we put it on ice, come round tonight, we can have a drink on the veranda."

"No thanks," Colt replied. "We don't drink," he said finally.

April cleared her throat. "But thanks for the invite, maybe just a jasmine tea or something-"

Clarissa trilled. "Well sure, honey-"

"Why don't you drink?" Miles dug impolitely.

April bit her lip, watching the exchange of terse comments like a tennis match, as the ball was batted from one side of the net to the other. They had practiced this, Colt was going to own up to being an alcoholic, they were here to clean him up, rather than go straight to rehab… Colt gritted his teeth. "Why do you think?"

Miles smirked. April could see what he was doing, what a dickhead. "I think you're the kind of guy who likes a good time, too much of a good time… hey, we've all been there, pretty girls, bringing around trays of booze, champagne flowing-"

She couldn't take it any more. "I drank," April butted in. All three heads turned to her. "It was me, I had a problem with alcohol and I…" She fizzled out, breathless.

Colt blinked at her. She'd stepped in and batted for him. April couldn't bear it. Why were these people being so judgmental? She didn't need to step in, Colt wasn't embarrassed. He couldn't care less what these people thought of him, she knew that. He wasn't surprised that they had assumed, out of the two of them, it was him that had the alcohol problem. They didn't drink, and all eyes were pointed at Colt. He had to be the reason, the cause, the culprit. Because he had tattoos and long hair. And a leather jacket. Because he swore and did not form all of his sentences with perfect grammar. Because he looked rougher, different. April hurt for him. She wanted to challenge this, stand up to it. For him. She didn't need to, but she wanted to. She wanted to rage beside him. In this and everything else.

Chapter 42
COLT

He loved her for it. He was the happiest man on the planet. He was flying high. She really did care. He tried not to grin. Instead he put his hand on the top of her head, her warm, wet head. She flashed him a little smile that was almost apologetic. He'd dreamed of pulling her into his darkness, but she was showing she'd step into it willingly for him. His cock plumped up, but not as much as his heart. Something in him swelled with joy, filled his soul with pride and, fuck it, love.

He growled under his breath, just for her ears only, but he didn't care if Miles and Clarissa heard, "home. Now. Bed, Kitten."

And that was how he found himself hovering over her naked body minutes later. In their cabin, on the bed. She was very wet, lying on her back, eyes half closed, aching with anticipation, her hands reaching out for him. And he fell, drawn into her grasp like a magnet. He couldn't have fought it if he wanted to. But something had changed. It wasn't fast and physical, eating his fill, or satiating her. It wasn't about feasting on what he wanted and buzzing with satisfaction afterwards. There wasn't a build up, foreplay, then a peak and a release. This time felt different. He held his throbbing cock to her warm, wet pussy, and pushed in, inch by inch. Slowly, agonizingly slow. He pushed deep, excruciatingly deep. Keeping eye contact with her. More than skin touching this time. His balls were nestled against the roundness of her ass cheeks. He curled so he could kiss her hard little nipples. Then he rested his forehead against her chest. Her heartbeat kicked his mind into a new plane of reality. More than wetness flowing between them. She reached a hand up to his chest and laid it on his heartbeat. His heart beat her name. Ap-ril. Ap-ril. Could she hear? Did she know?

He lifted his head up from her chest and really looked at her. She was gazing back up at him. And he saw it. Yes, she knew, she felt it, too. The wild look in her eyes told him she hadn't been prepared for this, hadn't expected this, but here it was, raw and real.

Her hands on him, skimming over his chest tenderly. His arms with appreciation. His shoulders with love. She lightly tapped his nipple bar, giving him a beautiful burst of stardust pleasure, then skimmed her nails smoothly down the center of his stomach, over his hip, to his butt cheek. It wasn't hard and rough, it was gentle. It was her hands telling him she loved him. He knew it. He could speak that language, too. The language of touch. He touched her with his forehead, his lips. He wanted to keep both hands on the mattress, to control the pace. He could keep this up for hours. It wasn't about coming anymore. He might come, and he would just carry on, forever. He wasn't worried about blowing too early. Or being too rough. Or being unworthy. Or not deserving her.

He loved her, that was all there was to it. And he fucking deserved to love and be loved, because he was a man, not a monster. Each deep stroke inside her said it. Each ragged breath from his lips onto her hot, damp skin, spoke it. They would roll on, coming together, all night, all the nights. It wasn't climbing to the top of the cliff and jumping off, it was rolling and tumbling together forever.

He licked his lips, moving slowly, deeply. "April," he began.

"Colt I-"

"Wait, let me say it first, April, I want to say-"

"Colt."

"I love you. April, I fucking love you," he whispered. And now he had spilled the truth, it tumbled off his lips like it had always meant to. Like the words had belonged there all along. Had been there all along. And they would always be there. They felt right at home there. He trusted her, with every fiber of his being. He respected her, everything he did was for her. Every breath in his lungs, every beat of his heart, hers. He loved her, and he would always love her. He got it now, they went to bat for each other. Her fights were his fights. Her victories were his, and his were hers. And together they would take on the world.

"Colt, I love you, too, I don't know how to say... how much I..."

He sighed. He roared. His heart flipped and soared. She loved him. April. Ap-ril, Ap-ril, Ap-ril.

Her hips continued to rock against his. They moved against each other, he felt they were perfectly wet, perfectly in sync. He got it now, this felt right. This was the truest thing in the universe. She was completely enough for him, and together they formed something that was all encompassing. He was a man, in love with his woman. And he didn't need to chase anything else. He had it all, right here. And he had the courage to dream it would be like that forever. For the first time, he wanted something to endure, to stay like this, raw and new and pure. He wanted to keep it safe and treasure it. He wanted to treasure her now and forever. He didn't want to even consider the possibility that something could threaten it. They were safe, in love, hiding from the chase in their bubble in the Pines. And he was happy thinking of nothing else.

CHAPTER 43
APRIL

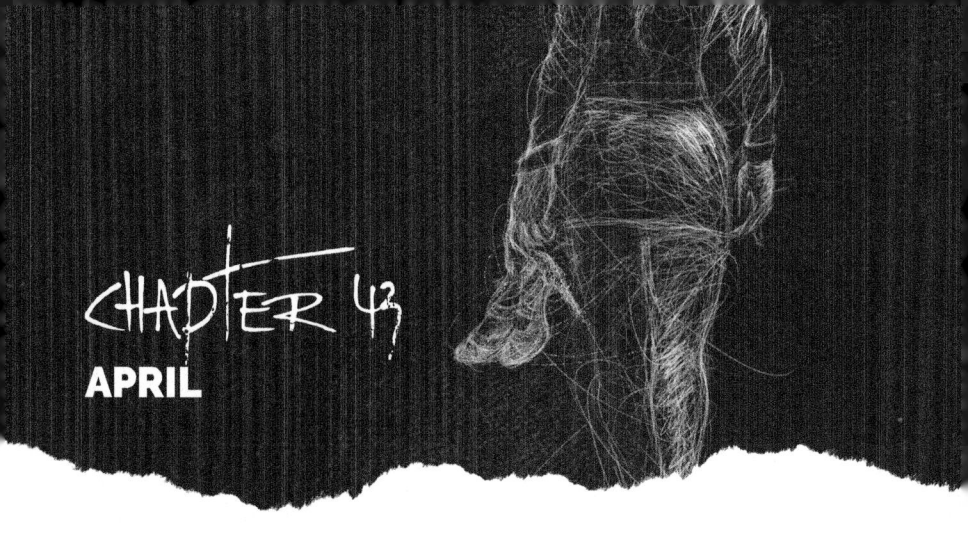

April felt the safety of their little bubble, too, and loved it. But she knew, deep down, it couldn't last forever. They had fallen into a cozy night time routine. They would lock the door and light the log burning stove. Sometimes they just lay there. April sometimes read a book, curled up on the sofa. Colt often stared into the fire, either lost in thought or existing in the moment, she couldn't quite tell. They'd talk very little, just content in each other's company. Sometimes they made love; slowly, sweetly, lying together spooning on the sheepskin rug in front of the fire. Other times it was fast and hot, with her straddling him on the sofa as he sat there, legs splayed wide apart, hands on her ass, pumping her up and down, slamming into her. Eyes locked onto each other, always.

A few nights ago she had warned him she was on her period. She hadn't been sure how the conversation would go, how he would take it. She knew he would respect her, if she said no, he'd do as he was told. Except she didn't want him to say no. Colt had come up behind her when she was changing, he'd put a hand between her legs, his thumb skimming close to her anus, his fingers massaging her folds over her panties. He'd growled in her ear that he wanted in. She said she'd pleasure him instead. He countered, saying he loved getting blown by her hot little needy mouth, but that he wanted to be deep inside her. Inside her body, her core, her soul. She was a sucker, she'd agreed as long as they did it in the shower. Colt smirked and joked that he could pretend he was popping her cherry like he should have done years ago. She'd rolled her eyes and shoved him playfully into the shower cubicle. It had been a very light period, she'd stopped bleeding just the next day. She scratched her head over it and Colt had drawled that maybe he'd fucked it all out of her. She told him not to be a sick bastard. He'd smiled lazily and said that with her, nothing was off limits. They'd done anal, too. Her first time. He'd nonchalantly called Ash and barked down the phone that he needed lube. April had scoffed at the ridiculous request. But Ash, the ever helpful concierge had delivered a paper bag with a bottle of lube in it, minutes later. April had bared her all to Colt, and he wanted more. And she gave more, with Colt, she had no limit to how much she would give him. And he always lapped it up. She wasn't talking about sex anymore, it was love, irrefutably.

To surprise him, she'd changed into a lace playsuit, again, Ash had met that shopping request with aplomb, and donned the original 'fuck shoes' as he called them, from that very first time they'd met. Her gold Manolo Blanik stilettos. He'd told her they were fuck shoes. She had been outraged and turned on. And outraged that he'd turned her on. So she thought it would be fun to put them on and wait for him on the bed while he went outside for a smoke. His only smoke of the day, she noted proudly. When he came back in she'd been lying on her stomach, her knees bent, bouncing her feet back and forth playfully. She asked him to show her what he meant by fuck shoes. His eyes had blacked out, so they were just giant dark pupils. He warned her that he wouldn't be gentle, she was counting on it. He had been merciless. She'd been thrown against or on top of every piece of furniture in their room. The desk, the chest of drawers. Bent forwards, bent backwards. Commanded to scream, commanded to sit on his cock. She'd done it all, she'd taken it. She had wanted to feel what he was capable of. Now she knew.

He'd revealed the tattoos he got for her. She couldn't believe it. The little kitten, playful, on the sensitive, pale flesh inside his hip bone, on his lower groin. Then the large, fierce looking lioness, staring back at her with a look of haughty imperialism, over his butt cheek. Peeking above the top of his waistband, inviting intrigue, and also peeking below on his upper thigh. She was speechless. They were for her, and they looked incredible on his skin. "For you, my kitten, my fucking fierce little spitting kitten. My lioness, queen of the Savannah, ruler of my heart," he whispered as he nipped her ear lobe, then her collarbone. She stifled a gasp and took that moment for her own reveal. She'd shown him the bandage on her own lower hip area. At first he frowned and looked concerned, asking if she was hurt. She shook her head, peeled off the gauze and revealed her own tattoo. A skittish young horse, a colt, galloping forwards. He hissed in satisfaction, a look of pure bliss on his face, and kissed her continuously for the rest of the evening. Eyes closed, reckless kisses, that had gone rolling on and on. He slipped inside her but hardly moved, it had been bliss and agony at the same time for her until finally, he'd picked up the pace and finished them both off, their marks on each other's skin fueling them for eternity.

April was laying on the sofa, her head in Colt's lap. She was staring into the fire, watching the yellow flames light the wood, turning to orange and red embers. She was tired, so physically tired. The yoga, fresh air and calmer pace made her feel sleepy. But her mind was whirring away. She had a plan. She knew what she had to do. She thought about it every evening they had been here. Run it through a thousand times in her mind, trying different scenarios and variables, like a computer trying to work out a math problem. She had alighted on a plan, but she was scared. It would involve divulging something that she hadn't told him, that she should have right from the beginning. She knew it was a form of betrayal, what she kept from him. She didn't want to jeopardize what they had. She knew he'd be angry, hurt, and she should have revealed it earlier, much earlier. Like at the beginning. Why hadn't she? She put it off, hadn't wanted to give him any excuse to leave her behind, or to not get involved with her. Because she had known this would bother him.

And she couldn't even tell him about it now. She was going to wait until the last possible moment. She wanted to eke out as much blissful enjoyment from this as possible. Was Colt going to like this plan? Maybe he'd come around, after time. But at first, he would not be happy.

It was a starting point. And they had to go with that.

"Colt," she said, her voice sticking in her throat after a long stretch of silence. His eyes met hers and they were filled with such love. She felt sick.

"April," he replied, calm intimacy dancing in his eyes.

She cleared her throat before speaking again. "I've got a plan."

He perked an eyebrow up and his gaze dropped to her lips. "A plan? To get the MC off our backs? To end the chase?"

"Yes."

"You did say you'd think our way out of this... I'm all ears."

She traced her tongue around her lips nervously. "We have to meet someone," she began.

He frowned, "Who?" he said, an octave lower than before.

She felt her guard coming up. That shutter slamming down. Going into siege mode. Isolate and survive.

"Colt, you have to trust me on this. I can't say, I'll just message him and we'll arrange to meet-"

"Him? Who, April?" he growled. "If it's that fucking college douchebag ex-fiancé -"

"No! Colt, trust me, why would I go running back to him?"

"For money? I dunno, you've had your fill of dirty fucks with me and you want to go back-"

She raised her hand and cut him off bluntly. "Never going to happen. Don't even go there, Colt, I know you're angry but don't pick at that scab again-"

"Then why can't you say-"

"I just can't, okay? And when we go to meet him, you'll understand why. You're not going to be pleased-"

"I'm not pleased now."

"-But this person will be able to fix things. I'm confident of it," she said, trying to sound certain.

He looked anything but pleased. He looked furious. "So we're going to meet someone, who isn't your country club cock and isn't the cops..." He paused and looked at her pointedly.

She tilted and rolled her eyes and shook her head. "I can't believe I have to reassure you. I'm not turning you in or dumping you."

"Oh, well, that's fucking good to know," he ground out cagily.

She grabbed her phone. Colt eyed her with mistrust. Instead of texting, she navigated on the internet to a gardening fan blog site. Colt raised his eyebrows. She let him watch. April logged in, knowing her email address and password, typing them out furiously. She navigated a few pages. Colt peered down at the screen. Something about planting blue dahlias. She flung a look at Colt, who was watching what she was doing intently. He must think she'd gone mad. She quickly scrolled to the comments section and typed a question; can you plant blue dahlias in April?

Colt now flicked his look up to April. Clearly, he was confused. She wanted to allay his fears, but truth be told he had every right to be mistrustful. She felt she had broken his trust. The moment to speak up, to say something, would have been back in the MC clubhouse when they were being taken into that inner room. That had been the time to pipe up. Or later, when it transpired the MC had intel from somewhere about where to look, what vehicle they were in. She'd been so caught up in the chase that it had never seemed like the right time. She'd been selfish, she hadn't wanted Colt to get angry and drive off without her early on, then later, she hadn't wanted to ruin the mood. Relinquish an opportunity for them to be intimate. She realized now the full repercussions of it all.

"Now what?" Colt asked, cutting through her thoughts. He nodded down to the phone in her hands.

"We wait for a time and place to meet. Then, we meet," she said.

He stroked his stubble, the dissatisfaction clear on his face. "Well, fuck," he said finally.

She sighed. "Colt, I'm sorry-"

"Cigarette," he ground out, cutting her off before she could try to begin to explain. He heaved himself up from the sofa and crossed the room in a small number of strides.

She sighed, what could she say? "Please, Colt."

He shrugged on his jacket, patted the pockets to check he had his lighter and the pack inside them. She pulled herself up off the sofa.

"I'm trying my hardest here, Kitten, I really am, but this is just... shit," he said.

"I know, I promise, trust me-"

"April, fuck, I do trust you... but this... it's not that easy for me to

THE CHASE

just... say okay... after everything..."

"I know, I get it, I do, just know-" She was in front of him, she reached up, putting her hands around his head, deep in his hair and she kissed him. Hard. Just lips. A hard, pure, simple kiss where she attempted to convey all she felt for him. She poured her heart and soul into that kiss.

He froze at first, making her work for it, and she did. Then he warmed up a little, squeezed her lips back, and then even opened his mouth, flicked his tongue inside hers for a moment. He pulled away first and she let him.

She stared up into his eyes. "I think we have a couple of options, and this person we meet, he will be able to make them happen for us," she said, nodding to reassure him. Trying to reassure herself.

He grunted, his face passive. He gave her a flick of the head and stomped out of the cabin. She let him go.

CHAPTER 44
COLT

THE NEXT MORNING, Colt stood at the bus stop on the main square in the town, arms crossed. He had no intention of getting a bus. After a shitty sleep last night, he was pissed off. April stood beside him, fidgeting nervously. They were pretending to check the bus schedule, but Colt wasn't paying any attention to the times and bus routes in front of his eyes.

Who the fuck was this guy they were going to meet? Why was April nervous? She'd been distracted all morning. Last night she tossed and turned in bed before finally dropping off into a fitful sleep. But she didn't seem full of dread, she was almost... excited. Flitting about at breakfast, unable to settle on one plate of food.

Colt sighed. "What are we-" he began, but April cut him off.

"Colt, I told you before, we've got to check the bus times, bear with me just a moment," she said, her eyes scanning the minute details of the schedule, behind plastic in the bus shelter.

Colt ground his teeth. Fucking fine. She was saying they needed to do it her way. He'd follow, for now. He'd tried to ask a thousand questions about this meeting, but April had refused to answer. She just told him to let her take the lead. So he would. He'd play ball, but he hated not being in control, not calling the shots. The hairs on his arms bristled, he felt cold sweat on the back of his neck. He had the overwhelming urge to run. His guard was up. Adrenaline pumped through him. He knew he shouldn't fly off the handle, he needed to keep control of his temper. He knew it with his rational mind, but his body was telling him something else.

He was aware of someone else loping up to the bus stop. Slightly outside of his field of vision. Just on the periphery. He sensed their presence. There was no one else at the bus stop. The streets were quiet.

April turned beside him from the timetable and looked up. Her face changed as she took in the arrival of the stranger. Colt watched, trying to gauge how he should react, too, when he turned and faced whoever it was. April looked on in awe and warmth. Colt frowned. Who the fuck was this guy?

"You have got to be fucking kidding me," a gravelly voice cut through the morning air.

Unfamiliar to Colt, and yet so familiar it hurt. It physically pulled at his heart. A bodily thing. A chemical thing. His breath caught in his throat. His brain scrambled to make sense of it, yet his heart leapt.

Joy.

Relief.

Confusion.

Hurt.

Betrayal.

He wanted to hug the man and punch him at the same time.

"Daddy, don't swear," April quietly muttered, her arms coming up.

Colt turned around fully now to look straight at the man they were meeting. "You've got to be fucking kidding me," Colt echoed what the other man had just said.

The other man gently embraced his daughter, giving April a kiss on her forehead, then letting her go again. That was probably the only thing this man would be gentle about. He was a tough, rough bastard. He was the only man Colt was afraid of. The only man Colt idolized, adored, respected. Colt's savior. Colt's President.

Blue Rodgers. Former Black Coyotes President.

It was fucking Blue, alive and breathing, in the flesh.

Blue cleared his throat. "I goddamn well got you to guard April to avoid her falling in with the likes of you-"

"Yeah, but then you went and fucking disappeared, so someone had to step up and do your dirty work-"

Blue snarled. "Dirty work... I wanted April to be kept clean from-"

"Well tough shit, I got her dirty." Colt smirked.

"Fucking animal, I'm going to cut off your dick and shove it down your-"

"Not before I slice your-"

"Enough!" April boomed, stepping in between them because they'd squared up to each other and she could clearly tell neither of the men would back down. "Colt, I'm so sorry, I couldn't tell you my father was alive... in fact, I almost blurted it out at the clubhouse, but I'm glad I didn't because that would have probably caused more problems... I was so confused why everyone kept harping on about his ghost... I had to sign something to say I'd never disclose... anyway, I'm sorry."

Colt's ears heard the words, and his brain began to rationalize what April was saying, but his body still raged with emotion.

"Daddy, Colt saved me, the MC kidnapped me and were going to keep me there at the clubhouse as a whore but Colt came back and rescued me and has been keeping me safe ever since. We're being chased by the MC-"

Blue sucked his teeth. His gaze had been fixed on Colt, the most blue, piercing eyes you could imagine. Now his gaze flicked to April. Blue reared back. "Cleaver?"

"Yes," April tried to explain, flustered. "Cleaver is the President and excommunicated Colt, put a price on his head, so they could do some new deal with the Guardians of Purity or something... then Cleaver wanted to keep me as his sex slave. He said it was so the money from your cut of the pie could go back into their pot rather than paying me..."

Blue tutted. His gaze flicked back to Colt. "They cut off your colors?" he muttered, eyeing Colt intensely, knowing what that would involve.

Colt sniffed nonchalantly. "Nah. April persuaded them not to. Got it tattooed over."

Blue nodded once, seemingly appeased. Why they were suddenly answering to Blue, Colt had no fucking clue. But that was the kind of guy Blue was. A leader. Wearing an unmarked leather jacket, his steel gray hair still thick and long, pulled back in a ponytail. He had a long earring in one ear. A little silver charm dangled from it, an arrow. In jeans and well worn boots. He had a hawk-like face, April's delicate bone structure, Colt now recognized, but on Blue's impressive stature and in his wizened, male skin, it came across as chiseled, handsome. But deadly. Like Niagara Falls, powerful, draws you in. Then sends you plunging down to an icy cold death.

Blue had a few extra wrinkles around his eyes than he had when Colt had last seen him. His hair was fully gray now. And, Colt noticed with a slight puff of smugness, Blue had thickened out around the waist and sported a little paunch. Whereas Colt was in the best shape of his life. Colt took a breath in and drew himself up to his full height, shoulders back, stomach in. Blue was the same height as Colt. Colt had no idea if Blue had all of his muscles under that easy living

THE CHASE

blubber or not. Colt had seen Blue shirtless, back in the day, fucking women in the clubhouse, or working out in the club's gym. Colt had a flashback to being a skinny, malnourished kid, looking up to Blue, everything Colt wasn't and wanted to be. And now Colt stood in front of his idol. And Colt looked at Blue now as his equal, Blue saw it too, knew it. He acknowledged it with a chin lift.

Colt realized he was at a turning point, a crossroads in his life. He was on the cusp of seizing everything he had ever wanted. April was sleeping in his bed every night. Taking his cock bare every night. Wearing the fucking ring he'd bought her. Yeah, he was going to claim her. Right here, right now. And their freedom so they could end the chase and get on with living their lives. He had to seize it.

Blue cleared his throat and looked back at April, any previous aggression doused. "I've been trying to track you as soon as I heard Cleaver had brought you in-"

"I wondered if you were in communication with them somehow. They've been tracking us, they seem to find out what van we were in, what route we were taking..."

Blue tutted. "One of the members has... close relations with the FBI..."

"You fucking with me?" Colt said, eyes wide.

"Wait, who? Someone in the MC you are in touch with?" April asked.

"Yeah," Blue rasped. Clearly he still smoked more than he should. "We got a man on the inside-"

Colt hissed. "A rat? We? Who's we?" Colt let out a roar of frustration, of impotence, he let it all go. "Why the fuck did you disappear? Why didn't you come back? Why didn't you come back for me?" Colt realized he was almost choking, he realized that he sounded like that lost, scared fifteen year old boy again.

Blue heard it, stepped forward and put his hand on the back of Colt's neck. Despite all his anger and posturing and bravado, Colt let himself relax into Blue's chest. And damn it, it felt good. The comfort, safety. Blue smelled the same, felt the same. He was the closest thing to a father Colt had ever had.

Blue knew that, too. "Son, I'm sorry." He cleared his throat. "I wanted to tell you, but I couldn't, still shouldn't but fuck it, this family reunion and my old age is turning me into a sentimental old bastard. I kept tabs on you in prison. Why do you think you only did five years for what should have been a double digit stay? I pulled all the strings I could."

Colt silently shook his head and stayed pushed into Blue's chest. Leather, smoke and home filled his nose. Filled his chest and his soul. He snorted it up like it was the purest cocaine money could buy.

"I'm FBI," Blue said finally. "Always have been. Undercover agent. Organized Crime and Gang section. But the bosses decided enough was enough, so I was pulled in. I didn't want to go. They said I was in too deep as it was. That night when the Guardians of Purity betrayed us, the FBI brought me back."

Colt was aware that April was snuggled into Blue's chest, too. They both clung to him like abandoned orphans. They practically were.

"You could have at least told us, we couldn't even find a body, Blue, we couldn't mourn properly, we couldn't move on..." Colt said, lifting his head, putting his hand on April's shoulders as she, too, nuzzled into Blue. It became an unconventional family hug.

"Ah shit, I... trusted you with my MC, Colt. I'm sorry I thought you'd all get over it and get on with life."

"We did until that raid five years ago. It was meant to be vengeance, for what happened to you. We were going to raid their gun stash.

THE CHASE

Instead, it turned into a shit show, bullets everywhere, fuck…" Colt growled. "Your FBI buddies do that?"

Blue raised a hand then. "That was part of a bigger play, Colt-"

"I'm not a fucking pawn in your game of chess-"

"No?" Blue raised his voice now, took a step back. "Then stop acting like one. You're just running and running Colt, someone chases you, you turn and run. That raid wasn't supposed to end with you doing time but it meant we got an undercover agent in the Guardians of Purity, so it was a sacrifice that had to be made-"

"Fuck, you're still FBI?" Colt snarled.

"Yes, fucking running the department now, so you better play the game."

"I'm not your pawn, Blue".

"Then pick up the queen or something, you dick. Master the game." Blue poked Colt hard in the chest with his hand, his four fingers.

April stepped in front of them again. "That's why I asked for a meeting, Daddy. I have two ideas, well one main one and one slightly wacky one… two plays that I think could end this chase. I want a permanent solution, I'm not running forever, I'm not spending the rest of my life worrying that the MC might kidnap me again."

Blue flexed his jaw. "I'm sorry that happened, April, I'm sorry I failed you."

She shook her head, dismissing his apology. "It doesn't matter, it happened, and now we move on."

"Let's hear your ideas then," Blue said, raising his chin, folding his arms over his chest.

April flicked her gaze to Colt, who nodded, he wanted to hear this, too. "Okay…" She licked her lips. "Well, first idea. We testify against Cleaver and the MC. You've got kidnapping, assault, forced imprisonment-"

"They imprisoned you?" Blue snapped.

April bit the side of her cheek. "Only for a bit."

"They tied her to the bed for a gang bang. Lucky I went back for her, eh?" Colt interjected. Blue's face went thunderous.

"So then," April continued quickly, "we get witness protection…"

Blue's head snapped back as if he'd just been punched. "You wouldn't want to go back to San Francisco? You had everything… good job, nice apartment, that college guy at your beck and call-" Then he paused. "Wait, We… as in you and Colt? Fuck me," Blue muttered.

April raised her eyebrows. "Yes, Colt and me. That's right, witness protection together. I'm not going back to San Francisco and my boring job and my poky condo and that college douchebag-"

Colt interjected now, "He really was a douchebag."

Blue looked at Colt. "You met him?"

"I tipped a tray of drinks all over him," Colt said smugly. Blue grunted with approval.

CHAPTER 45
COLT

"I can organize witness protection for you, new IDs, new life. We could set you up anywhere… a job, a house, a quiet life." Blue cleared his throat.

Colt felt slight panic. Not because it involved a future with April. His heart danced for joy at that and at how she'd defended him to her father. Reminding him he wasn't that little gutter rat anymore. Colt flexed his powerful body again to reaffirm it to himself, like how they'd taught him in one of the yoga classes. Fuck him but it worked. He squeezed his glutes and felt brave again. Powerful. Stronger than this old man in front of him. But the panicked feeling formed because of the mention of a quiet life. No more MC drama. No more belonging to something bigger than himself. No more playing by his own rules. He'd have to conform to society. Sit down, shut up, pay taxes. He'd have to answer to something else, someone else. It felt like defeat, somehow. Yes, the MC wouldn't be chasing them anymore, but something would be missing.

Blue's voice cut through his musings. "What's wrong, Colt? Getting cold feet? Not loving the sound of playing house with my daughter?" he snarled.

April snapped her head around to take Colt in.

Colt cleared his throat and shook his head. "No, that's not it at all,

I want April by my side forever, Blue. I'm claiming her. She's mine."

"Fuck me. There is no table to claim her at-" Blue groaned.

"Fuck the table!" Colt yelled now. "You were the only one at the table that mattered to me. So now I come to you and tell you that I'm claiming April. See that ring on her finger? I put it there and I mean it." Colt crossed his arms over his chest, a challenge laid out now in front of Blue.

April smiled warmly at Colt, then bit her lip and tried to hide it when she turned back to Blue. He'd seen it though. He saw it all. Blue might be old but he wasn't stupid. He sighed in resignation.

"I always did trust you with my daughter," he said quietly now.

"Always will?" Colt probed.

Blue flicked his eyes over them both before nodding. "Always will," he agreed.

Colt took that as permission. His confirmation. Declaring it to someone else felt good. The pride he felt was tangible. He couldn't help himself, he reached for April. She returned an equally elated smile and leapt into his arms with a squeal. He'd claimed April. And fuck him, he couldn't stop grinning from ear to ear.

"I love you, Kitten," he found himself murmuring into her ear.

"Love you, Colt," he had the joy of hearing her whisper back.

Yeah, he could sacrifice MC life, being part of a brotherhood for this. He could stand in line and pay taxes for this. If this was what was waiting for him at home when he'd finished a mind numbing day doing some shit job. Wherever she wanted to go, he'd go with her, he'd follow her to the ends of the earth.

"Sorry to break up the romantic scene but before you two start fucking and doves fly overhead..." He shot them both a pointed glare. "What's your second idea then?" Blue's voice cut through his haze.

He shook himself, putting April down. He was hard, of course.

THE CHASE

He didn't make any attempt to hide it. Blue noticed and rolled his eyes.

April nodded and smoothed down her T-shirt after it had rucked up in Colt's embrace. "Sure. My second idea," April said, a little breathy, smoothing down her hair now too. Colt couldn't help but smile, she was equally turned on by their embrace. "Plan number two. It's harder, but I think greater pay off..."

"Right..." Blue said slowly, gesticulating for her to continue.

"Bring down the MC. Reinstate Colt as President. Wipe the slate clean," April said.

In the silence that followed, Colt could have heard a cloud passing overhead. He suddenly took a gasp of air, because he'd forgotten to breathe.

"April... you're talking about a strong MC full of thugs who are currently chasing us. You want to, what?"

"Turn around and chase them back. Hunt them down. Do whatever needs to be done to get them off the face of the earth," she said simply, like she was talking about rearranging the living room furniture.

Blue scoffed. Colt gulped. Fucking bold idea. Him, Prez again... the Black Coyotes... his brotherhood, his kingdom. He rolled his shoulders back and down and turned to face Blue.

"I give you my queen." He aimed a half bow at April. "I told you, Blue, not your pawn. I play my queen." Colt raised his chin in challenge.

Blue raised an eyebrow. "If we put the legal and moral issue of somehow killing twenty or so men aside..." Blue rubbed the back of his neck, under his ponytail.

April merely blinked. His lioness, Queen of the Savannah, was fucking fierce. Terrifying, beautiful, determined to get what she wanted. At all costs.

"Why do you want this, Kitten?" Colt quietly asked.

April didn't break eye contact with Colt. "I want it because you want it. I know it, Colt, you want your MC back."

Colt melted all over again for her. "Well fuck me Kitten-"

"Enough, very heart-warming, let's talk," Blue cut in. "If, big if, we do this, there are a few things you need to know. The MC will still need to work with law enforcement, we need an undercover agent or an informant at the very least."

"You are shitting me," Colt said, crestfallen.

Blue shook his head. "No, the buyers of your guns and drugs are all high priority targets. Homeland Security will need the MC to keep supplying the bad guys who buy your shit for our other sting operations to work out. We've got multiple fingers in multiple pies and the Black Coyotes MC is a key lynchpin for that."

Colt bit the inside of his cheek.

"I love the idea but I don't love having rats under my feet. Undermines the brotherhood. The trust-"

"My Black Coyotes had informants-" Blue began.

Colt shook his head. "And look how well that worked out, huh? It's a fucking mess of a club that allowed scum like Cleaver to float to the top."

"Only 'cause you got trigger happy during that raid…"

"That was your fault in the first place-"

"Hey." April slammed the heel of her fists into both of their chests. It was enough to knock some of the wind out of their sails and a lot of sense back in.

"I'd help you with the 'wiping the slate clean' bit… the current members, including Cleaver… they're expendable. The MC isn't, as an entity. I have access to resources that can be used for expendable targets," Blue explained, matter of factly. Colt had to remind himself they were talking about taking men's lives here. Scumbag men, yes, but still…

"He was the one who wanted to keep me as his whore," April said. Colt nodded. He heard what that meant. April wanted him dead.

"It's a heavy thing taking a life," Colt began quietly.

April shook her head passionately. "I know my mind, Colt. You can critique me for lots of things but not this. I want him to pay. For what could have been if you hadn't come back for me. Twice dammit, since I turned you down that first time, who was I kidding? They would have found me. And they would have hurt me. I want revenge." She said that last word with clenched teeth and fire in her eyes. She burned with it. Colt recognized it because he burned with the same. Cleaver took his brothers. Poisoned what was good. Desecrated Colt's holy place. Yes, Colt recognized that if it came to it, he knew he had it in him to end Cleaver.

"Well," Blue said, "Black Coyotes MC can have its slate wiped clean, but that still leaves us needing an FBI agent in the fold."

Colt's frustration simmered.

Blue shrugged smugly. "Welcome to the chessboard, now you have to sacrifice a pawn or two of your own, Colt." Blue cracked his neck. "It would need to be a clean club, we've had too many incidents with informants being bribed by drugs from dirty agents in other departments. No pills, no powders." Blue nodded.

April nodded, too. "Okay, well, I'd personally be very happy with that rule…"

"And you'd need to establish links with whoever we say, the Armenians, Bratva, the Columbians, if I say sell a hundred thousand dollars worth of guns, you do it-"

"And we could have legit businesses, too?" April interjected.

"I couldn't care less about any other businesses you want to run, so yes, sure-"

April practically giggled. She turned to Colt with such glee in her face, wide smile, eyes sparkling, cheeks flushed. But she clearly caught sight of his face and her smile slipped. "Colt, you've been awfully quiet, what's wrong?"

Colt took a slow, deep breath, and rubbed the back of his neck with the palm of his hand. He didn't want to pop April's high, or let down Blue, but he had to speak his mind.

"They are pretty big compromises," he said in a flat voice. April's mouth fell open.

He expanded. "I mean, being in the pocket of the Feds, doing whatever jobs you tell us to do, we'd be trapped between a rock and a hard place if shit went south. Which it is likely to do quickly if we're whoring ourselves out to every crime gang in the area... it involves too many other people calling the shots, and if there's one thing I hate, it's-"

"...Not being in control," April finished, dejectedly. Colt put his hand on April's shoulder.

"Playing Mr. and Mrs. Average Joe Miller in the middle of nowhere would be the easier, safer route," Colt said, his voice not sounding like his own.

Blue raised his eyebrows. "I never knew the unstoppable Colt Kincade to take the easy, safe route. Just saying."

April looked into Colt's eyes, drilling deeply. "I thought you would have wanted to be Prez of your MC again?"

"I would, I do, but April... fuck, I can't believe I'm here trying to talk you out of this... it's not a glamorous life; it's dangerous, even with FBI backing, it would still be dangerous."

Blue shook his head. "Colt, seems like you're talking yourself out of it. Sure, there's aspects of this plan I need to check up on, get budgeted, line up resources, but, fuck, it's everything you ever wanted, right?"

"Colt, are you running from this, too, now?"

"Fuck April... it's just... a lot to take in right now..." Colt stammered. He felt dizzy, he felt his world spinning. He felt himself trembling again. Was he strong enough, or was that wind going to blow right through him and take him off and away?

Blue cleared his throat. "Get back to me tomorrow. Take today and tonight. Think about it. I'll check on things on my end. If you want to disappear, testify and get placed in WITSEC, fine. Easy. But that would be it then, no more visits. Sever all ties."

April gulped. Blue continued, "Or you go back, claim what's rightfully yours, raise hell with those fuckers until they're history, and your ass is back in that head of the table seat where it belongs."

"But you are pulling the strings," Colt sneered.

"You'd just have to be smart enough to know when to follow through and when to pull back," Blue countered.

Colt felt the politics already. He'd have sleepless nights trying to figure out Blue's agenda, trying to work out who to trust, worrying about April not being safe... and yet... President of the Black Coyotes again. April at his side. Fuck.

He cleared his throat. "We've got to run, we have no choice-"

"There's always a choice," April said quietly. Colt heard it echo through his ears within his brain.

"If you run now, you'll be running forever; they will always be chasing you. Even if Cleaver gives up... your mind, your soul will always be being chased," Blue said.

Colt took a step back. "Yeah, we need to talk, think about it, sleep on it..." He let that fade out.

"Alright then," Blue said finally.

"Alright then," she repeated through pursed lips. Man, she was pissed at him. Well, he was pissed at her. She knew this whole time that Blue was alive, she'd kept that from him, knowing how much Blue meant to him, knowing how much of a father figure he was.

"Well, looks like we part ways now," Blue said.

April latched onto him, hugging the air out of him. "I love you, Daddy."

Colt felt like a dick.

She pulled away and Blue turned to Colt. Colt wasn't sure what to do, shake his hand? Give him a high five? Flip him the bird? Blue decided for him. He pulled Colt in and held him pinned against his chest.

"Love you, son," Blue muttered. Colt thought his heart exploded. His mind had exploded earlier when he'd seen Blue. His soul had exploded earlier when he'd claimed April. Now his heart was a goner, too.

Colt let out a strangled sob. Then Blue pulled away. And, without a backward glance, he strode away. Down the sidewalk. An old man in a too tight leather jacket.

"Colt." Her quiet but steely voice pulled him back from the edge of a deep downward spiral. "We need to talk."

"April, at the risk of sounding like a grumpy bastard, I don't want to talk. I don't want to think, I want to fuck you until neither of us can walk. I want to pound into you until I am seeing stars and then until those stars are bouncing around off other stars like that fucking air hockey arcade game."

"I see. I'll call a taxi."

CHAPTER 46
COLT

Colt flicked his lighter and lit up his cigarette. The tip glowed red in the inky, cool evening sky. He took a deep drag, relishing the burn, and tipped his head back to blow the plume of smoke upwards. As he did so, he noticed the moon. A full orb of whiteness. Beautiful. Untouchable. Mocking him. He scratched his forehead with his thumb nail, and began to limp over to the steps up to their cabin porch deck. Limp because, yes, April and he had fucked each other into next year. She was asleep, or passed out in a post orgasmic haze on the bed. She was a fighter. She hadn't complained, and he knew he was being too rough with her. No, she'd let him have his way with her, she'd begged him for more. And he'd complied. The lactic acid build-up in his quads though... So he limped stiffly and sunk down with the sigh of an old man onto the steps. He was hoping to have a quiet cigarette before ending up beside April and sinking into sleep alongside her. He stretched out his legs and groaned.

Another groan answered his. Colt looked up. What the fuck? There it was again.

"Argh..." A drawn out, groggy kind of groan. Coming from the flower bed by the side of the cabin. Colt got up tenderly, and peered into the gloom.

"Huhh... I don't feel so good." A body lying on the ground

moaned and stirred.

Colt raised his eyebrows. Someone was lying face down in their flower bed. "Fuck." Colt sprang into action. Tossing the cigarette, he lurched forwards, hunkered down awkwardly and grabbed the shoulders of the person on the floor.

"Miles!" Colt exclaimed, surprised. "What the hell are you doing out here, man?"

"I thought this was our cabin," Miles slurred. Colt caught a whiff of puke on his breath. He tried not to grimace as he helped the other man sit up. Colt sat beside him, groping the ground quickly to check he wasn't about to lower his ass into a puddle of Miles' vomit.

Fuck, Miles was drunk. Really drunk. His eyes were barely open, his head lolled about. "My cabin," Colt said, correcting him. "Yours is next door, about 100 yards that way. Come on, I'll help you get there." Colt started to drape Miles' arms over his shoulder and heave him up.

"Nooo..." Miles howled. "Is she there?"

"Who, your wife? Clarissa? Probably."

"No, we can't go, she'll kill me, Colt, she'll send me to rehab-"

"Er..." Colt said inanely, but Miles babbled over him, saving him from thinking of anything else to say.

"I promised I wouldn't get into trouble, this was my final strike, it was this as a last ditch attempt to prove I didn't need it but now she'll send me to rehab and divorce my ass and suck me dry, my money-"

"She might not." Colt attempted to reason with him but mainly he attempted to maneuver Miles over to his own cabin and avoid his stale breath.

"Oh God, she'll be so fucking pissed-"

"Well, just apologize, give her the best head of her life in the morning-"

"Easy for you to say, your April is a stunner..." Colt smirked.

Miles continued, "I bet you both have incredible sex-" Colt simply grinned. "Well you know what's better than sex? What I have that's incredible every day?" Mile whispered like he was drawing Colt into a conspiracy plot.

"What?"

"Cocaine," Miles slurred.

Colt paused, frowned, and looked him over. He didn't seem high, he seemed drunk. "You have any tonight?" Colt asked.

Miles shook his head like a child. "No, they didn't have any-"

"Who didn't?"

"The men in the bar. I snuck into a bar, shit, don't tell Clarissa," Miles said, showering Colt with spittle as he loudly shushed, despite Colt not making any noise.

Colt wiped his face with the back of his hand and murmured back, "You went into town?"

"Yeah, I said I had a headache and needed aspirin but I didn't go to the pharmacy. I went to the bar. And there were these men in there that looked like they could hook me up-"

"What men?" Colt asked, his hackles beginning to rise.

"Men. Actually, they looked like you."

"Like me?"

"Yeah, they had hair like yours and the jacket like yours, only they had a picture on it. A gross looking animal skull-"

"Fuck."

"Yeah, it was pretty ugly really. Anyway, I asked them if they had any blow but they told me to fuck off-"

"Was it an old man, with long gray hair, in a ponytail... fat?" Colt asked, desperately hoping it was Blue.

Miles shook his head. "Nope. Two guys. One young and skinny. The other guy was drunk. Really drunk. Like he passed out on the bar, the skinny guy called him a funny animal name…"

Colt sagged. "Skunk?"

Miles chuckled. "Yeah, which was funny 'cause he was drunk as a-"

Colt practically shook Miles in his frustration. "Did they talk to you, or you to them, other than about blow?"

Miles pouted up at Colt. "Ouch, you're hurting me!"

Colt relaxed his grip and forced himself to breathe. "Sorry."

"No, they were rude, so I got myself a drink, or three, ha!" Miles guffawed.

Colt rubbed a hand over his face. "Okay, what happened next, did they leave?"

"Well, Skunk passed out at the bar and the skinny guy couldn't lift him, then there was some argument about paying, I don't think the drunk guy could pay for the bottle, so the bartender kicked them out."

"Okay, probably got a few hours then until Skunk sobers up…" Colt thought out loud.

"Why can't I be like you, Colt?"

"Huh?" He looked at Miles like he'd forgotten the other man was there.

"You're so badass, I wish I could be as strong as you, do things my way… I bet no one messes with you."

"Oh, you'd be surprised," Colt said with a tinge of wry amusement. They'd made it to the other cabin. No lights were on. "Listen, Miles, you definitely didn't say anything to those men, right? About this place? About who you'd met here?"

Miles nodded sloppily.

"Okay, here's what's going to happen. You are going to go into your cabin. You're going to get a bottle of water and down it, okay?"

Miles nodded again. "Then you're going to get into bed, and sleep, and pretend we never had this conversation. You're going to wake up, tell Clarissa you love her, stay away from the blow, and go on living happily ever after, got it?"

Colt didn't wait for Miles to respond, he slapped him on the back in a friendly gesture, propelling him forward to his front door. "Bye Colt!" Miles whispered loudly.

Colt forced a smile and waved.

"Love you Colt!" Miles whispered again.

"Fucking... great work, Miles," Colt replied sarcastically, with a thumbs up. Colt waited with baited breath as Miles opened his door and swayed through. Colt listened out for the possible bang of Miles hitting the floor. After a few seconds and no bang, Colt released his breath, turned, and stomped back to his cabin.

Well, fuck, that changed things.

CHAPTER 47
COLT

He had to get out of there. He had to run again. April deserved better, so much better than this. Maybe he should let her find something better, maybe he should lead the MC away from her, so she could escape. Blue would look after her, put her in witness protection, she could go anywhere, do anything... It stabbed at his heart and his soul.

He reached into his back pocket, grabbed his phone and hit the dial button. The one number that he had saved into that burner phone. It picked up after one ring. "Mr. Black, how can I help?" Came the easy confidence of Ash down the line. Colt forced another breath in and out of his lungs.

"Ash, I need a favor. We're checking out."

"I... what? You're paid up until the end of the week."

"I know, but we got to go, now."

"I can send a maid to help you pack-"

"No, fuck it." Colt shook his head.

"It's the middle of the night!" Ash's smooth confidence wavered.

"I know, fuck, I know, look... the less you know, the better. But my wife and I... we gotta go. Right now."

He heard Ash draw a breath in and out. Please Ash, Colt silently prayed. Please don't make this a big thing, don't ask a hundred questions.

"Alright. Alright. What can I do?" he asked.

Colt almost cried with relief. He took a breath and closed his eyes and made a decision. "I've gotta drive... me and my wife, we have to get out of here... I need your help."

"Just ask."

"Ash, can you lend me a car?"

"Umm... I don't have one... I'll borrow my uncle's, I'll say a friend was in trouble-"

"That's great, it has airbags, right? Recently serviced?"

"Yeah."

Colt swallowed the bile in his throat. "Good. I need you to drive our VW van out of state, while we take the car..." Colt winced. He knew it was a big ask.

"Okay... This sounds like trouble."

Colt pursed his lips. " Honestly, it is. Hang up now and go back to sleep if you wanna stay out of it-"

"Ha! No chance. At fucking last. Just what I was hoping for. I'm bored out of my fucking mind. Get me out of here and get me in fucking trouble with a capital T."

Colt smiled. He liked Ash. "Meet me in the driveway in five," Colt instructed. "And there is one other thing I want you to get for me..."

After talking to Ash, Colt hung up and shoved the phone back in his pocket. He jogged up the steps now of his cabin and opened the door. He slunk over to the bed, that giant white cloud of heaven that had been something so good Colt had never thought he'd have in his life. There she was. April, fast asleep. Blonde hair splayed out on the pillow, face peaceful, gentle breaths. He took this moment, right now, to appreciate her. He almost had everything. He wasn't sure what would happen now. But right here, right now, for these final few seconds, he still had April. For a few seconds longer, they existed in this happy bubble.

Now he needed to burst it.

He came up to her, buckled down onto his knees by her side of the bed. He gently caressed her forehead with his thumb. Cupped her cheek with his palm. Her eyelids fluttered open, as she calmly took him in, in front of her. She didn't startle, just blinked up at him. Fully trusting him. Fully loving him. Colt was hit by the enormity of what he had to lose if he wasn't careful.

If he didn't play his cards right. Or his chess pieces.

"April," he breathed, aware he probably smelled of cigarettes and whatever booze Miles had consumed and breathed all over him.

She simply smiled up at him and reached up for him. He knew there wasn't time, but he knew he couldn't resist her, either. He bent forward, brushed his lips over hers. They were warm, sleep swollen, ripe. He groaned and kissed her, loving the feel of her lips kissing him back. Then she opened her mouth. Her warm tongue invaded his mouth, taking him, owning him. He let her, welcomed her, bit her lip slightly begging her not to go. She groaned now, and shifted in bed, pulling him down, pulling him in. For a moment he was tempted to fall. To just tumble down on top of her. To kiss her, love her, lose himself in her. To spend the night in her embrace, and continue as they had done. Doing yoga, eating, fucking, sleeping. Bliss, unburdened bliss.

But no, he knew he couldn't. The MC was closing in. So far just the drunk guy and a prospect. Hopefully they were out of action for a good few hours. But Colt didn't know how many others were nearby. How had they found them? Was it Blue, had he snitched on them?

No, Colt dismissed that thought as soon as it crossed his mind. The conversation they'd overheard a few weeks ago suggested one of the MC members had connections that he was using for intel...

"April, we gotta go," Colt breathed. April moved in the bed, making room for him. The beautiful soft bedding rustled, whispering invitingly to Colt.

"No, Kitten, the MC are in town. We gotta move."

She went rigid then, wide eyed.

"What? Here?" she stammered.

Colt took her hand off the back of his neck. "Yeah, Kitten, in town, only two guys so far, but we're going." He kissed her hand.

She rubbed her face with the other palm and then pulled herself up. "We need to pack-"

"No time, listen Kitten, Ash is getting a car. He's going to drive the van outta here, create a diversion, drive a different route," Colt said through gritted teeth.

"Where are we going?" she asked, flinging off the duvet.

She was naked. Colt bit his lip, sitting back on his heels, giving her space to get up. He felt like he was on his knees, praying to his goddess. He was. April was his goddess. Colt felt his cock flaring up in his jeans despite the imminent danger they were in. She threw on the leggings and T-shirt she'd been wearing earlier, then she turned to him.

Colt gulped with a throat as dry as the Sahara. "I was thinking, maybe I should lead them away, and Ash could get you a taxi, get you to safety, Blue could get you into witness protection-"

April held up a hand, stopping him. "No chance, I'm not leaving you Colt, if we go, we go together, we run together, we fight together."

Colt breathed and he felt like heaven breathed with him. "April... you deserve so much more..."

"I don't want more, I just want you. Now stop fucking around Colt, we don't have time for this," she said authoritatively.

He gulped. Yeah. That was his fucking brave, strong lioness talking now. "Colt, just shut up, let's get in the car and drive us out of here."

"Okay. Okay," he huffed. "Where do you want to go?" he asked.

"Where do I want to go?" She repeated his question. She used her fingers to comb through her hair, then started tying it up in a messy bun. "I want to go back to the clubhouse and I want to tell them all to fuck off and leave us alone. I want to chase them back, chase them down," she said, the lioness in her roaring, staking a claim, laying down the gauntlet. He fucking loved it.

"Then let's ride," Colt replied.

Chapter 48
April

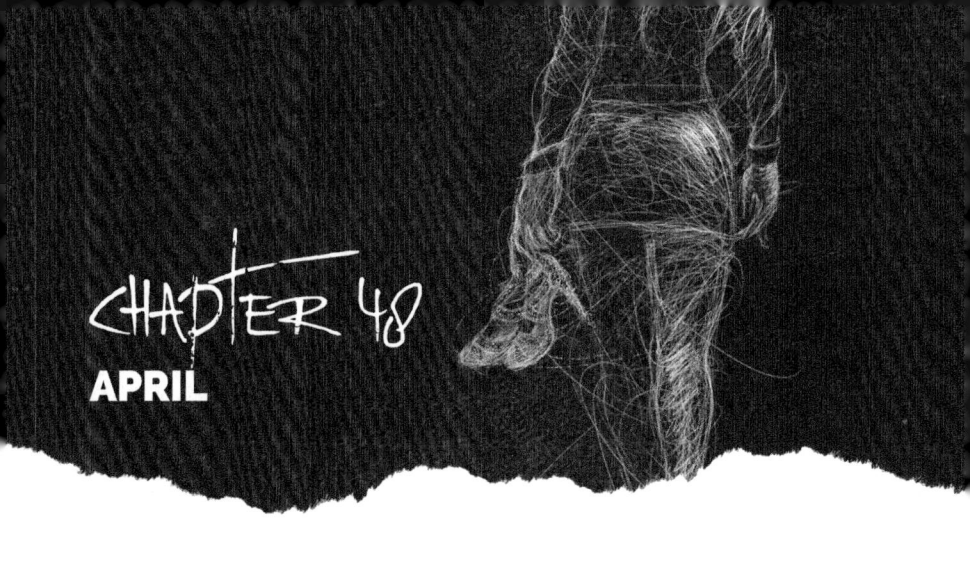

April was perched in the passenger seat, eyeing the inky night suspiciously. He had caught her up on what Miles said. The MC guys were close, in the town. A few members anyway. She couldn't believe it, she had felt so safe. The view across the lake that she had looked out at fondly, she now watched with suspicion. Colt hadn't turned the headlights on. April wasn't sure if that was necessary but she'd not said anything. Colt had his saddle bag slung in the back still. Both pairs of her fuck shoes in there. He was such a sentimental soul. He'd never admit to it though.

    They hadn't had a moment to talk any further about what they planned to do, after their meeting with Blue earlier. They had gone back to the cabin and talking had been the last thing on their minds. They had been at it for hours, it had been blissful. But she was sore, thoroughly spent. They had collapsed into sleep and hadn't talked further.

    His reaction to her ideas had surprised her. His hesitation. She thought Colt would've been more in favor of going back and reclaiming his MC. She'd thought long and hard if she could be the 'ol' lady' of a biker. She'd listened to his stories of life in the MC before. The parties, the roughness, the sweet butts. Women who belonged to the club, who were shared by the men. Who did the cleaning, the cooking, but who counted for nothing. She couldn't be one of them. And she didn't like the sound of it, at all, for anyone else, either. Then there was the illegal activity, the guns, drugs, the turf wars. Even if Colt changed this, made a better club, April knew there would be violence. She knew there would be catty women eager to dig their claws in. If April did find herself in the position of 'Prez's ol' lady', she would have to be strong, brave.

She would have to trust Colt to do right by her and the interests of the club. But then she'd weighed it against the other side of MC life. One big family having each other's backs, belonging. Living how you wanted. Making your own rules. Maybe she could convince Colt to ban sweet butts or something. She wanted a sense of warmth, creativity, of building something worth having. A mini society of their own making was appealing. She wanted a pool and a vegetable garden. She wanted to escape the rat race of her white collar world. Where success was measured on how much your salary was and how recently you got promoted and how many square feet your apartment was. She wanted to be surrounded by people who were good. Who cared about their family, about each other, about what they built together. In San Francisco, she'd regularly push people out of the way to get a place on the subway train, a place that involved standing in someone else's armpits, on her way to meet people she didn't really know or like. No, to hell with that.

She wanted roots. She wanted something amazing. She had a heart full of love to give and she wanted to create a family to share it with. Kids, yes, but friends, aunties and uncles of their choosing. Brothers and sisters. An amazing place to bring up those kids. Colt's kids. Trials and tribulations. Getting a cup of coffee and always having someone there to chat with, to share laughter or tears with.

So before she'd suggested it, she'd thought about it. She could see it in Colt when he spoke about Ash, how he would make a good prospect. There was light dancing in those dark chocolate eyes of his. He became animated, gesticulated, and talked more. He became alive. She thought he'd have been more up for it, though, when she'd suggested it. Yes, Blue's reappearance had obviously shocked him. She had bargained on Colt's anger, but not his pain. The embrace with Blue... she'd teared up herself. She hadn't realized her father had meant so much to Colt. Had been so much of a father figure to him. So maybe that had been too much of a shock. Too much to process on top of the other things, too. She thought Colt would be more angry at her, for keeping it a secret. He had been angry, but more at Blue. And more confused and hurt, she'd seen a glimpse of the scrawny, lost fifteen year old who showed up at the clubhouse, and it had melted her heart.

However, when she'd shared her idea of reclaiming the MC, she thought he'd jump on it. But he hadn't. He didn't seem willing to compromise on the things Blue had said. A MC with FBI backing, it sounded ideal to April. But she'd seen it in his eyes. Fear of being cooped up again, not free. Not in control. Fear of being betrayed. Answering to someone else's call. Fear of being imprisoned again. Even if it didn't involve walls and fences this time, but other people's agendas. It had really changed him. April was beginning to see how the time he was incarcerated affected how Colt felt about pretty much everything. His decisions, actions and reactions. He needed stability, trust. He needed people around him who he could rely on. April wanted to be that for him. He needed a home. To block out memories of prison. He needed roots, so he could feel grounded and safe. He needed routine, to ward off the emptiness. Warmth to block out the frostbite from the cold. April wanted to give him all of that.

She honestly didn't think it would come to anyone dying. Maybe she was naive, but she thought once Colt read them the riot act, they'd give up. Go home, find a new MC. They'd leave quietly. Wouldn't they? Cleaver was different. April felt burning hate like she'd never felt before for another human being. She'd stewed on it, how he'd orchestrated her kidnapping, directed the prospects to take her. Driven her in the back of the car for hours, then basically trussed her up. All because he wanted that money. To become a sex slave, to be used and abused. It didn't bear thinking about. The loss of her dignity, her freedom... if Colt hadn't come back for her... she shivered involuntarily.

Colt saw and put a hand on her arm. Silly man, now that she'd refused his foolish notion of them separating in different directions, he wasn't flapping anymore, he wasn't the self-doubting ghost she had first met. The Colt who had been ballsy bravado one moment, then a shriveled wreck of a man the next. No, he was gone, and in his place was her fierce, brave biker bad boy. Her Prez.

Colt licked his lips and continued, "Going back... this wiping the slate clean... you know what that means, right?"

April rolled her shoulders back and down. "I don't think it will be the bloodbath you fear, Colt." She tried to sound brave, too.

"I don't fear it, I've killed before, and I'll kill again, I know this," he added evenly. The simple way he said that sent a different shiver through April. "But I'm just checking if you know what it means... I don't believe in heaven or hell, or God, I don't believe my soul is damned, but it changes a person... it has a weight... and some people can't carry it."

April heard what he was saying and thought about her next sentence carefully. "The anger, the rage I feel, Colt, that's too heavy for me... it's too hot, it burns too ferociously. That's what I can't carry. I don't want to burn in that rage anymore."

THE CHASE

Colt took his eyes off the road to look at her. Really look. Search her soul for the truth in her words. Search for the strength it would require.

"Okay," he said simply.

April sat back in the car. Yes. She felt ready to start the chase, as the hunters this time. The chasers. Hunting them down and getting rid of the threat they posed. Once and for all. Any means necessary.

Colt set his jaw. "Can you call Blue, let him know?"

April cursed under her breath. "I don't have his phone number. We used that gardener's website to arrange a meeting."

"Fuck," Colt said. "Well, we'll do it ourselves."

The driveway came into view, the parking lot, the main lodge building, the way out. Ash was there, waiting for them, unfaltering Ash.

Colt pulled up next to Ash and his uncle's Mercedes, parking the VW in beside it. Ash had his arms crossed over his chest, baseball cap on backwards. April could see his face, curious and excited, lit up in the outside lighting that was casting a soft orange glow over him.

"Well, I'm going to be honest, I knew your real names weren't Mr. and Mrs. Black," Ash said, as Colt jumped out of the VW. Colt grabbed the saddle bag.

April climbed out slowly, letting her hands trail on the dashboard, on the door. She said a swift little goodbye in her mind, bitter sweet, to the van she'd come to love. The van they'd basically stolen in the first place. She suddenly had the urge to cry. Remembering how she'd been so unsure about taking the van in the first place. She didn't feel like the same woman now. That was before. Before Colt had made her his. Before she had become undone by him. And re-made. She set her jaw and climbed out of the van.

"Ash, drive this to this address I'm about to text you, just over the border in Oregon. A guy called Millhaus runs the garage, this VW is his, he'll be happy to get it back. If you get that far, there's a beautiful custom Triumph waiting for you there."

Ash nodded slowly. "Sweet. Where do you want me to drive the bike?" he asked.

Colt shrugged. "It's yours, wherever you like."

Ash gaped for a second, then snapped his mouth shut. "Seriously? A custom Triumph? I could keep it?"

"Sure."

Ash fist pumped the air.

"But you gotta make it to Millhaus' garage first. That's an all night drive. And you'll have company."

"Some people are chasing you? You owe money or something? On the run from the police?" Ash asked excitedly.

"Something like that. Not the police, bad people. Don't fuck about with them, if you see them, you just drive faster, okay?"

"Okay."

"And we can take your uncle's car?" Colt turned to eye up the Mercedes.

"Yep, I'll tell him I had to borrow it for a friend, he won't know it's gone until the morning, I'll take the rap for it which will probably involve working another month here, maybe taking on the role of janitor, too...." Ash smirked and shrugged his shoulders.

Colt nodded. "Okay fine. Is it in good working order? Brakes? Airbags? Seat belts?" he asked again.

"Yep," Ash said with a pop to the P. "He's all about ensuring stuff is clean, safe, blah blah blah." Ash moved his hand about.

"Fine." Colt produced a package of notes from inside the saddle bag. He caught April's eye, a silent check with her. April nodded and Colt then thrust it into Ash's hand.

"Wow." Ash saw the wad of crisp clean bills and froze.

"For your hard work, Ash. I know we haven't been the easiest guests and you've been good to us," Colt said softly.

Ash looked up, Colt's tone catching his attention. April heard it, too. Colt sounded proud. Fatherly. Ash almost choked. April realized Ash probably hadn't been praised, told he'd done good, for too long. By the sounds of it, his family had villainized him and cast him out. He had fucked around, yes, but he had a good heart, he had a good head. He wasn't into taking advantage of people. Unlike Cleaver and company. April felt all the emotions bubbling up in her. God, she'd actually cry before the night was out, she knew it.

Ash cleared his throat, looked at the money, then at Colt and April. "Thank you," he said quietly.

Colt slapped him on the back, then pulled themselves together in a brief hug.

"Time to drive," Colt said. April nodded. She gripped Ash's shoulder in her own emotional display before turning from the van and climbing into the passenger seat of the Mercedes. Ash had put water and granola bars in the seat pockets. She smiled.

She looked around and Ash slipped Colt one final thing. A gun. April did a double take.

Colt took it, handling it with care, inspecting it. She watched it in his hands, she wanted to look away, like he was touching something dirty. But she couldn't. She wanted to watch him handling it at the same time. She realized she hadn't breathed. She wasn't meant to see this, she realized. Colt looked up and nodded at Ash, and tucked the gun into the saddle bag, too. It was coming in the car with them. She felt the weight of that, she felt how it changed the air in the car, how it made it heavier, in her opinion.

Colt slipped in beside her, into the driver's seat. He turned on the engine and paused for a moment.

"You sure you want to do this?" he asked quietly.

April blew out a breath. "Yes," she said simply.

Colt nodded and took the car out of park. They were moving, at last. He purred it slowly at first, tapped the brakes, revved slightly. The security barrier came into view. In front, Dwight, the security guard, swaggered over. Colt swore under his breath.

Then, suddenly, Colt hit the accelerator pedal. The car shot forward, noisily, jerkily. April gripped the seat beneath her with both hands.

"Colt!" she squealed. The barrier was streaking toward them but Colt didn't slow.

Bam. They hit the barrier. Smashed it out the way. It snapped and folded easily, the car hardly slowed down.

Dwight was left looking on from a safe distance, aghast.

Colt was grinning from ear to ear, and he chuckled wildly.

"That was so unnecessary!" April chided. In truth, now her heart was pounding.

"That's MC life, Kitten… revenge and vengeance."

She'd felt too emotional before, saying goodbye to Ash, The Pines, the van. Now she felt Colt's wild energy, the pump of adrenaline in her body. Fear, yes, for she should be afraid. But also the thrill. She couldn't wait for them to get on the highway, for Colt to put his foot on the pedal and for them to streak off into the night. Back to California,

THE CHASE

back to where it all began.

She threw a glance over to Colt, and the thrill of the chase was gleaming wildly in his eyes again. She recognized it because she felt it, too. "So bad, Colt," she said, but the smile in her voice, the tease, was clear. He heard it.

"I'm a bad boy, April, what can I say?" he replied, before flooring it down that narrow driveway. The night air ripped in half, in the wake of the roar of their car.

CHAPTER 41
APRIL

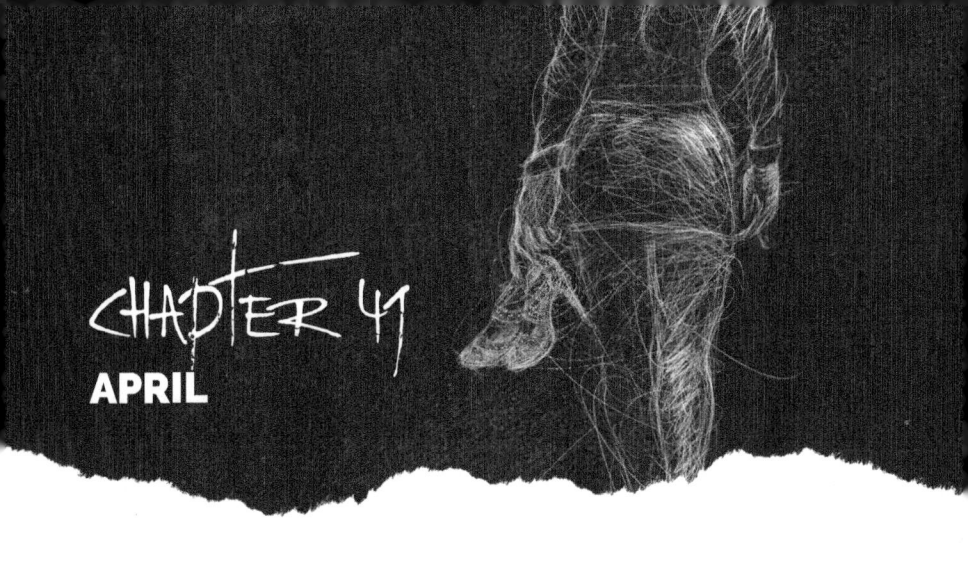

APRIL'S FINGERNAILS BIT into the car seat with desperation. Her palms were sweaty but the leather seat did nothing to absorb it, and probably made it worse. She flicked a glance at Colt. He looked like a teenage boy who had spent too long in front of a gaming monitor. Wild eyed, strung out, manic. They had been driving for three hours, non stop. April felt a tick in her eye. She must have strained it from staring so intently at the road. Both in front and behind. And she wasn't even driving.

It had taken about an hour before they spotted the first rider. A huge, black Harley Fat Boy. The man on it, wearing all black. Colt had spotted him first. He'd done a double take into the rearview mirror. A slight tilt of his head, but April had seen it. And their carefree, excited mood had just flipped slightly. Just a little switch. But it was no longer about driving fast and enjoying the buzz. April had swallowed and it had suddenly taken on a sharper edge. There was a bite to the air in the car that there hadn't been before. April flipped down her passenger side sun visor and angled it so she could use the vanity mirror to look behind. The highway no longer felt like the fun, safe place it had, moments before. She asked Colt if the biker was definitely Black Coyotes.

Colt hadn't answered her immediately. Instead, he changed

lanes on the highway slowly, casually, like they were on their way to a shopping mall, or church maybe. A casual morning drive. Not a second later, the bike behind switched lanes, too.

Colt tilted his head. "There's your answer," he ground out.

It had been inevitable, she tried to remind herself rationally, as she watched the biker follow them. It was bound to happen. She barely blinked, Colt gradually sped up. And so did their shadow. They followed at the same distance, but discreetly. A few hours later, she was burned out. Her face muscles felt sore and her neck hurt. Not to mention the pounding pulse in her throat. And of course her sweaty palms.

They'd continued for a few more hours. Colt gradually increasing his speed from the speed limit, to just above. How she would drive if she was late for work, on a normal day, perhaps. Colt had then pushed to a definite speed increase. How she'd drive if she was late for a very important appointment. Then to an unmistakable speed. April wouldn't have driven at that speed. It was the kind of speed that had other drivers shaking their heads and pulling out of the way. And Colt had taken it up a notch even after that. How she felt now would be appropriate for a rollercoaster rather than in a car on the highway. She was dizzy, like she wanted to squeal except her throat was frozen tight. Waves of adrenaline slapped against her. The dizziness was making her feel sick. So she gripped the leather seat even tighter.

Then two other bikes turned up. Flanking Colt and April's Mercedes. The police joined for a while, inevitably, too, a cruiser with its reds and blues flashing, bringing up the rear. Colt didn't slow down. True to his word, Colt drove hard and fast. So did the other bikers, though. April had felt a surge of relief seeing the police. Maybe they could arrest the bikers, once April and Colt had explained who they were and what the situation was. They could explain her father is a

THE CHASE

senior FBI agent. But no, the police cruiser turned its lights off, and turned around, having been more like an escort than an additional threat or active participant in the chase.

Colt tutted but didn't look surprised. He'd muttered something about 'dirty pigs' and carried on driving.

Then a large Ford van joined the bikes. It was black, April did a double take in her vanity mirror.

"That's the van they took me in!" she exclaimed. Colt flashed a glance in the rearview mirror. He set his jaw but said nothing. April looked back to the front.

She saw something out of the corner of her eye. Bam. They jolted. The car twisted ninety degrees. Another car had plowed in their side.

"Fuck!" Colt swore, as he fought to control the steering wheel.

April shuddered. "Colt, I think we should-" The rear windshield exploded, a hail of glass shards suddenly dusted the back seats.

Colt hit the gas pedal. The car hesitated then shot forward.

"That was a gunshot… that was a gunshot," April chanted to herself as the car spun, she could smell burning rubber now.

More shots.

"Colt… hit the gas, hit the gas!" she shouted. Colt ignored her, swerving around a corner rather than hitting the accelerator. The car screamed in agony, protesting. April forced herself to peer into the rearview mirror. One of the bikers couldn't make the turn to follow, they were going too fast. The bike slipped out from under him as the biker wiped out on the road and slid.

"Oh shit!" April heard herself swear. She locked her eyes on the biker, she couldn't tell if he got up or stayed down. Did that mean he was dead? Her heart thudded.

"One down," Colt ground out, handbrake turning around another corner. "Hold the wheel, April."

"What?" she stuttered.

"Hold it straight."

He let go, reached down, and pulled out the gun. April felt the air change around them. Danger. It even smelled different now. April gulped.

He eased off the gas a little, the car slowing painfully. April reached over and grabbed the wheel with claw-like fingers. White knuckled. She looked ahead, swerved a little, realizing she was steering now. He'd chosen a stretch of long, straight road, very few cars. He knew what he was doing with all of this. She should feel worried, terrified, but she didn't, she felt safe. Like she was on a rollercoaster that was way above her thrill threshold, but ultimately no matter how it thundered and twirled and looped, it was safe. That was how Colt made her feel, that was how she felt on this fast, dangerous ride with him, this chase. Thrilled, safe.

Colt leaned out the driver side window. He held the gun up, paused for a moment. She dared a glance at him. He was silent, still, calm. He aimed down the barrel of the gun.

And crack. It went off.

April wobbled the steering wheel involuntarily and whimpered. She flicked her eyes to the rearview mirror and saw another biker, much closer than she'd expected. Red liquid exploded from his shoulder. She heard him yowl and swerve off their trail. She let a breath pass over her cracked lips. She glanced back again, the biker couldn't control the bike, he was drifting into the other lane, into oncoming traffic. It was like slow motion. Closer to that double yellow line, over it, a box truck blared its horn.

She closed her eyes. Now she understood "wipe the slate clean".

THE CHASE

She swallowed, but set her jaw. If this is what their freedom cost them, then this is how she paid for it. She'd recall that noise for the rest of her life in the quiet, small hours of the night. But at least she'd have a life to be haunted. She'd judged the MC harshly at first for its outlaw status, its lack of moral compass. How the men, including Colt, set their own rules. Turned out, she was as ruthless and dark as them.

The hair-raising chase continued.

"Two down," Colt said as he pulled back into the car and took control of the steering wheel. He sat the gun down into the drink holder between them. She clung onto the leather seat again, focusing on the horizon, throwing glances at Colt. He drove like a man on the edge, determined, as if his life depended on it. She saw his aggression now, he could be cold blooded. And he refused to lose.

He ran a red light.

They hurtled onto an empty road that suddenly filled with cars. Red, blue, moving fast. Colt swerved. April had never had such a near miss. But then-

Bam.

She turned back to look out of the empty space where the rear window used to be. The biker sprawled in front of a car, lying still on the ground.

"Three down," April said for him. He threw her a look this time. She returned it, determination in her eyes. He saw it, turned back to the road and stepped on the gas.

They just had the black Ford van bearing down on them now. Colt did a U- turn. "Colt! Colt!" April screamed. Colors flashed by in the window. Shapes. She didn't see anything else. Tires screeched. Gunshots cracked outside the car. April ducked automatically.

Colt frowned and hammered the gas, doubling back down the road they'd just come from.

April blinked and looked out. She recognized the street. "The clubhouse-"

"Yeah. Seat belt tight, yes?" Colt spat out.

She checked hers. "Yes."

He nodded grimly. "Hold on."

April gripped the seat until her fingers felt like they'd never open again. The car streaked like a bat out of hell toward the clubhouse. The gate was open.

He didn't slow. The gate slowly began to close. The iron railings, forcing the gap closer.

"The gate!" April yelled unhelpfully. She knew he'd seen it.

Colt had his gaze fixed on the rearview mirror, the black van behind them. It began slowing. A little jerk left, the driver overcorrecting right, then left again.

Colt took his eyes off the back now, his mind made up. He set his sights on the gate, the gap into the MC compound getting smaller and smaller. He angled the car straight at it and floored it. The car lurched forward.

He didn't slow. He didn't stop. The car hit the curb, much faster than intended.

The gap looked too small. Colt didn't slow.

April closed her eyes.

The car dragged against the gate. Metal scraped, but they made it through.

April opened her eyes, a victory whoop quickly silenced. Colt still didn't slow. They bulleted into the parking area. April blanched, she saw his plan.

There was a loud crunch from behind. Guess the black van didn't make it, April thought.

But she didn't turn to look. Her eyes were dead ahead. Because they were still hurtling forward. Unstoppable, plummeting onwards. Straight toward the clubhouse. Toward the wall.

April took a breath.

Bam.

Chapter 50
COLT

Colt had been ready for the impact. That punch to the face from the airbag hadn't surprised him. April had said she wanted to take the fight to their door. He'd literally done that.

He knew this section of wall was old, he knew with impact it would all come down. Anyone left inside would be history. What he had been surprised by was the noise. It was an almighty crash. Metal, glass, wood. Then the dust. He hadn't anticipated them being covered in a blanket of white insulation dust. It felt like he couldn't breathe.

Coughing. His ears were muffled, the crunch of metal still ringing in his ear. But over that, he heard coughing. He turned to look beside him. April.

Thank fuck the airbag had deployed. She had a graze on her forehead. Her eyes were wide. Wild. But she was fine. They were fine. She was fine.

Colt spluttered, too, now, the dust in his mouth. His throat.

"Gotta get out," Colt wheezed.

April nodded. His voice still sounded far away to him. Had April heard? He began to fumble for the door handle but realized he'd never get the door open, building debris piled high.

Colt pulled himself out of the car window, clinging to the roof to do so. The glass in the window was long gone.

"April? You okay?" he asked into the oddly deafening silence now.

"Yeah, I, oh, God, I'm okay, I'm okay-" she replied, wincing, but pulling herself out of the car through the smashed out window like he had.

"I'll come around and help you," he said, treading gingerly over the debris.

But then there was a roar.

A motorcycle, starting up.

Nearby.

Colt turned.

It was fucking Cleaver.

He sat on a bike, revving it, triumph in his eyes. He thought he was getting away.

"Colt! Get him!" April shrieked. Colt didn't need to be told twice. Turning from April, he stalked toward Cleaver who was obviously thinking he was getting away. Cleaver was on a bike. Colt didn't hesitate, didn't think. He planted his feet firmly in the way. Cleaver would have to go right at him to get through the now mangled gate. Cleaver practically shrugged, a game of chicken, clearly he thought Colt was going to get out the way first. Run from him on the bike.

No fucking chance. A voice in his head yelled to him to run at it. Colt didn't think. He felt pure rage. The animal in him roared.

Cleaver streaked closer.

The sound of the bike was loud.

Deafening.

Both men glared into each other's eyes, they were that close now.

Colt lunged.

Cleaver's eyes widened.

Colt clotheslined him off the bike with a mighty swipe, his fist connecting with Cleaver's throat.

THE CHASE

The bike slid away to join the remains of the gate, stuttering throatily.

Cleaver buckled to the ground, the air knocked out of him and struggling to breathe.

Colt was on him in a flash, fist flailing wildly. "You fucking dirty-"

"Colt, why won't you just die already?" Cleaver wheezed.

The two men fought.

Cleaver, driven by the urge to run, to escape, he looked at Colt like he was the devil. His worst nightmare brought to life. Colt was driven by an all consuming urge to kill. Cleaver had taken one too many things from Colt. He'd taken his home, his place in the world, his brothers. Cleaver had nearly taken his woman, nearly done atrocious things. Hell, Cleaver had nearly taken the very skin off his back. It ended now.

Colt took a punch in the nose. And another to his kidneys. Shit.

Cleaver overplayed his advantage, though, surging forward. Colt used it, followed Cleaver's momentum and crashed down on top of him. The two men kicked, Cleaver went for Colt's eyes, throat. Colt pulled his head free.

Colt was on top.

Then Cleaver.

Then Colt.

Who was more angry? Who was more desperate? Who had more to lose?

It wasn't going to be Colt. He wasn't going to let that happen.

Colt finally got Cleaver in his grip. He had his hands pinned above him. Colt on top, pressing him down onto the ground. Both men were panting. It was almost erotic. Except it wasn't. It was deadly.

Cleaver was exhausted. He wheezed, "Bastard... you've just destroyed-"

"It ends here, now, Cleaver."

"Oh yeah?" Cleaver's eyes mocked him. "Are you going to strangle me with your bare hands?" He laughed. "I know you're a caveman but even for you-"

"No, you're going to take a bullet in your head." April's calm, clear, soft voice came from right beside him.

Colt turned. There she was. Gun in her hands, the gun. His gun. Fuck, she must have picked it up from the drink holder. She held it steady with both hands, barrel right under Cleaver's chin. She had determination on her face. Cold, calculated detachment. Unlike Colt, who'd been all hot fury and flying fists. She was crouched beside him, gun pressed in a deadly position. Completely still. Colt swallowed and kept his grip on Cleaver. His heart was galloping.

But Cleaver didn't fight it. No, he raised an eyebrow and laughed. "Sweetheart, if you expect me to believe you are going to pull that trigger, then you're dead wrong-"

Bam.

She pulled the trigger.

Hot liquid spattered onto Colt's face. His reflexes kicked in, forcing him to shut his eyes and his mouth.

He heard a slow, steady breath, in and out, beside him.

April had pulled the trigger.

"No, you're dead wrong," she whispered softly to Cleaver's lifeless body. "In fact, you're just dead."

Colt felt his heart stutter. She had killed. For him. They'd killed. Together. She turned and she was covered in a splatter of blood, too. Cleaver's blood. Colt released his grip on Cleaver's dead hands. They weren't straining against him now.

"April," Colt managed to croak.

She stayed in business mode. "Colt, I think the car is on fire, we should move. Also, I'm bleeding."

Colt's throat stuttered, his gaze roving from the smoldering car, to her hands, which were indeed covered with blood.

"Let's move April, come here-" He reached for her, and she gave him a blood covered hand. It slipped in his, he had to adjust his grip to hold her.

Sirens were creeping closer. They were loud now. The car was not just smoking. There was fire. A raging inferno. The air was poisonous. Flashing red and blue lights outside the compound walls could be made out through the black smoke.

Colt didn't care anymore, he held April to him like she was his oxygen. His life raft. His everything. She clung onto him with the same vigor.

There was too much blood. It was all over her trousers, the bottom of her T-shirt. Something was wrong. She was going limp in his arms. Colt peeled away, holding her still to him. He peered down, examining her, concern etched into the dust and sweat on his face.

Boom. And it was at that moment that the car exploded.

Colt was knocked back. He hit the ground. April's hand was no longer in his.

He felt heat. He heard sirens. His vision swam. And blackness took him.

CHAPTER 51
COLT

COLT LAID ON the narrow bed and stared up at the tiled ceiling. He'd counted the tiles already. He'd counted the swirling patterns on the tiles. He'd multiplied the number of swirls by the number of tiles to get the total number of swirls in his room. His small room. He'd pace it later. Wall to wall. That was something to look forward to, he thought wryly. This felt too familiar. His soul was screaming. His body felt numb. He was trapped.

But then the door opened. He felt relief, he was not trapped, he had to remember that. Never trapped again, he vowed to himself. Not prison, instead a hospital.

"Ah, Mr. Kincade, good morning!" A doctor marched through the door with a nurse following not far behind, far too upbeat for Colt's grumpy mood. April would tell him off for it. April. His pulse quickened.

"April?" he wheezed, trying to sit up, suddenly aware his voice was like sandpaper, his lips so dry they'd stuck together. When was the last time he drank water? That's why he was on an IV drip. His eyes darted to the needle taped down to his forearm.

The doctor tilted his chin. He was a decent looking, if slight, man. Colt couldn't help but size him up. Colt was confident he could knock him out cold in one swipe if he had to.

"She's recovering, in the next room," the doctor explained. Colt tried to move. Tried to pull himself up further. "Oh no, you've got to rest, too. You can see her later, she's resting anyway-"

"She's okay?" Colt nagged.

The doctor's smile turned to a slight frown, which set Colt's mind whirring away. "She's recovering, just like you, but she'll be fine. I'm Doctor Singh, I'm your-"

"When can I see her?"

"When she wakes up, now please don't be difficult, Mr. Kincade."

"Colt."

"Very well, Colt. You had smoke inhalation and a concussion, you passed out at the scene of your accident, do you remember?" the doctor asked, while grabbing his stethoscope, checking Colt's breathing. The metal plate was cold on Colt's chest. He indicated for Colt to sit forward and slid the metal plate onto his back.

"Take a deep breath," Dr. Singh said, listening.

"I don't remember," Colt said passively and breathed in and out slowly. The doctor was satisfied with what he heard, and took the stethoscope out of his ears and off Colt's chest.

"Well, the police are here to talk to you anyway, so save any memories for when you speak to them."

Colt pursed his lips. Fuck.

"In fact, you've got a whole group of visitors waiting to speak to you."

"I do?"

"Yes." The doctor leaned in a little and glanced at the door. Colt braced himself, what the fuck was he doing?

"Between you and me, the members of that biker gang and that eyesore of a HQ or whatever it was, is gone now and that is not a bad thing in my book." The doctor's face flashed in the ghost of a wink.

"Less gunshot wounds in the ER, less overdoses, less DUI incidents... all fine by me. And the rest of the residents of the town, I'm sure."

Colt licked his lips. He didn't want to risk saying anything, but gave a subtle chin lift to him.

The doctor stood up and stepped back, clearing his throat.

"Right, well, I'm happy that you're okay. A few bruises but otherwise… I'd like to just monitor you this morning, get some breakfast in you. Then we'll take out the IV, and you can be discharged later in the afternoon."

"Thanks, Doc," Colt replied.

The doctor nodded and fixed him with a pensive half smile, then turned and marched out the door.

Colt laid back. Mind reeling. Heart flopping like a fish out of water. He closed his eyes. But seconds later there was a knock at his door, and his first visitor came into his room. Colt eyed him up, gaze flicking critically up and down, assessing him.

He was young. That was Colt's first thought. His uniform was that of a police Sergeant, the most senior police officer in the city's police force. Which is why Colt had particularly noticed he looked young. He was shorter than Colt. But well-built. He worked out, obviously. He was stocky, sturdy looking, broad shoulders, pecs that hugged the sleeves of his uniform. With a face that no doubt could get him into ladies' panties. Cute chipmunk features, a smile to melt butter. Eyes like Colt's own, chocolate brown. Short, dark brown hair, neatly trimmed.

Colt's gaze flicked to the name badge on his uniform. Rossetti. It rang a bell, sending Colt spiraling down memory lane. Fuck. He felt suddenly dizzy. The pizza place just down the street from the clubhouse. The old clubhouse. Rossetti. The place Colt had scrounged for food when he was a skinny homeless mutt. The place he'd been kicked out of; just before Blue had seen him, invited him into the MC... fucking fate. What were the chances?

Colt cleared his throat. "I didn't order a bacon pizza," Colt said calmly, not letting his internal emotions show on his face.

Sergeant Rossetti set a half smile onto his face. Yep, Colt could see women finding that fucking cute.

"I get what you did there. I'm a pig, right, that's the slang term for the police, anything related to being a pig, like bacon." He sauntered closer to Colt. "And if you want a pizza, it's my father's place you want to hit up... and my brother's now, too, nothing to do with me." He frowned. Colt noticed, clearly a point of contention, did the Sergeant secretly want a slice of the pizza place instead? Colt stored that. It might come in handy one day. The Sergeant cleared his throat. "Name's Carmelo. Carmelo Rossetti."

Colt looked at Carmelo's proffered hand. Colt itched. The uniform immediately raised his hackles, he didn't like it. But he knew slighting the local police wasn't a smart idea. He hesitated as long as he dared. Carmelo didn't lower his hand though, he waited. Bold, Colt thought, suitably impressed.

"What happened to old Hughey?" Colt asked Carmelo, finally taking his hand. Both men grasped each other firmly, solid and warm.

Carmelo shrugged. "Got too old. Retired a few years ago."

"You're young," Colt said honestly.

Carmelo smiled. "Jealous?"

Colt raised his eyebrows. "No, probably not much younger than me, a few years maybe?"

Carmelo sniffed and rolled a shoulder. "A year." He caught Colt's slight frown. "I read your rap sheet. I know your age. Don't worry, give me a few years and I'll be Captain in no time, give me a few more and I'll be Chief. "

Colt grunted. Ambitious guy. "If you're here to arrest me or question me for what went down..."

"No, no." Carmelo held up a hand. "That's not why I'm here-"

"Then what do you-"

Carmelo huffed. "Chill out, dickwad." He then looked horrified about what had slipped out of his mouth, and rubbed the back of his neck with his palm, cursing under his breath.

Colt raised his eyebrows. "You quoting *Terminator* to me but realized you probably shouldn't call me a dickwad... Sound about right?"

Carmelo smirked and raised his chin. "Alright. You got me." He sighed and perched on the side of Colt's bed. Colt frowned some more at the proximity and familiarity but Carmelo didn't seem to notice, he carried on talking. "Truth is, the Black Coyotes MC disappearing is no bad thing for me, for the town..." Carmelo crossed his arms on his chest.

"They're all gone?" Colt wanted to confirm.

Carmelo nodded. "All but one. Guy passed out across the road from the clubhouse drunk as a-"

Colt almost smiled, he dropped his head and sighed. "Let me guess, Skunk?"

"Yep. His name's Lyle Peterson. We've had him in for a run of DUI's, drunk and disorderly-"

"Guy's got a problem," Colt said.

"Yes siree," Carmelo agreed. "Anyway, he's a few doors down, alcohol poisoning."

Colt laughed once, dryly. "Well, it saved his life this time."

"Yeah, him and one other thing survived, some skanky old leather sofa-"

Colt barked out a harsh laugh then. That old sofa, his home, his sanctuary, his starting place.

"Fuck me."

"Yeah, we had to take it to the evidence lock up but-"

"Nah, I want it."

"What, the old sofa? It's probably infested with lice or something-"

"I'll take it, you can sort that for me as a goodwill gesture, our welcome gift, if you like-"

Carmelo turned to Colt then, his previously casual pose suddenly stiff. "Welcome gift? Look, I'm just going to ask it... are you going to start up the MC again? You were president, right? Before Cleaver?"

Colt sighed. He needed time. He needed to think. He couldn't commit right here and now. "I was Prez. What gave you the notion I was going to start it up again?" he asked, trying to sound neutral. His heart pounded.

"You wanting the sofa for one thing." Carmelo leaned in. "There are two other visitors waiting outside your door, one of them is this FBI agent with long gray hair." Carmelo paused. Colt immediately guessed it was Blue. "And the other is the goddamn mayor." Carmelo sat back with a challenging look on his face.

Colt almost stuttered at that. "Mayor Harris? She's here?"

Carmelo raised an eyebrow. "Yes, to see you. Why would those two VIPs be here to see you, if you weren't going to start up the MC again?"

"Ah... fuck," Colt said out loud, looking at Carmelo with chagrin. He should hate this guy, the local police Sergeant and the MC Prez should be arch enemies, rivals. But he liked Carmelo and he sure as fuck wasn't going to waste any time doing what he felt he should be doing. He lived by his own rules, if he wanted to be friendly with the Sergeant, he damn well would be. "I dunno," Colt replied honestly.

Carmelo pursed his lips, drew himself up to his full height, all business again. "Well if you do, don't fuck around with my town, okay?"

"Oh, your town?" Colt countered.

"Yes, my town."

Colt set his jaw, they could bicker but not be enemies, right? "From where I'm sitting, if I did start up the MC again, it would be my town." Colt laid down the gauntlet.

"Don't go pissing in my pool, Colt…"

"Oh, you fresh out of chlorine?" Colt jumped in again.

Carmelo stopped in his tracks.

Colt smiled. "You quoting Die Hard 2 now? You may be a fucking pig but your taste in classic movies isn't too terrible."

Carmelo shrugged. "It's a good sequel to a great Christmas movie."

"You think Die Hard is a Christmas movie? Controversial." Colt grunted. "Now, Die Hard 3…"

"Not even worth talking about. Not even worth the title Die Hard." Carmelo shook his head.

Colt couldn't help but grin. "I agree."

They both looked at each other. Colt felt the warm rivalry, the start of a solid friendship.

"Well, if you did start up the MC again, I'd be your liaison point, with the local PD. Our captain and chief want to keep their hands clean, I've been given full latitude to collaborate with you as I see fit." Carmelo gave Colt a playful flash of his eyebrows.

A nurse came in at that moment. She was curvy, blonde, chatted sweetly with a bubbly little laugh as she took Colt's blood pressure and temperature. Colt smiled politely and chatted back and watched Carmelo. He smiled at her with what Colt was learning was his signature smirk, and eyed her up, from the top of her head to her feet, his gaze devouring her. The nurse bustled out and Colt waited to speak again.

"You're not getting any then."

Carmelo blinked. "Any what?"

"Sex," Colt replied bluntly.

"I-" Carmelo's eyes widened. "Not recently, how did you guess that?"

"The way you were eye fucking that lil miss blonde and curvy-"

"I wasn't eye fucking-"

"Yep." Colt cut off any further argument.

Carmelo arched an eyebrow but smirked and looked down. Colt smiled at him. But before he could reply, Carmelo's phone rang.

He sighed and answered it, without his smirk, back in business mode.

"Yeah... kids trespassing at the Creekdale Hotel? Again?... Third time in as many days... okay, okay... Yes, alright... and what else? A cat? A... disabled cat? How...? Back legs fucked up... okay... well can you get the fire department in... Yeah you're right, fuck them, they'll shove our noses in it... we'll get it... okay, let me... give me a minute. I'll call back, hang on..."

"The Creekdale hotel?" Colt asked when Carmelo had ended the call.

"Yeah," Carmelo said, "An absolute shit show that's been... there was a fire... in fact the rumor is that the MC started it somehow... then it turned out the insurance wasn't valid so the fire damage was too extensive... then half the staff were illegals... now it's condemned and uninsurable, owner is trying to sell it but no one wants to buy it... kids keep trespassing..."

"And to top it off someone has found a disabled cat?" Colt summarized.

Carmelo sighed and rubbed a palm across his forehead. "Yeah, out on the highway, back legs are all fucked up but it's causing a traffic jam, now we have to take it to the pound but they'll put it down..."

"I'll take it," Colt found himself saying. Carmelo opened his mouth and gaped at him. Colt reeled himself. What the fuck was he doing? But he felt it. In his gut. Colt shrugged, styling it out. "Get well soon present, for April."

Carmelo raised an eyebrow. "A disabled kitten?"

Colt grinned. "Yep. I'm going to take your phone number, too. Your personal one."

Carmelo raised his eyebrows, a hundred questions swimming in his eyes. "Does that mean you are going to take on the MC-"

"No comment."

Carmelo sighed. "Right, the disabled kitten and the health hazard of an old sofa. Got it. I'm gonna make some calls. I'll be back."

Colt rolled his eyes. "Alright Arnie," he said dryly, as Carmelo flipped him a wave over his shoulder without looking back.

Despite himself, Colt found himself smiling. Carmelo may be a police Sergeant, but Colt had a distinct feeling that despite the stereotype pulling him to hate him, they could actually be friends.

Chapter 52
COLT

Colt wasn't left alone long. As soon as Carmelo had exited, Colt's door opened again. And in strode Blue.

Colt sighed. The man had an aura about him, a presence. You could take the Prez title away from him, but he still carried himself like he was the President. Regal. Demanding respect. Colt's insides gripped, like they always had done around Blue, like they probably always would do.

He came close, sat down on the side of Colt's bed.

Colt wasn't sure what he could say. Something like, 'Hi Blue, we decided to come find danger after all. I crashed the car she was in into a building then she shot the former Prez…' Fuck.

Colt was painfully aware of the danger he'd put April in. He'd crashed a car with her in it into a building. On purpose. She was now bleeding, hurting. They could have asked him for witness protection, rode off into the sunset and lived a quiet, happy life. But they didn't. They'd borrowed a car and pointed straight at the monster's nest. Colt had done that. Colt looked down and nervously plucked at the edge of the blanket in front of him.

Blue reached out his hand and let it rest on Colt's shoulder. And Colt felt it, right to his core. The heat of Blue's palm. The weight of his arm. Like the weight of the world. A father's love. For both him and

April. So he just felt Blue's hand, the heat, the weight, both luxuriated in it and also cringed under it. And the shared silence hung around them, like fog.

Blue cleared his throat and spoke first. "You know, I met April's mother when I was VP," Blue began. Colt could tell Blue was in storytelling mode. His voice was deep, strong, like a fine whiskey. And in Colt's book, it was never too early for whiskey. He sat back and breathed out, happy to listen. "She was beautiful. You know, that smile... lit up the whole fucking bar. Her hair... long, glossy, so fucking soft, all the way down to her ass. And that ass of hers..." Blue let out a long whistle. "She hung out at the clubhouse all summer. And we were all panting for her, I can tell you. Dogs in heat. But I was the one to bag her. She was young, too. Turns out she'd run away from home. Too many arguments with her mom. She attracted trouble, like bees to honey. She was beautiful, but boy, Marisa could make some terrible decisions. Terrible judgment. She saw good intentions and wanted to be nice to everyone and it landed her ass in trouble with the wrong kinda people. Fuck, and I'd run around trying to fix her, and the trail of devastation behind her. That summer... the best time of my life and the fucking worst...one minute on cloud nine, the next raging at something stupid she'd done. Anyway, she gets pregnant. It's mine of course. She told me she was on the pill, turns out she wasn't... we argue. I claim her, try to make a go of it. I thought sticking a 'Property of Blue' label on her back would calm things down. It didn't. She fucked up and fucked off. It was September. I thought I'd cut my losses and get on with my life. She turns up again next summer with a little baby in tow, and fucking track marks all down her arms. She said she didn't use during the pregnancy. It was only to help calm her nerves afterwards. To help her sleep. Raising the baby was too hard... yada yada. Excuse after excuse. We took the baby, we made her go

THE CHASE

cold turkey sober..." Blue teared up.

Colt hadn't heard all of this before. Hadn't seen this side of Blue. A young man in love. A young father, trying to do what was best for his little baby.

"Marisa fucking died. Seizure, her body couldn't cope without the drugs she'd been taking." Blue paused, cleared his throat. Colt saw a single tear fall off his face. It created a damp stain on the bed sheets. "I took the baby to Marisa's parents. They nearly died of heart break. They didn't know. They said to come back on the baby's birthday. Baby April. I did. I fucking came back every year on her birthday. I took her out when she was older, to the mall, to the ice cream parlor. I sent all my money to her. Told Marisa's parents to send her to good schools. Keep my little girl far away from low lives like me. I wanted her to have a good life. Full of happiness. Her own family, one day. A good job, nice house. That's what I wanted for her."

Colt felt himself cringe, guilt eating his flesh. He looked down. "Blue, I-"

"If that ring on her finger is there for real, to stay-"

"It is."

"If you can keep her safe, make her happy..."

"I will."

"MC Prez or not-"

"MC Prez or not, April comes first."

Blue paused, cleared his throat and took a breath. In and out. And again. Blue regarded Colt carefully. His ice blue stare inspecting him with a fine tooth comb. Colt stared back almost defiantly but trembled inside. "I trust you to do right by her, Colt."

Colt let out a breath. Shaky. "I'm... grateful. She's... everything... always has been."

Blue shook his head. "I was stubborn and blind, I didn't see it... I mean, I saw you were panting after her as a kid but I didn't see much more..." Blue shook his head, awash with emotion. "Marisa, April's mother, I should have chased after her, stopped her from leaving in the first place. If I hadn't been so proud... hell, I was VP at the time, life was good. I thought I was the cat's pajamas, booze every night, the town respected us, money, good times... I thought she'd come back. I should have fought for her, supported her. Like what you did for April. I should have gone back and made her battles my battles. I should have chased her to the ends of the earth-"

"Sometimes it's hard to know what we are actually chasing," Colt said.

"Amen to that brother," Blue said, nodding slowly, lost in thought. Then he seemed to remember who he was talking to and flicked Colt a look.

"What?" Colt asked suspiciously.

Blue cracked a smile then, for the first time. "My boy's got me in check mate. Well done, son, well done."

Colt didn't feel like he'd got Blue anywhere near check and didn't think he ever would, but took that as the compliment it was meant to be, nodded a little and sighed.

Blue cleared his throat again. To business, the intimacy and tenderness of the previous moment passed now. "So... if you did start the MC up again, you'd need informants. They'd come in without you knowing... maybe you'd be able to guess who they are. Maybe not."

Just then, the door burst open. It banged against the wall behind it.

"I've got to meet him," the lady who strode in declared. She was African American, with short hair close to her head. Wearing trousers, a blazer, and loafers. Not heels. She was wiry and petite, but the atmosphere in the room changed as if she was taking up most of the space. Most of the air.

Blue seemed put out that she had interrupted him.

"Colt, this is the Mayor, Maxime Harris."

Blue nodded at Colt and addressed Mayor Harris. "This is the potential new President of the Black Coyotes."

She looked him up and down. Colt wished he wasn't meeting her while he was in bed wearing nothing but a hospital gown with his face stitched up. He imagined he was looking slick and flashed her his best devil-may-care smile.

"Ma'am," he said silkily, then he offered her a hand. She raised her eyebrows and took his.

"I've heard so much about you, Colt Kincade."

"All good, I hope?" Colt replied.

She smiled wryly and shook her head. "No, indeed not."

Fuck. Colt fixed his smirk in place but inside his heart was rattling against his rib cage.

She shook her head. "But the past is irrelevant. It's what you are going to do next that I'm here about. Mr. Kincade-"

"Colt," he corrected her.

She looked at him sternly, as if she wasn't often interrupted. After a long pause, where Colt had to force himself not to squirm, she continued. "I've worked hard to make our city a good place to live and work, for hard working, law abiding citizens. For them to buy houses, for their children to go to school safely… for this place to be an exemplary American dream."

Colt thought he knew where this was going. She was going to say she didn't want his kind in this town-

"I want you in this town," she said finally.

He must have misheard. "What?"

"I want to know everything that goes on in my city. That includes the illegal aspects, too. I want to know about the gangsters and mobsters, and I want them working for me, too. That's why I liaise closely with Special Agent Blue-" Colt almost snickered. Special Agent Blue. He'd never get used to that. "-To ensure everyone's pulling in the same direction. My direction. You and our charismatic police Sergeant may pound your chests and measure your dicks and think it's your town. It's not. It's mine, and if you get too big for your boots, it's the end of the line for you. Do I make myself clear?"

Colt glanced at Blue, wondering if this was some sort of joke. Mayor Harris wanted a finger in all the pies. She was as corrupt as they come.

"Ma 'am," he wisely replied.

She nodded, satisfied. "I'm cut in on every deal going on around here, and I call the shots on some, too. The Black Coyotes MC is a useful pawn in the game we play-"

Fucking chess again, Colt thought. "We need you working with the local Mexican cartel, a group called the Demonios, and we like them doing business in our town. They pushed out the other gangs while you were on your sabbatical, Colt-"

Sabbatical? Colt caught himself just before he rolled his eyes.

"And that's a good thing for now because the Demonios deposit a large amount of money in the town's coffers and keep the crime rates low, drug use low, keep the drugs and arms moving up the coast and not sticking around here…"

"That's why you put up with Cleaver?" Colt asked.

Blue nodded. "That's why we left Cleaver in situ, but we didn't fucking like it."

"So, if you did set up the MC, you'll be informing for us. On the Demonios, on what they are doing for who. We'll loop back around to the Guardians of Purity and that gun deal later. They won't want to work with you, Colt. But we've got our man planted there, we'll see if there are other avenues for that... Special Agent Blue will be your contact, and I'd be fully in the know about everything that is occurring. You'll be under the full protection of the FBI, immunity for you and whoever in your club is working for us."

Colt hadn't bargained on this.

Carmelo burst back into the room at that moment, tucking his phone into his pocket. It was a fucking circus in here, Colt thought.

"Is he doing it or not?" Carmelo asked bluntly. "If he doesn't, the power vacuum could upset the balance-"

Maxime interjected. "If he doesn't, he'll find himself facing charges for what he's done, smashing into a building, reckless driving, injuring others-"

"Stop," Colt said quietly, but they all heard him. They all paused. "Just stop. Save yourself the embarrassment of making any ultimatums or any attempts at blackmail or entrapment. For fuck's sake," Colt burst out, letting his anger show through a little. Keeping his fear far from their nosy peers. "Look, I'm not deciding anything without first speaking to April. I don't like the idea of answering to you, any of you. Nothing personal, I'm just not liking the idea that you could tell me how to run my MC. I'm not liking the idea that my brothers would be rats and roaches. Slick FBI agents would be strolling about, undermining trust."

Carmelo piped up. "The agents are not good boys, they're the dirtiest, meanest guys..."

"Rosetti, you aren't selling it." Blue sighed.

Colt shook his head. "No one's selling me anything. If you're all here for an answer today, you won't get it. I'm going to see my fiancée -" he caught Blue's eye. "And I'm going to do whatever it is she tells me to do. 'Cause she owns my ass, and I'm happy to admit that. My dick, my balls, my heart-"

"How romantic," Carmelo muttered sarcastically.

Colt continued, "So you can all just fuck off for now and I'll get back to you."

Carmelo pursed his lips, pissed off. Blue frowned, frustrated. The mayor looked on with stony-faced disappointment.

He shrugged. Fuck 'em. It was his decision, and he'd decide based on his little kitten lioness in the next room, not because of politics, or for the sake of reducing crime rates, or to assist in other investigations.

A loaded pause followed.

"Fine," Blue said after staring Colt down to no avail. Colt returned the stare with as much ice as Blue sent his way. Blue pushed himself up, he'd had his ass perched on a table in the room. He held his hands wide, in a gesture designed to herd the others out. Carmelo smirked, shrugged and sauntered out. Mayor Maxime fixed Colt with a 'do what I say or I'll have my people kill you' kind of glare. Colt returned a bored blink her way. Even if they ended up working together, he wouldn't be threatened, he needed to set that precedent right fucking now.

The door closed with a soft click. Finally, Colt could process it all. He wasn't sure whether to laugh or cry, or fucking pinch himself that he was really alive and it was all real. Fuck, because it felt like some sort of bittersweet parallel world. Where he had everything he'd ever wanted within his grasp, and yet everything he'd ever feared hanging over his head. April, Prez of the MC, freedom from prison... yet answering to others, trapped in an arrangement that involved traitors.

Fuck Blue and his talk of chess pieces and pawns. It all felt like a game of snakes and ladders to him. A roll of the dice and he could be up at the top of the board, set to win big. Or sliding right back to lose it all.

Chapter 53
APRIL

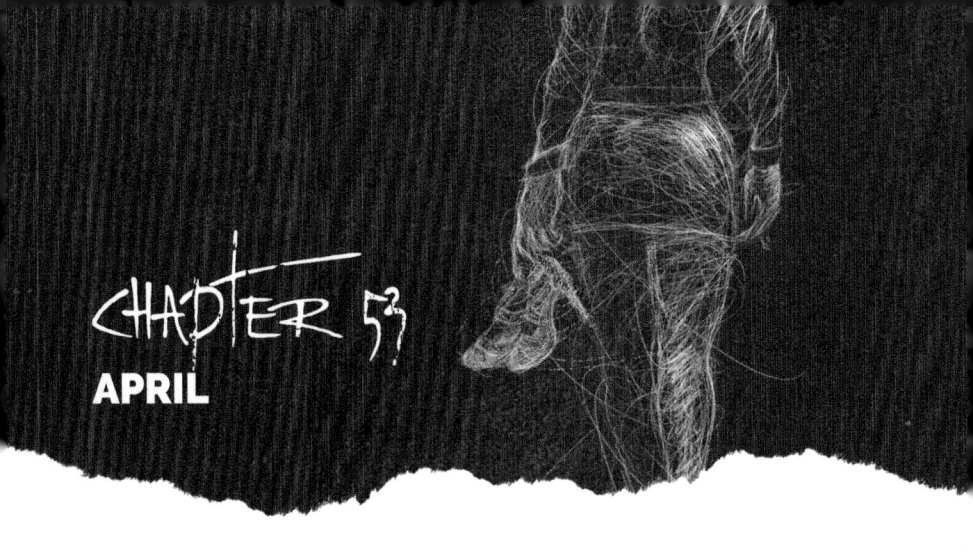

April felt a warm hand skim her head. It was a rough hand, but it stroked her so gently. A caress across her forehead, a gentle swipe down her cheek. She awoke slowly. She leaned into the stroke, reveling in it. But then the hospital sounds intruded. The roughness of the sheets against her skin. The smell, a whiff of floor cleaner and antiseptic. The aching in her body. The numbness. She kept her eyes closed for as long as she could, prolonging the momentary simplicity of the sensations around her. She knew, when she opened her eyes, things were going to get a lot more complicated.

"I'm sorry, Kitten," she heard. That voice, deep and rough. Colt's voice. She opened her eyes, and was met with his, peering over her. He was sitting by her bed. His eyes were so brown, such a rich chocolate coffee. His beautiful face was covered in little scrapes, scabs, a bruise, a bigger cut stitched on his forehead. His long, brown hair hung forwards, tenting them. She smiled up at him. He was wearing his clothes again, he'd changed out of his hospital gown. She was still wearing hers. He dipped his head and let out a breath of air. She saw his pain, his indecision, but also his patience. He just sat, stroked her head, and waited calmly.

"What are you sorry for?" she asked, her voice quiet.

He grinned wryly. "For waking you just now. For crashing the car with you in it... for... driving you halfway across America in a van, for pulling you away from everything that was comfortable and safe-"

"Colt, you can apologize for waking me up, but the rest is nonsense. And you know it," April said with a gentle sleepy smile. She was happy he was here. He tutted above her, but a slow smile caught on his lips, too. She gazed at them. She loved those lips. She loved him. "You saved me. And we did it all together. We agreed on the road trip, on the idea to come back, we did that. I heard they are all dead."

Colt nodded. "All but one, the drunk guy. He was, ironically, too drunk to make it into the clubhouse, passed out outside across the road."

"Wow, lucky him."

"Yeah, well, he's being treated for alcohol poisoning but otherwise, he'll live. The police Sergeant said Skunk was the one who tracked us down. Apparently he has some link to someone who could trace us, or something like that..."

April could see Colt's mind ticking over. "What are you going to do to him?" she asked.

Colt looked lost in thought for a second. "What am I going to do? Something his brothers should have done a long time ago, check him into rehab," Colt said with a wry smile.

April started to smile but it slipped, despite her best efforts. She licked her lips, unsure how to say what she had to say. So she took a page out of Colt's book and all that she had learned from being with him over the last few weeks. She just plunged right in. "Colt, you know I was bleeding... a lot?"

He nodded and stroked her forehead, the same, calm, unfaltering strokes that had woken her. "Well... they think it wasn't because of the car crash... they think it was a miscarriage."

Now Colt's hand paused on her head. "A..." he choked.

"They think it was early, maybe like five weeks, and it could have just miscarried naturally, it might not have been related to the crash..."

"The crash..." Colt stammered, she dared to look at his face. He was white.

"It was yours... just to be clear, that first night, on the back of the bike..."

He looked like his world had just been turned upside down.

April pulled her hand out of the sheets and rested it on Colt's. "No, don't even think... It was very early, only a few weeks in, and a lot of pregnancies miscarry, one in four they said, so while crashing into a building in a car that then caught on fire and blew up probably weren't too conducive for an early pregnancy, this is not your fault. This is no one's fault."

"What... how... what..." Colt couldn't form the words.

"I'm being kept in for observation tonight, you are being discharged later today..." She drifted off, unsure now of what to say. Maybe he wouldn't want to stay with her after all. Maybe he'd get on another bike and ride off into the horizon without her. She recognized this insecurity within her. She'd seen it in Colt. That fragility shivered through her. She'd never felt it before. But she felt it now. Colt had trembled with it when they'd first met, it had held him back. She felt the all-encompassing pull of it now. Because now she had lost something, and now she had more to lose. She understood why Colt hadn't pursued what he had wanted, which was her, his MC, his freedom. It was easier and less scary not to fight, to turn away and make do.

"Not going anywhere, April. Not without you." April felt her heart swell at that, she felt the tremble die down, she felt it being banished and his warmth seep into her veins once again. "April, the...

the baby-"

She swallowed a lump in her throat. "I know, Colt. It could have been a baby, it was so early-"

"I know but it still hurts-"

"I know."

"I'm sorry for that, too. I didn't realize-"

"I'm sorry, too, Colt, I didn't know, I feel stupid for not knowing… I should have realized, what with how tired I felt, emotional, hungry, beginning to feel sick… that bleeding, I thought it was a period, it was actually probably implantation bleeding, the doctor said… I'm…" She reached up her hand to caress his face now, too. She saw his pain. She had to comfort him. They had to banish the darkness from each other, she saw that now. They had both been hurt and lost, and now they would be forever working to stop that cold wind of self doubt from blowing through their souls. But they would work at it together.

Her eyelids fluttered. "We can try again, when the time is right, when I feel better, when you feel better, when you want, if you want…" she began.

"Yes, April, I do want… a family with you, fuck… yes."

"Me, too." She ran a hand through his hair and he closed his eyes, savoring it, laying his head down on her lap. They stayed like that for a while, their breathing synchronizing, calming each other, grounding each other. She took a moment to mourn the loss. The little life that could have been. For a moment, she let herself dream. They could have gone into witness protection, ended up somewhere hot and carefree. They would have had a little condo, something small and simple, she imagined dated kitchen counters and a few electrical sockets that didn't work properly. But none of that would matter. Colt would have a job doing something physical, locally, she'd have a blossoming stomach, and then a little baby. The three of them would have been happy. She

THE CHASE

imagined going to the local market, picking out ripe, fragrant fruit, sitting out on the porch in the evenings, afternoons on the beach. She held that sunny dream in her mind for a few seconds.

But it wouldn't have lasted, she knew. Something would have happened. Every man in a leather jacket, every motorcycle they heard, she would panic. Always looking behind them, always worrying, living in fear. She was ambitious, that hadn't changed. She hadn't wanted to settle for a quiet little life. They would have been happy but not fully living. They would have been making do. Whereas she wanted it all. She wanted family trips to the market, carefree afternoons and intimate evenings enjoying the sunset. She wanted it without the fear, the fake IDs, without having to be forced away from her father. She wanted to be happy and fearless, what she felt she deserved. She had gone after what she wanted and it had cost them. She sniffed and raised her head. No, they had needed to deal with the threat, they needed to do what they did. She had no regrets, she'd do the same again. For her family to thrive, their family, she needed to be unafraid to live life each day. And now they could be.

He sensed her stirring. "What do you want to do?" he asked her, lifting his head, opening his eyes, glancing right at her, into her soul.

She knew what he meant. About their life, about the MC. She cleared her throat. "It was all a lot more violent than I'd thought. Messier. The blood... the pain..." she began.

"I know, I'm sorry, I know..."

"But I don't feel guilty, I feel better, Colt, knowing they aren't here. "

"The MC?"

"Yes, Cleaver, all of them, out there, doing bad things, hurting others... I feel a bit proud... we did that... we took action, took things into our own hands..."

"Yeah. I've seen your father." Colt shrugged, pouted. "Police Sergeant, the fucking Mayor-"

"Harris? She was here?" April's eyes widened.

"Yep."

"What do they want with you?"

"Just explaining the terms of the offer. Running the MC again... complete immunity... if we play ball. By their rules, their game..."

"But ours to win," April finished. Colt sighed.

Suddenly, a phone rang. Colt frowned. It was only him and April in there, no one else, no one else's phone, but one of theirs. April's was turned off on her bedside table. He patted his pockets, and fished out his phone. It lit up and rang. No one knew this number. Who'd be calling him?

He looked at April. She widened her eyes and shrugged. Colt pressed the green button to accept the call and put it on speaker phone.

Chapter 54
COLT

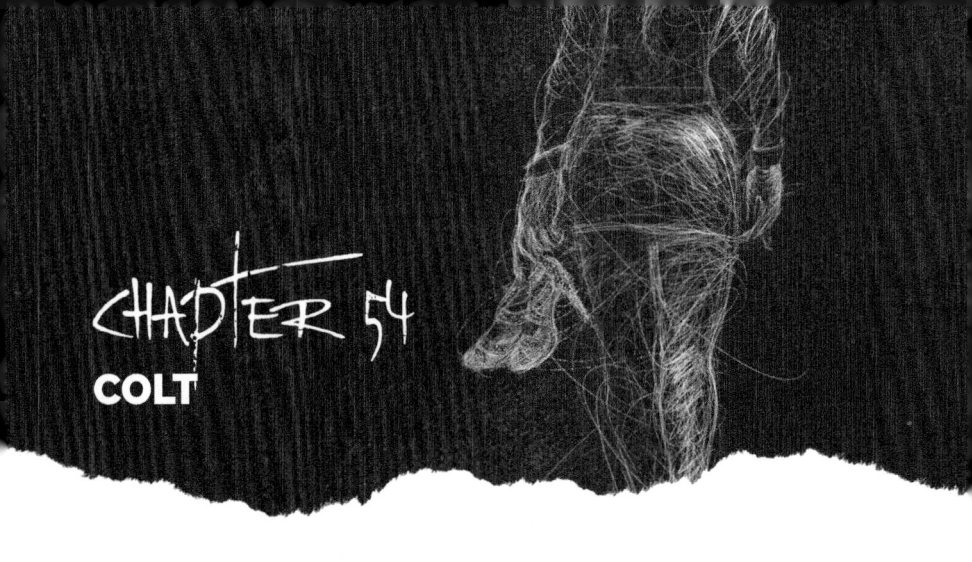

Colt cleared his throat. "Yeah?"

" ... Mr. Black?"

Colt jolted when he heard the voice. "Ash?"

"I... didn't know who else to call, I..." Colt flashed a look at April. Confusion and concern juddered through him.

"Name's Colt," he said. Then left a quiet pause, left space for Ash. He took some loud, deep breaths over the line, he took his time.

"I was going through my contacts and I didn't think anyone else would answer. I've pissed off everyone, Colt, I've really fucked up..."

"Don't worry, everyone fucks up at some point," Colt answered. April smiled sadly. "What's up?" Colt continued.

"This is my phone call... I don't know what to do now..."

"Where are you Ash?"

"Police station."

"Why?"

"My uncle... he's pressing charges... I explained I borrowed the car but he's called it in as stolen, I've been arrested for grand theft auto-"

"Fuck." Colt bit his lip.

"I... my parents already messaged saying not to call, or come back... they said they don't have a son anymore..."

"Oh for fuck's sake," Colt muttered.

"What mother could do that?" April hissed.

"Sorry, is that April? Are you busy, or-" Ash said.

Colt focused back on his phone. "We're in the hospital-"

"Shit, are you okay?" Concern caused Ash's voice to shake down the line.

Colt rubbed the back of his neck. "Yeah, April is... we crashed the car... Ash, I'm sorry-"

"Fuck the car, you both hurt?"

"Nah, we'll be fine, April... she's in overnight but we're okay," Colt said, putting his hand on the top of April's head. She smiled gently back at him. He didn't want to tell Ash about the baby, that was between the two of them, Colt and April, not for anyone else to share with them.

"I'm sorry." It sounded like Ash sniffed. "I shouldn't have called…"

Colt shook his head, even though he was on the phone so Ash wouldn't see it. "No, you should have, I'm glad you did... April, too-"

"Yes, Ash, we're happy you called us," April said, leaning forward a little so her voice traveled clearly to the phone in Colt's hand. He appreciated how April was still ready to help, open to give her emotions to others, despite being in need herself.

A big sigh from the other end of the line filled the room. "I got no one else. Yours was the only number I had left..." Ash's voice got quieter.

Colt looked at April and she looked back. He knew what he had to do. He wanted to do it. This was that missing piece in the puzzle. It fit now. He wasn't doing this just so he could be Prez again. He wasn't doing it just for April and him, so they'd get off any criminal charges. He sure as hell wasn't doing it for the cocky police Sergeant, or the ambitious mayor, or for Blue and his grandiose plans to hunt down bigger bad guys. He would do it for the brothers. For the guys, like Ash, who had no one else. Who had been dealt a bad card, or had made a mistake, and were now paying for it with more than they could afford. For those who had no one else left, no other person in their life who'd take that call for help, who'd lend a hand, who'd be there for them if only to lend an ear. That's what it had been about for him from the start. Family, a home, when he had none. A hot meal and a roof over his head, a physical place to go. People to give him a smile or a hug, or a punch in the nuts when he fucked up or stepped out of line. Someone to fight his fights with him, to stand shoulder to shoulder with and defy the odds. Flip a middle finger up to fate, who'd dealt the shitty hand in the first place. To rage against the forces trying to put them down, keep them down. To the people who'd forsaken them. To society who wouldn't help a stranger. To the status quo that helped the rich stay rich and the poor stay poor. It was about a place, a family, a haven. A club of brothers. Who did their own thing, and stood by each other. Who lived for each other, rode together, died together. Loved together, shared together.

That was what the MC had always been for Colt. He knew Blue had led the way for him. He could do this for Ash, too. It was a survival instinct kicking in. But not for himself, not for his sorry ass hide. For his fellow man. He'd felt it as soon as he'd seen Ash being bullied by his uncle. He'd felt it when fucking Cleaver and the others of the old MC had just left Skunk to suffer alone. Colt wanted to welcome, provide a safe space and protect. Create a family. Set things right. Give second chances. Forgive, forget, move forward. Live life on their own terms, saying fuck you fate, I've got a team of brothers battling on my side now. And we are going to rage and kick and bite and fight against whatever shitty path you put me on. I'm finding my own path with my new family at my back, so fuck you.

That's what the MC life was all about. That's what the Black

Coyotes were to Colt. And he wanted that for Ash and others, too. Going forward, together, farther than the cards they were dealt had intended to get them. Further than they ever could have alone.

April saw it in him, she had a look of recognition, of understanding, on her face. In her eyes, he saw pride at the choice she had seen he'd already made.

Colt cleared his throat. "Ash, this phone call is meant to be to your lawyer-"

"Right, right, I know, I didn't know who to call-"

"It's okay. You were right to call me, Ash. This is what we are going to do... We're going to get you a fucking good lawyer... You may do time, Ash, prepare yourself for that but we'll get you out as soon as we can."

"We? You and April? I can't ask you to do-"

"No, we, as in the MC, my MC." Colt fixed his gaze on April. April nodded. That was all it took. Colt's soul soared.

Ash's voice shook again. "Your MC? Like... motorcycle club..."

"Yeah."

Ash paused for a moment. "You're a member of a motorcycle club?" he asked, his voice rising at the end with incredulity.

"I'm the Prez," Colt said, and couldn't help smirking like that fucking police Sergeant.

Colt heard Ash take a breath. He thought he could almost hear Ash's heart beat. That was what it meant. The life affirming realization that you aren't alone. Colt was giving that to someone else, and it felt good. Colt felt a warm hand squeezing his. April's. Though she was hurting, she still offered comfort to him. His heart slapped its own beat. That felt life affirming for Colt. He wasn't alone. She wasn't alone. Ash wouldn't be alone. And any other fucker who stumbled upon hard times and crossed Colt's path in life, they wouldn't be alone, either.

"What's the MC called?" Ash asked breathlessly.

Colt felt adrenaline creep into his veins. like sinking into a warm bath at the end of a cold walk. Like putting the cherry on top of a cake you've just drenched in homemade icing. Like finishing the thing you've worked your whole life for. Except really this was just the beginning. "The Black Coyotes MC."

"Fuck... this is..." Ash's voice cracked. "This is a dream come true..."

"You want in?"

"Seriously?"

"They'll be a leather cut with your name on it waiting for you."

"I... yes! Hell fucking yes!" Ash yelped. Colt chuckled. Actually fucking chuckled at this kid's reaction. "Black Coyotes will get you out, kid, we'll put our lawyer on it-"

"Can I tell people I'm a member?"

"Here's the thing... you might hear shit about the MC, some of it might not be true. Some of it might be... the old Prez was a dickwad and did bad shit...and we do things a bit differently to other MCs... but yes, you're part of the family, Ash, part of our family." Colt gazed at April, she smiled and nodded.

She silently mouthed back to Colt. "Our family." She gripped his hand. She was excited. Fuck she was perfect.

"I'm a member of a MC? The Black Coyotes MC," he said it like he was trying it on for size.

Colt smiled. "You'd normally have to prospect for a year... do the shit jobs before you could call yourself that-"

"Could I stay with you, when I come out... is there a place?"

"Clubhouse? Sure," Colt said breezily. April's eyebrows rose. Colt swallowed. "I mean, it's a fixer upper but we're working on it, you can have your own room..."

"Yes, man! Just fucking yes... I can't tell you how much this means to me," Ash said, elation in his voice.

April stifled a smile. Colt winked at her. "Good. Then leave it with your MC, give me your details, where you're at, and I'll get our lawyer to get in touch..."

After Colt hung up, April took a breath. "Got a clubhouse? Jeez, you have the confidence of a champion, I'll give you that... the clubhouse we just blew up?"

"Nah. I'm more ambitious. The Creekdale Hotel," he said, looking up at her gaze, checking for approval.

She burst out laughing. He kept a straight face.

She raised her eyebrows when she noticed. "You're not joking," she spluttered.

"Nope. Gonna buy it. Perfect clubhouse for a modern, expanding MC. It would need a hell of a lot of work, we'll take the penthouse suite... there'll be a bar downstairs... it's got a pool...we can dig up the golf course and plant your vegetable patch..."

April threw her head back and laughed out loud with glee. He felt like the king of the world for giving her that. "So... it's settled then, you're doing it?" she asked, breathless, tilting her head back to his.

He shook his head. "We're doing it." He came in for a kiss, a firm press of his lips on her mouth. She opened her mouth. Colt hadn't intended to take it there but she led, and so he followed.

"And you've got a member already, Ash."

"Yes, I guess so."

April paused for a moment. "You know who else could join? Lyle?"

"What? Drunk as a Skunk guy? He's the one who tracked us down somehow, apparently."

"Yes, it would be a good connection to have. You know what they say, keep your friends close, but your enemies closer… He's obviously smart, well connected, the enemy of your enemy is your friend, isn't that what they say?"

"He's an alcoholic, he's got liability written all over him… Ash will need a good role model-"

Colt stopped himself mid-flow and suddenly grinned. "This is what I've been chasing this whole time. Us, the MC, setting up our family, discussing this shit with you, Kitten, my lioness…"

She looked down and smiled bashfully.

"So, we've got the new logo sorted, got a clubhouse… you know what else a MC Prez needs?" he whispered into her hair.

"What?" she asked, closing her eyes contentedly and leaning into him.

"An ol' lady." His voice rumbled above her. She raised her gaze up to meet his. "Be mine, April," he said. It wasn't a question, it wasn't a demand, it was a statement of fact. He felt it within him. Confidence in the way ahead. His way.

He held her hand, stroked it. "I know I got nothing now… I'll get you everything. You want to live in a nice place, hell… I'll get you that. Be my wife, Kitten. Be my ol' lady. You want a family. I'll give you that. We'll have babies, we'll have sisters and brothers around us, and a kickass clubhouse, and legit businesses coming in-"

She beamed. "Colt, I-"

He felt manic with excitement, like he was going to explode. "I got to make some calls… let's get on a plane and get married… flights to Hawaii…"

"Flights to… Colt I-"

"… I'm going to get that guy, Skunk, Lyle… get him into rehab… I'm going to call Carmelo, I want that sofa out of the evidence lock up and into our new clubhouse…"

"The sofa?"

"Fuck yes, Kitten, the sofa, from the old clubhouse, it survived the fire, the one I slept on when I was a kid..."

"Colt, I haven't given you my answer yet."

He stopped in his tracks, eyes widening, feeling sick, feeling like his legs didn't exist, like nothing else existed. He stared at April. "What do you say, Kitten?" He managed to gruff out. His heart pounded. Ap-ril. Ap-ril.

She raised a hand to her hair and smoothed it down. "I mean, I'm saying yes to that but..."

Colt's heart flipped. "But-"

"Colt, you are getting ahead of yourself. I don't need all of that, I don't want all of that..."

"What do you want, Kitten?"

April smirked now, and looked him right in the eyes. "I want what you promised me from the start... a fast ride and a hot fuck. For the rest of our lives, Colt."

He smirked back. The world at his feet. "I can give you that." He smiled.

"Colt, that's all I want, for now and always, every day."

And that's exactly what he did.

EPILOGUE TO THE CHASE
& PROLOGUE TO THE TASTE
CARMELO

"Welcome to the party, pal," Police Sergeant Carmelo Rossetti muttered to himself as he stepped out of his police cruiser. Yes, he was quoting *Die Hard* to himself. He felt the situation was fitting for a movie quote that he held in such high regard. He'd pulled into the parking lot without any problems. He thought he'd be held at the gate by the guard, or flat out turned away, but no, the guard had eyed him up and down, taking in the car, his uniform, his determined face, and beckoned him in with a nod of the head. Carmelo stood tall, brushed a hand down over his uniform, straightening it out. He knew he looked good in it, he wanted to look good for this. Like a man who got his own way. He slid his sunglasses over his eyes. He was here on business.

He had just finished his shift at the police station. He turned back and locked the car that he had just parked up in the front parking lot of the former Creekdale Hotel. Now, it was the new clubhouse for the notorious local outlaw motorcycle club, the Black Coyotes. He looked up at the building ahead of him, a former high end, five star resort hotel. He took a breath in and out. He was here on unofficial business. Perhaps that was a better description for his visit.

He hadn't met with the President of the MC for a month or so. Last time, of course, things got heated. Neither man liked to back down or lose face. They were both stubborn. It's fair to say their relationship was one of healthy rivalry. Mainly around how many quotes from action movies they could slip into their conversations, as both men had similar taste films. Carmelo knew he should hate the Prez. He knew it wasn't the way between the local police, who had "serve and protect" wired into their blood vessels and a MC president. He had seen first-hand the ups and downs of having a local MC, and that MC's new leader, its President, was an ex-con. A rough, blunt man who lived to take what he wanted. Carmelo shouldn't like him at all. But he did. Carmelo saw that he was also loyal, brave, and loved fiercely. Frankly, Carmelo liked Colt, a lot.

Yes, Colt and Carmelo often butted heads, each wanting the best for the town and their families. Having slightly different views on the route to get there. Carmelo knew the MC was involved with the local gangs, he knew they were involved with drugs, guns, illegal activities. He ground his teeth as he started striding across the parking lot to the front door. He also knew the MC was involved with the FBI. Above his pay grade, so he was kept in the dark mostly. All he knew about that arrangement was the MC had pretty much carte blanche as long as they kept the bigwigs at the FBI informed on various underground criminal activity. Some of the members of the MC must be informants. He'd heard a rumor that some of them were even undercover federal agents.

Carmelo didn't know, but he did know it felt particularly galling when he thought he'd caught the bad guy over some misdemeanor or chaos that had ensued, only to find he had to let them go again. When they sped through town on their loud bikes, parked wherever they wanted.

Oh yeah, it got him going alright. Colt stood for everything Carmelo fundamentally believed was bad. He found it a moral quandary, however much he liked Colt, he wanted to hate him. He hated his lifestyle, this whole idea of a select club of men who could basically do what they want, illegal stuff, take what they want, act how they wanted. Carmelo was all for law and fucking order. But here they were, and now it looked as though Colt and his gang, no, club of bikers might actually be able to help out. Do some good hopefully.

Hence why he was here, in person. Carmelo was also curious, he had to admit. He wanted to see the infamous local landmark himself, The Creekdale Hotel. The Black Coyotes motorcycle club HQ, their clubhouse. A former five star hotel on the edge of town. Swimming pool, gym, even a nine hole golf course. It had been high end, the place to be for glittering parties, fancy cocktails, anyone who was anyone in town had to have been to some event at the hotel. But a fire last year had made it uninsurable. The hotel's paperwork wasn't correct. Then they found half the staff were illegal immigrants and hadn't been paid properly. It had stood abandoned for a while, being a thorn in the side of the town… there was a rumor that the fire was even caused by the MC originally, the former members of the MC. The bad members. Before Colt had chased them out of town, or before most of them had unfortunately died in that explosion at their old clubhouse that Colt had managed to stagger out of, sole survivor, and his wife, April. Carmelo had no idea what the new and improved MC had been doing at the hotel under Colt's leadership. Carmelo had asked Colt about the fire, Colt was suspiciously tight-lipped about it, and that usually meant he'd been involved in some way. The fire was just days after Colt got out of prison… not that Carmelo knew half of what was going down. No, Colt and the MC had a pretty cushy deal with the FBI which basically granted them all immunity. As long as they toed the line. And Colt didn't like doing that. Colt had bought the hotel with an actual truck load of cash that he just rolled into town with. Fuck insuring it, the MC didn't need to do that. To be fair, the hotel had been in desperate need of a cash buyer, it was languishing with trespassers and becoming unsafe, a blight on the edge of town.

Carmelo's steps rapped on the concrete in his boots as he approached the entrance to the former hotel, now MC clubhouse. It had been painted a dark charcoal gray. It was striking, a sprawling facade of large windows, in a seven or eight story building, walled off all around. It had been a respectable white color previously. Or off white... ivory or magnolia or some shit like that. He stepped up to the big door with the brass handle. The building looked good, actually, from the outside. He paused and turned, taking in the line of sleek, gleaming bikes, the security camera fixed to the wall, the little booth with a security guard inside it. Carmelo had to hand it to him, Colt knew what he was doing, from the outside at least. A professional set up.

Carmelo swallowed, he had been unsure about coming, he normally met Colt on neutral territory. They got along but often tried to pretend they didn't, Colt was blunt anyway, but turning up unannounced at their own place... Carmelo hoped Colt didn't see it as overstepping. But Carmelo had been let in the gate, the MC knew he was here, and the fact they'd let him get this far told him Colt was willing to listen. Carmelo took a breath and pulled on the heavy door.

It opened silently, accompanied by a blast of blissfully cool air-conditioning.

He stepped in. He stood in the foyer, blinking. It was dark in there. The lighting was low; small spotlights twinkled from above but it was soft and calm. He tugged off his sunglasses and began tucking them into the breast pocket on his shirt. And it was then he noticed some wide, green eyes staring back at him. Carmelo froze.

They moved closer. Then he heard a little mewl. A cat. Fuck, it

THE CHASE

was that little kitten he'd let Colt take off his hands, the one with the crushed back legs. Carmelo had received a call about it being stuck on the highway causing a huge traffic jam and one of his officers had rescued it. They should have taken it to the pound where it would have been put down, poor little dude, due to its injuries. Colt had overheard and had said fuck that and taken the kitten out of his hands. Now here it was, eyeing Carmelo with that condescending, defiant stare that cats manage to grace people with. It meowed again and moved closer, and Carmelo noticed it was strapped into a little cart with wheels where its back legs should have been. The cat pulled forward with his front legs to get himself around. Carmelo huffed. That was so Colt. His spirit, his inability to give up on things, his force of will, summed up right there in that little cat. Colt had somehow gotten a little wheelchair for it.

"Hey little one, glad to see you're still here," Carmelo said softly, and crouched down to give the cat a ruffle on its head. The cat tilted its head to let Carmelo have better access, closed its eyes and purred. Carmelo smiled.

"He likes you," came a soft voice through the darkness.

Carmelo almost wobbled off the balls of his feet, caught off guard. April, Colt's wife, his "ol' lady", as she was known in the MC world, came out of the inner door off to his left.

Carmelo steadied himself and looked up. April was beautiful, no mistaking it. Long, blonde glossy hair, clear skin, a body to die for. Carmelo tried to stand up too quickly and jarred his knee. "Ah, Mrs. Kincade, ma'am," he stuttered, embarrassed to have been caught squatting down, talking to a cat.

"Call me April, I always tell you this, Carmelo," she said breezily, her hands coming down to scoop the little cat up, wheelchair and all.

Carmelo noticed April had a little round stomach, an early baby bump. She was glowing. She obviously caught him staring as she put one hand over the perfectly round little globe of her stomach and smiled.

"I'm halfway there. It's a boy!" She smiled and Carmelo felt lucky to be coated in the warmth of that glow. "You're having a baby brother, Shadow," she said in a sing-song voice to the little cat. The cat turned his head and gazed up at April with wise eyes, like he already knew, like he had always known.

She stroked the cat fondly, then looked back at Carmelo and nodded to the door on his left, where she had just come from. "Colt's in there, interested to hear what warrants a visit in person." She raised her eyebrows but smiled at him, the complex mix of fraternity and animosity he felt for her husband did not reach how he felt about her. He liked her, for who she was on the outside and the inside. She was a good person, kind, smart, good for Colt, and fucking hot, too.

"Sure. Take care now, ma'am. April," he corrected himself with a half smile. April smiled and waved and drifted off to a door on the right with the cat. Carmelo watched them go. He'd be a lucky bastard if he ended up with a woman as beautiful -

"If you're done eye-fucking my wife, get your ass in here and tell me why the fuck you've come, pig."

Carmelo tipped his head back and sighed. Of course Colt was standing there in the doorway. Of course Colt had seen his gaze lingering on April's neat little blossoming behind as she'd sashayed into the other room. Of fucking course.

Carmelo turned around and gritted his teeth into a half grin, half snarl. The Black Coyotes President stood with his hands on his hips, eyes flashing fiercely, blocking his route ahead with his tall body.

Carmelo licked his lips. "First, congratulations, Colt, and second, I wasn't eye-fucking-"

THE CHASE

"You were, don't fucking lie to me. I don't blame you for it, I know my woman is hot as fuck. And thanks, she's due in the fall." Colt's deep brusque tones cut through Carmelo's protest.

Colt stared hungrily at April's retreating back. "You need to get lucky Carmelo, you can't just stare at women like they are your next meal. You still haven't got a girlfriend? You need to get some, my friend."

Carmelo bit his tongue.

"My Lioness, Queen of the Savannah... so fucking hot, knocked up..." Colt faded out and seemed to be talking to himself, seemed to have forgotten he stood in the foyer with Carmelo. Colt even reached a hand down and grabbed his junk. Carmelo thought it best to say nothing and avert his gaze. Their sex life must be off the Richter scale, Carmelo thought wistfully as he stared at the ground.

A good few seconds passed then Colt suddenly turned back to Carmelo, aware again of where he was. Colt took the other hand off his hip and placed it on Carmelo's shoulder. Carmelo was shorter than Colt, he knew he was stockier. Well, unlike Colt, Carmelo had a job and hadn't spent time in the slammer with nothing better to do than lift weights. Unlike Colt, who'd served five years. Colt steered Carmelo through the foyer and into the common room of the clubhouse.

Carmelo immediately stopped and gazed around. He was impressed. It looked more like a chic urban bar rather than a dingy MC clubhouse. Polished concrete floor. Hanging chandelier made out of recycled clear and green glass beer bottles. Upcycled vintage furniture. Big leather sofas, obligatory pool table and bar. It was clean. There was a good sound system installed, currently acoustic guitar music was playing. Could he smell sandalwood and bergamot?

Colt eyed Carmelo's face and seemed pleased with his obvious awe. "Yep, this bit's pretty much ready to go, we've just finished painting it, got the bar fully stocked, got the furniture in..."

A gaggle of incredibly scantily dressed, heavily made up women sat around one of the tables, it looked like they were having some sort of boardroom style meeting. Colt saw Carmelo staring.

"We've got a new business, the old strip club in town, we're giving it to the twins, they're going to get it back on track, refurbish it, open it again. These girls are some of our new adult entertainers." Colt nodded to them as he and Carmelo passed.

"Strippers?" Carmelo questioned, raising his eyebrows.

Colt smiled and shook his head. "Oh, they do so much more than strip."

Carmelo rolled his eyes. "Great, just what the town needs, sounds like more trouble if you ask me."

Colt looked at him with a deadpan gaze. "Then it's good no one asked you," he replied. "Anyway, the twins will make it a success, don't get your panties in a twist, pig, they know what they are doing."

Carmelo sighed. The twins. They weren't trouble, they were double trouble. They had showed up in town a few months ago and raised hell already. Like parading the Rio Carnival into a quiet church coffee morning. Yes, the twins were infamous in town. Rita and Rafe, fraternal mixed race twins who were thick as thieves together and had been welcomed into the MC like long lost cousins. Ridiculously good looking, both of them, half the town wanted to either be them or be with them. Getting any form of acknowledgement that you existed from either was a sign you'd made it big. He remembered Rita had blown him a kiss once from her perch on her custom bike as she'd waited outside a shop sucking a popsicle and he'd driven past in his cruiser, staring at her. He'd nearly come in his pants.

"Well, it's been quieter than I expected with you in town, Colt, I

THE CHASE

have to admit. I know you've taken on new members, but you're more like a construction company that rides bikes really. You being in town hasn't been the carnage I thought it was going to be," Carmelo teased.

Colt looked at him evenly. "If that's what you think, then I'm running a very successful MC. Below your radar, at least."

Carmelo fumed silently.

"What'll it be?" Colt asked. "To drink?" Colt nodded to the bar, where what looked like a thousand liquor bottles of all colors and sizes twinkled under the spotlights against a background of mirrors.

Carmelo's eyes caught and lingered on one of the top shelf whiskeys. It was a well stocked bar, he'd love to try a glass of some of the labels they had. But he shouldn't, even though he had a day off tomorrow, he needed a clear head for this.

"Oh, no, thank you, I'm here on business. Well, actually, not official business… that is, I mean…."

"Look pig, do you want a drink or not?" Another man yelled out. He stood behind the bar, wearing the MC leather jacket, or 'cut', as they called it, wiping a glass.

He was younger than Colt and Carmelo, but no less sure of himself. Carmelo's eyes dropped to the name tag below the club's insignia, on the guy's pectoral. Ash, his name tag said. Sergeant at Arms, his position in the club. Sergeant at Arms was normally the biggest, meanest, toughest guy, the one who kept everyone else in check. This young guy looked like the slightest guy in the MC so far compared to the others.

Carmelo gathered himself. "No drink, thank you," he replied more decisively.

Colt indicated to a bar stool, but Carmelo stayed standing. The other guy behind the bar, Ash, shrugged, poured whiskey into a glass for Colt and came out around the bar. Carmelo tried not to feel outnumbered. He didn't know much about Ash, except he had been put in jail for helping Colt escape the old MC, when Colt was on the run from them. Ash had lent them a car to escape but it turned out his family used it as an opportunity to get Ash locked up and out of their hair. Colt had put the town's local law firm on retainer to represent the MC in all things legal, and Ash had walked out of jail a few months later. Carmelo was usually unfazed by miscreants like this. They were both acting up today, Colt and Ash. It was because Carmelo had come to the clubhouse unannounced. His mistake.

"You think you can just pop on over for a drink?" Ash chimed in. Colt crossed his arms, a neutral look on his face. Carmelo felt it was some sort of test, how he reacted to this young upstart called Ash. "You think you can just call in, wearing that uniform?"

Fuck, Carmelo hadn't thought of that, it was because he was wearing his uniform. That's why they were being off with him. He'd just wanted to try to get this issue resolved, and coming straight from his shift at the station had seemed like the best course of action. Carmelo tried to remain undaunted. "Look, we've got an urgent situation that I wanted to talk to you about as soon as-"

"We can't let that go, I hope you realize?" Ash interrupted again.

Carmelo glanced sideways at him, determined to keep his cool. He continued stoically, "I really need to get your view on this issue we've got, your help-"

"Oh, our help!" Ash piped up again. Colt didn't even blink but stayed still, silent, staring Carmelo down. They had a good double act going, Carmelo had to hand it to them.

"You come dressed in that pig outfit to ask for our help?" Ash mocked.

Carmelo was beginning to lose his patience now. He turned to Colt. "Can this guy leave us to it, do you think?" Carmelo snapped.

THE CHASE

Colt raised an eyebrow but Carmelo spotted a faint smile on his face. "Ash, calm down," Colt said quietly. And true enough, Ash crossed his arms like a moody teenager, but said nothing else.

Carmelo took a breath and got down to business, talking directly to Colt. "We've got a guy in custody, we picked him up last night. He skipped a red light, passed out, skidded off the road-"

"In a car?" Colt asked, curious now.

"No, motorcycle, some sort of custom thing, you'd like it-"

"Under the influence?"

Carmelo shook his head. "No, he's clean, no alcohol, no drugs-"

"Injuries?" Colt barked, interested, leaning forwards.

Carmela nodded, emboldened by Colt's reaction. "Major road rash from his fall, he wasn't wearing gear."

Both Ash and Colt winced. Colt spoke up, "Fuck, everyone wears leather pants from now on when out on runs, okay? No more fucking around with denim or whatever the fuck people want. If we are being a MC, then we'll fucking wear the right gear-"

"Black leather? For the Black Coyotes? It can be like your signature…" Carmelo trailed off. Ash and Colt looked at each other, nodding slowly. Huh, this outlaw MC shit wasn't so hard after all.

"Anyway," Carmelo carried on, "so we pulled him in, kept him overnight. He's okay, we checked him out, but something's wrong, Colt, something's very wrong. He hasn't said a word."

Colt frowned. "Nothing?"

Carmelo shook his head. "Not even nodded or made eye contact."

Colt ran a palm over his jaw. "So you have no idea who he is, where he came from, why he skipped the light…"

Carmelo nodded once and cleared his throat. "Yeah, he doesn't have a record, he's said nothing but he's refusing food and water, too. Our medic reckons he passed out from dehydration, that's how he plowed through the light-"

"Fuck," Colt muttered. "How old is he?"

Carmelo shrugged. "He could be anything from twenty to early thirties, hard to tell. It's like he's lifeless, Colt. Like he's already a ghost, a phantom, passing out of this world. Like he's already kind of... given up." Carmelo took a breath and let it shudder within his chest. Colt and Ash heard it and exchanged a glance. Colt ran a hand through his hair, seeming uncomfortable.

"Poor bastard," Colt said, empathetically. Ash gave him a tilt of his chin in solidarity. Carmelo nodded, the men united for a moment in their emotion.

"There were no witnesses, or victims, he was in front of an officer, it was just after one this morning... his charges will be dropped. We can let him go but I think he'll just pass out in the parking lot, to be honest."

"Hospital?" Ash injected, Carmelo shot him a glance. Ash looked worried, concerned. Hell, all three of them did.

"Well, the road rash is gonna leave a mark, and... he's got... scars... on his body. When our medic checked him over... treated the road rash... it's something else, it's self-inflicted, or done by someone else, all over his chest..."

Colt riled, getting angry now. "What the..."

"What's it look like?" Ash asked.

"Like... tally marks... like he was keeping a tally, in scars... you have to see it to believe it..." Carmelo licked his now dry lips before continuing. "And a brand... Colt... burnt on..."

Colt set his jaw. "The Demonios?"

Carmelo nodded. "Yes, but that's not all..."

"What else could there possibly be?" Ash huffed.

Carmelo took a breath. "The brand is old, it's healed... like he was branded years ago. The oldest I've seen…"

Colt pursed his lips. "But if he's only in his twenties… like when he was a child?" he asked, already knowing the answer from the tone of his question. Carmelo nodded. Colt and Ash exchanged a loaded glare.

"So the hospital is a no-go. Too many questions, too much heat." Colt let out a hiss of air from between his teeth. "Have you approached the Demonios about this? Horatio and his men? They might know, or should be able to answer for our Mr. Phantom here?" Colt asked, leaning back, elbow on the bar.

Carmelo frowned and began to gesticulate as Colt was saying the words. "That's another weird thing, I can't get hold of them. My usual contacts… their phones are dead. I've asked around… no one has seen or heard from Horatio's men for a few days now. They were all having some big meet-up, I don't know if it was business or pleasure but I know there was some sort of big shindig and it seems like they've all just… disappeared. And another thing," Carmelo continued quickly, "Horatio's own personal limo driver has just turned up in the hospital, stab wounds all over him, practically bled out… he's in a medically induced coma, they aren't sure he's going to make it…" Colt looked thoughtful, and took a sip of his whiskey. A small sip. He winced, like it pained him to taste it. Carmelo wished he'd asked for the same, the excitement and drama of his shift catching up with him now, he felt tense.

"You're working with the Demonios, right?" Carmelo thought he'd try his luck at getting some info out of Colt. He was kept out of the loop of their FBI involvement, but he knew the FBI basically told Colt which gang they wanted him to get into bed with. And the Mexican Demonios were flavor of the month.

Colt simply growled in response.

Carmelo sighed. "The whole thing is a fucking headache to be honest…" Carmelo trailed off.

"Fucking scum, fucking Horatio…" Colt muttered darkly.

Carmelo opened his palms. "Look, I get it if you don't want to get involved, I mean, if you can't take this guy in… he's a bit of a wild card…"

Colt rolled his eyes to the ceiling. "Christ, Carmelo, we aren't a fucking homeless charity for stray dogs-"

Carmelo tilted his head down and raised his hands." I know, I know, I get it if you say no-"

"I don't want to say no," Ash spoke up from the sidelines, quietly yet with certainty.

Carmelo and Colt both silently turned their heads to look at him. "I don't want to, either," Colt admitted finally, then he blew out a deep breath and nodded slowly. "We aren't saying no," he said with certainty.

Carmelo raised his eyebrows. Had he just done it? Successfully convinced these guys to take the poor bastard in? He thought it would be harder, he thought these bikers would be loath to help, but they weren't.

Carmelo stammered on. "I mean, he could be a complete psycho, I know you're not really set up or qualified to cater for-"

Ash interrupted. "Qualified? We're fucking humans. That's all the qualifications required to help a brother in need." He frowned at Carmelo.

"Well, okay then." Carmelo nodded quietly. "You could come pick him up today."

Colt pursed his lips and sighed. The world weary sigh of someone setting off on a long trek up a steep hill.

"Ash," Colt barked, snapping forward suddenly, "make this

happen, we'll get him today and get him back to health at least. He can stay if he's a good 'un, or he can go."

Ash nodded, then turned and roared out, "Prospects!"

Carmelo almost jumped, but three guys in newer, plain black leather jackets loped out of the swinging kitchen doors. They formed a huddle around Colt and Ash.

Colt spoke first. "We got a new brother that needs our help. We're going to make it happen. No questions asked," he said.

Ash then took over. "So you," he pointed to the first prospect, who was listening intently. "Get the van ready, we'll need to load up a bike. Colt, me and you will be going down to the station to pick him up."

The first prospect nodded. Carmelo did a double-take. It was Lyle, former member of the MC before Colt had taken over. He'd been an alcoholic, they'd not so affectionately named Skunk, as he had literally been drunk as a skunk all day, every day. He was the only one who had lived after the explosion at the clubhouse, mainly because Lyle had passed out drunk outside the compound, half a block down the road. Colt had sent him off to rehab and then taken him into the new MC. A ballsy move, Carmelo had thought, as Lyle kept his loyalty close to his chest, and didn't share any opinions on his time in the former Black Coyotes under their old Prez, the ruthless Cleaver. Lyle was older, much older than the other prospects, older than Colt, but he looked better than when Carmelo had last seen him. He looked sober, for a start.

Ash turned to the next Prospect. "You, get a room ready, one of the bigger ones, and an easy chair in there, too."

"Ash, sorry man, but there aren't any more rooms ready, there's some still being refurbished but-"

"He can have mine," Ash returned in a heartbeat. "I'll move into one of the half finished rooms…"

Carmelo was impressed at his generosity.

Ash turned to the third prospect, rapping out orders in quick succession. Carmelo had to hand it to Ash, it was military precision.

"You, draw up a rotation schedule, 'round the clock care for our new brother, everyone does a shift, and I mean everyone-"

"Even... April?" the prospect piped up.

Ash glanced at Colt who gave a subtle single nod, and then Ash nodded back to the prospect who had asked the question. "Yes, but she does afternoons, no nights. Everyone does four hours on, for the next two weeks..."

Carmelo turned to Colt as Ash continued to brief the prospects. "He's good," Carmelo muttered, talking about Ash. "Is he ex-military?"

Colt shook his head. "No, ex-concierge," he said with a straight face.

Carmelo's mouth opened and a single bark of laughter escaped him before he could shut himself up. He had no idea if Colt was joking or not. "I'm surprised he's not your VP," Carmelo added, as Ash continued to dole out instructions to the eager prospects, guys who were basically apprentices in the MC, getting all the dirty, degrading hard jobs until they proved themselves and were formally welcomed, or patched in, earning their name patches for their leather cut.

Colt smiled then, and shook his head. "Ash isn't VP material yet. He's an excellent Sergeant at Arms." Colt paused. "Ash is good at punishment," Colt added in a deep, almost husky voice.

Carmelo gulped, hoping not too loudly. Colt continued like he was talking about a delicious cake recipe. "So good at punishment," he added, amusement now clear in his dark eyes. Carmelo didn't get whatever was so funny.

"Jared is ex-military," Colt added, returning to Carmelo's original question.

Jared Jennings ran the small construction company that Colt was using to refurbish the hotel. Carmelo thought it was funny because he looked the most like a biker out of all of them, with his long beard and his giant stature, covered in tattoos. He had a slight limp too, which only added to his swagger. Jared and his team practically had been absorbed into the MC.

"You know who the FBI informant is yet?" Carmelo asked. He knew he sounded like a petulant child, but it had been bugging him for months, who the mole on the inside was.

Colt sighed wearily, the ever-patient parent. "No fucking clue."

Carmelo pursed his lips. "I bet Jared," he whispered. "I mean, it's obviously not Lyle, is it? The twins... I doubt..."

Colt grunted, keeping his face neutral. "I'm tempted to take that bet on Jared, but you know I can't. Until I know, everyone's treated the same," he said. A man of principles, Colt was, through and through.

"And Lyle looks well, or Skunk, I should say?" Carmelo said.

Colt nodded with a smile on his face, it almost looked like pride. "Yep, Lyle's ex-military, too, did you know that? Keeps it on the down low but has let it slip out now and then... he's sober now. He forgave me for sending him to rehab and was happy to re-join the MC. As a prospect. He has to prove himself again. To be fair, he has, he'll be patched in next month, get full membership. He doesn't go by Skunk anymore."

Carmelo raised his eyebrows. "I thought you all had road names, or something, you had to go by a different name-"

Colt interrupted, "You just go by whatever fucking name you want to be called in the Black Coyotes MC. We do what we fucking want to do, Carmelo. We make our rules."

Carmelo nodded. "Well, I should be going-"

"Whoa, not so fast, pig," Ash butted in, dismissing the prospects with a wave of his hand. They loped away to do Ash's bidding.

"You're forgetting what I said... you can't get away with wearing your fucking pig uniform into our clubhouse," Ash reminded him. He leaned over and grabbed Colt's forgotten, barely touched whiskey, and downed it in one. Colt and Ash were brothers indeed. Ash knew Colt wanted the whiskey, but wouldn't finish it, and he knew Colt would be comfortable with Ash grabbing it, they bounced off each other, a solid partnership.

"But I need to go now–" Carmelo began, his heart started beating faster.

"We told you, we can't let that go unpunished," Colt said, too calmly.

"Look, it was an honest mistake, I won't do it again." Carmelo tried to laugh it off, though he felt his palms get sweaty. They'd all been getting along so well. He knew these men, they could be violent, they didn't take well to being slighted in any way. He felt for the taser in his utility belt. He still had his gun, his club even. He swallowed. He'd use them if he had to.

"Ash, what shall we do with him?" Colt continued, calm amusement leaking out of him.

Ash clicked his neck by tilting it to the side and stared at Carmelo fiercely. "Oh, there are many things I'd like to do with him," Ash practically hummed.

Carmelo blinked. Hell, Ash was looking at him with... desire? "I'm not gay," Carmelo suddenly felt the need to announce.

Ash didn't seem in the least bit put out. "Ladies!" he suddenly barked, keeping his eyes fixed on Carmelo hungrily. The women on the other side of the room, the strippers, looked over, stooped their heads and conferred, then four of them stood up. Ash beckoned them

THE CHASE

over with a nod and a devious smile. And they came. Prowling toward Carmelo, practically in formation. Carmelo couldn't drag his eyes off them. They were hot, half naked and heading his way. Christ.

The nearest one eyed him with distrust when she got closer. "What's bacon boy doing here, honey?" she asked Ash with a sultry voice. She tossed a mane of long, straight blonde hair over her shoulder. What would it be like to stroke that lovely soft hair while fucking her from behind, Carmelo thought to himself, then tried to shake himself. He had to focus, he might need his wits or even his fists to get out of this situation.

Colt spoke first. "Ladies, there's been a mix up, he's not a real cop," Colt said, winking at Carmelo. The blonde raised a perfectly manicured eyebrow.

Ash spoke up, "Yeah, he's a stripper."

Carmelo almost choked. "I'm-"

Ash continued over Carmelo's shocked sputter. "He got the wrong address, he's meant to be stripping for some girl's twenty-first birthday but he's here instead, only now that he's here, he's refusing to get his costume off."

Carmelo simply gaped at Ash. It was Ash's turn to wink at him. "That seems like a missed opportunity, doesn't it ladies?" Ash added.

"Oh sugar," the brunette to the left of Carmelo chimed in now. "Yes, it does."

"We'll help get your little costume off you," the third girl with shorter, darker hair said, too, draping an arm over his shoulder.

"Course we will," the fourth lady said, yanking his hat off his head and putting it on hers instead. "What a funny mix up."

The blonde lady placed her hands on Carmelo's chest. The air whooshed out of his lungs as blood rushed to his groin.

"Ah, ladies, sorry I can't-"

"You're not single anymore?" Colt suddenly piped up.

"No, no... still single..." Carmelo stuttered through a sharp intake of breath, as the brunette lady grabbed a handful of his shirt and yanked. Buttons pinged off.

"Oh fuck." Carmelo winced, aware of his swollen dick now digging into his trousers.

"Has it been a while, Sergeant?" Ash leaned in close to Carmelo's ear.

Carmelo felt nimble female hands now undoing his trousers, the teeth of the zipper coming undone one at a time.

"Ah..." he had to focus to continue to talk, desire and heat colored his face. "Yes, yes... it has..." he wheezed, as the blonde lady planted a kiss right on his cheek. The brunette went straight for his lips and kissed him while the dark haired lady didn't hesitate to suck a hickey on his neck. Carmelo groaned.

"Too bad." Ash smiled mischievously. Carmelo closed his eyes, but then snapped them open when he felt his utility belt coming off.

"Ladies, this is dangerous equipment here-" Carmelo tried to express his concern, his thoughts going to his gun, his taser.

Colt shrugged. "The girls can handle that," he said, nonchalant.

"Colt, at least take my gun, my taser, someone could get hurt-"

Colt shrugged again. "Maybe you'll like it."

"I'll help you with your... dangerous equipment, sugar..."

"No, I'm not joking -" Carmelo tried to remain in control but it was as futile as holding a handful of sand on the beach. He felt grains of his resolve trickling out from between his fingers.

"So will I, baby, you think we don't know how to handle that? You're fully loaded, big, hard-"

"Oh fuck Christ," Carmelo breathed, eyes rolling to the back of his head.

He heard Colt's voice in his ear now. "I told you, Ash is so good at punishment." Colt chuckled darkly.

Carmelo forced his lungs to breathe air in. He opened his eyes and stared at his reflection in the mirror behind the bar. He had a perfect pink lipstick kiss mark on his cheek, a smear of bright red lipstick all over his own lips and chin. A purple love bite shining strongly by his Adam's apple. His hat was on the head of a lady now licking down his chest, exposed as the tatters of his shirt hung off his shoulders. His pants were around his ankles, his dick hard and oozing a little wet patch of pre-cum onto his silk navy blue boxers. Fuck him. He heard a click and realized the blonde had clicked his handcuffs, one on his wrist, one on hers. The lady with the short hair took his utility belt off and flipped it over her shoulder. She handled the gun like she knew exactly what she was doing. She emptied the bullets out onto the floor. Carmelo sighed, the immediate danger removed at least, so he could relax and try to enjoy himself. The brunette yanked her top off and her full breasts bobbed in front of his face. Oh, he could relax and enjoy himself for sure.

"I'll keep the handcuffs on when you fuck my throat later..."

"I'll let you fuck me, sugar, thrust that oh so dangerous equipment of yours in my hot, wet cunt..."

"While I lick your rim, have you ever had that, sugar?"

Carmelo reeled from the images flashing through his mind. This was wrong. Dangerous. But now he felt rising heat and tautness in his stomach, in his soul. Fuck. Things were about to get kinky.

Carmelo groaned, dragging his gaze over to Ash. "You dick, I'm going to fucking love this and I'll never be happy with vanilla sex again after this, will I?"

"Nope," Ash chimed mirthfully. Ash reached up behind the bar and grabbed the bottle of whiskey Carmelo had been eyeing up earlier.

He slapped it into Carmelo's open palm.

"Here, to wet your whistle after they've wet your..." Ash winked. Colt snickered and slapped Ash on the shoulder, congratulating him on a job well done.

"Ladies, take him up to a bedroom," Carmelo heard Colt's voice through his looming haze of arousal. "Sergeant, we don't want to see you this side of midnight," Colt instructed.

Carmelo gaped at them both as hands began to roam more freely and grope with purpose. "But it's not even lunchtime," he wailed, half with despair, half with delight.

Colt shoved Carmelo on the back playfully, in the direction of the stairs to the bedrooms. "Welcome to the MC, pig."

Acknowledgements

Thank you to everyone who has helped me on my journey to getting my debut novel out there in the world. I've been incredibly grateful for the patience and professionalism of everyone I've worked with so far, and the unwavering curiosity and unconditional support of friends and family.

Artwork: Erick Centeno
Not many serious artists would be open to working with an author who gives you feedback on your work like "can you make him more hunkier? Really smouldering? Yes I like it but can you make him really steaming hot? Thank you!

Editors: KDL Editing, Proofreading By the Page
For all the UK English slurs and for doing basically every speech mark wrong, sorry and thank you so much!

Formatter: Books and Moods
The book looks better than I could have imagined, thank you!

PR: Foreword PR & Marketing
Linda, thank you for such a professional, guiding hand, for answering my thousands of questions and for your honest and open approach.

If you enjoyed this book, please leave a review online, this is a massive help to indie authors like me!

Check out www.rubybloomauthor.com and subscribe to my newsletter or find me on social media for information about me, upcoming book releases, and news!

The Black Coyotes MC story continues in the next book in the series, The Taste!